THE RAISING

THE RAISING

The Torch Keeper Book Three

STEVEN DOS SANTOS

To my dear father, Alvaro. Thanks for always being there, Dad, and helping to keep the fires burning, especially during the dark times.

ACKNOWLEDGEMENTS

The Torch Keeper series has been quite the ride! When I first wrote *The Culling* back in 2009, I had a very clear vision of how this third book would end. Little did I know what an adventure it was going to be to finally be able to tell the whole story as I had envisioned it. When the original publisher of the first two volumes in the series decided to pull the plug before the conclusion was released, it was one of the most devastating experiences in my life. In those dark times, when it looked like Lucian's torch would be snuffed out for good, it was the encouragement and enthusiasm of the awesome fans that kept me going and motivated me to find a way to get this story out there. Thanks to super fans Corey Henio, Bazz Krycek, Kameron Haggard, Matthew Pavia and all the rest for your continued support. This is for you!

I'd also like to thank my awesome beta readers and besties, Stacie Ramey, Joyce Sweeney, and Marjetta Geerling for your invaluable input, and endless pep talks. Love you guys!

And I also couldn't have released this book without the selfless contribution of my fantastic editor, Diana Stager, who I'll be forever indebted to for her key role in this book's ultimate release.

Jay Aheer? What can I say? Thanks so much for yet another fantastic cover, which embodies the spirit of the first two volumes of the series and takes it to an exciting new level!

Much thanks to my rock star agent, Ginger Knowlton, and the staff of Curtis Brown, Ltd., including Marnie Zoldessy and Steve Kasdin, for helping me to realize the dream of a completed trilogy.

And last, but certainly not least, a big hug to my partner, Jeffrey Cadorette, for his never-ending support and patience throughout this entire process. My torch will always burn for you!

PART I

ENEMIES

CHAPTER ONE

Dawn finally bleeds through the night sky. I wipe the sting of ice-cold rain from my eyes, committing every shade of color, every nuance of purple, pink and orange, however slight, to memory. It'll probably be the last morning of my life.

Dozens of other smaller ships like mine flank the enormous troop carrier in a V formation, a lethal arrowhead surging through the choppy seas toward the cape.

The camera closes in on my face once more. I'm tempted to tear it from Valdez's hands and hurl it overboard. Instead, I just glare at the lanky war correspondent who's been tailing my every move like a pesky mosquito for days now, documenting everything for posterity's sake.

Valdez clears his throat. "You mind talking about what's at stake here today?"

I stare right at the lens. "I guess if there are any future generations left after this bloody war, they should know the world's in real shitty shape right now. The survivors of the Clathrate apocalypse, which released methane into the earth's atmosphere centuries ago and nearly destroyed all of human civilization, have divided into three factions: The corrupt Thorn Republic, formerly known as the Establishment; the religious zealots of Sanctum and their army of human-machine Flesher hybrids; and us, the resistance, known as the Torch Brigade, fighting for control over what was once known as the United States of America, trying to restore some order to this living hell. If the Brigade loses this offensive today, then the other two sides will pick at our remains like vultures, and all hope for a free and just society dies." I take a swig of water from my canteen. "Does that work for you?"

He notices my dirty look and shifts his eyes from mine to the view-finder on his camera. "The Thorn Republic forces are comprised of human soldiers. What can you tell us about these Fleshers defending Sanctum? They appear monstrous, with no eyes, protruding biomechanical append-ages, and regenerative capabilities."

"They aren't *monsters*. They're *people*. People just like you and me that have been subjected to nano technology and grafting experiments, and turned into hideous slave machines with a hive mind. In some ways they're just as much victims as the rest of us."

"Just one more question. What are you feeling right now?"

I lean forward and stare right into the camera lens. "Considering it's my eighteenth birthday today and I'm heading into battle, my death would bring my existence full circle, the natural end to the life cycle of Lucian Spark. How's that for a sound byte?"

Valdez sets the camera aside and clears his throat. "I think that'll do it for now." Avoiding my gaze, he fiddles with his tablet, slick with rain, and makes a show of reviewing his notes. "Looks like we've covered every-thing…Lucian Spark… betrayed and recruited by Cassius Thorn and forced to choose between the lives of his loved ones during the Culling…became a resistance figurehead known as The Torch Keeper…currently leading the charge to retake the strategic shipping lanes of the Cape from the restruc-tured Establishment, now known as the Thorn Republic…," he glances up and gives me a nervous smile. "I think that just about covers it, Spark?"

"Just about." Except, I'm not even sure Lucian Spark's my name any-more, much less whether or not I was actually born, at least in the tradi-tional sense. According to what Cassius Thorn told me during our last encounter, I was *Sown*, the ghost of a centuries old dead man, recreated in a lab.

But not just a copy of any dead man. Oh no. That'd be too easy. I run my fingers across the palm of my other hand, feeling every ridge and groove of the cool skin, slick with rain and sweat. I'm the exact replica of Queran Embers, the founder of the tyrannical Establishment, right down to every last putrid gene.

If what Cassius told me was true, not even the vast ocean surrounding me can ever wash away all the blood from these hands.

The earpiece of my com-unit crackles like far-off thunder.

"Initiating climate camouflage."

Valdez picks up the camera again and aims the lens at me.

I wave it away and slash a finger across my throat. "We're done here."

Valdez fumbles with his gear as he packs it up. I feel guilty. It's a dangerous job, risking one's life to report on the war and keep hope alive. He's just as terrified as the rest of us.

Despite the stabilizers on our retrofitted stealth boats hovering over the water, my company's boat lurches. On the starboard side, Corin leans over the rail and throws up. And I'm pretty sure it has nothing to do with succumbing to seasickness. At just under fourteen, he's the youngest member of our squad. In an ideal world, he'd be safe at home, maybe doing some schoolwork, helping out with chores.

This world's anything but idyllic. When Corin begged our commanders for a shot to be on the front lines, I didn't fight it, despite the gnawing in my gut. After everything he's been through, he's earned the right to fight for his freedom without me or anyone else telling him otherwise.

Corin finally slides back into position, looking paler than a full moon, and wipes his mouth.

"You good, Kid?" I call.

He just nods and bites his lip.

Normally, the others in our company would be slinging their own good-natured taunts at him—or any of us—for tossing under pressure. But today's different. You can smell it in the air. It's fear, seeping from everyone's pores, mixing with the sweat and body odor of the soldiers cramped into this small boat. This isn't a hit and run op. A search and rescue. Or a supply raid.

If we fail today, we lose all access channels for resupplying resistance forces and our little revolution is wiped out.

"Almighty Deity," someone mutters from the bow. Sounds like Valdez. "Forgive my sins. Grant us your blessings and watch over us..."

A hiss, generated by the massive battleship in the center of our perimeter, rises over the sound of the waves, drowning out the prayer. Soon the entire area's smothered in a thick fog, hiding our approach to the rocky shoreline.

Someone grabs my arm. I can feel hot breath whispering in my ear. "You didn't think we'd forgotten, Spark, did you? Now you're really in for it, Mate."

Cage's voice.

Before I can respond, there's a sharp crack, and then a small glimmer appears in the darkness.

"Surprise," Arrah says, holding out a small object, approximating the size of a lumpy muffin, complete with some sort of icing and the tiniest candle I've ever seen, which casts the faintest of glows on her smooth, caramel skin. "Baked it myself." She smiles, her hand cupped over the top of the makeshift cake to protect it from the rain.

Beside her, Drusilla gives me a wink. "Don't even ask what's in it."

Arrah gives her a playful shove before Drusilla leans in and gives her a peck on the lips. Then the levity's gone, and their hug becomes more of a clutch, before they reluctantly break apart.

Dahlia squirms her way into the ring and nods. "Better make a wish and blow out that candle before we get busted by the commander for giving away our position."

With everything going on, the fact that they—that my friends—would remember this day…

I close my eyes and move my lips silently, pretending I'm formulating some sort of wish. But I'm not. I can't. Not all of us are going to get out of this alive. So why ask for something that will never come true?

When I open my eyes, I blow, snuffing out the candle and the illusion of normalcy in one fell swoop.

Taking a small sliver, I pass the cake on down the line, the final meal of the condemned. But the sight of even the most miniscule piece of food is enough to send those teetering on the abyss of nauseous anxiety over the edge. A few down the line lose it over the rail just like Corin did, while some let loose right at their feet.

Cage's grin fades. The gears of the metal prosthetic that replaced his real hand grind as the fingers open, revealing a tiny box resting in its palm. "No birthday would be complete without a present, Mate."

I shake my head. "You guys, you didn't have to—"

He grips my arm with his other hand. "You're right. We didn't. But we did. It's from the entire company. Open it."

I rub my rain-soaked fingers against my uniform in vain before untying the string and removing the soaked wrapping paper, which looks like nothing more than the remnants of an old canvas bag. I smile.

Inside the box there's a ring. Even in the dark, I can see that it's in the shape of a small, flaming torch. I slide it onto my finger.

"Happy Birthday, Torch Keeper," Arrah says.

I swipe at the annoying rain pelting my eyes.

Glancing around the crowded Stealth boat at the others in my regiment, I wonder what they'd think if they knew the very enemy they were currently on a mission to strike against could actually be hunkered down beside them. Would they be so quick to follow me into battle against the Thorn Regime one more time given everything we've shared as fellow rebels? Or would they toss me overboard into a watery grave?

"Prepare for ground assault," the command issues over our com units.

"Here we go," Valdez mutters with a nervous laugh, pulling out his camera again.

His head disintegrates in a spatter of bone and blood, like warm hail. Those unfortunate to be directly behind him are flung backwards, one of them slamming into me. As I crash against the bulkhead, I catch sight of Corin hunched down beside a wounded soldier, just as the bow erupts in a fireball, flinging him overboard.

The explosion is deafening. I'm spinning, muffled shouts and screams of agony all around me. I try to breathe but begin to choke, realizing that I'm now underwater. Through the murk, bodies writhe all around. Live rounds of ammunition whiz through the sea, silent serpents striking all about me, tearing apart bodies as if they were twigs. A crimson veil spreads. My lungs are about to burst. I swim upwards, breaking the surface just long enough to take in a lungful of smoke-tinged air and orient myself toward the shore.

As bad as things are underneath the surface, they're even worse up here. All around me, Stealth boats erupt into fireballs. Crews abandon ship, scattering into the sea. Hundreds of our soldiers descend on the beach from above on jetsails and glidechutes, many of which are blasted out of the sky, the pilots careening to their deaths like burning fireflies. The air reeks of smoke and charred meat. I spit out a mixture of salt water, blood, and ash, desperately searching for signs of Corin, Arrah, Cage, and the others.

A female soldier treads water beside me. Hobbes.

"Spark—" A smoking hole appears in the center of her helmet and she slumps against me, dragging me under again.

The straps of her pack have caught in mine and for a horrible moment, I don't think I'm going to be able to cut loose. But I tear the strap away and swim toward the beach as fast I can, my muscles tensing for the crippling blast that'll tear through me at any second.

Up ahead, a familiar body floats lifeless, narrowly avoiding the blasts knifing through from the surface.

It's Corin.

Despite my aching lungs, I grab hold of him, dragging him with me toward the beach.

As soon as the water becomes shallow enough, I'm on my feet, slinging Corin over my shoulder and trudging through the surf. Crimson waves of tangled bodies crash all around us.

Once on the beach, I drag Corin under the shelter of a sand dune. Pinching his nose, I cover his mouth with mine, alternating with chest compressions. Soon he's spitting out gobs of sea water.

"You're going to be okay, kid." But his eyes remain closed.

I hail one of the med drones zipping through the firefight, little more than a set of blinking lights attached to a transparent capsule. "Get him to shelter!"

The drone is still scooping Corin's body into the protective capsule when I sprint away to join the fight.

The beach beneath me vibrates. At first I think it's just the rumble of the explosions and the debris ricocheting everywhere. Pockets of sand erupt like small geysers all along the shoreline, one within a few feet of my position. A shadow falls over me. I look up as something rises from under the surface.

It's a sleek, black machine with a bulbous, metallic center. Four enormous barbed appendages twist about it like tentacles, giving it the appearance of an Octopoda from the ocean's depths. But instead of two eyes, it has only one, a targeting device. It glows red as it homes in on victim after victim, spraying them with volleys of powerful energy, ripping them apart, reducing them to smoldering, unrecognizable husks.

Two soldiers from a different company run by, weapons raised, firing at the atrocity towering over me. But the blast of their guns barely penetrates. Before they can flee, the Octopoda's tentacles lash out, grabbing both men, its steel barbs sawing through them, dicing them alive.

Before this abomination can turn its attention back to me, I'm burrowing through the sand, scrambling to get as much distance between me and it before its targeting sensors can reacquire my position.

But even if I do manage to get away from this one, the entire beach is swarming with those things. And if they're impervious to our weapons, what the hell chance do we possibly have?

Bursting from the sand, I zig zag up the beach, stumbling and rolling my way toward the metal remnants of a beached stealth boat. Several oth crs are hunkered down there, using the mangled hull as a shield against the continual enemy onslaught.

I recognize one of them instantly.

"Cage!" I leap over a trench toward the makeshift shelter, just as a shower of blasts strike around me. To my left, a soldier's leg disappears in a blur of red and a piercing scream. Another soldier takes a hit right through the chest, leaving a gaping hole of cauterized flesh. I tumble into Cage and feel an impact slam into the back of my skull.

For a horrific second I think that I've been shot through the brain. I pull away from Cage to feel the back of my head. Aside from a throbbing and trickle of blood, which quickly washes away in the cold drizzle, it feels like I'm intact. One glance at the smoldering dent and twisted gears in Cage's metal hand tells how I've been spared.

We sink to our knees behind the crashed hulk. Blasts continue to bombard the beach around us.

"They knew we were coming!" He shouts over the chaos. "Someone sold us out!"

I grip his shoulder. "Arrah, Dru—"

Cage shakes his head. "Haven't seen 'em." He grits his teeth as he picks up a nearby helmet, rinses out the blood with the rain, and places it back on his head. "Dahlia, neither."

"I pulled Corin from —" The memory's knocked away by another blast. Half our cover's gone, replaced by a rain of shrapnel.

Two of the Octopoda machines close in on our position, creeping nearer every second.

There's no time to wonder or grieve now. Besides, our friends could still be alive. I point up toward the tower. "We have to get up there and knock out the power before these things wipe us all out."

Cage digs into his pack and pulls out several silver grenades. "Got these. But from the pounding I've seen those machines take, I don't think they're going to do the trick, Mate."

I grab one of the grenades from him. "I had something different in mind."

He grins. "You little ripper."

"We can't penetrate their hulls but we can destabilize them, blow openings into those holes they popped out of, and maybe find access up to that tower."

"I'll give it a burl." Cage reaches for one of the grenades with his damaged metal hand and nearly fumbles it. "Figures they'd knock out the dominant one."

Cursing, he tries with the other, but I shake my head and take the pack from him.

"If you wanna help, I need you to distract them."

He opens his mouth to protest, then stops himself. He knows I'm right. Instead, he grips his particle rifle and aims it at the nearest Octopoda. With his back to me, he mutters, "When this is over, you and I are going out and gettin' rotten, Mate."

"First drink's on me." Then I turn to the half dozen shaken and anxious soldiers in our group. "Take a grenade and follow my lead."

More explosions rock the beach. The searing heat of the blasts dries the cold sweat on my skin. Another chunk of our makeshift shelter disintegrates.

Cage lets out a guttural roar and emerges from the corner of the shelter, firing multiple rounds at the nearest machine. The Octopoda's sensors immediately fix on his position and it swerves, firing. I grit my teeth at the sound of his cry of pain and the sight of his prosthetic limb hurling through the air in pieces.

Grenade clutched in my hand, I bolt from my hiding place, sprinting in an arc around the machine, almost colliding with another soldier. She's dragging a wounded comrade—at least what's left of his wriggling upper half. "I want my momma…," he mutters .

Before the Octopoda can shift its focus from Cage to me, I rip out the pin and lob the grenade, not at the machine itself, but by the ground beside it.

A fireball erupts beside the contraption, displacing the sand around it. It wobbles for a second and tumbles to the ground. Before its stabilizers can readjust, I dodge and leap over its weaponized appendages, pouncing on the bulbous head before tumbling into the chasm it emerged from.

In the darkness, I activate my helmet's shadow imaging tech. The infrared images highlight a series of interconnected semicircular mazes leading far off into the distance—the same direction as the control tower.

Doing my best to ignore the sound of muffled explosions still coming from above and their terrible implications, I rush down the sleek, steel corridor, the only pounding now coming from my heart and lungs.

Even though it seems like hours, my chron tells me it's only a few minutes by the time I reach the other side of the tunnel. I scramble up a long, metal ladder, twist open a small hatch, and squeeze my way through.

I've made it to the control tower at last.

Banks of blinking monitors, gauges, and controls surround me. Panoramic windows look out onto the beach below, a bird's eye view of hell: human fireballs writhing in agony, thick, black smoke. At least it appears some of the others have taken down more of the Octopodas. And as soon as I punch in the override codes our spy in the Parish, gave us…

Something's not right. This is too easy. Why aren't there any other personnel around?

Approaching the controls for the installation's defense grid, I begin to input the codes. If they've already been changed, this whole operation will have been for nothing.

At first nothing happens. But then the lights on the instruments go from green to red, and I let loose a trapped breath. It's working. Only a few more seconds and I'll transfer control of the automated station's drones and weapons to the rebel armada. With the Cape under our control, it may just turn the tide of this war.

I toggle a few switches at the communications bank. "Torch Keeper to Base 1. The key has been turned. Repeat. The key has been turned."

"I should have known it would be you."

Cassius Thorn's voice is like toxic adrenaline in my veins.

I whip around, weapon raised.

CHAPTER TWO

It's only a full-sized holo of Cass behind me, not the real thing. The image is low res, flickering and strobing, replaced by a blizzard of static every few seconds. Despite the poor quality of the projection, I can make out the conflicting emotions in the turbulent green of those terrible eyes.

"You've lost the Cape, Cassius. And it's only the beginning."

"You still haven't embraced the truth. Who you really are. Tell me, Lucian. How many rescues of helpless children do you think it will take to wipe away all the atrocities you've committed? A hundred? Two hundred? You still think that by aiding the misguided rebels that you are somehow cleansing yourself? Saving your soul?"

"More lies. I'm not who you say I am."

He sighs. "There's proof. I wonder what your friends would say if they saw it for themselves."

I clear the lump from my throat. "Where's my brother?"

"If you are referring to Cole, he's safe. Now that he is finally away from your influence." He shakes his head. "You think this is easy for me, especially knowing how I've always felt about you? Can you even fathom what it was like to find out that the one person I cared most about in the world is a mass murderer? Is the one responsible for making me destroy my own father?"

I'm trembling with rage. "Shut up. You're delusional. Whatever happened to you during your own Trials has warped your mind."

He sighs. "Despite everything, I am not going to give up on you. Yet. I'll keep your secret. But you have to help me end this war now. Telling me who your spy is amongst my advisors will be the first step in true contrition."

"Never." I'm surprised he's not threatening to use my brother as leverage.

My hand goes reflexively to my abdomen and the knife wound scar hidden underneath my uniform. He obviously has other plans for him.

"This conversation is over." My finger hovers over the coms panel, ready to cut him off. "I'm not telling you a thing."

Cass's image leans closer. "Will you tell *him*?"

A flash of movement in the darkness above me.

I grip my weapon tighter. A figure descends from the shadows, like a giant arachnid. It's absolutely silent. No footfalls. No breathing. No telltale sounds of humanity.

Even before his features come into focus I stifle a gasp at the familiar silhouette.

It's Digory Tycho—yet it's not.

Digory's golden hair, long and full the last time I saw him, has been shorn into little more than a platinum, almost pure-white, buzz cut. The skin-tight black jumpsuit he's wearing can barely contain his muscular frame, even bigger than it was before. His skin, once bronze, seems almost the color of chalk. Even from here I can make out the greenish hue of his veins pulsing in his hands and neck. But it's his eyes that fill me with dread and despair. Once a brilliant blue brimming with warmth and compassion, they're now a luminescent gray, dark clouds glowing with hidden lightning, heralding the approach of a violent storm.

Cass's experiment to create the Ultra-Imposer has succeeded. And once again, I've failed Digory, the man I love with all my heart, cruelly torn away from me by this terrible war.

"Digory." My tone is the epitome of despair.

He steps closer. "Who is your informant at the Citadel?"

His voice is like sleet, emotionless. The fact that he's not holding a weapon somehow makes his presence even more menacing.

"I'm not sure what they've done to you, Digory. But you're stronger than they are. You can fight—"

"This is the last time we're going to ask. Who is the mole feeding our intel to you rebels?"

I search his face, trying desperately to find some trace, however minute, of the old Digory. Maybe this is all for show. Maybe he's just pretending so Cassius won't suspect. But there's nothing there. It's like gazing into the eyes of a corpse. Except this corpse has the ability to kill.

Fighting the pain knifing through my chest, I raise my weapon higher with a trembling hand, trying to target the place where his heart should be, made all the more difficult by my blurred vision. "I'm not telling you a damn thing."

Digory takes a step closer—

The trigger's slick with sweat. "Don't make me do this, Digory. I'm begging you. Please." This can't be happening.

Cassius must be relishing the irony of me being the one to end Digory's life.

Digory moves in. An avalanche of emotions rips through me. At the last second, I shift my aim to his thigh, instead, and fire, just as his fist connects with my arm. It's like colliding with a steel club. The impact sends my gun flying from my grip. I hurtle across the room, smacking my forehead against the instrument bank.

Dazed, I try to sit up. I wince. Pain shoots up from where he struck me. I brace myself against the wall with my other arm, hoisting myself up, wiping the mixture of blood and tears from my eyes.

Digory's sprawled several feet away, his thigh still smoking from the shot I fired. But you'd never know he'd been wounded. His face is expressionless. He lifts up the tattered fabric surrounding his injury.

I must have hit my head harder than I thought. The torn skin begins to knit together, like finely woven fabric. In seconds the dark wound's gone, replaced by brand new flesh.

That nanotech Cassius subjected Digory to back at Sanctum has given him regenerative properties. The perfect, unstoppable killing machine.

Dragging myself across the console, I try and ignore the pain, both physical and mental. The only thing that matters is inputting the last of the control codes.

Something yanks me away. I can tell from the *pop* that my shoulder's been dislocated. The pain is excruciating. I whirl and slam a fist into Digory's jaw, but it has little effect. Then I spin and catch him in the gut with a roundhouse kick. But he grabs my foot and twists, flinging me to the ground. Before I can get my bearings, he hauls me to my feet from behind, squeezing so hard it feels like he's cracked a rib. He twists my body around to face him. One of his large hands clamps around my throat, squeezing.

"Tell us the name of the traitor. Now."

If I betray Valerian, the rebellion will lose one of its most valuable assets, deep undercover in Cass's inner circle.

"N-not...a...chance..."

As he squeezes tighter and it becomes almost impossible to breathe, he goes out of focus. I try to imagine his face as it used to be. It's the last thing I want to remember before I die.

There's a muffled burst. The pressure around my throat disappears. I try to make sense of fragmented images. Troops bursting into the control center. Someone pulling me to my feet.

"Tycho's rigged to explode!" A familiar voice shouts.

Arrah.

"He's sealed us all in!" Someone else shouts.

I snap to my senses. Arrah, Drusilla, Dahlia, and Cage surround me. The other soldiers are backing away from Digory, who's standing tall and erect like a marble statue. The top of his suit's been ripped open, revealing the explosive device strapped to his body. The digital counter reads thirty seconds...twenty-nine...twenty-eight...

"If we fire at him, it could set off the explosive," Cage mutters in my ear.

So this was Cass's failsafe. If he couldn't get the traitor's name, he'd blow us all to hell...including Digory, a disgarded tool that's served its purpose.

I grab Arrah's weapon, dispel the cartridge, and replace it with ampules of anesthetics from Drusilla's medpack. Then I push past the others, aim my weapon at Digory and fire, round after round. He staggers and falls. I'm not sure how much of the medicine his system can take, but I'm on him in a flash.

"Lucian there's no time!" Dahlia shouts as she and the others try to batter down the door to escape the blast radius.

With only seconds to spare, I splice the wires to the detonator, wincing as I cut, hoping I've remembered enough of my training to cut them in the right sequence.

The timer hits zero. And no explosion.

"Get Tycho restrained!" Cage orders.

Half a dozen soldiers bind Digory with all manner of shackles.

Arrah and Dru kneel by me. "We did it Lucian," Arrah says. "We won this round."

I stare at Digory's body as it's dragged from the room for imprisonment and interrogation. Then I focus on the panoramic windows overlooking the beach. They're filled with black smoke and littered with hundreds of dead bodies, stacked up like a fishing trolley's catch of the day.

"Yep. We won."

CHAPTER THREE

I maneuver my way through the chaos of the Medical Ward's stark white corridors, marred here and there by splashes of crimson. The stench of blood and death is suffocating. Despite my best efforts, I can't help but keep a mental tally of all the body bags I pass, each one cutting a deeper notch into my brain as I examine the I.D. tags on every last corpse. Hundreds dead. Almost as many dying. The steep price for freedom these days.

My breathing's on rapid fire mode. The last transport of survivors and bodies from the battle of the cape has already checked in without any sign of Corin. I force a swallow. Maybe his body was never recovered.

That's when I spot him, sitting up in a cramped, corner cot at the very end of the ward. His skin's very pale and his eyes are like glass, staring at a small holo-globe. He doesn't acknowledge my presence in any way as I approach. Pausing, I glance at the holochart by his bed which some medtech left on projection mode.

Patient: Corin Totus (Male), Age: 14

Diagnosis: Shock, multiple contusions…

I breathe a sigh of relief as I scan the rest of the readouts. I'm no medical expert, but it doesn't look like he suffered any serious injuries at the Cape. He's going to be just fine.

"I really messed up."

Corin's voice startles me with its emptiness.

"How you feeling, Kid?" I switch off his chart and sit at his bedside.

"Can't really complain, compared to all those others," he mutters, nudging his chin toward the body bags filling the hallway. "At least *they* died fighting." He turns to me, his eyes dark pools. "I panicked. I should be in one of those bags. The rescue drone said you were the one who fished me out of the sea. Why'd you risk your life and do that?"

I grip his shoulders firmly to steady the trembling. "You don't think everyone was scared? You don't think *I* was?" My grip turns into a hug. "The day war stops being a scary thing is the day we all lose."

He pulls away, swiping his eyes with a forearm. "I promise I'll do better next time, Sir."

"I'm sure you will." I grin and pick up the holocube that's resting on his lap. The palm-sized device has obviously seen better days, judging from the scratched and dented chrome casing, and the static-filled resolution of the projected image of two young people.

The first is a tall, lanky, grinning youth with acne-covered cheeks. I recognize him immediately. Boaz, the resistance member who perished at Infiernos during the Trials last year. Corin was his Incentive. The second figure is a girl of about eight or nine, with wild hair, dirt-smudged cheeks, and skinned-knees. She springs from a tree onto Boaz's shoulders. The child's eyes and smile are unmistakable. It's Corin, before he Aligned. The two laugh and tumble to the ground. There's a burst of static and the scene repeats itself on a loop.

"You and Boaz look very happy." I offer Corin back the cube.

"I really miss him." He takes it from me. "After my folks were killed in that Establishment raid, he did everything he could to make a home for me. He's the only thing worth remembering from that part of my life." He shuts off the projection and stares at the cube. "I would have gotten rid of this, but it's the only image I have left of Boaz." He stuffs the device under the sheets. "I wish I could see him for real again."

"I know how you feel."

"There you are! I've been looking everywhere for you two blokes."

We both turn to find Cage flexing a new, if somewhat battered, metallic replacement hand. "Spare parts are a bit of a luxury right now. It's not as pretty as the last one, but I've still got pretty to spare." A wide grin spreads across his handsome face, framed perfectly by his long, thick brown hair. "Besides," he grips one of the cot's metal frames and twists it easily in his fist as though it were made of rubber, "it'll get the job done."

I crack a smile. "I'm sure it will."

Cage hands Corin a small white box. "Sssh. Don't say a word. I smuggled some chokkie past the nurses."

Corin tears open the package and stares wide-eyed at the bar of chocolate. Treats like this are rare, if not impossible, to come by these days.

"I'm not even going to ask where you got that, Cage."

He sidles up beside me and puckers his lips. "Hmmm. A little pashing on might loosen my tongue."

I push him gently away and grin back at him. "My fist might have the same effect."

Cage's wink can't hide the weariness in his eyes.

I guess we're all putting up a front these days.

Corin stuffs a piece of chocolate in his mouth and nods. "Yeah. You two go make out and I'll take care of all of *this*."

After making small talk with Corin for a bit, Cage and I glance at our chrons and exchange pointed looks. Cage announces he and I've been summoned to a briefing.

Corin grips Cage's arm as we're saying goodbye. "Thanks again for the chocolate. I'm sure Tristin's okay. If there's anything I can do to help find your sister—"

Cage ruffles the boy's hair. "Thank you. You just concentrate on getting out of here quickly, Mate."

We file out of the medical ward on our way to the briefing room.

"We *will* find Tristin, Cage." Looks like she and Corin really got close back at Infiernos.

He shakes his head as we round a corner, the heaviness in his eyes more pronounced now. "I hope you're right, Mate. There are rumors she's been stirring up the masses back at the Parish and has been taken into custody. I'm worried sick. Things between my dad and me are different now. It's like he blames me."

I squeeze his arm. "It's not your fault. Whatever happens." I nod toward the briefing room ahead. We pause just outside the doors. "Do you think they'll be open to my proposal?"

He slings his arm around my shoulders and squeezes. "Why not? I think it's ace."

"What about…the prisoner?"

Cage's face clouds over and he lets go of me. "We'd best get inside, Mate."

———

The mood in the cramped, spherical briefing chamber is gloomier than the murky ocean depths visible through the three oblong portholes surrounding us. During the past year, the rebellion's been forced to establish several different Base Ops, fleeing every time Cassius and the Fleshers get wind of our latest hiding place. This latest locale is a retrofitted submarine refueling station, abandoned after a Category Five hurricane rendered it unviable years before.

While Jeptha briefs us on the improving state of our supplies thanks to our success retaking the Cape, I focus on the construction taking place through the windows behind him.

Two Aero-Mantas plunge into the sea from the sky. They're small, triangular craft named after their undersea counterparts, except they're adaptable to both air and water, with flexible, curved wings and long metallic tails consisting of sensor arrays.

The Mantas deliver supplies to the construction team busy soldering beams and reinforcing support girders.

Repairs have been a bitch, costing too many precious lives in the process. But we're running out of hiding places and options real fast. As we strategize in the eerie, silent, calm, it's hard to believe in all the chaos taking place just above the surface.

"…consideration of your latest proposal, Commander Spark?"

Jeptha's direct address cuts through the depths of my brain.

My eyes break from the sea to take in the four others seated at the circular steel table. Besides Jeptha, there's General Garvin Rios, tall, ebony, and imposing; Jebez Croakley, now the Chief Rebel strategist whom I was once apprenticed to at the Parish library; and Cage, who shoots me a stern look and nudges me under the table with his leg.

I clear my throat. "Thank you, General."

Standing, I place the small holodisc I've been clutching in my palm into a slot in the center of the table. A three-dimensional map appears, hovering in the air between us, outlining the areas in red still controlled by Cass's new Establishment forces, known as the Thorn Republic, as well as the regions in green overrun by Straton and his Flesher battalions from Sanctum. Much smaller pockets of blue represent the scattered areas which our Torch Brigade has liberated and is currently holding and protecting.

I nod toward Jeptha. "Our recent victory at the Cape has dealt a significant blow to Thorn's troops. Now that we're in control of the region, the shipping and supply lanes belong to us. But as you can see, it's not enough."

Rios shakes his head. "You're not telling us anything we don't already know, Spark."

His contempt bleeds through his words. He's never liked me, and I'm sure at least some of that's because his son Rafé was married to Digory.

Can't even imagine how much worse it would be if he knew Digory let his son die in order to save my brother.

Avoiding his glare, I continue. "Thorn's forces outnumber us, but they're spread far too thin. I think I've come up with a way of evening the playing field."

My words have the desired effect. Even Rios now seems interested in what I have to say.

"Go on," Croakley says.

I point to an area of the map central to all. "If we can seize control of this area here, it would cut off both Thorn's and Sanctum's forces on either side of our borders and act as the perfect hub from which to launch attacks against them. There's no way they could approach without us seeing them coming from hundreds of miles away. With the drones we now control thanks to our success at the Cape, we could strike them before they ever got close."

Rios slams his fist on the table and shakes his head. "Except for the fact that the *little* area in question just happens to be a military base currently under Thorn's control."

Jeptha nods. "He's right. Fort Diablos was the primary military base where the Trials were held prior to them being brought back to Infiernos. It's still utilized as a training ground, with considerable weapons stockpiles."

"Exactly," Rios continues. "We don't have the resources for such an attack, and even if we did, it would be suicide." His gaze shifs from Jeptha to Croakley. "To even consider such a strike would be absurd—"

I jab a finger to a region west of the base. "Not if any strike would just be a diversion to draw troops from the base and hit them with their defenses down from a direction they're not expecting."

"The work camps at the Gorge," Cage says. He grins. "They wouldn't be expecting that, Mate."

I nod. "Security is relatively low tech at the camps, just enough soldiers and firepower to keep the unarmed workers in line. Slaves who I'm sure won't hesitate to join our forces and help launch an attack against the fort while Thorn's troops are engaged in a diversionary attack to the east."

"And what good will nutrition deprived civilians be against trained soldiers?" Rios snorts.

Croakley smiles. "Except they aren't all untrained civilians, are they, Spark?"

I shake my head. "Many of those interned at the camps are former recruits who've gone through rigorous training and competed in the Trials."

"And obviously failed," Rios growls.

"The point is these former recruits have military expertise, and reports from our spies indicate they've spent years secretly training their fellow civvie prisoners in the art of combat, just waiting for the right moment to strike. The fact that Thorn has all but forgotten them during his coup against Talon ensures they won't be loyal to his cause." I sweep the room with my gaze. "Valerian, our spy in the Thorn Republic, is prepared to end her cover and personally provide the security codes to navigate through Fort Diablos and give us automated control of the entire arsenal. If this strike succeeds, not only will it replenish our regiments of troops, but also give us access to an invaluable cache of weapons, not to mention a key strategic vantage point. It's a win-win."

Rios sighs. "But if it fails—"

"Then at least we'll be doing something instead of sitting on our asses waiting to die." Now it's my turn to glare at him.

"That's enough, Spark," Jeptha says. "I want detailed specs on this Op on my desk as soon as possible for presentation to the council."

"Thank you, Commander. And if the committee decides to implement my plan, I'd like to lead the team that infiltrates the Gorge and Fort Diablos."

Jeptha's expression softens. "Of course, Son."

"I'm right there with Lucian, Father," Cage announces. But Jeptha never looks his way.

"Thanks, Cage," I cut through the awkward silence.

Rios's eyes avoid mine. "And what of the last matter on our agenda?"

Jeptha scans his tablet. "Yes. So far we haven't been able to obtain any useful intel from the prisoner. I'm afraid his resistance to our interrogation methods is quite considerable."

I slump down into my chair. The thought of Digory being locked away, isolated, subjected to round the clock grilling makes me nauseous.

"Then might I suggest we implement unorthodox methods in our questioning of the traitor." Rios's words are measured, but his meaning cuts deep.

I focus on him. "You mean torture, don't you, Sir?"

"I prefer to look at it as *intense debriefing*. We're at war, Spark. Despite your significant accomplishments, your sentimental school boy crushes are an embarrassment and unacceptable."

My fists clench under the table. "If we start torturing people to get what we want without any regard to human life, then Thorn has already won, General Rios."

"If we don't utilize any method at our disposal to extract vital information from one individual for the greater good, then we all may as well surrender now. To beat the enemy, we can't afford to be weak." He dismisses me with a wave. "Besides, that thing in holding is hardly what I'd call human."

I'm about to spring from my seat, when Cage's hand grips my arm .

I take a deep breath. "Maybe you should let me, speak with Digory. We—we trained together. I know I can get through to—"

Jeptha shakes his head. "According to your own statement, Commander Spark, the last time you were alone together the prisoner tried to kill you. I'm afraid we can't risk another attempt on your life on the minute possibility of gleaning any useful information."

"But—"

Jeptha continues. "Both Commander Spark and General Rios make valid points on a highly complicated moral issue. As such, I move for a vote on whether or not to take more proactive measures in extracting information from the prisoner." He motions to the computer screens inlaid in the table in front of each of us. "All those in favor of more arduous questioning techniques, place your hand on the scanner on the right of the screen. All those opposed, on the left."

I shoot a look around me. It's a no brainer the way Rios is going to vote. Croakley has always been a pacifist. But Jeptha? He didn't seem persuaded either way.

I press my hand on the left side of the screen. One by one a vote tally corresponding to each of our names is projected in the center of the table via holo.

My vote, *Nay*. Rios's expected *Yes* vote, followed by Croakley's *Nay* vote. I look up at him and he nods. I knew he wouldn't let me down.

The next vote is Jeptha. Disappointment floods through me when I see his *Yes* vote. But that quickly washes away. It's a tie. And Cage is going to break the stalemate and definitely going to vote—

Yes.

I'm too stunned to move. There's got to be some mistake.

One glance at Cage's face confirms that there isn't.

"By a vote of three to two, the motion to vigorously interrogate the prisoner passes," Jeptha announces. His voice seems muffled. "In the interim, Commander Spark is ordered to refrain from any contact with the subject until such time, if any, it is deemed necessary. This meeting is adjourned."

Jeptha doesn't have a gavel, but the finality of his last words may as well have been hammered into my brain. To make things worse, Rios is staring pointedly at me, his face barely able to contain its satisfaction.

Croakley leans in close. "I'm sorry, Lucian."

I can barely nod, unable to respond, choosing to squeeze his hand instead as I bolt from the room.

"Spark! Wait up!" Cage calls. "Lucian!"

But he's the last person I want to speak to, let alone lay eyes on. And I can't trust what will happen if my fists get anywhere near his face.

I'm halfway down the hall, and through the doors to the lift, when I hear someone running to catch up. I smash my palm against the button and the doors begin to close—but not fast enough. Cage squeezes into the elevator beside me as the doors slide shut and it begins to descend.

"I know you're bloody pissed off at me, Mate," he says. "Just hear me out."

"I thought you were my friend," I hiss at him.

"I *am* your friend. That freak tried to kill you at the Cape. Kill all of us actually. And he would've if you hadn't tranked him. And don't even get me started on how he betrayed the rebellion before and let Rafé die. It's no wonder Rios wants to see his son's murderer pay."

That's it. I grab him by the throat, slamming him into the wall of the cab. "You don't know what the hell you're talking about. Digory never betrayed the rebels. He was working undercover to gain intel on Cassius—"

"...or so...he...says," Cage hisses.

"I've seen the proof myself. And as far as Rafé goes, he and Digory married in the event either needed an Incentive. It wasn't for love. You know that."

Cage tears at my grip with his metal hand. "Then why...did he let Rafé...die...?"

"So he could save my brother!" I blurt out. "Because he loved me. Maybe that's what's eating at you. Because of the way you used to feel about Digory. Because of the way you feel about *me* now."

I was purposely going for the jugular. But the look on his face tells me I've gone too far.

He rips my hand away. "You really think I'm that petty, Mate? Screw you, Lucian."

The doors slide open and he disappears down the hallway.

As bad as I feel, I can't worry about Cage now. Despite Jeptha's and Rios's warnings, I'm going to see Digory. I abandoned him once before. Not gonna happen again. Even if it kills me.

CHAPTER FOUR

I bite down on my tongue hard enough to smother the scream of rage and anguish threatening to burst from my throat. The last few days have been a real test of willpower, sneaking into the holding cell's observation room, riveted to the other side of the two-way mirror, where Digory's being tortured. Despite being barred from seeing him, I've technically not broken any of Jeptha's commands as far as making actual contact goes—not yet, anyway.

It's fortunate that Arrah and Dru have pulled guard duty. They have no problems sneaking me in to observe between my other duties. With no other prisoners to watch over, it makes the assignment pretty cushy for them and allows me access—at least visual—to Digory. But based on the knowing looks and glances I've gotten from Croakley, I'd bet anything that luck didn't have much to do with two of my best friends being assigned to the brig. Except each day that goes by watching Digory's increasing suffering, I'm not sure I should be grateful.

Arrah rubs my shoulder. "How're you holding up?"

"Been better."

Digory's strapped to an X-shaped platform, his arms and legs spreadeagle. Streaks of blood stand out against his chalk-white skin, and his face is a series of black and purple splotches, as if someone's worked it over with a club. One of his hands is a bandaged clump. His naked torso is covered with electrodes plugged into an ominous looking rectangular device clutched in the thin, meticulously dressed interrogator's hand. I swear by the look on Devlin's face, he's actually getting off on the pain he's inflicting.

"Let's try this again, Tycho." Devlin's voice is low and gravelly over the speakers. "Where is the location of Thorn's hidden bunker?"

Digory turns his head slightly and looks at him with one of those strange, iridescent gray eyes. The other is swollen, crusted shut with dried blood. Despite his battered appearance, there's no anger registered on his face. No fear. Nothing. It's as if he's staring at Devlin the same way he would study a specimen under a microscope.

Like clockwork, the change in Digory's physiology begins to manifest, the same way it does every time I observe these hideous torture sessions. Little by little, Digory's cuts start to heal and the swelling in his face subsides, as if a sculptor were remolding him into that perfect specimen, only to be tortured and destroyed all over again.

What was that story that fascinated me so long ago in the archives? Prometheus. Molded from clay, he stole fire from the gods, only to be punished by being bound to a rock, where an eagle devoured his newly regrown liver day after day, an eternity of endless pain and suffering.

Digory's crime? Loving me.

Digory's regenerated flesh, along with his pointed silence, is much more powerful a rebuke than if he'd have shouted a taunt at his tormentor.

"As loquacious as ever," Devlin mutters. His fingers hover over the controls of the shock box in his hand. "Where is Thorn's bunker?"

Digory just stares, now through both of those storm cloud eyes.

"Why doesn't he just give up Thorn and be done with it?" Arrah whispers to me.

"He can't, even if he wanted to. I think it's part of his programming."

"I'm sorry. I know he means a lot to you." She takes my hand.

"You have no idea."

Devlin hits the switch on the gleaming black unit.

Digory's body convulses. It feels as if the powerful electric current's surging through my own body as I watch him thrash about like a fish on a hook. Foam pools at his mouth and drips from his lips.

"He's going to *kill* him," I squeeze through clenched teeth. I take a step closer to the door leading into the cell.

Arrah grabs my arm. "You can't. If you do, you'll only make it worse for him and you'll be taking his place in there."

The seconds tick away like lifetimes. Finally, Devlin shuts off that infernal device.

"Stubborn to the end," he says, his tone as chillingly indifferent as Digory's expression.

Devlin reaches into a black leather case and produces a gleaming pincer tool. My face twitches as he approaches Digory and rips off the bandage from his hand.

It appears to be fine.

He grabs Digory's other hand. "You may be able to mend quickly, traitor, but I'm sure it's excruciating every time one of those bones goes *pop*."

Devlin positions one of Digory's fingers between the pincers. "Where is Thorn's enclave?"

No response.

"I figured that's what you'd say." Devlin squeezes the tool.

Snap!

Digory winces. I can tell he's struggling not to cry out, as Devlin proceeds from one finger to the next.

Snap. Snap. Snap.

Devlin's finally rewarded with a yelp. But still Digory refuses to tell him what he wants to know.

A flash of anger cracks Devlin's cold exterior. He packs up his tools, slamming each of them into his case. Then he's lowering Digory from the platform, careful to keep his distance as it retracts and Digory drops to the floor. Devlin starts to leave, then turns to him one more time.

"We've played out the bone breaking routine. Tomorrow we find out if your appendages actually grow back when they're cut off. Same for your eyes when they're ripped out of their sockets. Should be interesting."

Then he jabs at the control switch on the other side of the door. "I'm done here."

"That's your cue," Arrah says, hustling me into an equipment locker.

I'm still trying to contain my own rage and pain as I hear the cell door open and Devlin march past Arrah and out into the corridor.

She opens the locker door. "You look like Devlin's taken a go at you, too."

"I'm going to kill him." I push past her into the outer room and press my face against the cell's glass. Digory's laying there in a fetal position, manacled to the wall like a rabid canid. Regardless of his earlier composure, I can see the weariness through the rapid rise and fall of his chest. "In spite of his genetic enhancements, he's not going to last much longer if Devlin starts cutting away."

The door to the observation room slides open once again and I tense—but it's Drusilla, clutching a small, silver box. "Sorry. Just me. Devlin looks pissed." She flinches when she sees Digory through the glass. "Damn, they've really worked him over."

"Dru…," Arrah cocks her head toward me.

Drusilla clears her throat. "Sorry, Spark."

I glance at the object she's carrying. "Is that it?"

"Yep." She opens the box and removes a small data drive. "Once I plug this into the system, it'll create an audio-video loop on the feeds to Tycho's cell. Anyone monitoring the system will only see him in there while you slip in and have your chat." She strides over to the computer terminal and positions the drive into a slot before glancing my way. "I can only maintain the loop for a few minutes. If we keep it going too long, security will detect it and they'll be able to trace it back to us."

She jams the drive in and the monitors flicker for just an instant. To the casual observer, it'll appear to be a slight power glitch.

I manage to crack a smile. "Good work, Dru. I'm not even going to ask how you managed it."

Arrah gives her a squeeze and a quick kiss. "My woman knows what she's doing."

I head for the cell, then turn back to them at the last minute. "I appreciate the risk you guys are taking letting me do this. It really means a lot. Nobody here trusts Digory. Not that I blame them. If I get caught, I'll take full responsibility."

"You'd do the same for your friends," Arrah says. "Besides, if you believe in Tycho, that's good enough for us."

Drusilla takes Arrah's hand and kisses it. "All I know is if that were Arrah in there like that, there's nothing that would keep me away from her. You go on and do what you need to do. We've always got your back."

I nod, grab a first aid kit, activate the cell door's release mechanism, and slip inside.

Digory's still curled up in a fetal position. Despite the manacles, I approach with caution. After all, he did try to kill me before. The lacerations and bruises cut much deeper than my skin, and I doubt they'll ever heal.

I hunch down and reach out a tentative hand.

"There's no need for you to be afraid, Lucian."

His voice startles me more than if he'd grabbed me. I pause as he shifts about to face me with those strange gray eyes.

"We're not going to hurt you." His voice is just as cold and emotionless as before.

"I've got a few scrapes on my body that would say otherwise." I move a little closer. "You did try to murder me back at the Cape, after all."

"We were trying to extract information from you about the rebel spy. Pain is usually a good inspiration for truth."

"Now that sounds like a Cassius-ism if I ever heard one." I pull out one of the cloths from the first aid kit and begin to wipe away the blood from his skin. He doesn't try to stop me. "You keep saying *we*. You mean you and Cassius?"

He shakes his head. "We as in the Hive. We are as one."

I pause. "The Fleshers."

"We do not refer to ourselves so crudely. We are beings of order and reason."

"I suppose that bomb you had strapped to your body wasn't meant to kill us all?"

"When it became obvious you were not going to cooperate to end this destructive conflict, we activated a failsafe to prevent this vessel's capture and interrogation."

The timbre of his voice is cavernous and empty. There's no trace of the warmth that defined Digory.

There was a possibility you would make it out of there before the detonation," he drones on. "You were not the target. You were—"

"Collateral damage," I finish. "Another Cassius catchphrase. Not sure if that's supposed to make me feel any better."

"It was not intended to make you feel anything."

"Doesn't it bother you that Cassius was willing to sacrifice your life? That you're nothing but a disposable tool to him, Digory?"

He stares at me so intently that I have to look away. Now I realize what else is so unnerving about those eyes.

They never blink.

"We were following our orders. It is not up to us to question."

I let out a hollow laugh. "Right. Just following orders like a good little slave. Cassius really did succeed in creating the Ultra-Imposer. A perfect killing machine that heals itself and doesn't have a moral compass."

"Morality is subjective."

"What makes you say that?"

"You did not think twice about breaking protocol and disobeying direct orders from your superiors just to satisfy your own selfish desires to visit with Digory Tycho's former vessel one last time."

And in that moment, the full realization of what Cassius has done hits me like a concussion charge. If he can destroy all the good, all the compassion, all the love in a soul like Digory's, then there's truly nothing left to believe in.

I grab one of his manacled hands trying to infuse my warmth into its stark coldness. "You once asked me to never forget you. Surely you must remember who you were? Who you still are?"

"That person no longer exists, Lucian," he says. "Any fragments of irrelevant data that remain should be flushed in this vessel's next upgrade. We serve only the Thorn Republic now."

I let his hand slip through my fingers. "Then we have nothing to discuss, ever again." I force myself to stand on unsteady legs, trying to avoid his eyes so I won't lose it completely.

"Actually, we do," he says.

"What're you talking about?"

Without using his hands to brace himself, he rises to his full height, not making a sound. "We know that our stay here is about to be terminated prematurely."

"There's nothing I can do about that. If you tell them what they want to know, they may let you live. Please, Digory. It's your only chance."

"We are afraid that is not possible. However, there is something you can do. We have something you want. If you help extract this vessel from here and provide us with the name of your spy, we will let you have it."

I shake my head. "I'll never do that."

"Not even if in exchange we will let you have your brother, Cole, back? Think about it."

I swipe at the hot tears threatening to betray me as I bolt from that cell.

CHAPTER FIVE

"There it is again." Arrah points to a small blip on the spherical holographic map of the base's perimeter, hovering above her data terminal.

Jeptha and I lean over her shoulder to get a better look. The other dozen officers and personnel on duty in the communications hub crowd around us.

The radar screen displays one more faint *blip*, which disappears as if it were never there.

I turn to Arrah. "You say these unidentified bursts have been appearing in irregular cycles?"

She nods. "At first I thought they were just randoms, ghost images of our own transmissions bouncing back. But the intervals between each ping are growing shorter and the signal itself is getting stronger." She turns to Jeptha. "Sorry. I should have reported them sooner, Sir."

If she was trying to assuage her guilt, it has no effect on Jeptha's rigid face.

"When did you first become aware of this?" he finally asks. "Bring it up on the main console."

Arrah types in a few keys and a graph appears and hovers in the center of the room.

"Seems like the first was shortly after the battle of the Cape."

Jeptha shoots me a look laced with concern. "When Tycho was captured."

I turn away. After that last conversation I had with Digory the implication is more than a little unsettling.

"Someone's got to go take a closer look." I'm already on my way out. "I'm on recon patrol," I call behind me.

"Take Bledsoe with you," Jeptha commands.

———

The cockpit of the Manta is dark, except for the faint glow of blinking lights on the dash. Dahlia's sitting in the co-pilot chair beside me, her face ensnared by a web of alternating shadows as she studies the instrument readouts.

"This is Manta 5 to base," she says into her com-unit. "We're going radio silent, over."

"Copy, Manta 5," a voice crackles on the speaker. Cage. "Let us know as soon as you have a visual. Over and out."

She flicks a switch on the console and turns to me. "Okay. Just what the hell's been eating you, Spark?"

"Don't know what—"

"Spare me the bullshit. It's obvious you and Cage are pissed at each other. You barely mumble hello anymore." She softens her gaze. "It's got something to do with Tycho, doesn't it?"

She's gotten to know me pretty well this last year. The tension between Cage and I has just gotten worse since he cast his vote to torture Digory. Not only don't we speak, but I can barely stand to be in the same room with him. This coupled with Digory's proposal is all I've been obsessing about. Sleeping and eating are overrated anyway.

I toggle a few switches on my control panel. "I think we have a hell of a lot more important things to worry about right now." Pausing, I look her in the eyes and try my best to smile. "Your concern is duly noted and greatly appreciated, though."

She winks at me. "Anything for my favorite Fifth Tier." The smirk disappears from her face. "I'll always be grateful to you for being there for me, Lucian …when I was assaulted…the procedure afterwards…everything."

We continue gliding through the black sea in silence, until one of the screens on the instrument panel begins to ping.

Proximity Alert.

"Looks like we've found it," I say.

Just outside the cockpit windows floats an oblong metallic cylinder. It's about ten feet in length, slowly revolving end over end in eerie silence.

Dahlia activates the com-unit. "Base 1, this is Manta 5. We've made contact. Are you reading this? Over."

"This is Base 1. Your signal's…breaking up….interference…"

I study the instruments. "The whole system's gone screwy. Whatever this thing is, it must be putting out some kind of interference…jamming our coms…"

"It looks like some type of beacon."

"Yeah. But is it a warning, or a guide?"

"Time for a sweep." Dahlia grips the control yoke and steers the Manta around the cylinder. "This is interesting."

Gazing out the cockpit window, I get a better look at what's captured her attention. It seems the cylindrical device is hovering just at the edge of a dark trench that seems endless.

"Any idea how deep?"

She shakes her head. "Can't get a strong signal because of the interference, but I'd say it's at least several miles deep."

"Perfect place to hide something."

At that moment, the oblong shape emits a piercing sound that practically burns out the Manta's speakers, accompanied by a blinding flash.

"What the hell was that?" Dahlia rubs her temples as she attempts to make sense of the crazy readouts.

In the gloom of the trench, dim silhouettes appear under the scant beams of the Manta's lights. First one. Then a dozen, long, sleek metallic shapes.

A fleet of Eels, the latest submersible warships of the Thorn Republic.

They found us. But how did they know we were here? It couldn't just be a coincidence.

A sickening possibility hits me. This oblong cylinder isn't a beacon. It's a relay.

The real beacon is lying manacled in a holding cell back at the base because I let him live.

"Time to get out of here."

Grabbing the yoke, I bank the Manta hard to swerve out of the trench, just as the silent behemoths come to life and a thousand lights flood our cockpit with artificial day.

Dahlia's already on the horn. "Base 1 this is Manta Five. An attack fleet has located the base and is on its way. Repeat. An attack fleet—"

A concussion rocks our tiny craft, jostling us about. Sparks fly from the instrument panel.

"We've lost one of the stabilizers, but we're still watertight," I shout after a quick check of the Manta's systems.

I gun the craft toward the base with the enemy in hot pursuit.

More blasts rock the Manta, increasing in power and frequency while I weave the tiny craft through the dark seas.

"I still can't get a signal to base!" Dahlia slams a fist against the control panel, as if that'll somehow break through the frequency jam.

Dozens of blips appear on my radar screen closing in around us way too fast. "They're almost right on top of us."

The thought of flying the Manta up to the surface crosses my mind for a split second. No. If this armada has air support, as I suspect, they'll shoot us out of the sky as easily as swatting a fly.

Just ahead, the Manta's lights pick up a silhouette of an undersea rock formation. The wreckage of ancient sea vessels that have formed a coral reef from the looks of it. I hit the throttle hard and drop the Manta into a cave-like opening, just as another series of blasts barely misses us. The combination of the near hits and the g-forces created by my sudden dive are almost too much for the Manta to handle. The console crackles, metal whines and creaks.

The radar screen flickers and dies. Navigating on instinct now.

Dahlia's eyes grow wide. "Pull up!"

I'm squeezing the yoke so tightly, I feel like I'm going to crush it in my sweaty grip. With only a limited amount of visibility ahead, I pull back on the stick and narrowly avoid crashing into a cluster of mangled metal and jagged coral as I veer the Manta upright again. The tail of the ship screeches and another screen fades to black.

"We've lost the sensor array tail!"

But Dahlia doesn't respond as she continues to try and raise the base on the com.

"Base One. This is Manta Five. Come in…"

Cold sweat seeps from my pores. I maneuver the Manta through the seemingly endless maze of twists, drops, and climbs through the claustrophobic blackness, wondering each second if just one tiny miscalculation in my trajectory's going to end with us joining the scattered debris.

Just as it seems the ship's about to tear apart, we burst out through the opening and back into open sea.

Up ahead, I can just make out the familiar outline of the resistance base in the distance.

"I see it," Dahlia says before I can ask. Then she's toggling more switches on the com. "Base One, this is Manta Five. Do you copy?"

Now that we're in such close proximity and with direct line of sight, maybe there's a chance we'll break through the Republic's communications jam.

A second of silence stretches into infinity. We shoot each other a panicked look.

"…this is Base One…" a voice crackles. "What is….position?"

As I continue to gun the ship toward home base, Dahlia activates the emergency beacon. "We're under attack. Republic fleet is approaching the base. Activate defense shields and seal off the perimeter. Over!"

Another explosion rocks the Manta, the worst one yet. The craft banks sharply, hurtling into a tail spin as we careen toward the base.

"We've lost coms!" Dahlia shouts. "Better hope they got that last transmission!"

Maybe it's a blessing that we've lost radar and can't see the crafts closing in. Judging from the number of blasts all around us, it's like we've kicked a hornets' nest.

I'm barely able to maneuver the Manta. Smoke's filling the cockpit, even as numerous leaks spring, spraying us with icy sea water. "Structural integrity's down to twenty percent," I mutter, just before that gauge sparks and dies, too.

Dahlia points to a spot just outside the cracked cockpit window. "Looks like they heard us."

Before us, the lights of the defense grid are blinking from green to crimson. The shield doors leading into the hangar bay are already closing.

In a few seconds we'll be sealed outside. The way the Manta's groaning, we'll be done even before the Eels get to us.

With what little ship's power I have left, I channel all the remaining system functionality into the craft's turbo boosters. The hangar doors continue to close.

Another blast takes out the last of the Manta's power reserves. The cockpit lights flicker and die.

But the course I've set and the ship's forward momentum are enough to thrust most of the Manta through the narrow gap of the shield doors which slam shut, blocking out the Eels' firepower, but also crushing the back of the ship.

Ocean bursts through the cabin. I hit the pilot seat's eject button, joining Dahlia as we're spit out of the wreckage and tumble through the turbulent water until we surface in the hangar bay.

"You did...good...Fifth Tier," Dahlia says. We cling to each other, breathless.

Hands are waiting to pull us up and out. Corin and Cage.

All around us, emergency sirens blare and Jeptha's voice booms throughout the complex on the intercom system. "Attention. Base One is under attack. Repeat. Base One is under attack. All personnel report to battle stations. This is not a drill."

The whole station rocks and vibrates as the bombardment commences against its shields. Personnel scramble every which way.

Cage grabs my arm. "Time to suit up and get to our flight squad—"

I wrench myself free. "You all go on ahead. There's something I need to do first."

Then I'm pushing past them, ignoring their questioning shouts, heading in the exact opposite direction of the fighter bays, through a maze of corridors, down a flight of stairs several levels, until I'm standing at the entrance to the holding cells.

With the entire base in a state of chaos, there's no sentry on duty. Good. That'll make what I have to do much easier.

I hurry inside the cell block. There's one thing I need before going through with this insanity. Rummaging through an equipment locker I find it in seconds.

A gleaming silver neuro-stim collar, complete with the small rectangular remote activator.

Dashing to the cell that holds Digory, I activate the door's release and it swooshes open.

He's standing there calmly, almost bored, staring with those tireless eyes.

"Took you long enough," he says.

"It was all a set-up, wasn't it?"

"If we are to make the rendezvous for the exchange, we should get going."

More explosions rock the base, sending deep vibrations that rocket through my core.

I storm into the cell stopping just short of him. Wrapping the collar around his neck, I squeeze it shut until it locks into place. This close, I can almost feel a wave of cold radiating from him. "You sent out a signal to the Thorn Republic. That's how they found us. Hundreds are going to die. Perhaps more."

"We needed a diversion. Besides. It is for the best. This insurrection is a virus that needs to be contained if any peace is ever to be achieved. We cannot sacrifice the greater good for selfish reasons. We have evolved."

To hear those words coming from Digory fills me with regret and disgust—especially because, in some perverse way, the part about the greater good and being selfless ring true.

I grip my pulsator and place the barrel of cold steel against his temple.

"I should kill you right now." My voice barely registers.

His blank eyes remain fixed on mine. "Maybe you should."

"Spark. Why aren't you with the rest of your squad?"

I turn to face Rios. He's accompanied by Devlin and a burly escort. He looks as if he could skewer me with his eyes.

My eyes flit to Digory then back again. "I wanted to make sure the prisoner wasn't going to escape."

Rio's anger coils into a smug grin. "So you've finally come to your senses. You realize this *thing* has to die."

"And you realize that killing him won't bring back your son, Sir. Rafé's never coming back."

His smile is engulfed by fury. "Tycho could have saved my boy, but he chose not to. He's got to answer for that."

I shake my head. "He's beyond emotion now. Killing him won't have any effect."

He considers this for a moment. "You're probably right. But maybe the key to breaking him is to destroy someone he once cared so deeply about. Isn't that right, Devlin?"

The words take a moment to sink in. Instinctively, I lower the gun from Digory's head.

Devlin shoots me a look. It's the first time I've ever seen him appear to be unsure. He turns back to Rios. "Theoretically, it's possible that the shock—"

"Let's test that theory," Rios says. "I'm sorry, Spark. It's not personal. But by trying to free this prisoner you've committed an act of treason. Shoot him, Devlin."

Devlin's gaze swerves in my direction, then to Rios's, then back to me again. "Sir, we need to evacuate the base before—"

"Do it, Devlin. That's an order."

I exchange a look with Digory, who has been observing the entire scene with the clinical detachment of a scientist studying a new strain of virus. But there's a momentary flicker in those eyes, a faint ray of sunlight trying to filter through the turbulent gray. Maybe it's a trick of the light or just my nerves. But at this point it's a gamble with nothing to lose.

Click.

The sound of Devlin cocking his gun snaps me back to attention.

He aims his weapon at me, and I brace myself to spring into action.

But he shakes his head and lowers his gun. "I- I can't do it, Sir. Spark is one of us. He's done nothing wrong."

Rios holds out his hand. "You've disobeyed a direct order. That's treason. Surrender your weapon."

Devlin hands over the gun, relief registering on his face.

Rios's expression is one of extreme disappointment and regret. "Guess if I want something done right, there's only one person I can rely on."

He fires, hitting Devlin in the chest. The impact sends him crashing into the wall and in that split-second of confusion, I whirl and unlock Digory's manacles, just as Rios opens fire on us.

It's over in seconds. Once free, Digory leaps into the fray, pummeling Rios's bodyguard until he's writhing in a fetal position in the corner, and then relieving him of his weapon.

Before Rios can fire again, I roll across the floor and my boot snaps up, kicking him in the gut. But he's a seasoned soldier, and despite the pain, is on me in a flash, the two of us punching and tearing at each other as we grapple for the gun.

Then we're locked in a death clutch, each of our hands wrapped around each other's throat. I don't want to kill him, even after he tried to murder me. I know what deep loss feels like...

"He...killed...my son..." Rios's slobbers out the words, drool running from the corners of his lips.

"He's already...paid...the price..." Before I can fade, I sink my teeth into his wrist. The moment his grip weakens, I rip myself free of his hold and punch him hard enough to send him careening into Devlin's prone body, lying in a growing dark pool.

"Attention," a voice echoes through the base's com system. "The installation has been compromised. Proceed to evacuation areas stat. Repeat. Proceed to evacuation areas stat."

I can't bring myself to look into Digory's eyes. "Looks like your people have crashed this party. The further you're away from the resistance, the less chance there is they'll be able to use you to track our forces to the rendezvous point. Time for us to get the hell out of here."

CHAPTER SIX

We rush into the chaos that's engulfed the base. Bodies litter the corridors, awash in the continual lightning of strobing emergency beacons. Many of the walls are cracked and scorched by enemy blasts. The stench of blood and flames stings my eyes, disorienting me as we dodge through the haze of destruction. Dashing through the flight crew's quarters, I twist open a mangled locker and rip out some weapons and two flight suits, tossing one to Digory. "Keep your helmet on." Not that anyone's going to be paying too much attention to us.

In seconds we're both suited up and bolting for the hangar.

The bay's filled with smoke from the crisscrossing blasts. Thorn Republic agents are engaged in a firefight with my fellow resistance members, who are struggling to protect a large transport vehicle loading the last of the base's personnel onboard for evac.

"Damn it," I curse under my breath. We duck behind a cargo container for cover against the ricocheting onslaught. My people are outnumbered, and I don't have time to give them any back-up—not that it'd make much difference.

And to make things worse, my stomach sinks when I recognize two figures caught in this increasingly one-sided cross-fire.

Arrah and Dru. They're giving it their best shot, but they're vastly outnumbered. Their defensive posture is quickly becoming a last stand.

"I should be with them."

Digory grips my arm. "No time. We must go."

He nods toward the far corner of the bay where several Mantas still remain. Our ticket out of this hell.

There's a *click* behind us, and we whirl.

Two Thorn agents, weapons drawn, aim and fire.

Everything happens in a blur. I brace for the impact, but Digory shoves me to the ground with superhuman speed and takes the full brunt of the blast. Instead of toppling over, he lunges at the first agent, snaps his neck, and uses the deceased's weapon to gun down his shocked comrade.

Wasting no time, I grab the downed agent's grenade and lob it at the bulkhead directly above the strike team that's got Arrah and the others pinned. The blast almost blows my eardrums out as the ceiling above the enemy collapses on top of them, burying most in a flaming mound of screams and rubble.

I stumble over to Digory. He staggers toward me. I wince at the sight of the scorched wounds on his side and leg, oozing dark tissue. Even with his regenerative abilities, it's going to take the nanotech quite some time to regrow, and that's something we don't have much of.

"We will recover," he says in that monotone. But he collapses against me. Swinging his arm around my neck, I haul him to his feet and half-carry, half-drag him through the debris toward the remaining Mantas.

Looks like my little trick with the grenade worked. The surviving resistance personnel are scrambling aboard the transport vessel, its engines revving for take-off.

After making sure everyone's inside, Arrah and Dru are the last two to board. Just before the hatch seals, they spot us. With Digory's head slumped, I hope they don't realize who I'm carrying.

"Lucian, come on!" Arrah calls, waving me over.

But I shake my head and continue to heave Digory toward the Mantas.

"Where the hell are you going?" Dru shouts.

Another explosion rocks the far end of the hangar. A swarm of Thorn agents filters through the gap. Reinforcements.

Arrah and I make eye contact one last time, and in that moment, I can see a mixture of shock and understanding dawning in her eyes. Dru pulls her aboard and the hatch seals.

Reaching the first Manta, I drag Digory inside and strap him into the co-pilot's chair before hopping into my own seat. My fingers fly over the controls, gunning the engine. The Manta soars out of the hangar directly behind Arrah, Dru, and their transport ship, barely missing a blast from the invading army.

The gray sky's filled with Mantas, Squawkers, and Vultures, zipping around like angry insects intent on stinging each other to death. The flotsam and jetsam of debris from the compromised base bobs on the ocean's surface, slick with oil and the blood of countless bodies. I try not to think that most of them belong to people I know and care about.

At least it looks like most of the resistance forces have escaped during the evac.

The last remaining Mantas surround Arrah's transport vehicle, zooming toward the resistance rendezvous point. But with so many enemy ships in the air, it's going to be too close.

I switch on the radio and static crackles through the cabin. "— is Manta 3. Setting coordinates for rendezvous."

It's Cage. He's not out of the woods either.

Beside me, Digory shifts in his seat, his eyes wide open. "We are locked onto Thorn Republic radio frequency coming from the bridge of that Eel class command vessel. They are preparing to fire on the remaining transports. We will be destroyed in the blast radius unless we flee to coordinates—"

"No. Prep the escape pod."

I may be abandoning my friends, but I can't accept a front row seat to their deaths.

As I check my gauges, Digory shambles to the small emergency escape craft. I reset coordinates to my new destination.

A collision course with the command center bridge on the Eel.

I toggle the com switch. "Manta 3. I've bought you some extra time. Get everyone to safety."

The speakers crackle. "Lucian?" Cage asks. "That you, Mate?"

In reply, I hit the cut-off switch and join Digory in the pod.

"This is a mistake," he says.

I sigh. "What's one more to add to the list?" Taking a last look out the cockpit, I see it fill with the Eel's bridge. Then I seal the pod, strap in, and hit the *Purge* switch.

The g-force plasters me against my seat. Outside the pod's windows, the Eel's bridge erupts in a fireball as the last of the resistance transports whiz by it into the infinite sky, leaving me to wonder when, or if, I'll ever see my friends again, as we crash back into the ocean's depths.

CHAPTER SEVEN

We spend the next couple of days drifting through the darkness of the sea, with only the occasional ray of light filtering through from the surface to cut through the gloom. With Thorn Republic forces possibly still hovering in the area, I thought it best to shut down all of the pod's systems except for life support, using the craft's limited supply of fuel to propel us in short, measured spurts toward land.

We had a couple of close calls when a few enemy craft entered our zone, but we managed to seek camouflage in some reef formations until they'd passed. That last time was over twenty-four hours ago, and there hasn't been another sign of pursuit since.

The pod's cramped, with barely enough room for the two of us. Without the coolant engaged, it's hot and humid, the air stale. Even though we've both shucked our flight suits and are only wearing tanks and shorts, my body's glistening with dampness. But Digory hasn't even broken a sweat.

Most of our time's spent in silence. Digory has entered some kind of hibernation repair mode, I guess. He sits rigidly; blank, unblinking eyes transfixed on the small porthole. Were it not for soft, unsettling sounds of his skin knitting back together, I'd swear he was dead.

Part of me thinks it would be better if he really was. At least if he were actually dead, I could deal with the pain, mourn, maybe go on.

But having him so close, staring at him and knowing I've lost him forever is agonizing, a festering wound that'll never heal.

"We are not dead," he says at one point, startling me.

Then we sit in silence again, for endless hours.

The next day, I'm forced to propel the pod to the surface when the oxygen supply finally runs out. We bob on the sea, and I brace myself for the worst as I spring the hatch. But the ocean is mercifully empty, and I can't get enough of the cool, fresh air and early morning light streaming through. "No sign of the enemy."

Digory's awoken from his hibernation, clearly not as relieved as I am. The areas where he suffered wounds look perfectly seamless now. Only slight, pinkish patches remain, like a light sunburn. I'm sure they'll fade soon, too.

"Morning," I mutter.

He ignores the greeting and instead joins me at the hatch. When he propels half his body out of the opening to get a better look, his bare skin rubs against mine and the alien coldness once again jolts me with how different everything is now.

"There is land up ahead." He points. "Close enough to swim to. We should get a move on to make up for lost time."

Though his tone is emotionless, I can't help get the sense that his words are reprimanding me for choosing to crash our ride into the Eel rather than flee without trying to help my friends.

Screw him.

In a few minutes, we've packed the survival kits and our suits and strapped them to our bodies. I hit a few switches to flood the pod, so it'll sink and erase any evidence of our presence. We both dive into the choppy sea and swim toward shore.

By the time I make it to the beach, I'm winded from the pummeling of the rough seas, despite being a pretty decent swimmer. Digory's already standing on the shoreline, legs spread, arms crossed, staring at me, almost bored-looking.

"We suppose you will need a rest period before we can continue," he says.

I spit salty sea water at his bare feet. "Hazards of still being human, I guess."

I know what's happened to him isn't his fault. But I'm hungry. I'm tired. I'm angry.

And this pain deep inside me just won't go away.

Unstrapping the supplies clinging to my body, I collapse in the damp sand and tear open a ration pack. Chewing the tasteless brittle bar, I force myself to swallow before taking a few gulps of water from the canteen.

I offer him some and he takes it, sitting down to face me, just staring as if I'm a newly discovered species.

"*What* are you?" I finally ask. There's no malice intended in my question. More like frustration and desperation.

He finally drops his stare and says nothing, just continues to chew his ration bar.

But I can't let it go. "Digory Tycho. Do you still have all his—your—memories?"

When he looks up at me again, I'm surprised to see a hint of confusion and uncertainty in his face. "We think so. Yes. Like dreams mostly. Sometimes they are very clear. Most of them are about you. Possibly. But the more we try to recall them, they fade away. We do not really try much anymore. It is counterproductive to our orders." He stares right through me. "But we still hear the screams."

I lean in closer. "Screams? You mean during the Trials? Or when they were holding you for torture and experimentation at Infiernos?"

He shakes his head. "Those dreams, like the ones about you, feel different. Fresh. The screams…they are something else. A glitch from a very long time ago. In time we will learn how to eradicate every trace of them. Purge them from our collective. Just like we are discovering how to do with the fragments involving you."

A wave of pain and bitterness washes over me, followed by a pang of fear.

Who knows what kind of memories are locked inside my own head, just waiting to tear free from their prison, a cancerous tumor hiding, ready to burst at any moment and flood me with the thoughts of Queran Embers, a depraved dictator responsible for so much horror and death?

How can I blame Digory for blocking out painful memories of us, when I would give anything to rip away all proof of that cursed life lurking inside of my own existence?

Who the hell am I? And do I really have the nerve to discover the truth and face it head on?

I spring to my feet and start packing up the gear, checking the compass. "Better make the most of the day before it gets dark."

For the next few days, we trudge inland, trying to stick to wooded areas to conceal ourselves from prying eyes. Our progress is hampered because we travel mostly at night, seeking concealment and rest in the underbrush during the days. After the ration bars run out, we sustain ourselves on edible roots and berries, with an occasional long-eared lepus providing protein and bad memories of my long-dead fellow recruits.

We replenish our canteens with drinking water from streams along the way but at this rate, it'll take too long to get back to the Parish undetected. We're simply too far away to make it on foot. By sacrificing our Manta, I might have already doomed this expedition before it's begun.

The whole time Digory and I barely acknowledge each other's presence, and only speak when absolutely necessary, in which case it's more like a few muttered words, grumbles, and nods. I'm still processing the ramifications of what he's become—and what I'm becoming.

Even sleep has become a kind of burden. On more than a few occasions I'm jolted awake, gasping for breath, my heart thundering, unsettling fragments of barely remembered horrors plaguing my thoughts. I'm not sure if it's just my subconscious getting the better of me, or if it's a part of me—a part of that other life—struggling to emerge. And if it eventually does, what'll happen to me? Will Lucian Spark just cease to exist, snuffed out by the original owner of this mind I've leased?

Digory doesn't seem to be faring too much better. Some nights I awaken to find him staring into space, his pale, sculpted physique bathed in sweat, whispering cryptic phrases. Most of it's unintelligible, but I could swear I heard *Why won't they stop screaming* and *There was no choice*.

Once, as we hiked through the cool night and stopped to take a rest, we stared up in silence at the blanket of shimmering stars sprinkling us with twinkling light. It reminded me of a time so long ago when we had such innocent hopes and dreams, despite the fact that the world seemed to be closing in on us. Sitting so close, I found my hand absently wandering toward his, longing for its natural sheath—until it stopped just short. That time...those two people...it was all over now. And the moment passed, carried off by the wind and dissipating into nothingness.

After almost a week of travel, my weary body starts to wonder how much more it can take when things come to an abrupt change.

It seems like I've only been asleep a few minutes when Digory roughly shakes me awake.

"What the hell—?" I start to mutter, until I see him jam a finger across his lips.

I'm instantly alert, shaking off sleep like an old blanket.

I join him peering down from the ledge of our hillside perch into the clearing below.

A sleek, black and silver craft in the shape of a dagger is hovering there. I've never seen a vessel quite like it, but from the markings and crest it's unmistakably from the Parish, and more specifically, from the Priory. The ship's surrounded by several dozen monks cloaked beneath their hooded, crimson robes, the vibrant scarlet giving the appearance the ship is floating in a pool of blood.

Turning, I whisper to Digory, "Those markings on the ship are religious. According to our informants still risking their lives in the heart of enemy territory, Prior Delvecchio has ascended to the role of Chief Spiritual Caretaker, a position even more powerful than Prior, placing him as one of the top three most powerful men in the Thorn Republic's inner circle. Doesn't look like a prayer circle down there, though. What can you tell me?"

Digory's staring blankly ahead. When he speaks, he doesn't whisper. It's more like he's turned the volume of his own voice down. "Since assuming his newfound position, Delvecchio's initiated a nationwide *Depuration*, a series of tribunals intended to cleanse the souls of those who have defied the Deity's commandments and fallen from grace."

"That doesn't sound too comforting."

"As part of this cleansing process, monks are sent to the outlying territories to fight the evil of the Non-Acceptors, those who worship other gods, or worse yet, no god at all."

I sigh. "Why do I get the feeling that in this holy battle, anything goes?"

Digory nods. "It seems any method toward accomplishing this goal is permissible by the acolytes, no matter how hypocritical it appears to be."

"I wonder what brought them this far away from home?"

Before he can offer an answer, there's movement below, and the assembled part to admit several more of their brethren, escorting two captives, whose filthy white jumpsuits are a stark contrast in that sea of red.

I recognize the clothing these newcomers are wearing in an instant.

They're refugees from Sanctum.

It's a male and female in their early twenties, maybe. They look haggard and malnourished like so many other casualties in this bloody war.

"Please," the young woman's saying. "We come in peace. It's not too late to accept the healing power of the Begetter—"

Zap!

She falls to the floor, writhing in agony from the acolyte's neuro-stim blast.

Her companion rushes to her side, but another monk kicks him so hard in the ribs I can hear the sharp crack from up here.

The acolyte that appears to be in charge steps forward. "Blasphemer. There is only one true divine power, that of the Deity. But you shall have time to repent when you are brought before the tribunal and face our beloved Caretaker." He motions to the monks guarding the prisoners. "Load them in and toll the bells. It is time to return."

As the prisoners are corralled inside the ship, the distinct sound of bells, just like those of the Priory, are broadcast from the ship. The acolytes, heads bowed in prayer, begin filing into the ship.

I turn to Digory to relay my idea, but he's already nodding and pointing toward a couple of acolyte stragglers, still in the woods.

It just takes a few minutes to knock them unconscious, don their robes, and creep aboard the ship. The vessel takes off a few minutes later with a roar of engines. Soon I'll be with my brother.

Provided I survive the evils of the Priory.

CHAPTER EIGHT

Fortunately for Digory and me, these acolytes must have taken some vow of silence which, coupled with our hooded robe disguises, makes it easy to slip into the ship's shadows with little or no interaction with our hosts.

During the hours it takes to return to the Parish, we keep to our dingy, windowless cubicles, heads bowed and faces concealed. The air reeks of synthetic incense, seeping through the vents. When a couple of chanting acolytes pass us, I mutter unintelligible words into my clasped hands until they pass. The irony is, I do find myself actually praying. Not to the Deity or Delvecchio's glory, but to the universe itself. Praying that Cole can still be saved, that my friends in the resistance have survived.

Several times I sneak a peek at Digory, kneeling just a few feet away. I can't see his eyes, but I wonder what he's thinking, if he's thinking anything at all. Or is he just being tortured by the sounds of that mysterious screaming in his head?

Once the ship sets down, I can barely contain my excitement. I spring to my feet, despite the aching in my knees. But I force myself to tug at the reins of my impatience and follow Digory's lead, slipping into the end of a queue of monks disembarking the vessel. With the acolytes' heads still bowed and their focus on a rhythmic chant, it's easy for the two of us to slip from the end of the line into the shadows of an alcove.

We slink from pillar to pillar in the flickering light of the candelabras, under the canopy of the huge, vaulted ceilings.

"You seem to know where you are going," Digory whispers in the gloom.

"I've been here before. We should be able to make a break for it out the back and through the courtyard."

As we dodge a few sentry anchorites gliding past on their hover discs, a rumbling reaches my ears. It's getting louder, like a pregnant storm. Only there's nothing natural about this commotion.

Creeping up to the piazza doors, I crack one open so we can peer outside, and suck in my breath.

The vast courtyard is filled to capacity. Most are citizens, looking more worn and disheveled than I remember at the height of the Establishment's power. Interspersed throughout the crowd are armed agents of the Thorn Republic.

Just as in town square during the Ascension Day and Recruitment Day rituals, jumbotrons have been set up throughout the courtyard allowing scrutiny of even the most minute detail.

The entire assembly is focused on the center of the square.

A long, lavish table draped in red velvet has been set up. Seated at the center, in an ornate, golden chair, which seems more like a throne, is Delvecchio himself. His entire body glitters in the sunlight from all the jewels and rings adorning him. Delvecchio is flanked by anchorites seated at either side, his henchman from the Depuration Tribunals, I imagine.

More disturbing is the sight displayed before the tribunal. One is a coffin-shaped silver pod containing an upright human being, a young woman, whose head is bowed so that her hair obscures her face. The second is an X-shaped silver contraption with a young man strapped to it spread-eagled. And the third is a silver tank with a woman suspended just above the foul-looking liquid inside.

I've heard of these obscene devices, but I'd hoped they were just rumors. Each of these machines is an instrument of torture or punishment under the Depuration. What sickens me most are the words that have been etched into each of these infernal instruments in elaborate script:

The Deity's light shall free us.

Delvecchio clears his throat. "Each of these poor souls has been found guilty of heresy. As you all know, anyone who attempts to construe a personal view of the Deity which conflicts with the Priory's teachings must be punished without mercy."

The crowd remains silent, and it's not hard to read the fear in their faces. Attempting to stand up for any of these convicted victims will result in joining them to face the consequences.

"We are at war," Delvecchio continues, "against those from the dark regions who would attempt to blaspheme our beloved Deity in the name of their false god, whose corrupt name shall remain unspoken, lest we pollute this Holy place." He smiles. "Still, we are not entirely without compassion."

Digory and I exchange looks and as much as I'm loathe to admit it, I silently agree that there's nothing we can do for these unfortunate prisoners. Common sense says that instead of wasting any more time, we should seize advantage of this distraction and flee from the Priory undetected.

The thing is, I'm not feeling very practical today.

Gritting my teeth, I catch sight of the girl in the coffin-like prison on the screens. She's finally lifted her head and there's no mistaking who she is.

Tristin.

"We can't leave." I don't bother to look at Digory when I say this. He's probably incapable of understanding what I'm feeling at the moment. Even if Tristin weren't a dear friend, the fact that she's Cage's sister alone would make it impossible to leave her behind. I owe them both so much, and I'll probably never get the chance to let either of them know.

The anchorites flanking Delvecchio each grip one of his arms and help him rise to face the crowd. I'm not buying the frail act for a minute.

He turns to the two prisoners on the end. "Aestreus Hawthorne. You and your wife, Belinda, have both been found guilty of harboring a wanted fugitive from the law, who was spreading lies about this sacred order."

"We found him at our back door," Hawthorne replies, his voice laced with fatigue and pain. "He was nearly starved to death. All we did was feed him some soup and attend to his wounds."

"Isn't that what the Deity would want us to do?" Mrs. Hawthorne chimes in, a hint of defiance in her tone, as if the sound of her husband's protests have infused her with strength.

Delvecchio sighs and shakes his head. "Even at the end you do not understand the ramifications of what you have done. Evil has clouded your minds."

While Delvecchio drones on, I scan the area, the gears in my head working over-time trying to figure out a way to stop what's about to happen. With so many agents in the crowd, we're vastly outnumbered. Even if we could reach the prisoners before they nab us, we'd never make it out alive. What we need is a miracle.

I stare at the enormous stained glass window in the sanctuary behind us.

If there truly is a Deity, it would never set foot in this abysmal place.

"To show you how forgiving the Deity truly is," Delvecchio rambles on, "I will give you both one last chance. Whichever one of you speaks out against the other first, shall be granted clemency, a prolonged stay in the isolation chambers where you will have years to reflect on the grievousness of your sins and find true repentance."

In other words, years of abuse—if they should be unlucky enough to survive.

"The choice is yours," Delvecchio says, reminding me of the recruits' hellish instructions during the Trials, and the hopelessness of my stint as an Incentive. "I urge you to confess and safeguard your souls against the eternal damnation of the pit."

The Hawthornes look at each other, anguish carved into their tearful faces. The moment stretches out into eternity as the couple's eyes seem to urge each other to speak out and save themselves. But in the end, their love for each other appears to be much stronger than the survival instinct. Mrs. Hawthorne shakes her head while her husband bows his and closes his eyes, his lips muttering what I assume is a final prayer.

Delvecchio shakes his head and sighs. "So be it. May the Deity have mercy on your wretched souls."

He nods to one of his underlings, who activates a few switches on a control unit in front of him on the Tribunal table.

Mr. Hawthorne stretches out one of his bound hands toward his wife, who presses her own against the glass of her tank. They're both sobbing now.

If I could just find a way to cut the power source—

It's too late. The entire courtyard is filled with the sound of agonized screams. The beams binding each of Mr. Hawthorne's limbs spin like rotors, tearing his appendages from his body. Fountains of blood erupt from the severed arteries, dousing his screaming face and seeping into each of the letters carved into the machine's base.

The Deity's light shall free us...

Even as it tears us apart in blood.

Mrs. Hawthorne is wailing at the sight of her writhing husband. Then a glistening metal pincer plunges into her neck, probably hitting her carotid artery. Her body plummets into the tank. Immediately, she's entirely covered by the swarm of Serras, crazed with the scent of her blood. Their fangs are like scalpels as the tiny fish undulate over her squirming form, which disappears in the crimson cloud that engulfs the tank.

It's all over in minutes, leaving only the bloodless, dismembered corpse of Mr. Hawthorne, one of his severed hands still reaching for his wife. She's now nothing more than a fleshless skeleton, the carnivorous fish snapping at each other for the remaining tatters of skin.

Delvecchio turns his attention to Tristin. "And finally, we have Tristin Argus. My dear, you have been convicted of heresy. Spreading the word that there are many paths to the Deity is the most insidious way to guarantee a soul a direct path to the underworld. There is only one supreme being that will lead to salvation."

Tristin looks up at Delvecchio. Her serene expression is in stark contrast to the carnage just a few feet from her, the growing pool of Hawthorne's blood lapping at the base of her own prison. "Salvation is not limited to one particular god or adherence to any given dogma. All that any higher power cares about is the kindness and compassion we bestow on our brothers and sisters. That's all that matters."

Delvecchio's smile is almost paternal. "Consider your punishment a kindness to your eternal soul as you experience the burning fire of the damned from within."

Fire from within? Then it clicks. That capsule that Tristin's trapped in is the microwave cooker I've heard rumors about. They're going to boil all the liquids in her body—the water in each cell, the blood flowing through her veins, the fluid around her brain—with the human body being comprised of ninety-six percent water, she'll suffer unimaginable pain. Gruesome images of bursting eardrums, ruptured lungs, eyes popping from their sockets, and melting skin bombard my imagination.

Delvecchio gives the signal and the words etched into Tristin's death chamber begin to glow.

The Deity's light shall free us.

"What are you two doing here?" a deep voice from behind us rumbles.

Two of the sentry Anchorites hover on their discs behind us. They're both pointing weapons at us. The holy power of the Deity, no doubt.

Digory springs first, grabbing one of the monks and twisting his arm until he's rewarded with a sharp *crack*. Then he retrieves the anchorite's weapon and kicks him off the hover disc, taking his place. In seconds I follow suit, kicking the other guard as he fires. His stray shot misses me and I tackle him, ripping the weapon from his hand and hopping onto his hover disc.

Digory shows no emotion. He follows me as I zoom out into the square, already firing my weapon. The crowd erupts. There are screams and shouts as they rush the exits. Seizing the element of surprise, I fire at the mechanisms of Tristin's prison as I dive close. The door springs open and I swoop down, scooping her up onto the disc, which teeters at the sudden, added weight.

"Lucian?" she mutters.

"Hang tight!" I shout, as she wraps her arms around my waist.

Just below, Delvecchio glances up at me with a look of pure amazement.

"Spark," he hisses.

One of the anchorites flanking him raises a weapon to fire just as I point mine at Delvecchio. But another fleeing member of the tribunal blocks my shot, his body toppling onto Delvecchio, shielding him.

"Damn you," I mutter, barely avoiding the anchorite's blast.

There's no time for another shot. The Thorn agents patrolling the courtyard have gotten over their initial shock and are regrouping, firing at us from all sides. To make matters worse, a squad of anchorite sentries is zooming toward us on more hover discs.

Digory's blasts take out at least a dozen, but there are too many.

I turn to him. "Sermon's over. Let's move before they administer Final Rites."

We swerve through the sky in tandem, agents and anchorites hot on our tails, dodging energy blasts, one of which singes my shoulder.

I lead the way back through the sanctuary.

"Where are you going?" Digory follows my lead.

"Maybe this will slow them down," I call back.

As I whiz by a candelabra, I grab it and hurl it at the large tapestries adorning one of the walls. In seconds, it's engulfed in flames and the fire starts spreading throughout the rest of the Priory. Soon, it's a scene reminiscent of Delvecchio's Underworld and damnation rantings. Our pursuers are dodging falling rafters and black smoke.

The problem is, so are we.

Below, the agents are already setting up barriers to block the exits. If the flames don't get us, *they* will.

With the enemy closing in, there's only one way left to go.

"Brace yourselves," I shout to Tristin and Digory.

We crash through the huge, stained glass window of the Deity in a burst of jagged shards, out into the bright day.

The Deity's light shall free us, indeed.

CHAPTER NINE

During all the chaos engulfing the Priory and surrounding areas, we manage to lose our pursuers in the maze of shadows and alleyways dissecting the Parish. But I can already hear the sirens wailing in the distance. We're fugitives now. At least Tristin and I are. Delvecchio saw my face, and, if he survived, I wouldn't be surprised if there isn't already an All Points Bulletin being blasted on every jumbotron in the city, along with a towering close-up of my face.

Digory swerves over in my direction until we're gliding side by side. "We need to lay low for a while before proceeding to your brother."

My fingers dig into my pocket, hovering over the control to his shock collar. "That wasn't the deal."

Despite my threat, and with everything that's happened, he's still eerily calm, eyes cold, expressionless.

Then again, I've become so numb to torture and death myself, who am I to really judge?

"They will be searching for us now," he continues. "It is too dangerous. Especially with her and the condition she is in."

"Lucian…" Tristin's body slumps against mine, and I know she can't deal with much more of this turbulence. There's only one place I can think of where we might find cover, if only for a short while.

"This way." I pull away from Digory and surf toward an area of the Parish that is little more than a burnt out husk of its former self.

My old neighborhood.

The hover discs' power is already starting to fade. These gizmos were never designed for prolonged high speed chases. Hovering close to the surface, we double-check that the coast is clear, and slip through the alleys where I used to scavenge for food. Now they're nothing more than paths of rubble, marked by torn chunks of cobblestone and toppled buildings, protruding from rivers of sludge and sewage. Looks like the Thorn Republic never bothered to rebuild after the raid on the rebel forces during the coup Cassius staged last year.

I grab onto Tristin and hop off my hover disc as it putters and dies.

Digory springs off his, landing soundlessly beside us. "Where to?"

Slinging Tristin into my arms, I stare at her unconscious face and touch her forehead. She's way too cold. If I could only risk getting her to a medcen. But the only one I know of is in the Citadel, which would be suicide. I turn to Digory. "Not much further. Keep your eyes peeled in case we have a tail on us."

"As you wish." Before I can protest, Digory scoops Tristin from me. I don't have the strength to argue. We both know he's better equipped to handle the added weight through this crumbling maze.

Leading the way over broken posts that once flickered with gas light, we reach the intersection of Liberty Boulevard.

The only thing remaining is a statue—at least part of one—that sends winter's finger scraping up my spine. It's the effigy of Queran Embers, still standing sentinel over what's left of the society he created.

The society I created.

Half the face is gone, leaving nothing but crumbling, marble tissue.

I freeze. It's like glimpsing into the future at my own tombstone, a monument to a corrupt life. Irredeemable. Wasted.

"We have to find cover," Digory says.

But I kneel and force myself to touch the statue, freezing cold yet burning hot at the same time. My finger traces the base until I find the tiny chiseled letters hidden there.

C + L trapped in the outline of a heart.

My fingers recoil. Did Cassius know my true origins even back then when we were still kids?

Sirens blare a few streets away. The enemy's close.

"Let's go." I lead the way, trudging through a few more blocks, and there it is.

My old tenement, now no more than a scorched shell, but miraculously still standing. The last place Cole and I shared a shred of happiness. Hopefully, the last place they'd look for me.

We carefully skirt the debris and enter. I do everything I can to avoid looking through the threshold of Mrs. Bledsoe's apartment, gaping like an open wound. Slinking through the dust and cobwebs, we finally reach the remnants of my old home. I take a deep breath. Digory sets Tristin down gently in the splintered hallway. Together we push open the door, which is wedged in the canting floor, and then we're inside.

Despite what Digory's become, I can't help but notice how careful he is when he carries Tristin inside and sets her slowly on the floor. It's something the old Digory—my Digory—would do, like when he carried his rescued victims to safety during the Trials. I guess some instincts can't be eradicated, even by programming.

Like Queran Embers and the part of him that lives inside me? I suppress a shudder.

Hunching, I touch Tristin's icy skin again. "Tristin. It's Lucian. Can you hear me?"

Her eyes flutter open. "Lucian….where….?" Her face contorts.

"It's okay. We're gonna get you all patched up. You'll be back with Cage and your dad in no time."

Digory kneels beside us and offers the medical kit from his satchel. "Unless we can get her to a proper medical facility—"

Grabbing the case, I rummage through it. Bandages. Anti-bacterial ointments. All useless. I grab the only thing of any value. A vial of pain killers.

"Do you have any water left?" I ask Digory.

He hands me his canteen and helps me prop Tristin's head up.

"It's so cold," she mutters.

I press two of the pills against her lips. "Here. Take this. You'll feel much better."

It's an effort, but she opens her mouth and takes in the pills, barely able to gulp them down.

She manages a smile. "Thank you."

Digory eyes her in that curious, clinical manner that feels so alien. "In all probability those pills will not do much good. We were too late. No doubt, the microwaves have already caused significant internal organ damage. Her vitals are failing."

"Shut up!" I shove him, and he barely flinches. "We'll sneak her into the Citadel somehow and—"

"Moving her in her present condition will just hasten the inevitable."

I meet his iceberg gaze. "Then I'll just kidnap a med team and drag them over here if I have to."

He pulls himself up to his full height. "Be logical. There is no time for that."

I whip out the remote for his collar, my trembling finger hovering over the activation button. "I think I've had just about enough of you."

"He's…right…Lucian."

Tristin's trying to sit up, even as I do my best to steady her. "Take it easy, Tristin. You need to conserve all your energy."

She sighs. "Too late, I think."

I shake my head. "Don't talk like that. We're going to get you help."

Even as I say the words, I can tell we both know the truth. I've been around death so long I can sniff its stench like another sense.

Her fingers graze my face. "You're sweet. But it's okay. I'm ready now."

My hand tightens around hers. "I should have gotten to you sooner. I'm so sorry."

"I'm sorry, too."

I shake my head. "What do you have to be sorry about?"

She struggles to swallow, then smiles. "That you and the others are stuck to deal with this terrible mess while I get to go home." She caresses my moist cheek, wiping away my grief. "Don't you see? I'm the fortunate one."

"Tristin, I—"

"I know you don't believe, Lucian," she whispers. "I'll believe for both of us."

And in that moment, she appears more peaceful than I've ever seen anyone look. No fear. No pain. Pure bliss. She looks beyond me, past my shoulder, up through the crack in the roof, at something I can't see, and smiles. "It's so bright…"

The light in her eyes flickers like a candle burning through the last of its wick, and she slumps in my arms.

I pull her close, burying my face in her hair. Then I just sit there, rocking her slowly. My emotions cycle. Sadness. Anger. Bitterness. Until they peter out to numbness.

An hour goes by, maybe two. I can't be sure. I finally set her down.

When I look up, Digory's staring at me. He hasn't said a word this entire time. Maybe in his new incarnation the death of a friend is just another oddity, information to be stored and studied. Frankly, I can't seem to give a damn what he thinks right now.

His eyes flick to Tristin's body, then back to me. "Do you think she got there?"

Out of all the things he could have asked, his question throws me for a loop. "What are you talking about? Got where?"

"Home."

At first I think he's pulling my leg, playing on my emotions. A cruel joke at my expense. I'm about to unleash my pent-up anger on him in a string of colorful profanities, but the curiosity on his face stops me cold with its childlike genuineness.

"She's dead, Digory. Gone. She didn't go anywhere. She just doesn't exist anymore." Still, the innocence of his question nags at me and I soften my tone. "As much as we might want the opposite of that to be true."

He nods. "So you do not embrace the concept of an after-life or a supreme being that sees and controls all?"

"No. I mean—take a long look at the world around us. Suffering. Torture. Starvation. Death." I glance at Tristin's prone form and close my eyes for a moment. "If there is some kind of cosmic entity overseeing this whole mess, he or she definitely has a sick sense of humor."

He pauses and cocks his head. "Yet Tristin, and many other people like her, still choose to believe. Fascinating. She seemed to see something at the end there. A bright light."

I sigh and shake my head. "Yeah, *that*. I did a lot of reading when I apprenticed at the library. It's just a physiological response. Basically, when the body dies, the neurons in the brain fire off a surge of gamma waves, which create a kind of hyper-conscious state. It's sensory awareness overload, a hyper-realness. That bright, white light is nothing more than a combo of the dying brain's gamma waves and alpha waves, which heighten visual awareness, as well as internal visualization, also known as the imagination. None of it's real, Digory. It's the brain's final fireworks display before it's lights out forever."

Digory nods. "Prior Delvecchio would probably not agree."

My anger returns in a rush. "And that's another reason why I don't believe. What kind of Deity would invoke the likes of such evil and hypocritical people, like our Prior, as its voice to the people?"

He turns to gaze at Tristin's lifeless form. "The message can sometimes get garbled along the way. Tristin seemed to be able to separate the messenger from the message. She chose to believe, while others do not. We guess it will not truly be known who is right until we ourselves cease to function, and then it will not really make much difference."

"I'd love to philosophize with you longer, but we're running out of time. Those sirens are getting closer. We need to move." I stare at Tristin again. "I just can't leave her here." It's not because of any mystical being or afterlife. The idea of leaving Tristin to rot, or dumping her body in some lonely, unmarked grave sickens me. She and her family deserve so much more.

"Understood," Digory says. "There is a place not too far from here we can take her. And it is on the way to your brother. But we will have to wait until nightfall."

We pass the rest of the day in silence, Digory going into his regenerative, hibernation mode, sitting cross-legged in the corner, while I grieve for Tristin, wondering how I'm going to face Cage and Jeptha with the news of her death.

As soon as the sun sets, we wrap Tristin's body in several tattered sheets tucked away in an old trunk stashed under one of the splintering floorboards. Digory manages to find a wobbly cart in the wreckage, and we place her inside it. I take once last look at what used to be my home, and then we set off.

More than a few times we have to hide from passing patrols, in the shadows, or under rubble, but between Digory's improved reflexes and my Imp training we're able to avoid detection.

Digory leads the way through the ruins of my neighborhood until we reach the banks of Fortune's River. A short time later, we arrive at a wrought iron fence and follow its perimeter. Digory finally stops and tests a few of the rusting bars, which easily give. "We are here." He rips the bars free and helps me wheel Tristin through.

"Serenity Hill," I whisper. The cemetery where my mother begged Delvecchio to bury my father when he passed. Instead, he was dumped in a mass grave and burned. Only the wealthier among the Parish are buried here. Dignity and Eternal Peace are auctioned to the highest bidder.

Instead of stopping at an untouched plot of earth, Digory leads us to a square, marble crypt.

As we step over the mounds of dying autumn leaves churned by the mourning winds, they crunch like brittle bones. I crane my head up to decipher the inscription etched above the mausoleum's entrance. One word.

Tycho.

I'm more than a bit surprised. I always assumed Digory grew up like I did—parents who spent most of their days slaving away at some back-breaking job. Scrounging the alleys for scraps of clothing and food. Adopting the rats that infested his home like pets. It never even crossed my mind that he could have had it easier than most.

Though when I look at his solemn face now, the unnatural eyes, mutated, pale body, I realize the absurdity of this last thought. It just points out how little about him I really know. Or ever will.

"Just how much of your previous life do you remember, Digory?"

"There are gaps. But far too much."

"Your family was prominent. They would have had to be part of the Establishment's elite to be allowed burial in this place."

He gazes blankly at the inscription. "The Tychos worked for the government. As such, they were entitled to certain privileges."

"I guess this place belongs to you now."

He touches one of the two marble pillars flanking the entrance. "The Hive has no use for places such as these. Let us get inside."

I pry open the heavy, iron gate. The creaking grates on me like a worn razor. Digory carries Tristin inside and I wedge the gate closed behind us.

The interior of the crypt's cold and dank. Embedded in the walls before us are six plaques, four of which have writing on them, while the last two remain blank. I approach them to get a better look in the gloom. My fingers graze the cold stone as I brush away the dust on the first two.

Byron Tycho. Aurora Tycho. Based on the ages, these must belong to Digory's parents.

My index finger presses a button underneath their names. There's a flash of light and a holo appears of the couple. Both appear to be early thirties, the father tall and broad shouldered like his son. The two even share the same, infectious smile. But Digory definitely got his mother's golden hair and piercing blue eyes.

There's an audio feature, but I choose not to activate it, already regretting that I may have stirred up painful memories in Digory, however unlikely that might be in his present condition.

He's studying the images with that same distant expression, as if they were strangers instead of his blood. After a few minutes, he moves to the other plaques.

These are smaller and bear the names Oliver and Olivia. Twins, judging from their identical birth dates.

This time it's Digory that activates the holo of their images. Two giggling children appear, their eyes twinkling in the murk.

Digory's younger brother and sister. They were only five years old. And the dates of their death and those of his parents'—

It hits me all at once and I tug at my collar, finding it a little difficult to breathe.

Digory stares at the images for a long while, his face unreadable the entire time. Finally, he presses the buttons and the projections fade to black.

"Yes," he says, answering my unspoken question. "They all died on the exact same day."

My hand brushes his shoulder. "From these dates you must have been no more than twelve when it happened. I never knew. I'm so sorry."

"Do not be. It has been years. Besides. That was someone else's life." His hand touches the first of the blank slabs. "This was supposed to be Digory Tycho's tomb. But it is a little too late for that now." His eyes flit to the last, empty plaque. "And this one was for Digory's spouse." He turns away from me. "We can lay your friend to rest here. Her body will be preserved until her people come for her."

In silence, Digory enters the code for the last vault. The vacuum seal hisses, and the drawer slides open. Carefully, we lift Tristin's body and place it inside. Out of respect for Tristin, I try to recite a few of the prayers from my childhood, but I can barely remember them, instead piecing together a hodge-podge of mutterings to the Deity, trying to remind myself that it won't really matter to Tristin anymore. She's at peace now. Rituals like this are for the living.

I bow my head and give her a tender kiss on the forehead. "I hope you find it," I whisper. Then I hit the switch and the drawer slides shut, sealing her inside.

No sooner is our makeshift funeral over, when Digory grabs my arm and points to the gate. I can hear it too, now. Voices in the cemetery. The static and crackle of coms.

My heart's in overdrive. "It's a republic patrol. They've tracked us."

Cautiously, we peer through the bars of the gate. Sure enough, I can see at least half a dozen Thorn agents, a few astride Caballuses, the others on foot.

"—reports of a sighting on Serenity Hill," the lead officer's saying into her walkie. "We're checking it out now."

One of her companions trains a light on the mausoleum, and we duck back into the shadows. I scan the four corners of the small crypt.

"They have us cornered," Digory mutters in that strange, muted volume of his. "We will take down as many as we can before becoming non-functional. You get to the woods and—"

"Better idea." Before Digory can protest, I scramble over to the one remaining empty vault, the one intended for him, and open it. It'll be a tight squeeze, but we can do it. I don't need to motion him over. He's beside me in an instant. We both leap and slide into place, closing the drawer almost completely. Digory breaks off the locking mechanism as a precaution. There should be enough air in here to last until they're gone.

The gate creaks open as the patrol makes its way inside.

Our bodies are wedged together and I can barely breathe, aware that even the most minute sound will give us away.

Tense seconds stretch into minutes.

"Nothing here," one of the agents finally says. "Let's comb the entire cemetery again."

"Wait," the lead officer says, freezing my blood. "Conduct a thermal scan. I want to make sure there's nothing else alive in here but us."

This is it. No escape this time. At least they won't have to worry about disposing of the bodies when they kill us.

Digory surprises me by pulling me even closer and enveloping my entire body with his. As he stares deep into my eyes, I start to feel numb and lightheaded. My vision blurs and a wave of dizziness hits me. It's so cold...I can't feel my limbs...

I open my mouth to speak but no words flow past my lips, only frosty breath.

This is all Digory. He's lowering his body temperature...*our* body temperature...masking the heat signatures...

Everything's hazy...hypo...thermia...just want to sleep...

Scanners not picking up anything. It's clear.

The voice sounds so far away...

Creaking...gates slamming shut...

A rush of warmth on my lips. Starts coursing through my whole body. Fire hits my heart. My eyes spring open—

Digory's lips are pressed against mine, feeding me air.

He pulls away. "Sorry for any discomfort. You started slipping away, but I fed you oxygen and restarted your heart with an electronic pulse."

All I can do is nod.

"We should stay here for a while until the patrol is gone," Digory mutters. "Get some rest."

I don't think I'm going to be able to. But with my face pressed against his chest, the strong, rhythmic beating of his heart starts to lull me, and I finally give in to exhaustion—

I'm awakened by a gasp from Digory. His body's bathed in an icy sweat, his breathing heavy.

Because of our confinement, I can't sit up. "Digory, what's wrong?"

"The screaming," he says. "It was worse than it has ever been."

"It's okay. It was only a nightmare, that's all."

He turns his face toward me and grips me so hard, I think my ribs are going to crack. "It was Digory." He finally says. "His family. He killed them. He killed them all."

He buries his face in my neck and his body stills again.

But I can't fall back to sleep.

CHAPTER TEN

Hours later, we rise from our tomb, making sure to make as little noise as possible in case the patrols are still searching the graveyard. We peer out the gate and don't see any signs of lingering agents. Digory volunteers to sneak around the mausoleum's corner and climb up one of the tall trees to survey the area before we head off. I agree with barely a nod and he disappears. He hasn't mentioned his nightmares and what he said, and I haven't either. The implication of his confession, or whatever it was, is just too much to handle with everything else that's going on.

He slithers down from the roof, hanging upside down, his face appearing through the gates like an arachnid's peering through its web. "It is clear."

I glance at the last unmarked grave. As soon as I get the chance, I'll make sure her family gives her a proper burial. "Goodbye, Tristin." Then I turn to Digory. "Let's go."

He hops off the gate, barely making a sound, and I follow him out of the crypt. As he closes the gate behind us, he pauses for a minute and peers in at the vault, gripping the bars. Then the moment passes and we're off, trudging through the cemetery, trying to stick to the shadows of trees, following the maze of headstones to the far side before we slip over the fence.

About an hour after leaving Serenity Hill behind us, we finally reach the outskirts of New Eden, where the wealthy aristocracy of the Parish and its government officials reside. The entire area is secured by an invisible laser grid, which will burn through the flesh and bone of any poor unfortunate looking for more substantial scraps of food.

My heartbeat gains momentum. "So Cole's in one of those houses?"

"Number forty-seven."

I scoop up a handful of dead leaves and toss them through two of the columns. There's a puff of smoke. They're reduced to cinders in an instant.

I glance at Digory. "How do you propose we get through?"

He moves in closer to the laser grid. "A large enough creature attempting to cross the field will create a temporary disturbance as it absorbs the brunt of the blast. Theoretically, that should allow another living organism to pass through at the same time relatively unscathed."

I join him at the perimeter. "Theoretically? It still doesn't solve the problem of finding a decoy—"

Oh, hell.

"Digory, I can't let you do this. You'll never survive."

"You have seen our regenerative abilities first hand. We can handle the impact. This vessel's tissue and cells will heal." He holds up his palm, warding off my protests. "There aren't any other options. You do want to see your brother again, do you not? That was our agreement."

He's right. I've waited too long already. But still. Despite everything that's happened, I can't sully my hands with someone else's blood. Especially Digory's, no matter what he is now or what he may have done.

I shake my head. "We'll find another way."

"Move quickly," he says, stepping through the field before I can attempt to stop him.

The moment he does, his body doubles over and his face contorts.

"Damn you!" All I can think of as I dive through the field is the smell of burnt flesh, clogging my nostrils.

Then I'm rolling, curled into a fetal position, pain and nausea wracking my body. Burning moisture drips from my eyes. I try to get my bearings. Wisps of smoke rise from my singed clothing. After a quick check it looks like I'm still in one piece.

The shock wears off and one thought burns through my brain.

Digory's lying crumpled just on this side of the field. I crawl over and pull him further away from the deadly lasers. His skin is even paler than it was before, if that's even possible, a stark contrast against the vibrant red trickling from his nostrils and ears. A lot of his clothing has been burnt away, and I swallow hard at the sight of scorch marks burnt deep into his body. His breathing's shallow and frosty sweat seeps from his pores. When I touch his face, his eyes flutter open and I can see the grey obscured by burst capillaries.

"Told you…it would…work…" he groans.

And then it's like we're back at Infiernos and the trials saying our goodbyes before I set off to rescue Cole.

Only this time I'm breaking the cycle. I'm not going to lose him like I did before. Like I just lost Tristin.

"I'm staying right here with you until I'm sure you're going to be okay."

Despite my own depleted strength, I manage to pull him behind the cover of some perfectly manicured hedges. I cradle his head so he can sip water from the canteen. Then I swathe his body and cover the worst of his wounds in bandages from the medical kit. While I can see evidence of the skin beginning to knit itself together again, it seems like a much slower process this time, as if each of these instances of massive tissue damage are starting to finally take their toll on his system. In any case, if he recovers, there's no way I think he can withstand another episode like this.

Morning turns to afternoon, and his shivering becomes less and less pronounced. The burns fade from black, to red, and then pink. His breathing eases back into something resembling a normal rhythm, at least for him, and I finally start to let myself relax a little.

"You're probably wondering what we meant about…the Tycho family, back there in the crypt."

His words take me by surprise. I sit up from my slumped position. "Yes, I did. But you don't owe me any explanations right now." I crush up some of the pain pills into a powder and pour them into the water left in the canteen, mixed with some sleep meds. I tilt it against his lips. "Drink up. I need you in peak condition if we're going to make it through this."

He gulps it down in one swig.

"This place is heavily patrolled." His voice is low. "There is a security station in the northeast quadrant. You might be able to borrow a uniform there to blend in easier."

"I've heard rumors that these homes are now inhabited by the former Imposers who have pledged their loyalty to Cassius. What can you tell me about that?"

Digory's eyes glaze over as if he's scanning some internal hard drive. "Most of the previous residents, the once privileged elite that were loyal to deceased Prime Minister Talon during the Thorn coup, have been arrested and sent to the camps in an effort to purge the new regime of their tainted bloodlines."

I spit into the dirt. "Genocide. Your new boss, Cassius, is a real prize. The fortunate ones were murdered outright. There's been talk of these political prisoners being used as test subjects in horrific biological experiments. Who the hell knows what they've done to my brother?"

My rage cools. I take in the blank expression on Digory's face. With the UltraImposer conditioning he's been subjected to, he's just as much a victim as all the others.

"I should get moving. You going to be okay?"

"We will probably be functioning efficiently again and wondering what has taken you so long by the time you return."

I can't help but smile. This sounds almost like the old Digory's sense of humor.

Making sure he's concealed behind the hedges, I set off, skirting the perimeter of the laser grid, heading northeast, until I finally reach the valley just beyond the security station.

The palatial mansions of New Eden look pristine as ever, but with one major difference. Where once the emblem of the Establishment bloomed everywhere, it's now been replaced by the enormous banners of the Thorn Republic, a letter T, the vertical portion formed from an obsidian dagger, while the horizontal portion's in the shape of an ebony scale, in a mockery of justice. The symbol is encased in a diamond shape framed by a crimson backdrop. These banners are draped over the balconies, turrets, and gables, fluttering in the chilled, autumn breeze. A stark message that the remnants of the Establishment have been conquered.

I slink past a cluster of trees that look like they've been wounded in battle. Their blood red leaves spill all over the grass. I try to avoid crunching them under my boots while I creep toward the back of the patrol station.

In less than ten minutes, I've grabbed hold of a young, unsuspecting agent exiting the bunker to go out on patrol, knocked him unconscious, and slipped into his uniform. I use his own restraints to bind and gag him, hiding him in some shrubs. With his radio, I'll be able to keep tabs on the agents' movements and hopefully, move about undetected.

Taking a deep breath, I stride into the center of town acting as if I belong among the marching squads and agents bustling around.

The other personnel barely glance at me. Instead, their attention is focused on a gathering in the courtyard of one of the manors.

My heart skips a beat as I take in the number on the house.

Forty-seven.

Gripping my sidearm, I move in closer.

A family, consisting of two adults and one child, is being dragged from the home. They look haggard. But it's the abject fear in their eyes that makes me pause.

"Please," the woman pleads. "I just need to get my grandmother's ring. It's all I have—"

Slap!

She recoils from the agent's blow. Her husband breaks free of his own captor, shoving the brute away and shielding his wife with his own body. "Don't you dare lay another finger on her."

The bullet hits him right through the eye. He collapses on top of his wife's now gore spattered body. Her shrieks are piercing. But the son just stares in silence. He must be at least eight, but he's sucking his thumb.

"I'll give you something to scream about." The agent who slapped the woman tears at her dress. I realize where I recognize him from. Arch. The former Imp who was on duty with Valerian that long ago day when I met up with Digory in the alley before we were both recruited.

All around me the officers laugh.

"Filthy Stains," an agent mutters beside me. "Society will be a lot better off when their blood's filtered from the gene pool."

She claps me on the back, and I nod.

"Good work, Cadet Spark," a voice utters nearby, shocking me to attention.

I'm about to whip out my weapon and fire, when I realize it's not me being addressed.

The agent who slapped the woman and murdered her husband is saluting the head of a squad composed mostly of children, a boy of around six with dark, somber eyes.

Cole salutes the agent back. "Just doing my duty, Agent Arch, Sir!"

Arch turns to address the onlookers. "Let this be a lesson in loyalty. Cadet Spark did not hesitate to present evidence against the very family that was fostering him as soon as he discovered it. His uncle will be very proud of him." He turns to Cole again. "Any last words for your foster brother before he's taken to the camps?"

I feel like I'm trapped in a nightmare, unable to move. Cole pivots on his heel, turns to the boy, and slams a fist into his gut, despite the other's larger size. As the boy falls, Cole kicks him repeatedly, while the other agents cheer him on.

Soon the other kid's a bloody and prone clump.

"Do it, Spark." Arch commands. "It'll be your first Kill. An act of purification that'll bond you to the brotherhood forever."

I'm still reeling as I stare at my brother. All those years I tried to shield him from the horrors of this world, and now he's becoming one of them.

Cole rears his boot back, ready to deliver the killing blow to the kid's skull.

I bite my lower lip and clench my fists. Screw caution. I bolt from my spot, knocking agents over. "I taught you better than that."

Before they can take me down, I grab Cole, lift him, and throttle him. "What the hell are you doing?"

He glares at me as if he's been struck. "You're not my brother."

I glance at the injured boy's bloody body and turn back to Cole. "You're right. My brother would never do this."

"Looks like we've caught ourselves a bigger prize," Arch mutters. "Take him."

I'm surrounded by agents and dumped into a transport along with what's left of the doomed family.

As we drive off, Cole just stands there, staring after us amidst a swirl of dead leaves.

CHAPTER ELEVEN

The massive towers of the Citadel fill my eyes on our approach, but I can't get Cole's face out of my mind. The coldness in his eyes is even worse than Digory's because it's laced with hatred.

And what's become of Digory? Was he able to regenerate? Did he make it back here? Was my capture part of a trap he led me right into? No. That wouldn't make sense. He had plenty of opportunities to lead me into an ambush. He could have turned me over back at the mausoleum. But he didn't. Unless it's just another one of Cass's mind games.

I shake the thought. Digory's probably still lying there, dying, waiting for me to return to him in vain yet again. He may even be dead already. And with the Citadel looming so close, I'll probably be following soon.

The transport grinds to a halt on the landing platform, and the doors swing open. Arch is standing there, accompanied by two other agents, each tugging at the leashes of snarling canids. The beasts' massive jaws are open, tongues polishing their razored teeth and hideous snouts. As they stare at me, I get the impression they're deciding which of my limbs would make for the better first course.

"Looks like your flame's about to be put out permanently, Torch Keeper," Arch growls. "Get out!"

I match his contempt with some of my own. "I still have enough of a Spark left to burn you for what you've done to my brother."

My stomach muscles tense a split-second before his meaty fist slams me in the gut.

Before I can get my bearings, the agents grab and cuff me, dragging me between them like an unlucky wishbone, as we enter the complex.

I don't recognize this wing of the centralized knowledge tower of the Citadel of Truth. Must be a new addition after Cass's regime took over. It appears to be some kind of medical ward, but unlike any I've ever seen. From the number of agents patrolling the corridors, it's obvious the patients housed within are not here by choice.

There's a stench that underlies the antiseptic aroma, like meat that's just starting to go bad, mixed with the odor of sweat and bodily fluids.

Arch and the agents don't even flinch at the sounds of piercing screams and moans echoing around us. It's as if this entire facility is in its death throes.

I catch glimpses inside the rooms as I'm led along these hallways, snippets of horrors that have been ripped from nightmares and manifested into reality. One wing marked *Genetic Studies* seems to be entirely composed of twins, identical faces mirroring each other's suffering. Technicians jab needles into throats, right into their eyes—I have to turn away at the sight of another set of twins which looks like it's been grafted together, stitch by stitch, into some grotesque tangle of limbs.

In another wing labeled *Surgical Regeneration*, patients are undergoing what appear to be nerve, muscle, and bone transplantation operations—without the benefit of anesthesia. With my hands cuffed, I can't cover my ears against the agonized cries from these patients, restrained and forced to watch as their own bodies are cut open before their eyes.

Wing after wing unleashes one monstrosity on top of another: the *Head Trauma Center*, which tests patients' capacity to withstand cranial injuries; *Temperature Desentisization Testing*, where victims are forcefully submerged in tanks of freezing water to develop a resistance against hypothermia, resulting in frost bite covering most of their bodies; patients subjected to poisonous gases, infectious insects; chambers simulating high altitude pressure resulting in brain hemorrhaging; intentionally inflicted burns to test pharmaceuticals.

By the time I get to the *Desalinization Processing* ward, I have nothing but hatred and contempt left for the entire human race. Here, prisoners have been subjected to such extreme dehydration by being restricted to sea water, that one of them looks up at me in desperation and shame as he laps at the freshly mopped floor with his tongue, just to obtain one drop of drinkable water.

We all deserved to have perished in the Ash Wars. Every single one of us.

Arch and the other agents have smug looks on their faces as they watch my reactions. I'm sure they could have taken me wherever we're going without giving me the scenic tour. But they wanted me to see. A grisly preview of what fate awaits me.

Up ahead, the next wing is labeled *Sterilization Facility*. I force myself to peer through the glass. A line of hundreds of people is being herded by agents completely covered in protective suits through a machine emitting waves of radiation. Beyond this, some of the prisoners who have already undergone the treatment have collapsed, some vomiting, others covered in severe burns.

"Our methods can be somewhat crude at times, but they are highly effective."

I turn to face the owner of that voice. The tall, skeletal Prior Delvecchio.

He extends a bony hand, then catches himself at the sight of my still cuffed ones and retracts it. As if I would ever shake his hand. "Such an honor to see you again so soon, my son."

My eyes linger on the blood stains spattered on his white robes. Still look fresh. Wonder which of these cursed inmates it belongs to?

"If I said I'm not pleased to see you again, I'm sure you'd understand, Delvecchio."

Arch shoves me in the back, but Delvecchio waves him off. "That's enough, agent. Young Spark seems to think *we* are the monsters here." He peers at the sterilization queue. "There are your monsters." He turns back to me. "Every last, single one of the specimens in this facility. They are all members of the decadent and depraved bloodlines that turned a blind eye to the people's suffering and oppression under Talon's rule. Surely, you are only too familiar with the atrocities they committed. It's our divine purpose to eradicate their genes from future generations, so that we will be a purer, more noble people, worthy of the Deity's love, while at the same time building a stronger race. I would have thought the Torch Keeper of all people would understand this."

I can barely meet his eyes without throwing up. "Using evil to fight evil kind of defeats the entire point. No one deserves this."

Delvecchio blows his nose into a foul looking handkerchief and stuffs it back into his robes. "Filthy allergens. I told maintenance they needed to augment the air filtration systems. It's a viral paradise in here." Then he fixes his eyes on me again. "Perhaps, once you've undergone your treatment you'll be able to see things more clearly and appreciate the work we're doing here, my son."

These words rip through my chest with icy claws. "What do you mean?"

But instead of answering, he nods at Arch and his squad. They prod me down to the end of the corridor and shove me into a waiting elevator. As the car zooms upward, I keep seeing snippets of all those wards we passed and brace myself for the worst.

The doors slide open, revealing a sterile, circular chamber, with stark white walls and gleaming steel instruments. A trio of individuals, unrecognizable in their white smocks, surgical masks and caps, are waiting there, accompanied by a very familiar face.

Valerian.

Her stark features never once betray her allegiance. She glances at me with all the indifference of a pesky insect to be crushed.

"Got a little present for you, partner," Arch announces.

She shakes her head. "Lucian Spark. The Torch Keeper. Still can't believe that *this*," she looks me up and down, "is what all the fuss is about."

Arch sighs. "Well you did help train him, which is why we aren't going to take any chances."

One of the members of the surgical prep team hands Valerian a syringe. "This should help make him more docile before we begin. I'm going to need a vein."

"Screw you." When Arch's men grab me and he rips up my sleeve, I make a show of a struggle, trying to kick and punch, even bite them.

"Feisty to the end." Arch knees me in the gut.

With the wind knocked out of me and my stomach throbbing, the acting part's definitely over and I can barely focus on the syringe as Valerian jabs it into my arm.

"This ought to make you more cooperative, Fifth Tier." She glares at me, her eyes almost equally as cold as the liquid flooding my veins. Then she rips out the needle and turns to the prep team. "He's all yours."

I was hoping Valerian would have been able to switch out the anesthetic before injecting me, but I can already feel its effects, the bank of mental fog rolling in, clouding my thoughts, my eyes drooping against the lights, my tense muscles unspooling until I'm flopping like a rag doll.

Maybe Valerian didn't have time to switch the contents of the hypo or couldn't without blowing her cover.

Or maybe she's been playing us the whole time and she really is in league with Cassius and his new regime.

I must have drifted off, and I'm not sure for how long because by the time my mind's able to penetrate the haze, I find myself strapped to an operating table, hands and legs restrained against cold steel. In the reflection of the overhead monitors, I can see that I'm clad only in a pair of white medical shorts, and my entire body's been shaven, including my head, which has been marked up like a map.

My eyes flick to the tray of instruments in a cart beside me. Razor thin knives and saws with sharp teeth gleaming in the light.

A drill whose bit looks like it could cut clean through solid metal.

They're going to slice my head open like a ripe fruit.

I tug at my bonds and one of my hand restraints gives slightly. How thoughtful of Valerian.

Icy fingers brush against my skull, causing my body to erupt in goose flesh. I crane my neck to get a better look at the face that hovers into view.

Cassius.

"It's nice to see you in person again." His face is a mockery of concern. I turn my cheek away at his touch. "I hope you aren't too uncomfortable, Lucian."

"Just another day at the spa," I croak. My mouth's dry, and I'm disoriented and scared. But I'm not going to give him any satisfaction.

He leans in close. "I tried not to let it come to this. But I have no choice. This is bigger than you or I. I must think about the good of the people."

I force myself to turn to him. "What are you talking about? How is any of this for anyone's good?"

"This bloody war has gone on way too long. Straton and the forces of Sanctum are never going to give up. And your precious revolution is failing. It's only a matter of time before you're wiped out, too."

"Excuse me if I beg to differ. I seem to remember a victory at the Cape—"

"Followed by a loss of one of your main bases. Even as we speak, your forces are weakened, scrambling to stay alive. Is that what you want for the people you claim to care so much about, Lucian?"

As much as I loathe the sound of his voice, he's right about the plight of my friends. "What does any of this have to do with my being strapped to a table about to get my brain cut open?"

He strokes my forehead and this time I don't even have the energy to flinch. "The key to winning and ending this pointless war lies right *here,*" he taps my temple, "within you. Straton knows it just as well as I do."

"The hippocampus procedure that Straton wanted to perform on me back in Sanctum. He wanted access to my memories, but you stopped him then."

His expression turns grave. "I stopped him because once those memories are accessed the process will be irrevocable. Lucian Spark will cease to exist forever, replaced by your true self, Queran Embers. Pioneer of the Establishment. Then I'll have no choice but to put you down immediately."

"How are you so sure I'm *him*? How—when—did you find this out?" Even as I ask the question, there's a part of me that's not sure I want to hear the answer.

His eyes glisten, and he rubs it away. "When I was recruited. During my trials...I discovered a lot of things. Things that changed everything. I tried to spare you. You have to believe me. But there's nothing I can do now. Too much depends on it." He bows his head. "I'll always care for you, Lucian. No matter what you believe. Sometimes I wish I'd never been recruited, that I'd never left you and things between us could still be the same." He shakes his head against the wistful memories. "Then I realize, even if I hadn't learned the things I have, eventually, you will become

Queran Embers again. It's who you are. Your destiny. The only thing I'm doing now is hastening the process to save more lives."

The most disturbing thing about his rant is that I actually believe he's trying to be sincere. What could have happened to him to turn him into this stranger?

"Cassius, please. If you ever really did care about me don't do this. Just kill me now. I can handle death. But I don't want to be imprisoned in a body that's no longer going to be mine."

Tears stream from his eyes, dripping on to my skin. "I promise that as soon as I find out what I need to from Embers, I'll grant you the peace you deserve." He kisses my forehead and whispers into my ear, "I'm so sorry."

And in that moment, I'm sorry, too.

I catch the sound of the door opening and another silhouette approaches the bed.

"You have a few minutes," Cassius says. Then he leaves my bedside, and Cole takes his place.

By now the obviously diluted shot Valerian gave me is definitely starting to wear off. But even with one of my restraints loosened, I still have to pretend to be incapacitated, which is nearly impossible with my little brother so close.

His eyes narrow as he watches me. Then his finger reaches out and traces the faint scar where he stabbed me on the roof top last year.

"Cole. You came. You still remember who I am, right?"

He shakes his head. "You're going to hurt me. Just like you've hurt so many other people."

"I would never hurt you. How could you ever think that?"

"My brother's dead. You're evil." His fingers hover over the surgical instruments, settling on the power drill. He lifts it in his hands and presses the button to activate it. It comes alive with a loud *whirring* sound. Then he moves toward me. "I get to make the first cut. You're not going to ever hurt anyone else."

One of the surgical team pats him on the head. "Remember just like we practiced, Cadet Spark, during your lessons. Place the drill at the grid line and apply pressure…"

Cole moves behind me, out of my sight line, and I know it's only a matter of seconds before I feel that drill boring deep into my skull.

Mustering as much of my returning strength as I can, I bolt upright, rip my right hand free of my wrist strap, grab hold of one of the scalpels on the tray, and slice the left strap away. The element of surprise is on my side. As one of the surgeons tries to restrain me, I plunge the scalpel into his neck and tear it across. When he starts to collapse in a spray of blood, I fling his body into his two cohorts and proceed to slice open my foot restraints. Once I'm free, I spring to my feet and whirl, stabbing and slashing at the two remaining surgeons until they join their fallen comrades, still and lifeless.

Cole's watching me, eyes full of fury. Before I can stop him, he jabs the alarm. Sirens blare through the complex. He dashes toward the door. I reach him before he can escape, lifting him into the air, ignoring his kicks and screams.

"Let go of me!" His teeth sink into my arm.

"Aah!" I wrench my arm free and grab one of the hypos scattered on the counter, taking a quick glance at the label to make sure it's only a sedative. Then I pop the cap with my teeth and jab the plunger into Cole's neck. "Sorry, little brother. I need you to calm down."

While his protesting body loses its battle against the tranquilizer, I grab a pair of scrubs from the equipment closet and slide them on. Then I scoop up Cole, toss him into a hover chair with a blanket over him, and exit the operating room, just as a squad of agents comes barreling around the opposite corner.

I dash from ward to ward, activating the cell release switches, flooding the corridors with all those patients that are still ambulatory.

"Get the hell out of here!" I urge them.

"That's far enough, Lucian."

Cassius is blocking the hallway, his weapon trained right at my head.

I smile. "There's no way you're going to shoot me at point black range and risk losing all the precious intel trapped in my noggin, Cass."

He smiles back. "I don't need to kill you. Only disable you long enough for my men to take you into custody."

Before he can fire, my finger hits the throttle on Cole's hover chair, propelling it into him. The impact sends him reeling. I leap and grab the weapon from him. A quick check shows Cole's okay.

Now it's my turn to aim the weapon at Cassius. "Pick up my brother and let's move."

"You're making a big mistake, Lucian," he says, scooping up Cole in his arms. "If you really care about your friends, you know Queran Embers has to be destroyed."

"The only thing I know is that you're taking us to the rooftop and your private ship."

Jabbing the gun between his shoulder blades, he leads the way through the melee of fleeing patients, medical personnel, and pursuing agents.

In minutes we've taken the lift and emerged onto the roof. Cass's private ship awaits on the circular landing platform.

"Lucian. I beg you to reconsider," Cassius pleads.

Before we can get up the gangplank, the doors to the stairwell burst open. A squad of agents pours in with Arch and Valerian leading the charge.

Arch and the others aim their weapons at me.

"Do not shoot to kill," Cassius shouts.

I jam the butt of my gun against Cassius' temple. "Stay back or I'll kill him."

Cassius wraps his hand around the still unconscious Cole's throat. "Put down your weapon, or I'll snap your brother's neck before you can kill me."

My eyes flit from Cassius, to Arch and his team, and finally to Valerian. The nod she gives me is barely perceptible, but it's enough.

I drop my weapon, and she rushes over. But instead of taking me into custody, she aims her weapon at Cassius and fires. I wrench Cole from him as he collapses.

She opens her palm, revealing a sonic charge, capable of destroying this entire platform. "Stay back. All of you. Or I'll blow this."

Arch waves his hands to hold back his team. "So you're the traitor bitch who's been working with the insurrectionists. When I get my hands on you you're gonna wish you were dead."

I start up the gangplank. "Valerian. Let's go."

Another wave of agents swarms through the elevator doors.

She shakes her head. "They'll shoot you down before you get far. Don't you know anything, Fifth Tier?" She reaches into her pocket and tosses me a small computer chip. "You'll need this."

My eyes are burning. I thrust the chip into my own pocket and rush up the gangplank. I set Cole down gently inside the ship, before returning to drag the wounded Cassius up the gangplank, hurling him inside. I should just leave him to die, too. But I have to know what he was looking for inside my brain.

The last thing I see through the cockpit window as I lift off and gun the engines is Arch and his agents letting loose a blaze of firepower at Valerian, just as she activates the grenade.

The shockwave hits the ship, accompanied by a blinding flash which totally engulfs the landing platform, incinerating Valerian and the others. For a few seconds the concussion causes the instrument panels to flicker. I tense for the crash. Then the craft pulls out of its dive and soars into the horizon, leaving behind the Parish—

And Digory.

CHAPTER TWELVE

Not only does Valerian's chip contain a program that will temporarily scramble the Thorn Republic's scans and allow my ship to escape Parish air space undetected, it also contains data on the Resistance's mission to capture Fort Diablos. Looks like the council approved my mission specs after all. The attack's already underway.

Valerian's death won't be in vain. I'll make sure of that.

After plotting my course to the Gorge to rendezvous with the strike team, I set the ship on autopilot. A thorough systems check reveals I'll barely have enough fuel to reach my destination. The only refueling stations between here and the Gorge are deep in Thorn Regime territory, too much of a risk, especially with the hostage I'm carrying.

I glance at Cassius. He's still sitting on the floor where I left him, shirtless and barefoot after I searched him thoroughly for any hidden weapons. The shot Valerian inflicted was merely a flesh wound, which I crudely bandaged. He's trussed up in makeshift shackles. I also set up a portable force field generator around him to keep him in place. You can never be too careful with this one.

He looks up at me and holds up his bound hands. "Is this really necessary, Lucian? You already have me contained behind the energy barrier."

"I'm not taking any more chances than I have to. As it is, I'm taking an awfully big one just by keeping you alive. Your death could hasten the end of this war. But first, you have a lot to answer for."

He shakes his head. "Are we going to continue that charade? You don't care about bringing me to justice. It's all about you finding out what it is I want to extract from your dormant memories. We both know it. If you kill me, you kill any chance of ever knowing. And I'm going to go out on a limb and say that you wouldn't want your insurrectionist friends to have any inkling of what your true agenda really is."

I approach the force field. "Perhaps. I could just apply pressure and make you tell me before I even get you back to the brigade."

Cassius sighs, stretching his muscles against his restraints, as if he were preparing to take a nap. "There we go with semantics again. You mean you could torture me into giving up what I know. Perhaps you're already more like Queran Embers than you realize."

Anger and fear surge through me. "Just shut up." I turn away.

"No matter," he calls after me. "I'd die before I'd let whatever knowledge I had fall into your hands."

"Keep talking and you may get your wish."

Trying my best to ignore him, I march down the narrow bulkhead into the cramped crew cabin. The night light bathes the room in flickering shadows. Cole's still lying, unmoving, in the cot I placed him in after we escaped. At least it was an escape for me. More like a kidnapping for him.

I check the chron on my wristband. He should be coming to any moment now. Reaching into the pocket of the flight suit I changed into, I pull out a container holding a hypo and the next dosage of sleeping meds. As I approach him, I hate myself for having to keep him sedated. But he's been so brainwashed by the techniques Cassius has subjected him to, there's no way I can trust letting him wander around the ship freely. And I can't bring myself to shackle him like I did Cassius. Maybe once I get him back to the resistance they can figure out a way to deprogram him. Even if they can, it's going to be a long and painful process. I can't help but weep for him.

Sitting on the cot beside him, I stare at his peaceful face. At least in slumber he still bears a semblance to my little brother. "I'm so sorry I couldn't protect you." Reaching out a tentative hand, I stroke his hair. "There once was a Lady who watched over a magical city of lights…" I recite his favorite bedtime tale from memories and, in the quiet, I can almost pretend we're back home again, before I was recruited, before the start of this terrible war.

When I'm finished I look up to find his eyes staring at me, glassy and cold.

"I hate you," he says.

The words skewer me.

This isn't the first time he's said that to me. There've been other occasions over the years. When I would remind him to eat his vegetables or send him to bed instead of watching the snowflakes sprinkle from the night sky. When I had to explain why Mommy and Daddy couldn't take care of him anymore. When I couldn't stay with him because I had to go to work to earn enough money to buy meager scraps of food and clothing to try and squeeze out an existence. In all those other contexts the words were born of love. Or desperation. But now they are fueled by rage and contempt.

I recoil from his gaze.

"I love you," is all I can say. My fingers fumble with the hypodermic as I place it against his little arm.

His eyes open wide and he struggles against me, kicking and crying out. "No. It hurts me!"

I push the plunger, releasing the tranquilizer into his veins. I haven't sobbed like this in ages.

Holding him tight against me, I whisper over and over again, "It's going to be okay, Cole. I promise." Memories of other nights spent rocking him to sleep bubble up. Those long winter nights when we were practically freezing. Summer nights when he'd awoken, screaming, from another nightmare. And now I do what I did then.

I sing.

"*A spark does smolder deep within,*
While Winter's blow doth burn the skin,
Look toward the Sky, a flame held high,
The Season chars, its ashes nigh,
Keep it lit, Keep it burnin'
All the dreams, all the yearnin',
Ole leaves will fall, New moons arise,
The Keeper sings, the Season cries..."

The old Parish song that every kid grew up with works its magic again. His body settles down and grows still. Soon he's asleep again, clinging to my chest as he did when he was small.

Once I'm sure he's asleep, I tuck him in, leave the cabin, and head back to the craft's cockpit. If my readouts are correct, we should be in Gorge airspace within an hour or so, which is when things are going to get tricky. Unless I'm able to establish radio contact with the resistance, it's possible they could unwittingly shoot me down. Or worse, we might be spotted by Thorn agents requesting confirmation which could result in this craft being overtaken and boarded. The moment they find out Cassius is a hostage they'll either shoot me dead or take me prisoner and vivisect my brain. I'm not sure what Cassius is expecting to find, but whatever it is, I'm sure it can't be good for the resistance. And in either case, Cole's mind remains hostage to the Thorn Republic's depravities.

I reset the coordinates just outside of Fort Diablos compound and spend the next forty-five minutes getting my gear together and checking and re-checking that everything's in order.

As soon as the ship's in range, I decide to risk breaking radio silence to see if I can make contact with the resistance strike team, which according to the intel Valerian provided, should have already succeeded in making contact with the underground movement in the Gorge.

Hitting a few buttons on the dash, I tune into our pre-determined frequency, on what I hope is a scrambled channel.

"Storm Surge, this is Pilot Light requesting confirmation of your position. Over."

My only response is the crackle of static in the cockpit speakers. A few more attempts at hailing Storm Surge still yield no results.

Bleep! Bleep! Bleep!

"This can't be good."

A red light's flashing on one of the gauges on the console.

The fuel indicator. Looks like the reserve tanks are exhausted, too. We're running on fumes.

"*Attention*," the computerized voice on the data screen advises, "*fuel levels are dangerously depleted. Repeat. Fuel levels are dangerously depleted. Please proceed to refueling station immediately before systems are compromised, resulting in catastrophic engine failure.*"

"That so? I'm not sure how I'd manage without you, Sweets." I jam my fist against a button, snuffing out the warning. "We're just going to have to improvise a safe landing for this baby."

I re-plot my vectors and angle of descent. The instrument panel buzzes and beeps with all manner of warnings.

"Danger! Proximity Alert," another indicator blares.

My eyes widen when I catch a glimpse outside the cockpit window.

The airspace above Fort Diablos is lit up like a grandiose fireworks display. Streaks of blue, orange, and red burst all around me, buffeting the ship. Hundreds—maybe thousands—of resistance fighters and Thorn gunwasps are engaged in deadly battle.

With no gunner of my own, I have no choice but to concentrate on navigating through this ever-changing kaleidoscope of destruction, where any second, one wrong move will render my ship a smoldering mushroom of super-heated debris.

To make matters worse, I'm dodging blasts from my own people, who have no way of knowing who's piloting this ship. One missile takes out my communications beacon. The ship lurches violently. The cockpit's glass splinters with a sharp *crack*. I struggle to hold her steady. Another loud blast takes out my sensor array. I can barely see through the thick, black smoke obscuring the chaos out there.

"Lucian!" Cassius calls from his prison. "What the hell's going on?"

"Nothing I can't handle." An explosion slams me back against my seat. "Damn."

"You've got to let me out of here. I can help," he tugs at his bonds.

"Not a chance." I dart over and under squadrons of resistance ships.

There's one that I just can't shake, a resistance ship that's clinging to me like my own shadow.

Any moment it's going to vaporize us. And with my coms shot, there's no way I can even risk a warning.

The ship's getting closer. So close I can see its gun turrets swinging my way, already glowing as it juices up to fire.

That's when my ship's engines start to sputter. In just a few, we'll be free-falling and my pursuer won't even have to waste any firepower on us.

An idea hits me before the blast does. My fingers fly over the controls governing the ships external lights. I flash them in sequence, hoping that the other ship's pilot has the presence of mind to spot what I'm doing.

"C'mon. Remember your flight training." My muttering's drowned out by more explosions, one of which crack the vessel's windshield. Another hit and the cockpit will be flooded with shattered glass and other volatile projectiles.

It doesn't seem to be working. The pursuing craft moves in, soaring in so close I instinctively brace myself for the impact—

The oncoming ship swerves upwards at the last possible moment without firing.

They got my message.

My relief is short-lived. The controls freeze up. The engines are dead. We're just gliding on air now. It won't be too much longer before we go into a nose dive and that'll be the end of everything.

I rip myself free of the pilot's seat and sprint to the cabin where Cole still sleeps. Scooping him up, I secure him to my body with one of the harnesses.

The ship cants forward, and it's all I can do to grab onto cables and supports to remain upright. It takes me a few seconds, but I find the control panel to blow the outer hatch.

"So you're just going to leave me here after all," Cassius says. "Perhaps it's best we should all die here, right now. But I warn you, if Straton finds what he's looking for, your friends are going to suffer much more than you could ever possibly imagine."

My finger hovers over the hatch release button. It would be so easy to just take my chances with Cole and leave Cassius to his own fate.

I apply slight pressure—

And stop myself. Queran Embers would blow the hatch release without a second thought. But *I* can't. I'm not him.

At least not yet.

"C'mon." Deactivating the force field gennie, I drag Cassius to his feet, and loop the harness through him, too, just as the craft goes into a full nose-dive. Grabbing onto a support rail, I jam a fist against the hatch release button.

The panel blows, sending in a ravenous gush of air that sucks every-thing loose into the void.

I can barely hold on. It feels like my arm's about to be ripped from its socket, plunging all of us to our deaths. The resistance fighter that was tracking us zooms into view just beyond the opening. A hatch in its underbelly grinds open. It shoots a grappling hook our way. Grabbing it, I let go of the support and the three of us are sucked out the opening. For a split-second, I get the sensation of something heavy latching onto my leg. Then it's gone. We tumble into the open hatch of the other craft, just as our own ship crashes into a row of square, concrete buildings and bursts into flames.

At least Cole made it in one piece.

And Cassius.

"Spark!" Corin's crouched beside me, looking like he's seen a spirit. "Where'd you come from?"

I do my best to sit up. "Long story. Looks like I made it just in time. Nice to see you back on your feet, Kid."

"It *is* you," Drusilla calls from the pilot's seat. "For a minute, I thought you were going to miss all the fun. Welcome back."

Hauling myself up, I thrust my weapon into Corin's hands. "Keep your eye on these two." Then I dash over to Drusilla in the cockpit. "The resistance team—"

"They've made contact with the former recruits imprisoned in the Gorge. Their leader's some guy nicknamed Deal Breaker. Cage and his team slipped in on a prisoner transport they hijacked. Once inside, they were able to arm this Deal Breaker and his people and initiate a riot, over-powering the guards and breaking out." She stares at me. "Just like you said." Then she turns her gaze to the cockpit windows. "Thing is, we've lost communication with the strike team." Her steady demeanor falters for a moment. "Arrah's with them."

I grip her shoulder. "Reinforcements have arrived."

Her somber look morphs into a grin. She cranes her neck to look at the other two survivors. "Who the hell are they? Is that—?"

Before I can respond, a powerful blast rocks the ship. I careen into the sparking console.

The look on Dru's face tells me everything I need to know without checking out the gauges for a damage report. "We're going down. Strap yourselves in."

Running back over to where Corin's keeping watch over Cole and Cassius, I scoop my still unconscious brother up and strap him into a seat.

Cassius nudges his chin at Corin's weapon. "I'm sure you're no longer going to need that, son."

Corin's studying him with a mix of contempt and fear. He cocks his gun. "Don't take another step, Thorn."

Then I shove Cassius into another seat, cuffing his wrists to a support strut.

"I'm going to need both my hands, Lucian."

I ignore him. "Strap yourself in," I instruct Corin.

Turbulence rocks the cabin. We both lock our harnesses into place.

Another blast hits. The ship pulls a three sixty and slams really hard into something.

The overhead compartments burst open, spilling supplies and equipment everywhere. Shock cushions deploy in each of our harnesses to blunt the impact. Sparks fly and streams from cracked fuel and life support lines hiss into the compartment, shrouding everything in a thick, noxious haze.

At least we've stopped moving and have managed to land relatively in one piece.

Through the swirl of amber and crimson emergency lights, I spy Cole and leap from my restraints to go to his aid.

He's groaning but appears to be unharmed.

I free him from his restraints and lift him into my arms. "I've got you, Buddy," I whisper. While I'm rigging a harness to strap Cole to my back and free up my hands, I call out behind me. "Corin? You okay?"

"Not really."

I turn. Through the thickening haze I can make out Cass's silhouette. He must have been able to overpower Corin during the impact and is now aiming the kid's own weapon directly at him.

CHAPTER THIRTEEN

"I don't want to hurt this boy, Lucian," Cassius says. "As long as you do what I say, he'll be—"

Wham!

Drusilla knocks the gun from his hand, twisting his arm and jamming it into his back at an awkward angle.

"How about you do what I say, Thorn?" She kicks Cassius, and he drops to his knees. "What was that about the bigger they are?" she quips.

Corin retrieves the gun and jams it against Cass's heaving chest. "Time's up."

Cass's eyes lock with mine and I curse under my breath. He knows I won't let him die just yet.

"Corin, wait. We have to get out of here and take him with us." Moving toward the hatch, I hit the release and spring the door. The sound of twisting metal and grinding gears fills the air. The hatch only opens halfway and stops.

Corin's eyes dart to Dru's, then back to mine. "Take him with us?"

Drusilla wrenches Cassius to his feet. "Why would we want to do that? This bastard's responsible for every—"

"I don't have time to explain! Let's go."

Cassius gives me a smug, satisfied grin. Drusilla and Corin shove him past me and out the hatchway, both shooting me the dirtiest of looks.

As soon as I follow, it's obvious we've traded one chaos for another. Smoke and flames surround our crashed ship, accompanied by the overpowering stench of fuel and blood. All around us people are running, some shouting, others moaning. Shots ricochet amidst the crumbling remains of the building we've crashed into. We duck behind the remnants of a wall for cover.

"Our ship didn't do all this damage," I mutter.

Drusilla shakes her head. "We didn't. We're in one of the processing stations at the Gorge facility. I saw it overhead just before we touched down. Our strike team must have already set off their explosives."

"Why would you insurrectionists be wasting time with a labor camp?" Cassius asks, sounding truly surprised for once.

"Shut it." Corin slams him in the jaw with the butt of his weapon, causing him to double over.

I grip Corin's arm before he can do any serious damage. "Stand down."

Corin's eyes ooze venom, but he nods and spits a wad by our captive's bare feet.

Cassius looks up at him and grins, wiping a streak of blood from his lower lip and teeth. "When this is over, you and I are going to have a very serious talk, little man."

"Enough," I mutter, turning to Dru. "Any idea where we might be able to rendezvous with our strike team?"

Drusilla scans the readout on her holo-band. "There's a whole lot of interference screwing with the signal, but it looks like their beacon's transmitting from just around that junction." She nudges her chin in the direction of a fork in the smoke-filled corridor just ahead.

"Time to join 'em." I lead the way through the maze of sparking wires, dead bodies, and crumpled metal, pausing to allow the others to catch up with me.

"You know we could make a lot better time if we ditched the dead weight," Corin groans.

"Agreed. Go home while you can, little man." Cass's eyes reflect the blazing debris surrounding us.

My gaze flits between the two of them and settles on Cassius. "As soon as we meet up with the others you'll be relieved of your burden." Then I turn and continue, feeling too guilty to meet Dru's and Corin's glares.

It's frustrating me that I can't tell them why I need Cassius alive, especially when every instinct is telling me to get rid of him now, while I've got the chance I've been seeking for so long. But how do I explain to them what my reasons are without bringing up the whole Queran Embers thing? They'd never understand. In any case, I need to think of a reason for keeping Cassius around real quick because there's no way the others are going to go for it. They'll take him out as soon as they set eyes on him.

I round the corner.

"According to the readouts," Dru says, "the team should be just around—"

Shots tear through the corridor around us, blowing holes in the walls and tearing smoking craters into the flooring.

"Throw down your weapons!" A male voice shouts.

"Hands on your heads!" Another voice joins in from the opposite direction, this one female.

"Hold your fire!" I yell back, already on my knees with my hands clasped behind my head. The last thing I want to risk is Cole getting hit in any crossfire. "Stand down," I half-whisper, half-grumble to Corin and Dru.

Figures emerge from the shadows and surround us.

Figures outfitted in Thorn Regime gear. It's over.

I silently curse myself that I didn't take care of Cassius when I had the chance.

That is, until I look up at the shadow that eclipses the light above me.

"Where the bloody hell did you come from, Mate?" Cage stares at me, his expression alternating between shock, anger, and amusement. He lowers his weapon.

I could leap up and kiss him right now, but instead I grab the hand he offers and let him pull me to my feet. "Buy me a drink, and I'll tell you all about it."

Unstrapping Cole, I scoop him into my arms, patting his cheek. "How you holding up, Buddy?"

"You found your brother?" Cage asks. "That means you've been to the Parish. Any word on Tristin?"

"I—"

"Spark! It *is* you!" Arrah pushes past Cage and engulfs me and Cole in a fierce hug. "Didn't think I'd see you again," she whispers in my ear.

"Don't I get a hug?" Drusilla asks from behind me.

"Dru!" Arrah tears herself from me, dashes to Drusilla, and lifts and spins her around before planting a kiss on her lips. "When we lost contact I thought—" she backs away and jabs a finger in the center of Drusilla's chest. "Don't ever do that to me again."

"Affirmative, Sir." Drusilla gives her another squeeze before slowly letting go.

"Don't worry, I'm okay, thanks," Corin grumbles.

"Good to see you, kid." Dahlia ruffles his hair and he shoots her a dirty look, before his face reddens and he bursts into a grin.

An unfamiliar man pushes his way forward––bald, thirties, well over six feet of solid muscle. Unlike my friends, he still has his weapon trained on me. An angry, long scar carves his face from the corner of his right eye down to his lower lip. "Hate to interrupt your little reunion but we're on a mission here."

Behind him, a group of about twenty equally intimidating and armed men, women, and teens mutter their agreement.

I hold his stare and pick up my weapon. "Ready when you are, Mister…?

"Call me Deal Breaker," he growls.

I can't help let out a chuckle. "Lucian Spark here."

Cage steps between us. "DB here and his crew are the former recruits and prisoners who formed their own militia and trained right under the Gorge's noses. They've thrown in their lot with the resistance and have been pivotal getting us this far."

I nod and give Deal Breaker the once over again. "Glad to have you on the team."

Deal Breaker spits out a wad of tobacco, barely missing my boot. "How much longer till we breach that secured access door, Fontana?" he calls over his shoulder.

I crane my neck and take in the sight of a gaunt young woman with scraggly hair. She's hunched over a console, which is attached by wires to the digital locking mechanism of a huge, metal door. "Should just be a few more minutes to get the last two numbers in the code."

"Step it up," he barks.

Dahlia's able to read my confused expression. "Once our team infiltrated the Gorge and detonated the explosives, the militia got hold of the latest schematics. There's a newly constructed tunnel system through that access door. It's the most direct route to the installation's control tower."

Reaching inside my pocket, I pull out Valerian's chip. "This might help speed things up." I toss it to Fontana and turn to my friends. "A little gift from Valerian."

"I wouldn't go through that door if I were you." Cassius is still on his knees, muscles tense, coated in dirt and sweat. His head's tilted downward, obscuring his face.

"Who's that, Mate?" Cage asks.

Before I can answer him, running feet echo down the corridor, coming right at us.

Everyone snaps to attention, grabbing their weapons and aiming them in the direction of the newcomers.

But as soon as they come into view, weapons are lowered and hushed sighs of relief abound.

It seems I'm the only that's not feeling at ease at the sight of Rios and Jeptha, both breathless, their eyes brimming with panic.

"An entire battalion is headed this way," Jeptha announces. "They wiped out the rest of our team."

"How're we coming on that door, Fontana?" DB shouts.

"Almost there. The intel Spark provided is really doing the trick. Just one more digit to complete the code."

"I'm warning you," Cassius hisses. "Don't go through that door."

"And just who the hell asked you?" Deal Breaker shoots back.

As self-preservation seems to be Cassius's guiding force, my curiosity's officially peaked. "What's inside there?"

Rios finally takes notice of me and aims his weapon my way. "What the hell is this traitor doing here? He could jeopardize the entire mission." He turns to Cage. "Shoot him."

Cage's eyes go wide and bounce back between mine and Rios's. "I can't do that, Sir."

Rios turns the gun toward Cage and cocks it. "This scum is guilty of treason. Kill him. That's an order."

Cage takes a step back and Dahlia moves to his side.

Jeptha steps in front of his son. "Stand down, Rios. Spark may be guilty as you believe, but we can't execute him without a hearing to determine the facts. To do so would make us no better than the regime we're fighting against."

Deal Breaker smirks. "In case you people haven't been keeping score, there's no time for a hearing."

I hand over Cole to Drusilla and face Rios. "No need to involve anyone else. This is between you and me."

Rios unleashes his full wrath on me. "Very well then. I'll kill you myself."

Cassius stands and clears his throat. "That won't be necessary. I believe it's me that you want."

Everyone turns to him. They're just as shocked to see him as I am that he spoke up and diverted Rios's attention from me.

"Thorn," Rios seethes, shifting the gun toward Cassius instead. "Time for you to pay for all your crimes."

Before anyone can say anything, Cole leaps from Drusilla's grasp and dashes to Cassius. I move to pounce on Rios. Something drops from the ceiling and grabs Rios's gun hand. A shot rings out.

Then everything seems to happen all at once.

Digory's towering above Rios, having wrenched the gun from his hand.

"Tycho!" Rios shouts and lunges, but Digory grips him by the neck and lifts him off the ground.

I moved toward Digory. "How did you—?

"We completed our regeneration cycle. Upon tracking your accompanying squad back to the Citadel, we accessed the computer network, learned of the security breach, and stowed aboard the rooftop transport just before your escape."

I let out a long breath. "It was you that grabbed my leg and hitched a ride on Dru's ship before we crashed. You followed me."

Cage shakes his head. "I'm not following any of this, Mate."

"Don't...you...see...," Rios gasps, clawing at Digory's hand. "Spark's been working...with Thorn...all along..."

"I got it!" Fontana yells. The final digit to the security code flashes bright on her console. The access door swooshes open.

An explosion rocks the corridor, hurling us all about in a blur. It's accompanied by energy blasts from pulsators striking all around us.

"Into the access corridor!" Deal Breaker shouts.

I catch glimpses of Dahlia, Arrah, and Drusilla, stumbling through the opening, along with Jeptha and members of the militia crew. Cage is trying to haul Rios and me to our feet. I push away and crawl over to Cassius. He's shielding Cole with his broad back. Blood's oozing from Cole's arm where Rios's shot nicked him.

"Cole! You okay?" Shoving Cassius aside, I give my brother a quick once-over, making sure the injury's just a flesh wound. "You're good. C'mon. We gotta get outta—"

"Leave me alone!" Cole claws at me. I wrap my arms around his frenzied body, trying to pin his arms to his side, but it's like trying to hug fire.

"Let me try." Cassius holds out his hand and strokes Cole's hair.

As much as the sight sickens me, it seems to work. In seconds, the frenzied look on Cole's face dissipates. His face becomes vacant. Even his breathing slows down. He reaches out for Cassius. I can only stare, stunned, as he slips from my grasp and into Cassius's welcoming hug—just like he used to embrace me after he woke up from one of his nightmares. Only this time, he's seeking refuge with one of the very same monsters who have plagued our lives for so long.

"What have you done to him?" I mutter more to myself.

More blasts strike all around us, churning up chunks of metal and concrete in clouds of billowing smoke.

I wrench Cassius to his feet and drag him toward the access corridor, pushing him and Cole through.

"Wait, Lucian! I already told you. We can't," he protests, trying to go back.

"Shut up." I thrust him backwards, half in anger, and have just to escape the sight of this unnerving bond between him and Cole.

A split-second after I clear the accessway's threshold, another blast strikes, and the door slams shut behind me. Deafening clanks and hisses assault the air as a series of locking mechanisms engage with thunderous rumbling.

"That oughtta buy us a little time," I huff.

Cass's eyes grow wide. "You don't realize what you've done."

I stare at the rag tag group huddled close by. Cage, Arrah, Dru, Dahlia, Corin and the rest of my fellow resistance fighters. Deal Breaker, Fontana, and the rest of their militia team, all nursing their wounds, muttering among themselves, shooting glances at Cassius, then at me, eyes filled with suspicion and accusation.

Cassius sets Cole down, never letting go of his hand. Instead he glances upwards, and I follow his gaze.

The walls and ceiling stretch up and away into infinity. Thin grids of red laser light divide the otherwise smooth surfaces. On the ground, multiple pathways snake from our side across the vast field, disappearing into the shadows on the other side. There's something eerily familiar about this place, but I can't quite place it.

Drusilla's frantically adjusting the controls on her scanner. "I can't get a fix on our location."

Arrah cranes her neck over Drusilla's shoulder to study the screen. "Some kind of electrical field's scrambling the readings."

Cage points a finger at Cassius. "We need to take this bloody filth out now while we've got the chance."

Rising silently from the ground, Digory's limbs unspool until he's towering above Cage and standing between everyone else and Cassius.

"Thorn may be your only hope of escaping this place." His voice is as cold and devoid of emotion as the first time I heard it at the Cape.

Rios, arm slung around Jeptha for support, lets go and steps forward, still rubbing his neck, still raw with Digory's handprint. "Why should we listen to you? You killed my son. And you're not even human anymore."

Digory's eyes flit in my direction and hold for a moment before darting away again. He doesn't respond. Instead he bows his head and stares at the ground, as if daring anyone to step over an invisible line.

Deal Breaker's ear is pressed against the sealed access door. He turns to us. "Won't take 'em long to figure out where we went and come after us. We need to get our butts in motion."

"Let's go!" Corin chimes in. His face twitches. He bounces from one foot to the other.

Cass's expression looks grave. "It's not that simple."

Dahlia turns to him. "Why? Just where the hell are we?"

Before Cassius can respond, the lights grow dim and a high pitched vibration fills the air.

"What the hell is going on?" I lunge for Cassius, but Digory intercepts me, grabbing my arm in an iron grip. I glare at him and the pressure eases just a bit.

"We're being scanned," Cassius announces.

His voice is stripped of its usual cockiness and aloofness. I sense genuine fear and my eyes reflexively fix on Cole before settling back on him.

"Scanned for what?" I ask.

The red glow descends, engulfing each of us in quick succession. The sky crackles with a data storm. All our images flash, intercut with images of body scans, bio readouts, brain wave patterns, and a slew of other info before fading out.

New Recruit profiles complete, a voice announces over the com system.

The sound of it freezes my heart in mid-pump. That vague sense of impending doom crystalizes. This vast underground facility. Each of us being catalogued into the system.

Cass's warning.

Nightmares of Infiernos burst through the carefully compartmentalized walls in my brain. I can tell by the looks on Cage, Drusilla, Deal Breaker, and the others' faces they get it too. Even Digory, in his new, ice-cold incarnation, looks ill at ease, his former self responding through some primordial instinct to the memories of the horrors we once faced together.

It's happening again.

Cassius's lips curl into a bitter smile. "We've just been drafted."

My jaw drops and I turn to Cassius, unable to give voice to my shock.

"You should have listened," Cassius's voice is low. "The blasts must have shorted the system and locked in the start-up sequence. Once it's begun, there's no way to stop it except to make it through. All of us. Together."

Your Final Trial is about to begin, the computer voice blares. *Good luck, Recruits.*

CHAPTER FOURTEEN

A spherical containment field springs to life around us, crackling with energy, holding us at bay until the starting signal goes off. I've seen enough of these now to know that if we attempt to cross the field before the trial begins, we'll be instantly shocked to death or just plain vaped into an unrecognizable mound of goop.

I whip my head around to face Cassius. "What the hell have you done? The Trials are over. I made sure of that back at Infiernos."

He shakes his head. "We've scrutinized the recruitment process. Learned from the mistakes of the past. Refined it. This new experimental program will train soldiers more efficiently. Maximize their abilities without the barbarism of forcing them to choose which of their loved ones dies." His eyes soften. "I thought you of all people would be pleased at the lack of collateral damage."

Cage rushes toward Cassius, but Digory's hand shoots out and jams against Cage's chest, stopping him short.

"Stay back," he drones in a monotone.

"You get one pass because we used to be friends, Mate." Cage grips Digory's wrist, and the two stare each other down, one seething, the other like ice, until Digory lowers his arm, as if he's merely lost interest.

I'm still in shock. How naïve I was to think the Trials were behind me forever. Isn't this all life really is? A series of endless challenges until the day you die?

Deep rumbling vibrates through my core, jolting all my senses on the alert.

Above us, oozing gases have formed into ominous-looking clouds, dark and pregnant with destruction.

Attention, Recruits. Your trial will commence in one minute.

Cassius swallows hard. "Once the trial begins, I suggest we all head to the opposite end of the testing field and find cover as quickly as possible."

Jeptha and Rios move into position beside Cassius. Jeptha gapes at the artificial storm clouds. "What should we expect once the field becomes active, Thorn?"

"The unexpected." Cassius shrugs his shoulders. "No telling which of the myriad of final scenarios the short-circuited systems will unleash."

Cole sidles up to him. "Are we going to be okay?"

Cassius puts an arm around him and squeezes. "Yes. I'm going to look out for you." He looks up and his gaze locks with mine. "I promise you."

The collar of my suit becomes too tight, and I look away. Deal Breaker shouts commands to Fontana and the rest of his crew, moving them into position.

"This is all Thorn's fault!" Corin's trembling with rage. "What the hell are we waiting for? Let's waste this twisted son of a bitch right now!"

Deal Breaker cocks his weapon. "Sounds like a plan to me."

"I'm your only hope for making it out of here." Cassius sighs. "Kill me and the rest of us won't have to behold that handsome mug any longer. Isn't that right, Lucian?"

I turn to face the others. "We just need to make sure we keep Thorn alive long enough to guide us out of here. If he happens to lose a leg or an eye along the way, no prob. Less to carry."

Cassius shoots me a look, a barely perceptible nod, sealing our unspoken bargain. He'll continue to keep everyone in the dark about the whole Queran Embers thing as long as I ensure his survival in this trial.

Cage crouches, preparing to sprint. "And to think I thought my days of being a recruit and fighting my way through the trials were long over, mates."

"I hear you," Dahlia mutters, assuming a similar stance at his side.

"Twice in a lifetime is two times too many," Drusilla chimes in.

"Quit whining, you guys." I clench my jaw. "This makes Trials number three for some of us, if you count my brief stint as an Incentive."

Digory moves in beside me. He stares straight ahead at the trial field, his face blank, emotionless. "Technically, that would be the second time you served as an Incentive, correct?"

His words, so casually and distantly spoken, break through my growing anxiety.

I place a tentative hand on the mound of his shoulder. "You remember? The first time we were both recruited? How we became each other's Incentives?"

The containment field flickers and disappears.

This Trial has begun.

"Move out!" Deal Breaker roars.

In a split-second, we're all stampeding across the trial field like a frenzied herd, with Jeptha and Rios leading the charge. I know this place is a minefield of unimaginable booby-traps, but I don't have time to worry about myself. Through the blur of scrambling bodies, I catch sight of Cole, running hand in hand with Cassius. As much as it sickens me to see them together, I remind myself that Cassius is the only one in our group familiar with the layout of this hell-hole. And he's all about self-preservation. Ironically, Cole's probably safer with him than anyone else trapped in this mess.

I can barely distinguish between my pounding heart and the rumbling thunder. The artificial storm clouds are closing in on us from all sides. My muscles tense. Breathing quickens. There's something about those dark, swirling masses reaching towards us like skeletal fingers that's truly unnerving.

Sprinting beside me, Cage and Dahlia point at the gaseous nightmares and shout to one another. I can't make out everything they're saying over all the commotion, but they obviously sense what I do, too.

To my left, Digory shoots a look at the nearest cloud and then to me. There's a touch of urgency carved into his stone-like expression. He turns away quickly, before I can figure out if it's just my imagination. With his increased stamina and abilities, he should have already left me in the dust by now. Instead, he remains just a few steady paces ahead of me.

Up ahead, Corin stumbles. Arrah and Dru are at his side in a flash.

"No time for a break, Kid," Arrah grumbles.

"I got this!" he yells back, his tone a mash-up of fear and annoyance.

Arrah and Dru each grab an arm and haul him to his feet, half dragging him along.

The rumbling gets louder. One of the churning masses breaks off from the others and descends, oozing toward the opposite end of the field, where Deal Breaker, Fontana, and the rest of their militia are just arriving.

Deal Breaker pounds the door with his fists. He turns to his people and jabs a thumb at the locking mechanism. "Open this sucker up!"

Fontana and the others move in with their gear, rigging the door with explosive charges. They'll have it blown open in just a few and we'll be home free.

Jeptha turns and waves us forward. "Step it up! We're almost clear!"

Something's not right. This is way too easy.

A thin veil of mist obscures my vision. The cloud approaching Deal Breaker's crew lets loose a barrage of rain.

"C'mon!" Cole sprints forward, but Cassius freezes in his tracks and pulls him back.

Thin wisps of vapor form and rise where the droplets hit the ground.

There's something in the rain.

"Wait up!" I lunge and tackle Arrah, Dru, and Corin before they can reach the exit.

"What the hell, Spark—?" Dru flings me off them, but Arrah grabs her arm and points at the mist rising from the ground where the droplets hit.

Beside us, Digory's locked in a struggle with Cage and Dahlia, attempting to block their path. As soon as they, too, spot the vapor trail, they cease all movement and stare.

I cup my hands around my mouth. "Deal Breaker, move your people out of there now!"

He's too focused on the door. Without even turning around, he dismisses me with a wave of his palm. "We'll have this down in a—"

I spring to my feet. "There something in the rain, damn it!"

Deal Breaker whips around, just as the cloud reaches them and the droplets pelt him and his crew.

He shoots me a look like an angry dart and holds out a palm. "It's just drizzling. You newer recruits are really a bunch of—"

Deal Breaker's grin fades. His eyes grow wide. He opens his mouth in a silent scream. The vapor rises from his palm.

For a second, he's as still as a statue. He tumbles backwards.

Fontana rushes toward him. "What's wrong, DB?" She grabs his hand—and it shatters in into shards of crimson crystal.

"Liquid nitrogen," I mutter.

As Deal Breaker gapes at his crystallized stump, more droplets splatter Fontana's face. Her fingers tear at her jaw and cheeks, coming away with glass-like chunks of flesh and bone.

Deal Breaker collapses—and his body splinters into pieces.

Cage leaps forward. "Dad! Get out of there!"

Rios grabs Jeptha. The two dive and roll away.

And then it begins to pour.

Shrieks of panic echo through the field, accompanied by the earsplitting sounds of cracking bone. I've seen a lot of horrible things in my life, during these very trials. But the sight of writhing bodies tumbling to the ground and shattering like china dolls sets a new banquet for my nightmares to feed on.

In seconds, all movement of Deal Breaker's team has ceased. Everything is silent, except for the hiss of vapor rising from the shattered corpses and obscuring the carnage.

Dahlia slumps against Cage. "What the hell did it do to them?"

"It froze them to death."

Cassius, still holding Cole's hand, joins our huddle. "The temperature of Liquid nitrogen is well below the freezing level." He looks at Cole. "Do you remember your chemistry lessons?"

Cole nods. "The boiling point of liquid nitrogen is the temperature of the liquid when it surrounds the much warmer body and goes from the liquid state to the vapor state. As it boils it pulls heat away from your body, causing it to freeze solid. So solid that if we dropped you, you would break into dozens of pieces... like *those* people did." He looks up at Cassius, the way he used to look at me when I'd read him the story of the Lady. "Are we going to make it through?"

Cassius tousles his hair. "Yes we are. And you'll make one of our finest scientists yet."

Cole beams.

Part of me wants to throttle Cassius. The other part is too heartsick to even move.

The chaotic storm raging in my mind's compounded by more rumbling and flashes of thunder.

"Look!" Arrah points.

The swirling black mass of deadly clouds has begun to move again—directly toward us.

Cage takes Dahlia's hand. "Spread out people!"

"No, wait." Cassius' voice is calm, his eyes riveted on the approaching darkness.

"Like hell." I step toward Cole, who shrinks behind him.

Cassius grabs my arm. "If we separate and make a mad dash, the cloud's speed will increase and it will splinter, each segment hunting us down until it rains death on us all." His eyes lock deep. "You wouldn't want that for Cole, would you?"

I can't bear to look into my brother's eyes and see the hatred burning there.

Jeptha clears his throat. "So you already knew how this weapon operated but you said nothing to warn Deal Breaker and the others. You purposely let them die. You murdered them. But what's a little more blood on your hands, Thorn?"

"Would you have believed me if I tried to dissuade your team from blowing up the exit in order to reach the control room? Somehow, I think not. Besides, I wasn't positive the liquid nitrogen had been triggered. I had a theory but it needed to be tested."

Arrah shakes her head. "So they were nothing but lab rats to you, then?"

"Had I not stopped you from approaching Deal Breaker and the others," Cassius continues, "we'd all be crystallized corpses right now and you'd have no chance of ever completing your precious mission. The war would be over with your side being the unequivocable losers. I did you all a favor."

For a moment there's only the sound of heavy breathing. I don't know about the others, but there's a perverse logic to his words that simultaneously makes sense, and makes me disgusted and guilty to still be alive all at the same time.

"You've set us all up real good, Thorn. Time to do us all a favor and shut you up for good." Rios lunges at Cassius, but Digory is on the General in a nanosecond, flinging him to the ground. Rios scrambles to his feet, glaring at Digory. He wipes blood from the corner of his lips.

I shoot both Digory and Rios a glare. "Enough." Then I turn back to Cassius. "There's not much time. What do you suggest?"

Dru shakes her head. "You're not going to take advice from this asshole now, are you, Spark?"

"Yeah," Corin spits. "I don't care what he knows. He should be the first one of us to get a taste of what Deal Breaker and those others got!"

"Shut up! All of you!" I shout. "I don't trust Cassius either. But one thing I do know is that this son of a bitch is too much of a coward to let himself die just to try and stop us from reaching that control room. And right now, he's the only one that knows a way out of this shit. Once we're out of here, you can do with him as you please. Agreed?"

A chorus of reluctant approvals is practically drowned out by the advancing storm.

I turn to Cassius, avoiding Cole's eyes, those of a stranger . "What's the plan?"

We all huddle around him.

He nudges his chin toward the instrument of our impending doom. "The liquid nitro clouds are motion activated. The faster you go, the quicker they pursue."

"So we're supposed to just stand perfectly still while those killer clouds hover over us, waiting to spit?" Dahlia snorts.

"She's right," Jeptha whispers. "What good will immobility do us? We're running out of time to reach that control room."

Cassius shakes his head. "I didn't say we wouldn't move at all. It's *how* we move that matters." His eyes find mine and he smiles. "Up for a game of Dodge Piss, Lucky?"

Dodge piss. The old childhood game we used to play in the alleys back at the Parish. Leave it to kids to make a game out of avoiding human waste raining down from above. For a few seconds I'm thrust backwards in time.

Cassius is ten, and I'm eight. He's propped up on my window sill, legs crossed, proudly displaying the soles of his dirty bare feet. His green eyes peek through the scraggly auburn hair hanging over his face. We're alone. Mom and Dad are both slaving away at the mines, and Cole's still several years away. I'm cold but not lonely or afraid anymore now that he's here.

My stomach's rumbling. Haven't eaten since breakfast and dusk is already eating away the remainder of the day. Cassius reaches into his pocket and pulls out something that catches the last of the sun's rays and shines in the gloom of my hovel.

A shiny red apple. My mouth waters as he grins, cutting it in half with his pocket knife. When he reaches out and offers me the heart-shaped fruit, it's as though he's giving me his own. I curl up beside him, both of us munching away as he strokes my hair.

"I'll always look after you. For the rest of our lives." Then he wipes my chin and offers me his hand. "Up for a game of Dodge Piss, Lucky?"

"Lucky? Lucian?"

Cass's Prefect voice jolts me back.

"You're on." I stare at the hand he's offering and ignore it. "Something tells me this is going to be more like a game of Shit Dash." But I can't help but smirk. If those clouds move like he says they do, our childhood game may just save our asses. At least most of them.

"If we're gonna move, we need to do it now," Dru squeezes through gritted teeth.

Taking my cue from Cassius, I shush everyone. "Here's the deal. When I give the signal, we all charge the exit as a group. The Cloud pursues. Once we reach it, one of us stays behind, perfectly still, while the others continue to run in the opposite direction, acting as bait. The lone recruit hits the detonator, blows the doors and escapes."

Corin's eyes flare. "Then we all just make a run for it, right?"

"Not exactly," Cassius responds. "The explosion will redirect the cloud's vector toward the opening. If we all try to rush the exit together, the Cloud will overtake the group before we can all make it through, ensuring certain death for some. A safer bet for us all is to once again, run, en masse toward the exit, until the cloud reacquires our movement. Then when it begins to pursue, another person stays behind, the rest of us move off, then so on and so forth." He winks at me. "It'll be just like the old days."

"Except shit and piss wash off without taking your face off," I shoot back.

"What happens to the last person?" Dru asks the question that seems to be on everyone's faces.

I take a deep breath. "You let me worry about that."

Cassius nods. "Of course. Our little Lucky. Always the martyr." Despite the sarcasm in his words, his face is stern and worried.

The clouds are almost on our asses.

"Everyone remain perfectly still until the clouds pass over us. Don't even utter a single word."

The moment Cassius finishes his warning, the billowing mass of swirling maelstrom moves into position to hover above us, blocking out the overhead light and shrouding us in shadow.

My eyes dart around our circle. Arrah and Dru, arms wrapped around each other. Cage and Dahlia, backs pressed together. Stern-faced Jeptha and Rios flanking a wide-eyed Corin. Cole huddled against Cassius's side.

Something cold and firm brushes against my hand. Digory's standing close beside me. His jaw's rigid, his gray eyes examining the hovering mass above. I'm about to dismiss his touch as an accident, a mere reflex. Until it happens again. Maybe it's a trick of the shadows, but I could swear his eyes just flit in my direction. But I blink and he's staring resolutely at the cloud, with all the intensity of a scientist testing out a new hypothesis.

The cloud descends. This time there's no mistake. Digory and I grip each other's hands very carefully to avoid activating its sensors. Obsidian tentacles project from the oscillating center, weaving in and around our faces, our bodies. A cold trickle of sweat beads down my forehead. I tilt my head, ever so slightly, to stop its flow, unsure of how sensitive these things are to movement.

As the seconds turn to minutes, I sense tremors in the bodies huddling around me. My own leg cramps. If anyone should scratch and itch or fall...

After what seems like an agonizing eternity, the tendrils retract, and the cloud moves away, slowly at first, until it's gliding across to the far side of the field—in the exact opposite direction of the exit.

"Now's our chance," Cassius whispers through clenched teeth.

"Go!" I shout.

We take off like a stampede. I risk a quick look behind me and see the blackness swerve and speed in our direction.

As we all approach the locked door, I shout, "Corin! You're up first. Blow this bitch and start inputting Valerian's codes!"

He catches the chip and huddles against the exit door.

The ominous shadow moves in, blocking out the light.

"Move out!" Cassius commands.

Like a flock of wild birds, we veer sharply to the right, the shifting shadows hot on our tails. Except there's now one less of us.

I catch a glimpse of Corin pressed against the exit door. A stormy tendril zooms in—and moves past him. Then he inches toward the detonator, and I lose sight of him.

Just ahead of me, Cage trips in a pothole.

"Son!" Jeptha cries.

Cage goes down. Dru's at his side in a second. He wraps an arm around her while she hauls him to his feet.

"Not leaving you behind, Mate!" She shouts. He half runs, half limps beside her.

Cassius, Cole, and Digory are almost at the other end of the field, with Arrah, Dru, and Rios right behind them.

Bam!

Shrapnel rains down around us. At least hot metal fragments are a hell of a lot better than liquid nitro.

Corin's standing beside the smoking opening behind us. "C'mon!"

The cloud biting at my shadow suddenly veers away, heading full speed to block our escape path.

"Change course!" I yell, already altering mine and dashing toward the very horror we've been trying to avoid.

I slow my speed so the rest can catch up, and then we're dashing toward the cloud, trying to get as close to it and the exit as possible before it turns its sights on us again. We're less than ten feet away from the opening. Corin's peering out at us from the shadows.

The cloud reverses course, speeding toward us once again, seemingly larger than it was before, erupting in a mushrooming mass of thunder and lightning.

"Cage. You're up!" I bark.

"Bloody hell, Mate." He collapses, lying prone as the cloud approaches.

"Fall back!" Cassius yells.

The rest of us stop in our tracks and sprint in the opposite direction again.

Lap after lap we repeat this process. Losing one member at a time in quick succession. Dahlia. Rios. Dru. Then Arrah.

With each leg we're growing more and more exhausted, despite the training most of us have had. We won't be able to outrun the cloud for much longer.

Cole would have been the first one out and safe if I had my way. But he's joined at the hip with Cassius. And there's no way I can let Cassius out of my sight. He's always a few steps ahead of everyone else, and there's no telling what plan he's already hatched to escape and warn his troops.

I slow down to keep pace with Cassius, who's now carrying Cole. He's gasping for breath even more than I am.

"Give him to me." I reach out my hands.

Cole's too exhausted to protest, but Cassius shifts away from me. "I've… got… him…"

He trips and falls. At least he has the presence of mind to roll and absorbs the brunt of the impact. But Cole's sprawled half underneath him.

Trapped.

A loud crash of thunder nearly shatters my eardrum. A shifting shadow approaches from behind.

I dive and heave Cassius off my brother, scooping Cole into my arms, rolling onto my back and keeping him clutched close to my chest.

But my sudden move twists my ankle. When I try to get up, jolts of agony knife through me. I drop, taking Cole down with me.

The swirling vortex closes in from above. I crane my neck. Cassius is lying a foot away. "Get Cole out of here, now."

He's too groggy. Moving way to slow.

There's no time. The cloud pauses, almost as if it's taking sadistic pleasure in allowing me to process the impending horror. It rumbles. Droplets fall toward Cole and me. I push him as far away as I'm able.

Another dark silhouette eclipses the cloud.

Digory's torn off his upper armor, exposing his bare torso. He's using it as a shield to ward off the deadly rain.

"Hurry," he cries. The loud cracks and pops of his rapidly disintegrating armor fill the air.

For a second I think everything's going to be okay—

Until a large droplet dangles from Digory's armor—

Directly above Cole's skull.

I lunge to cover him, waiting to feel the ice cold liquid nitrogen bore through to my brain. My training kicks in instinctively. What was that theory we studied during training? I swerve my head in time to catch the droplet in my open mouth.

"Lucian, what the hell?"

Cass's cry is muffled. Concentrating on my training, I blow out the droplet on my tongue, creating a long plume of condensed water vapor. It worked! The heat of my body coming in contact with the liquid nitrogen has created a vapor flash reaction, forming a thin, protective layer and preventing actual contact, just like water beading up on a hot skillet.

The insulation only lasts seconds, long enough for Digory to grab Cole and me in his arms and scramble out of the way.

Cassius is on our heels. I manage to wriggle out of Digory's hold and sling my arm over his shoulder as we dash toward the exit. This is it. No more time to play it safe. We all need to make it through this time.

The trial field's systems have begun to malfunction. Searing lasers ricochet all around us, searching haphazardly for bodies to burn through and slice to pieces.

Above, the cloud's moving way too fast. We'll never outrun it this time.

Behind us, Jeptha's lagging seriously behind. Despite his strength, age is taking its toll. He'll be the first to go.

Unless…

I'm going to have to buy Cole and Digory more time.

"Everyone stop moving!"

Digory pauses with Cole. Cassius staggers to a halt. Jeptha drops to one leg.

I sprint in the opposite direction. At least they'll have a chance now.

"I can't let you do this, Lucian," Cassius calls. "I need you."

He grabs Cole from Digory. Then darts further away from me.

My heart clenches. Cole's face registers shock and betrayal.

The cloud pauses. Then the tendrils break away from the bulbous center, forming two separate predators.

"You bastard!" I reverse course and start heading back toward them at full speed.

Cassius stops running. The pursuing tentacles join together, ready to engulf us all.

I grab Cole and glare at Cassius. "I don't care what you know. You're dead now."

He smiles. "I need you Lucian. It was the only way. Forgive me."

"I'll never forgive you for what you've done to my brother."

Cassius shakes his head. "I meant, for *this*."

Just as the clouds are about to engulf us, he tosses his pack away from us, toward Jeptha.

The cloud swerves away, tracking the movement. It descends on Jeptha, dousing him in its lethal shower.

"Lucian! Move! You're clear!" Cage shouts from the opening.

Digory and Cassius tug at me, dragging me through the bulkhead.

But I can't tear my eyes away from Jeptha.

"Dad?" Cage whispers, catching sight of him.

Jeptha smiles and salutes him. "Take care, son. I was wrong about you. I was wrong about so many things."

His body's engulfed in vapor, and he shatters into nothingness.

Cage staggers against Dahlia.

Explosions rock the control room. The ceiling caves in. Circuitry sparks.

Corin's working the control board. He spots me and nods. "That's it. The code's a go. All arsenals are now under Brigade control. Our troops and the remaining Gorge militia are taking out Fort Diablos' primary weapon's systems." A big grin spreads across his face. "We're kicking their asses. Just like you said."

Through the smoke, I catch sight of Cassius running up the gangplank toward one of the landing bays, tugging Cole with him.

"Thorn's getting away!" Arrah fires several blasts that narrowly miss Cassius. Then they disappear from sight.

I turn to my friends. "Coordinate the attack. I'm going after him."

Before they can respond, I'm dashing through the maze of fallen girders and torn machinery until I reach Cassius. He still has a hold of Cole, standing on the empty landing platform. Explosions and shrapnel from the raging battle rain behind them.

"Give me back my brother, Cassius." I try to inject calm into my voice. Cassius is cornered. He's unpredictable enough as it is. There's no telling what he'll do when he's desperate.

He shakes his head. "Not until you give me what I want, Lucian."

"And what exactly is that?"

"The technology and scientific advances which were lost during the Ash Wars. Think of it. Cures for diseases, stockpiles of food that could save the precious population you claim to care so much about."

Now it's my turn to shake my head. "I have no idea what you're talking about."

He laughs. "But Queran Embers does. Every last spec and location of each of those hidden installations where the medicines, provisions, and research have been stored is lodged in that complex little brain of yours. I want that information."

"Why? Because being in control of the Parish isn't enough? You want the ability to control who lives and who dies? Besides I don't believe that's all you're looking for. Your motivations have not exactly been altruistic up to this point."

Footfalls behind me.

"Don't fight me, Lucian. You can't win." He looks past me. "Take him, Tycho."

More explosions rock the tower. Metal whines in protest.

Digory touches my shoulder. I tense to fight him.

I whip out the control unit to his shock collar. "Take another step and I'll activate this. I *mean* it."

He pauses for a moment. Then takes another step toward me, grabbing the collar around his neck.

My thumb jams against the control unit—

And nothing happens. He's still coming.

Digory rips the collar free. "It has been fried ever since the laser grid back at New Eden."

The control unit drops from my hand. "You tricked me. That's why you sacrificed yourself by going through the grid. You knew it would short the collar out."

"You see, Lucian," Cassius says. "I always get what I want."

My hands ball into fists, ready to fight Digory to the death to save my brother's life.

Instead of attacking me, Digory steps in front of me, blocking Cassius. "There's been a slight change of plans. Spark is coming with us."

Cassius's eyes look incredulous. Then he bursts into laughter. "So even after all your restructuring and conditioning in the UltraImposer program you're still a lost cause, Tycho. No matter. You'll find out soon enough your usefulness was always meant to be short-lived."

I push past Digory and we both lunge for Cassius.

He shoves Cole toward the edge of the gangplank.

There's a loud crack as it gives way—

"Lucky!" Cole cries, toppling over the edge.

I grab his hand just in time. Digory grabs me from behind, hauling us back toward solid ground.

But the delay's enough for Cassius. A Thorn Vulture ship zooms into view, hovering by the platform. Cassius jumps into its opened hatch. "If I can't have your secrets, no one will." He turns to a soldier. "Lift off and destroy this hangar."

The soldier salutes. "Yes, Sir."

The hatch seals and the craft veers away, preparing to blow us off the map.

"Looks like we're out of options." I press my head against Cole's.

"Not quite," Digory responds. He grabs hold of us and leaps off the platform, just as the ship fires. The hangar crumples into fiery ruin, as the Vulture soars away.

I brace myself for impact. But something snatches us up before we hit the ground. I look up. We're tethered to a ship.

A Flesher ship.

Digory stares at the craft then turns his gray eyes on me. "We need you, too, Lucian."

We speed away through the clouds of black smoke and the roar of explosions and into the troubled dusk sky.

PART II

MEMORIES

CHAPTER FIFTEEN

Traveling inside a Flesher craft feels like I would imagine being swallowed whole by a serpent would, wriggling around in its guts while it slowly digests me. Every trace of the vessel's surface is organic. No metal, plastic, glass. Just pulsating greyish skin, living tissue that's been genetically engineered out of the fusion of countless people unfortunate enough to fall onto the radar of Straton and the religious freaks in Sanctum.

I squirm, not just from revulsion, but trying to get comfortable in my seat, a grotesque mound of undulating flesh growing out of the equally disturbing walls. A glistening tendril's draped across my torso from right shoulder to left hip, some sort biomechanical seatbelt. But it doesn't escape my notice that it's also serving to trap me in place.

Cole's seated directly in front of me. Dark circles cradle his glassy eyes. In the strange glow of the Flesher ship, he looks even paler. But what disturbs me most is the expression on his face. The wide-eyed innocence that had been buried under brainwashed venom has now given way to the bitterness of someone well beyond his years. I think back to all those times in the Parish, countless nights of reading him stories, trying to protect him from the darkness of this world. What a waste. All of it's gone now. The darkness has touched him, too. And I've never felt as lost as I do now.

I lean toward him, the cold tentacle digging into my own flesh.

"I know it's very hard for you. With Cassius gone, you're feeling very alone and confused. But I'm here for you now. I'll always be here." I reach out a hand for his.

He pulls away, wriggling back into his own living harness. He blinks and stares right through me. "He said he'd never leave me. Ever. But he lied, too." His eyes focus on me at last. "You all lie."

"I've never lied to you, Cole."

"Yes you did. You're always leaving me. Just like Mom and Dad did. They didn't want to be around me neither."

"Cole—"

"You always promise I'm going to be safe. But I never really am. That place. The Priory. It was very scary. And so dark. So was Delvecchio." He turns away from me. "You said you were going to come for me the next day and get me out of that terrible place, but you never did. You forgot all about me. Left me to—" His lower lip quivers and for a millisecond he's exactly like the Cole I remember, sweet, vulnerable. But he bites down on it and the regression is gone. If it was ever there in the first place.

I could handle the anger in his eyes much easier than this. Just attribute it to more of Cass's brainwashing techniques and conditioning. It would be so simple to place the blame elsewhere. But his eyes are drowning in despair and it guts me to the core, especially since I know there's truth to some of what he says. I have promised to keep him safe, time and time again.

And I've failed at every turn.

"Why do you even care?" he asks. "You're not my brother. You never were."

I clear my throat. "Is that what Cassius told you?"

He nods.

"He lied. Just like he lied about not leaving you."

I instantly regret my words when I see the pang of hurt on his face. "I am your brother."

Cole shakes his head. "You're an evil monster, pretending to be my brother, wearing his skin like those Flesher monsters wear the skin of the dead. You're the reason everyone in the Parish is so sad and dying. You started it all. And when the time comes, you'll destroy me, too."

So part of Cole's conditioning has been Cassius filling his head with stories of Queran Embers.

"That's not who I am."

But what if it is?

My mind swirls with doubt. If there's even a slim chance that Cassius was telling the truth about Queran Embers, then maybe Cole is better off as far away from me as possible—

No. Stop it.

"Cole, listen to me. I'm not a monster. I used to protect you from the monsters. Remember when you'd wake up from a really scary dream, and I'd to read you the stories of the Lady and her City, the ones we kept hidden under the floor boards, so you could go back to sleep?"

His eyes are glassy again. He blinks a stream of tears, which trickle down his cheeks. "I can't dream anymore. Not about you. Not about the Lady. I try, but it's just black or full of static, like the old television in our room that never seemed to work right."

It's a struggle to swallow. "I'm so sorry, Cole." My eyes flick to the plate of food sitting untouched by his side. Not much. Just some bread and the dullest looking fruit I've ever seen. But considering their biological make-up, I'm wagering these Fleshers aren't big on four course meals. At least not of anything we'd find palatable. I shudder.

I push hard and my living restraint gives just enough for me to lean closer and pick up his plate. "Here. You need to eat something."

"I hate you so much." Cole's voice is barely a whisper.

Despite the pain, I force myself to tear off a piece of the bread and bring it to his lips. He doesn't protest and takes a tentative bite. Then another. Little by little we both eat in silence. Several times our hands touch. I avoid looking up at him, afraid of what I'll see there. But each time we make contact he doesn't pull away. And that's enough for me to hold onto.

When we're done, all I can hope for is to discover my own version of blackness and static as I finally give into exhaustion and grief, muttering to myself as I close my eyes.

"Keep it lit, Keep it burnin'
All the dreams, all the yearnin',
Ole leaves will fall, New moons arise,
The Keeper sings, the Season cries..."

———

I'm jolted awake by something cold and slimy crawling across the sole of my bare foot. I pull it away. Instantly, I'm disoriented. Instead of being tethered to my seat in what I'd assumed to be the passenger quarters of the ship, I'm someplace completely different, laying on a ribbed, vertical slab in what resembles that hive-like lab back at Sanctum.

With a stone-cold Flesher towering over me, its eyeless, bald head riveted at me.

I spring into a sitting position, wincing at the burning, pins and needle sensation radiating from my foot. "Where's Cole? And what the hell are you doing to me?"

"No need for alarm, Spark. The child is resting comfortably, and we were just treating your injuries," an unseen Digory says.

I whirl. On the other side of the chamber, a large, oval pod opens like a hatching egg, filling the room with a cloud of steam. A tall silhouette is visible beyond it.

Digory emerges through the swirling eddies of misty warmth. My breath catches in my throat. He's completely naked. His pale skin has regenerated again, erasing all his wounds. It's like staring at a perfectly sculpted marble statue. The soft, pulsing light and shadows of this organic chamber highlight every contour of every muscle on his body, from his broad shoulders and bulging arms, to his perfectly symmetrical chest, narrowing into a chiseled waist, expanding again to sculpted thighs—

I look away.

"What are you doing to me?" I ask again, focusing on the glistening goo covering my foot.

"We have applied a highly-concentrated bio-organic compound which should expedite the healing process. You will be back on your feet extremely quickly, with no adverse side effects."

I turn my attention to the Flesher, who takes it as a cue to apply more of the salve with some sort of sponge-tipped metal prong jutting out from its abdominal cavity, making soft, swishing sounds.

I'll never feel completely comfortable around these things. But I remind myself they were once like me, and I feel shame and pity.

After the initial burn, it actually doesn't feel too bad. "Thanks, I guess." I'm still avoiding Digory's eyes.

"We have no choice," he says with that eerie, matter-of-fact calm that I'm getting used to. "We need you to be in top form for what lies ahead."

His words override the awkward feeling. I turn in his direction. "And just what exactly does that mean? Aren't you taking me back to Sanctum so that Straton can cut my head open and find something he can use to destroy all opposition and win this war? I don't think standing on my feet will be of any help there."

Digory approaches. I glance at the floor and examine the grooves in between the tile, pulsing with liquid, like throbbing veins.

"We are not headed for Sanctum. Our destination is the place you know as Haven."

"*Haven*? You mean that sham community where the Recruit's surviving Incentives were supposedly sent to live out the rest of their lives in luxury? The paradise that turned out to be a death trap instead?"

"That is the very place."

"Digory, when we were in Sanctum, we discovered the evidence of the simulations they used to fake the Incentives still being alive. We both saw the holograms of Cole and Mrs. Bledsoe. Don't you remember?"

Digory doesn't answer.

"Haven turned out to be an internment camp for experimentation and...," I swallow hard, "human food processing. Why are we headed there?"

"Since the war broke out, Straton and his forces have taken control of Haven's
resources. Some of those resources are critical to the next stage of our plans."

I smirk. "Secret schemes? You and your Hive have more in common with the rest of humanity then you realize."

"You do not understand."

"It doesn't matter. The resistance has been searching for Haven's location for a very long time. But every lead always turns out to be a dead end."

Digory nods. "That is not surprising, given the uniqueness of its location."

"What is that supposed to mean?"

"You will know soon enough."

Before I can stop him, he kneels and cups my foot, examining every inch, gently probing and peeling away the layers of congealed regenerative balm. "Very good. Your body seems to be adapting quite well to the healing agents."

For a few seconds it's quiet, as his large fingers massage my foot. It's painful, but it also feels so soothing.

My breathing becomes heavy. A pang of self-consciousness hits me. Here I am, in basically nothing but a pair of tight underwear, with a naked Digory kneading away my pain—

I pull away and spin to face the side of the bed, clutching a layer of pulsing fabric to my midsection. I hope it's the Flesher equivalent of a blanket, and not one of the Hive's vital organs or something.

"Is something wrong?" Digory sounds genuinely confused.

"Yes! I mean no. Maybe you should get dressed." I conjure up as many unpleasant images as I can, which isn't too difficult. Anything to relieve my current condition.

I can sense him rising to his feet. "This unclothed form is disturbing to you?"

"It's a little uncomfortable under the circumstances."

He strides to a cavity in the wall and pulls out a pair of pants. I catch a glimpse of him sliding them up over his thick thighs. He turns to face me. "Is this better?"

"Yes. Thank you."

His eyes squint as if he's in deep thought, trying to solve some intricate mathematical riddle. "It is puzzling that your kind thinks nothing of tearing each other limb from limb, blowing each other up until your streets are nothing but rivers of blood, yet you find nakedness so offensive. Your social constructs are truly baffling."

"It's not like that Digory. At least not with me. It's just that—"

"Besides, we seem to have a vague recollection of—," he cocks his head at me. "Have we not seen each other naked before?"

I lower my feet to the warm surface and apply tentative weight, testing my balance, anything to avoid the topic. "As a matter of fact, yes. We have."

Pain knifes through my foot. I wince, and Digory's at my side in an instant, wrapping his hands around my waist and holding me up to face him. "For some reason, you found it pleasurable then, but no longer, correct?"

Despite what he's become, there's an innocence in his eyes that penetrates deep.

"Yes. Yes I did. We both did." I pull away, standing firmly on my own two feet. "But that was another time. And the past doesn't matter much right now."

He nods. "Agreed. It will be much less confusing when all traces of the past are purged from the Hive memory."

The words infect me. But I grit my teeth. As much as it hurts, I agree with him and wish I could do the same. There was never a chance for us and there never will be now.

"One other question," he says.

"I'm the one that should be asking you questions, but let's hear it."

"The child, Cole. Your brother. He is your family. And the family unit is supposed to function and support each other, just like our Hive, correct?"

I shrug. "It's supposed to work kind of like that. Why?"

"Those dreams we have been experiencing. Sometimes we wake, certain that we have abandoned the Hive. Then this hallucinatory data is gone, retreating into the recesses of the cerebral cortex, and we cannot quite grasp its meaning. But irrational impulses remain. It is like we have been hollowed out." He shakes his head. "Strange."

"Those graves. Back in the crypt. What happened to the Tychos?"

He breaks eye contact with me. "As you said. The past does not matter very much right now. We had both better finish dressing. We would not want you to feel more uncomfortable than you have to when you hear what must happen next."

CHAPTER SIXTEEN

Digory and I slip on a matching pair of gray body suits, made of some sort of biological material that shapes itself to adapt to individual bodies. He leads the way through a maze of corridors dissecting the bowels of the ship. It seems much larger on the inside than it does on the outside. Entering another corridor, I can see why.

The living walls and floors shift, blocking off chambers, creating new ones. It's like watching sinewy muscles and skin meld into each other, creating new tissue that silently knits itself into a different pattern.

Digory notices my amazement. "It maximizes efficiency by creating more direct paths to our destination, depending on our present location."

"Gotcha."

Yeah, and it also makes it impossible for any outsiders like Cole and me to reach any critical or restricted areas, much less find our way off the ship.

"But what if more than one of you decides to take circumventing routes at the same time?" I ask. "Won't that mess up your little flexible transit operation?"

He pauses for a moment, and eyes me with curiosity. "That would never happen. All of our thought patterns are synched. Unlike your kind, which seems to war and turn on each other irrationally, we operate as a cohesive unit."

"So as a result of that nanotech Cassius subjected you to, you can read each other's minds?"

"That is a very simplistic way of looking at it."

I roll my eyes. "Yeah, well, don't mind stupid little me."

"I did not mean to insult, Lucian. It is just that it is more like an instinct. I cannot quite explain it."

"And even if you did, I wouldn't be able to grasp it. I get it."

I hold up my palm before he can interrupt. "All this talk of Flesher Pride and Unity, yet I seem to remember something about you being Cass's bitch. How exactly does that work?"

"Thorn and Straton designed this vessel to be an obedient servant, carrying out all of their orders without question."

Is that the barest hint of a smile on his face?

He continues. "What they did not consider was that, despite the innovativeness of the UltraImposer process, the nanotech utilized in this body began to communicate with its predecessor models, eventually overriding Thorn's commands."

My eyebrows steeple. "So you're basically a mole in league with a rogue group of Fleshers. Busy little bees. Interesting. I have a pretty good idea what Cassius and Straton are after. Power. What exactly is on your agenda? Let me guess. Erradication of the human race? Not that I'm judging. We kind of have it coming."

He gray eyes bore into mine. "No. Freedom. Independence. Just what you claim to want."

I swallow, following him the rest of the way in silence.

As another wall ahead molds itself into a shadowy corridor, I tap Digory on the shoulder. "This tech seems pretty advanced, even by Flesher standards. Why do I get the feeling that Straton is not exactly in the loop on this?"

"We have been evolving at a much more rapid rate than the doctor envisioned. We prefer not to burden him with the cumbersome specifics of our daily development until such time that that it becomes necessary."

"In other words, you're keeping it a secret until you can use it to your advantage." I chuckle. "Like I said before. You may have a Flesher exterior, but you're still human at the core."

The wall before us oozes open, and I instantly eat my words.

Four Fleshers are suspended from the ceiling in oblong capsules. They're arranged in a semi-circle around a silver, opaque obelisk resting on a raised, round platform. There appears to be a body inside, but I can't quite make out who or what it is. The Fleshers' pods are connected with tendrils of pulsating, organic glop, forming a kind of web that seeps through the capsules and burrows into the back of their skulls.

My eyes open wide. "Wait a minute. Aren't those…?"

I don't need Digory's confirmation. I recognized these four Fleshers from Sanctum. The original prototypes that were once part of the Fallen Five recruits. The same ones that helped me escape.

The gasses swirling in the raised capsule thin. I approach it, rubbing the cold surface to peer inside.

This time, I'm truly shocked by this vision from the past. It's Orestes Goslin. Cypress's unfortunate brother. His skin is even paler than Digory's, his scraggly, dark hair is gone, exposing a shiny, smooth skull—except for the living tentacles burrowing into it from the undulating web above him. Everything below his chin is encased in layers of gelatinous fluid, covering the hideous wound Ophelia inflicted to his throat when she murdered him right before my eyes.

I turn to Digory. "I saw him die back at Infiernos. There's no way he could have survived."

"He did not. Not really. The Hive got to him as soon as the recruits fled. He had basically bled out. But they managed to preserve a portion of his oxygen deprived brain. That part of him has been integrated into our collective." His head bows and his fingers trace the glass. "We are all one, once again."

Staring at Orestes, I can't help but think of Cypress and her children, as well as Gideon. And even Ophelia. Such a terrible waste. A huge gash in my heart that'll never be filled.

I pry my eyes from Orestes and look up to find all of the Fleshers optical visors trained on me. Beside me, Digory seems to be in a trance, his eyes like frozen seas, riveted to something I can't see or hear, much less comprehend. The organic tendrils connecting all the Fleshers including Orestes, are glowing now, and Digory's eyes begin to as well. As the minutes pass, Digory occasionally nods.

Soon, the glow subsides, until it finally flickers out. Digory nods one final time, and then his eyes return to their new, normal gray. He turns to me, his face unreadable.

The tension is palpable. "So what did your friends have to say?" I finally ask.

"We need your help."

If it wasn't for the fact that he looks dead serious, I'd burst out laughing. As it is, I suppress a chuckle. "*You* need *my* help? Last time I checked, you and your Fleshy friends are engaged in all-out war with the Thorn regime, with the Torch Brigade caught right in the middle, and I'm a virtual prisoner aboard your creepy little living ship on my way to get my brain cut open. What could I possibly do for you, and, more importantly, why?"

"You have it all wrong, Lucian. You are not a prisoner. We are protecting you. And as far as delivering you to Straton and subjecting you to his invasive hippocampus procedure, there is an alternative we would like you to consider."

Despite my skepticism, my curiosity is definitely piqued. "Go on."

Digory places his palm on a scanner growing out of what looks like a control panel lodged in the nearby wall. There's a low hum, and a holo appears before us, flashing schematics of the human brain.

Digory points to a region of the brain I recognize as the hippocampus. "Straton believes he can vivisect your brain and isolate your memories, retrieving the genetically inherited memories of your original clone template, Queran Embers, who possessed valuable information that could help Straton defeat Cassius and win the war."

I nod. "I know. The locations of all the survivors of the Ash Wars who were placed in stasis, and probably their tech, too. The same thing Cassius is after. But what I don't understand is why Cassius left me in Straton's custody, when he was planning on double-crossing him. His plotting is usually very methodical. Why take the risk?" I pause to consider. "Unless…"

"Unless Thorn had deduced the unrest of those you know as the Fallen Five and tipped them off to your importance—"

"So they would break me out. Cassius knew Straton would never trust him to take me away from Sanctum. So he played him. That does sound like a Cassius move. But it still doesn't explain why your Hive would be interested in me one way or another. Don't you all want the same thing as Straton does?"

"No. We do not want war. We are not interested in violence, cruelty, or bloodshed. We want what all of you claim to want. What every living being desires and is entitled to. Our autonomy. Freedom to control the Hive's destiny ourselves."

For a second, he reminds me of the Digory I knew. The Digory I lost. "Haven't you already attained free will? I mean, no offence, but you are plotting behind Straton's back and you, yourself, infiltrated Cass's regime right under his nose."

"The original prototypes for our race, your Fallen Five Recruits, retained a certain amount of their original personalities and have managed to filter those attributes through to subsequent specimens. But it is not absolute. Straton has still embedded our collective with restrictions that prevent us from outright defying him without risking our complete annihilation. We need to terminate those fail-safes. Then, and only then, will we be free."

"I still don't understand how I can help you. Even if I wanted to."

He presses more buttons on the control panel and a diagram labeled *Bio-Mech Organisms* flashes into view. "During our analysis of the remnants of Sanctum's archives, we discovered that your progenitor, Queran Embers, held the knowledge to create fully-autonomous soldiers that could think on their own, and be spontaneous under stress, without relying on specific commands to carry out their missions. If we could access that knowledge, we would be free of Straton's influence."

"Suppose I agree. What's in it for the Resistance?"

"We would join your Torch Brigade to end this war as quickly as possible, minimizing the amount of casualties. However, without this technology, we will be forced to wage war and annihilate your kind."

I'm too stunned to speak. If what Digory's saying is true, the information locked in my brain is indeed critical in more than one aspect. It would be worth the sacrifice to my sanity. But what if it's just another ploy? A hidden Flesher agenda that I'm being manipulated into following? Betrayal has become as natural to me as breathing.

I force myself to speak. "What's to say that if I allow you to go digging in my skull and you find the keys to your handcuffs, you won't just decide to destroy the human race, including the Torch Brigade, to eliminate any potential threats to the Hive?"

"Because there is something else that you do not know. Something neither Cassius nor Straton ever revealed to you, which the Hive would not share if we were intent on decimating your race."

He pushes some more buttons. A map of a huge landmass appears. I recognize some of the areas. The region of Infiernos. The Parish. Fort Diablos. Asclepius Valley. The Fringelands. The western regions that once housed the Pleasure Emporiums. Sanctum. The map is labeled *Former United States of America.*

Wasn't that the place Straton referred to as where we all originated from? The one that was destroyed by the Clathrate Apocalypse and the Ash Wars?

Digory turns to me. "Do you remember the Nexus that Straton referred to during our first visit to Sanctum?"

"Yes. He said the Nexus was a hub of shelters built all over this country to protect the populace from the devastation of the Ash Wars, and that Sanctum was the only remaining installation."

"Straton lied to you. Our analysis of the encrypted files reveals that years ago, Sanctum cut off all communication with the Nexus when the first pioneers left Sanctum and returned to the surface, settling what became known as the Establishment. Straton's predecessors wanted to remain in absolute power and feared the other hubs would challenge their authority. They infected the rest of the Nexus with a computer virus and sabotaged all the other hubs' systems. The other survivors remain stored in underground facilities throughout the country, preserved in stasis, waiting to be awakened. Waiting for a signal that will never come. Waiting to die."

I slump against a breathing wall. "Queran Embers knew the location of every hub in the Nexus. The entire future of humanity."

Digory grips my shoulder. "And you possess this information, too. Our collective believes it has found a way to stimulate your cerebral cortex and retrieve those memories without a surgical procedure. But it cannot be done remotely. That is why we are headed to Haven. The equipment we need is stored there. We will have to access it right under Straton's nose, perform the procedure, and escape."

I sigh. "Is that all? Piece of cake."

He stares into my eyes. "We are not going to lie to you as others have. It is a risky procedure. You may still die. And if we are caught, you will not survive Straton's techniques. But we will not force you to do anything against your will. The choice is yours."

Those words should be the epitaph on my grave. Why do people constantly insist on maintaining the illusion of free will when there really is no choice?

If I choose not to go through with this brain procedure, the Torch Brigade could be wiped out in the crossfire, while the Thorn Regime and Sanctum blast each other into oblivion. No one wins.

If I do go through with it, however, I risk the dangerous knowledge contained in the memories of Queran Embers getting into the wrong hands.

But there's also the possibility of regaining contact with the entire Nexus of survivors and establishing a new, and hopefully better, society.

I feel like I'm facing the final and most important Trial ever. One in which, not just the life of a loved one is at stake, but my own identity and existence, as well as that of the entire human race.

"What about the Fleshers stationed on Haven?" I ask Digory. "I'm assuming since you're all a cozy little Hive that they're in on this plan and have our backs?"

"Negative. Until the Five can access the data that will allow us the autonomy to break from Straton's control, we cannot risk sharing this information with the rest of the collective. They would not be able to override their programming and would be forced to impede our progress."

"Keeping secrets from your own kind makes you no better than the rest of us." I bury my face in my hands. "I need a little time to think."

"Understandable. Sleep on it. But we have to check in with Haven in the morning. We will need your answer no later than that."

———

I get no sleep at all. Cole, on the other hand, rests peacefully. When he wakes up, he narrows his eyes at me. "You're still here? I'd have thought you'd be gone by now."

"Did you sleep well? Any bad dreams?"

He rolls his eyes. "I already told you. I don't dream. The nightmares always happen when I open my eyes." He turns away.

I know how you feel, little brother.

I stare at him for a very long time.

Do I really want my brother growing up in a world where dreamless sleep is a desperate refuge from the horrors of the waking world?

When I finally exit the room, Digory's standing outside the door like a sentinel. For all I know, he's been waiting here all night.

Before he can ask, I head him off. "Let's do it."

CHAPTER SEVENTEEN

Entering Haven Air Space.

The eerie, biomechanical voice oozes from every pore of the compartment. Since the Fleshers have no need for spoken language to communicate, the message has probably been run through some kind of thought-to-voice modulator for my benefit.

"What's that?" Cole points out the throbbing port hole. A gigantic dark mass lurks inside the thick bank of clouds we've just passed through.

I press my forehead against the living window, barely able to make sense of what I'm staring at.

Before us looms the most immense airborne carrier I've ever seen. Haven isn't a stationary land base like we all assumed. It's an enormous, mobile city flying through the skies.

I shake my head. "No wonder no one's ever been able to track Haven. Its location is constantly changing."

Steel gray towers and bunkers jut from the surface. An array of solar panels and radio towers are interspersed between numerous hangars and landing platforms. Squads of smaller craft zip by, some tethered to the behemoth by refueling cables.

"Those towers must house some sort of jamming tech which cloaks the facility from radar," I mutter.

My stomach sinks. The Flesher craft descends toward one of Haven's hangar bays. I'm not antsy about strolling into this vile nest. Facing Straton and his army of brainwashed, pious hypocrites is something I can deal with. It's tangible.

No. It's the fact that I don't know who or what I'll be after this memory retrieval business is over. What if Lucian Spark ceases to exist and becomes just a vessel to house the long-dead ghost of Queran Embers, like Digory and his integration to the Hive? Everything I've experienced, everything that makes me who I am, just wiped clean like a brand new hard drive, overridden with entirely different programming. It'll be like dying. Despite what Tristin believed about some mystical deity before she passed, I can't wrap my head around the fact that I'll just cease to exist.

An even more disturbing thought hits me. Maybe there'll be just enough of me left to be conscious of what's going on when the dominant personality of Queran Embers takes over, continuing his legacy of heinous cruelty. I'll be a silent witness to all the horror, but impotent, trapped in a vegetative state, worse than being buried alive.

The craft's nose shifts downward, and my fingers dig into the porous material of the clammy armrests.

"You're scared, aren't you?" Cole's glaring at me from across the aisle.

I shake my head. "I don't mind flying. Just hate landings." I lean in close. "Now remember what we talked about, Cole. When we get there—"

"Keep my mouth shut and just pretend I'm part of the latest shipment to Haven. Got it."

"Not a word. Our Fallen Five friends are tapped into the system and are fudging the new transfer manifest to account for our addition. Hopefully, no one will spot the discrepancy too quickly."

Cole stares past me, out one of the ever-shifting portholes. "I'm not doing anything for you. I just don't want to end up like those others. And you're my only chance of getting out of here and back to..." He bows his head and swipes a forearm across his face.

"Back to Cassius?" I lean in and touch his shoulder, but he rips it away. "Cole, you need to understand—"

"Don't you touch me. Don't even talk to me!" He shifts his body and continues to stare out the window. I can see the tears streaming down his cheeks in the reflective material.

The wall to the compartment wriggles open and Digory enters. Only he looks like a full-fledged Flesher, complete with eye-eliminating optical visor, buzzing and whirring tools jutting from his abdomen, and servomotors attached to his feet, allowing him to glide in and pause in front of me.

For a moment I'm horrified—until he rips off the visor and reveals he still has eyes.

"Pretty convincing disguise, do you not agree?" He flexes his muscles and tinkers with the ridges of his stomach, and the skins gives way, revealing the biological prosthetic emulating the abdominal cavity of the standard variety Fleshers. "The Prototypes put this gear together from the vessels of our fallen brethren." He wraps the belt around his waist again, the live skin stretching to integrate with his own so that it is indiscernible. Then he pops the visor back on. "It should be able to mask this vessel's identity. For a short while at least. One day, what remains of Digory Tycho will be completely absorbed by the Hive and will not require any false gear."

That thought does nothing to ease the wave of anxiety coming over me.

Cole's eyes narrow at him. "You're wearing dead people parts." He shoots me an equally disgusted look. "And you died hundreds of years ago. You two belong together."

The overhead lights hum and change color, from purple, to green, to red, the tones changing like the notes of a musical instrument.

I untether myself and spring to my feet. "What does that mean?"

"It's a proximity alert. We've timed our approach to coincide exactly with the other transport arriving at Haven. Our craft is communicating with the base and transmitting authentication codes. As soon as we have landed, we will exit the ship, and will herd you and your brother into one of the processing queues. Then we will slip away and follow the progenitors to one of the labs and begin the procedure."

"Sounds easy enough. I suppose I'd better change."

"I've taken care of that." His faux abdomen springs open and a pair of metal pincers clutching what looks like bunched up rags, springs forth and drops them at my feet.

I scoop them up, examining the threadbare material which is barely going to conceal my dignity. There's also a wig that looks more like a rat's nest. "Looks like fashion at Haven has seriously taken a nosedive." I toss Cole the smaller bunch, which he catches in one hand. "Time to get ready, Buddy."

Aside from his usual dirty look, he says nothing and begins to change.

"I don't suppose you have any shoes to go with these?" I ask.

Digory shakes his head. "Sorry."

Turning away, I start to peel out of my own clothes and pause when I become aware of Digory's gaze.

"Don't worry," he says before I can protest. "We are not going to peek." He swerves out of visor range.

A faint smile traces my lips. I finish undressing and slip into what amounts to a tattered loincloth. Sheesh. Even Infiernos had a better selection. These poor people were supposed to be living stress-free lives of luxury after the sacrifices all their loved ones made for them during the Trials. Instead, they were rewarded with the abominations of Straton. Another deadly bi-product of Cass's machinations.

The craft's engines gurgle and hiss like a massive beast's intestinal tract. The vessel settles on the landing platform and grinds to a complete stop.

"It's show time," I mutter.

The wall splits open and a gangplank unfurls like a slimy tongue.

"Try not to speak." Digory leads the way.

Cole and I creep behind him. The three of us slink into the shadows created by the aircraft's landing struts, while the rest of our crew rolls, glides, and marches off the ship and into the hangar to meld into the sea of Fleshers.

To our right, another ship has just docked, and its cargo doors slide open. Another crew of Fleshers busies itself with herding hundreds of prisoners off the ship, using silver tools jutting from their midsections like cattle prods. From the looks of the unfortunate captives, it's obvious that Digory wasn't exaggerating their condition.

Most of them look pale and haggard, their hair overgrown mottled clumps, skin scratched and bruised. The rags they're outfitted in look pretty much like the ones Cole and I are wearing, maybe a little dirtier. But there's one thing that really sets them apart from us. Their facial expressions are vacant. Must be from shock, considering all they've been through. It's probably best that they've mentally checked out, especially considering what's in store for them now.

As the Fleshers corral the new arrivals into formations, Digory turns to us. "Now is our chance." He flexes and a similar looking prod springs from his waist compartment. "Go."

Grabbing Cole's reluctant hand, I pull him after me from the safety of our hiding place. He rips his hand loose and steps behind me. Digory jabs at us from behind, moving us toward the nearest clump of catatonic humanity.

In seconds, we're assimilated into the pathetic flock, moving toward the bay doors leading into the complex. Digory's never more than a few feet away. We trade several glances along the way, at least I think we do, since it's impossible to be sure with his optical visor obscuring his eyes.

It's a real struggle not to keep turning and checking on Cole every few seconds. The instinct is overwhelming. But I fight it, knowing that if I attract any unwanted attention it'll be the end of the ride for the both of us.

Just up ahead, I glimpse the open doors leading into the heart of Haven. Only a few more feet to go and then we'll be able to make a break for one of the labs—

Two very large Fleshers emerge and block the door.

This is not good.

Digory strides up to them and pauses. Beads of cold sweat trickle down my forehead. I risk a glance at Cole. He's biting his lower lip.

Without speech, it's impossible to tell what's going on. At one point, one of the Fleshers projects a holo of what looks like some type of manifest. Probably the list of human cargo.

Digory gives a slight nod. Two of the entries near the bottom of the list begin to glow red. Those must be the entries for Cole and me, added during the system hack by the Five. I guess we're going to find out the hard way if it worked or not.

Cole surprises me by tugging my hand. He shoots me a worried look. He nudges his chin toward the opposite end of the bay, and it's obvious he wants to bolt.

It's too much of a risk. They'd swarm all over us in seconds. I clench my jaw and reply with a barely perceptible shake of the head.

The wait is excruciating. Then the holo *bleeps*—

The entries flash from red to green.

I let go of the breath I've been clenching with a soft hiss.

The prisoners shamble forward again. Only five more people ahead of us until we reach the door.

"Halt right there!" The familiar voice chills my blood, and invisible fingers clutch my throat.

Dr. Stefan Straton marches toward our group. I immediately bow my head, grateful for the ratty wig obscuring my face. If Straton decides to take a closer look, though, it's not going to pass muster. Maybe he'll just relay an order and leave.

Straton approaches one of the Flesher escorts. "Make sure the unit in Hangar D has been fitted with chutes for deposit in the valley."

The Flesher nods and speeds off on its wheeled base to carry out Straton's commands.

The doctor turns to those of us remaining. "Before you begin your new contribution to our society," Straton croaks, "I have randomly selected this group to test our new viability detector. It's a quick and painless scan that allows us to make an even quicker determination as to what your designation to the Haven community will be."

Great. Just a fancy way of saying whether or not we'll be selected as candidates for Flesher assimilation or get relegated to food source for Sanctum's crazed religious zealots.

"Let us begin." Straton points toward the two Fleshers, who begin their scan at the front of the line.

He tracks their progress via a pad in his hand. "Subject: Bazz K. Male."

A handsome, if disheveled youth, is scanned. His eyes are wide and flitting about like cornered prey.

Straton checks a readout and grins. "Excellent. You'll make a fine addition to our Bio-mechanical ranks. *Next.*"

The panicked youth is dragged through the doors. The next person in line, a frightened girl about my age, is scanned.

"Subject: Longchamps, M. Female. Begin." Straton commands.

The girl is scanned while Straton reviews the results. "Congratulations, my dear. You'll play a very important role in our nutritional and devotional processing."

Longchamps shrieks. She's hauled away. Then the next two are scanned. Until there's only one person ahead of me.

Shifting my weight from foot to foot, I make visual contact with Digory. His nod's very clear.

I brace myself. The person directly ahead of me is finished, an unfortunate girl named White.

"Next," Straton says.

I take a deep breath.

Last stand time.

My muscles tense.

"Don't I know you from somewhere?" Straton approaches. "Show me your face." His long shadow falls over me.

The last thing I'm going to do before I'm killed is choke the life out of him.

Cole bursts from my side and lunges at Straton. "You're not going to eat me!" He pounces and sinks his teeth into the doctor's wrist.

I'm coiled to spring, but Digory's there in a flash, pulling Cole away from the good doctor.

Straton clutches his bloody hand to his chest "You'll pay for that, you little bastard." He grabs the Flesher nearest him. "It seems our young friend here has volunteered to serve as an offering in our worship services. He'll become one with the Begetter and provide sustenance for us all. *Take him.*"

Cole shoots me a wink. Then he's dragged away into the darkness.

My brother's ploy worked. Too well. Straton's ignoring me now. His expression is a mixture of pain and rage. "I'll be in medical receiving inoculation against whatever infections that rabid little cur carries in his blood. In the meantime, get these others out of here." He storms off without another glance at me.

Digory pushes me through the doors and yanks me into a dark alcove.

I rip my arm free. "What the hell are you doing? We've got to go after my brother."

He shakes his head. "Cole bought us a window with his diversion. We may never get another shot at this. If you go after him now, you will both be destroyed."

144

I stare after Cole. My emotions are in a tailspin. Everything Digory's saying makes sense, but it goes against every instinct in my gut.

Digory's hand engulfs mine. "We promise you that once the procedure's underway, this vessel will retrieve your brother before he is harmed. We are running out of time, Lucian. You have to trust in our mission."

My entire body's trembling with fury and grief. I take a few deep breaths. "Let's get to the lab. And if anything happens to Cole, I'm holding you personally responsible. Not your Hive. You."

He nods, and we vanish into Haven's shadows.

CHAPTER EIGHTEEN

The interior of the cryogenic capsule is so cold against my bare skin that it actually burns. The Flesher med team has shaved my entire body, except for my scalp, in order to accommodate the spider web of electrode patches connected to countless organic tubes, wriggling like worms.

True to their word, they won't be actually cutting into my brain, allowing me to keep my hair. Instead, the tubules are filled with multi-colored chemicals designed to be absorbed through my skin and seep directly into my blood and neuropathways. As the Fleshers explained and Digory relayed, the theory is that this combination of fluids will stimulate the hippocampus and awaken the genetically preserved memories locked deep inside me like a dormant virus.

Considering how fast and furious my heart's pumping, it should take hardly any time for the serum to churn its way through my arteries.

The glow of the overhead lights hurts my eyes. I try to shift, but the capsule's cramped, a coffin of steel and glass that barely allows for any movement. It strikes me as disturbingly appropriate that this coffin-like container may very well be Lucian Spark's final resting place. When this is all over, who knows who, or what, will emerge from this bio-mech grave?

The lead Flesher leans in to my capsule to adjust the slug-like conduits attached to my temples. I feel a slight prick, then a burning sensation, as their tips burrow through and mesh with my skin.

"I don't suppose you put something in the mix to relax me a little, huh?"

The Flesher stares at me as if I were a bug, then disappears from view.

I attempt to swallow a couple of times before it takes. "Didn't think so."

Digory hovers into view and leans over my capsule. He's removed his visor so we can at least make eye contact now. "We are getting ready to begin, Lucian."

"What's the word on Cole? Did your hack into the security system pick up anything?"

I'll never get used to the way his eyes don't blink. "Not yet. As far as we can gather, he is still in holding at the Processing Station. As soon as the procedure begins, we will set about to retrieve him."

I lift my hand and grip the lip of the opened tube. "You have to get him out of here, Digory. That's the only reason I'm agreeing to do this. I never even had a chance to tell him I—" My eyes squeeze shut for a moment, then I turn to look at him again. "Whatever happens to me, make sure you get Cole back to the Brigade. My friends—Arrah, Dru, Cage— they'll look after him for me."

Digory nods. "You have our promise."

Now I push up as much as I'm able. Digory leans in closer to help prop me up. "One last thing."

"Lucian, there is no time—"

"Listen to me! If I should come out of this—if it should mess me up and I'm dangerous—promise me you'll extract whatever information you need by whatever methods necessary, and then take me out."

He doesn't even flinch. "Of course. It will be done quickly and painlessly."

Our hands clasp and squeeze tightly. Then his grip loosens and my fingers slide through his like the waning sands of an hourglass.

Maybe it's just the cocktail kicking in, but my muscles start to relax and a rare wave of serenity washes over me, filling me with warmth and a delicious tingling.

A smile spreads across my face. Guess that Flesher slipped me something after all…

I try to focus on Digory, but it's difficult. I see two shapes, one with a bright smile, piercing blue eyes, sun-kissed skin, and golden hair, the other with a smooth scalp, pale skin, and frost gray eyes. Both images blur and meld into one.

"Digory. I just wanted you to know. Whatever happens…I still…I'll always…" everything is dark…so tiredsoverytiredjustwanttosleep…

—falling down a dark well…spinning head over heels…

The alley is cold and dirty. Hiding behind a dumpster…they're gonna find me, and beat me up…Mommy and Daddy can't help me. They're at work. They told me to stay inside and lock the door but I didn't listen. The rain looks so fun…splashing in all the puddles…

They want my shoes. And my ration bar. So tired of running, being chased…

I hold my nose against the bad smells. The shadows fall on me. So scared. It's the three boys who've been chasing me. They're so big, like giants.

"We're hungry, little man," says the one with the missing front tooth.

The other two are also barefoot and dirty. They don't talk, just eyeing the ration bar stickin' outta my front pocket and the new shoes Daddy made me.

I pee my pants, and I hear that ugly sound. They're laughing at me. Getting closer, grabbing my hair, hurting me…

"Leave'im alone!" It's another boy, older like them. He starts kickin' and bitin' and punchin' back until the other three run away. But he's bleeding all over.

I'm cryin' real hard for my mommy and daddy.

"It's okay, buddy boy." He pats me on my back just like Daddy does when I'm scared of the thunder. The boy takes out a dirty rag from his pocket and smudges the cryin' from my face. "I'll take ya home. No one's gonna mess with you again. Lemme show you how to do that."

He shows me howta make loops with my laces and tie'em up.

"See? That's better!" He pulls me up and outta the garbage. "Name's Cassius. Cassius Thorn. But you can call me, Cass, got it? Not Cassie. Deal?"

I shake his hand. "Deal! I'm Lucian. But don't call me Lucy, 'kay?"

He chuckles. "How 'bout if I call you Lucky, on accounta it's a lucky day when you make a new friend?"

We both chuckle, and he takes me by the hand and walks me through the dark, scary streets til I'm safe at home…

Falling again, the well is so deep, like I'm never going to hit the bottom.

Another time. Another place.

Emergency sirens blare.

On the bank of video screens, people are rushing through the streets against the backdrop of a fiery sky.

There are others in the room with me. Watching the screens. Watching me. Waiting for my orders.

A female aide rushes up to me. "There's no more time. If we're going to do it, it has to be done now."

I nod. I've already been too generous as it is.

Another aide, younger and male, bolts from his chair. He looks very familiar to me. Where have I—? Of course he's familiar to me. A lover? An underling?

Both?

"We can't do it. There are too many of them out there. We have more than enough room to accommodate them. Leaving them out there to die is murder!"

I stare at the screens filled with panic and chaos. "Seal the bunker."

There's a loud explosion that drowns everything out.

Then my eyes spring open, and I'm gasping for air.

Someone—Digory is it?—is ripping off the tubes attached to my body. "The procedure is over. We have to go."

Sirens are blaring. Just like in…where was that? It's gone, the elusive fragments of a bad dream, always just out of reach.

Everything else comes rushing in like a mudslide. I spring from the pod, throwing on my clothes. "Did it work?"

The alarms are getting louder.

I grab Digory's arm. "What the hell is going on?"

Digory's already tugging me out the door. "It is your brother."

A lightning bolt of pain rips through my skull, doubling me over. Digory tries to hold me up. I push away and retch my guts out into a corner. My skin feels colder than his. I swipe at my burning eyes. When the wave finally passes, I grab onto Digory's massive thigh for support as he helps me to my feet.

"Unfortunately, there is no time for you to recover or to determine what effect the memory stimulation had on you. Can you stand?"

"I'm okay now," I lie. The nausea and pain might have subsided, but I definitely don't feel right. No time to worry about that now. "What's happened to Cole?"

He readjusts his optical visor and gear to resemble the rest of the Fleshers. "Apparently, your brother feigned a seizure and took advantage of the scene to seize one of his escort's weapons. He has broken out of the processing facility and is on the loose—along with the other detainees he managed to free."

Along with my shock comes a mixed sense of pride and guilt. Apparently, Cole's not as helpless as he once was, thanks to Cassius's indoctrination. But the loss of that innocence still cuts deep.

"There is a full scale search underway," Digory continues. "If they find him before we do, they will subject him to intense interrogation and discover who we are. This whole operation will have been in vain."

His words boost my adrenaline. "What exactly are you saying?"

He focuses his attention on his gear. "Our window for escape is closing. The diversion created by the child may offer the perfect opportunity—"

"Not a chance. We're not leaving without him." My blood's bubbling. "I can't believe you'd even suggest that. You once sacrificed everything so that I—," I turn away. "Would you sacrifice a member of your Hive to escape?"

Digory doesn't answer right away. "We are all a part of a whole. If it meant the survival of our kind, then yes."

My eyes narrow at the sight of this stranger. "Good thing it's not up to you. C'mon."

As we creep out of the lab, he mutters, "The more we learn about the illogical behavior of your kind, the more confused it makes us."

The complex is a scene of pandemonium. We rush to the armory to gather some weapons. White-clad worshippers are scrambling to get out of the way of the swarming Fleshers. It reminds me of the time they pursed Digory and our fellow recruits back at Infiernos, before we ever knew what they were. Now Cypress, Gideon, and Ophelia are dead, Digory's an honorary member of the Flesher force, and I'm—

Who the hell knows what I am now?

When we arrive at the armory, explosions rattle the chamber from one end to the other. Support girders come loose, toppling platforms and raining down debris.

I shove Digory under the cover of a cargo lift. "What the hell is that all about?"

His eyes glaze over, and he's perfectly still. Must be receiving a data transmission of some kind. "The detonations are being caused by mining charges that were stolen from this very armory after your brother and the others made a break for it. He has to be close."

Another wave of pain and nausea wipes the smirk off my face. I stumble over a few supply crates, unleashing a cache of weapons and grenades. Even as I scramble to get back on my feet, it feels like my head's about to burst open and splatter my brains across the catwalks.

"Cole…," I mutter through spasms. "We have…to get…"

Digory flings my arm around his shoulder. "Your brother seems to be taking good care of himself."

Composing myself as best as I can, we gather as many weapons as we can carry, slinging straps of firearms over our shoulders and stuffing explosives into our pockets.

A small, oval device, blinking red, catches my eye and I snatch it up. "What's this?"

Digory glances at it. "It's one of the specially designed beacons used to guide the fuel and supply ships to Haven's current position. Why?"

I'm already prying the device open and hacking the broadcast frequencies to match resistance channels. Once done, I hide the unit under one of the floor grates. "It's a long shot, but it may just guide the brigade to Haven at last, if someone doesn't find it first. Let's go."

We're just about to cross the access bridge when Digory halts, paralyzed. "It looks like someone has found your brother first."

Before us, a Flesher has his pincers around Cole's arm. He struggles, cursing and kicking his captor.

Straton enters with a squadron. His hand is bandaged, and his face smug as he approaches Cole. "Seems our little visitor here is more valuable than I realized. I just reviewed the analysis of your identity scans, boy. According to the data, your name is Cole Spark, recently a ward of my dear friend Cassius Thorn. And brother of Lucian Spark, a young man I'm quite eager to find. You're going to be quite valuable to me." He pulls out a long metal prod, crackling with energy. Its glow casts crazy shadows on Cole's anxious face. "Tell me. Where is your brother now?"

Cole spits at him. "You'd better hope you don't find him."

Straton's grin grows wider. "I was hoping you'd say something like that." He leans in with the prod.

"It's me you want, Straton. Let my brother go."

Straton glares at me. "This little reunion is long overdue."

"I'm sure you've been champing at the bit for the chance to cut open my brain."

He nods. "All you have to do is cooperate, and you'll avoid being made to feel uncomfortable." Straton nudges his chin in the direction of the lab. "I will have a surgical team prepped stat. Your brother will be safe." He brings the prod close to Cole's eye. "However, if you remain uncooperative, I can't promise that your brother's death will be quick and painless. As a matter of fact. I shall do my best to make sure that it won't be."

I sigh. "Tell me, Straton, just how rewarding is it being another one of Thorn's pawns? You do realize he'll destroy you once he gets what he wants."

"Not if I get it first. Please, do not force my hand. We of Sanctum are a peaceful people that follow the word of the Begetter—"

I rub my throbbing temples. "Peaceful people? Interesting. Yet you have no problem harvesting the survivors of Haven for food and genetic material to create your slave race of Fleshers, with you as their leader, of course."

His face flushes. "The Fleshers, as you call them, are the product of divine will."

"Damn you and your false gods."

Straton's lips curve into a toothy grin. "I would think Queran Embers would be appreciative of such strategy."

Cole and I exchange a quick glance, and he nods.

In a flash, I fling active grenades in every direction. Cole seizes the moment and thrusts the prod directly into the doctor's eye. Straton shrieks and flings him aside.

Digory follows my lead and tosses more grenades. Soon the entire level is a hell of deafening explosions, debris, and thick smoke.

Despite his injury, Straton is busy barking commands. I dash toward him, ignoring the blasts all around me. I grab Straton, wrapping an arm around his neck, and pulling his head back by his white mane. A strange calm I don't remember feeling in ages comes over me. This all feels so natural.

"What…are…you…doing?" Straton gasps. "I'll give you anything you want, Queran."

I yank Straton's neck. There's a loud *pop*. His body goes limp.

I'm stunned as he slides from my grip and onto the floor.

"Let's go!" Cole shouts.

The Fleshers advance on us. But from out of nowhere, another squadron, led by the Progenitors, appears, and the two sides begin battle. Blades buzz and whirr as the bio-mech hybrids turn on each other for the first time in their history. Sharp tools hack away at skin, appendages, spewing geysers of dark fluids every which way.

Digory's eyes grow wide. "It is not possible."

In that moment, there's no distinction between the Fleshers and humankind.

I truly pity them.

Grabbing Cole's hand, we race toward the hangar doors. "Digory! Move!"

His footfalls are directly behind us. Once we're through the doors, there's nothing but a long ramp leading into the infinity of blue skies. The only vehicle left on the landing platform is a beat up all-terrain Trundler.

A loud explosion rocks the platform. Behind us, Straton's legions are approaching, armed with portable cannons aimed in our direction.

We're cut off.

A thought hits me. "Wait a minute? What hangar is this, Digory?"

"Hangar D. But what does that—"

"Into the Trundler," I bark. The three of us race inside the vehicle.

"You do realize this vehicle does not fly?" Digory asks.

But I ignore him, trying to make sense of the control panel. "Strap yourselves in."

I study the dashboard. The strange symbols suddenly make perfect sense. Instinctively, my fingers fly over the buttons, entering a code on the keyboard. The vehicle's engines rumble to life.

Cole seems unnerved. "How did you know to do that?"

Though he doesn't say a word, I can tell the same question is on Digory's face.

"I'm not sure," I finally say.

Blasts rock the Trundler. Straton's crew showers us with canon fire, cracking the windshield and putting a huge dent in the hatch.

"Hang on." I gun the Trundler's engines, speeding toward the end of the runway.

"You're going to kill us!" Cole tries to wrest the controls from me, but Digory holds him back.

Another blast takes out part of the runway ahead of us. I swerve and take the Trundler to maximum firepower, sailing over the edge.

My stomach twists as we freefall in the sky. Cole's screaming. But my instinct kicks in. I hope I was right about the command Straton gave that Flesher when we arrived.

Toggling a switch, we're suddenly jolted upwards, as the chutes attached to the Trundler are activated, breaking our descent.

"Your brother knows what he is doing," Digory says to the now silent Cole.

As we drop, twisting and swaying to the surface far below, I wonder if it was my instinct that saved us, or someone else's.

CHAPTER NINETEEN

The engines of the Trundler transport vehicle grind to a halt at last with a clatter of clunky metal. I'm surprised it's made it as far as it has, considering all the damage it sustained from those cannons on Haven, not to mention the battering we took when the vehicle crash landed on the surface, despite the chutes breaking our fall.

Outside the viewport windows, the landscape is vast and bleak. Enormous, craggy mountains fill the horizon. The sparse vegetation is dry and brown. Funnels of dust flurries sweep the countryside, tossing spinning tumbleweeds to and fro.

The remnants of the road ahead shimmers with distortion caused by the intense heat. These were once called…*highways.* Yes. That's the word. Not sure how I know that, but I just do.

Or Queran Embers does.

I'm about to pop the hatch to go out and investigate, when Digory emerges from the cockpit with a tool kit and pushes past me. "We have almost reached the coordinates you gave me. If repairs cannot be made, we will have to hike the rest of the way."

He opens the hatch, letting in a wave of heat and dust, before slamming it behind him.

At first, Digory, who's a lot more familiar with the Flesher tech than I am, was able to patch a few holes and run some electrical bypasses to keep the systems functioning. That got us through the first few hundred miles or so. It was actually kind of eerie to watch him sit as still as a statue, eyes opened and far away, as he patched in and communicated with the craft via their shared consciousness. There was something very spiritual about it, at least more so than the hypocrisy at the Priory.

Eventually, the makeshift repairs began to give, beginning with the cooling systems. As the outside temperatures climbed to the hundred degree mark, it made the environment extremely uncomfortable, at least for Cole and me, who had no choice but to strip down to our tanks and shorts. Even then, we were both slick with sweat, while Digory remained relatively unaffected, except for when I caught him standing in the shadows of the cockpit, his right hand gripping his left, which was twitching uncontrollably.

"What's wrong?" I asked.

He quickly stuffed his affected hand out of sight. "It is nothing. Just a little recalibration of the nanotech, that is all."

Then he turned back to the exposed circuit board in front of him and ignored me.

I didn't buy it then, and I still don't buy it now.

Since then, he's been even more aloof than usual. And practically every night for the past week, I've awoken to the sounds of him thrashing in his bunk, muttering mostly unintelligible words.

Last night, I picked up a distinct fragment.

They weren't supposed to be harmed.

Not sure what it means. But when I try to approach him and broach the subject, he snaps at me, like he did earlier.

"You should focus your concerns on the welfare of your bother."

"Fine. I won't ask again."

"Maybe he's weirded out about you, too." Cole's voice startles me. I turn to face him.

He's pale. Dark circles under bloodshot eyes. His skin's slick and flushed.

"What are you doing out of bed? You need your rest."

"I can't sleep. It's too hot."

I hunch down and can't get over how he's at least a foot taller than he was just a short time ago. "I'm sorry. I saved you an extra replenisher packet. It should cool you down and supply you with a hefty dose of vitamins. You need to keep up your strength."

Despite his protests, I retrieve the pack from the melting contents of the cooler, open it, and press it to his chapped lips.

His thirst betrays his stubbornness, and his throat bobs as he gulps it down without spilling a drop.

Our situation's bad. Food we can do without for a while. But our water supply's seriously depleted.

When he's done, he stares at me for a moment before speaking. "Why are we here?"

"I'm sorry. I wish I could have gotten you back to the Brigade and not exposed you to any of—"

"No. I mean why are we *here*? A thousand miles out in the middle of nowhere. I saw what you did back at Haven. How you knew what code to input in the Trundler. What is it you know? Where are you taking us?"

At last, someone asks the questions we've all been avoiding ever since I gave Digory the westerly heading upon our escape.

The little bastard has no business meddling in affairs that have nothing to do with him. He should be punished. Severely. That'll make a man out of him…

The thought shocks me. It feels alien and all too familiar at the same time. But the venom behind it is truly palpable, and it frightens me. I try my best to push it away.

Concentrating as hard as I can against the unexplainable, nagging impulse to strike him, I gently grip Cole's shoulders instead. "I'm honestly not sure. Ever since the procedure in the labs, I've been remembering things. Fragments. Like some deeply ingrained instinct. I can feel that it's important that we be here. But I still can't make sense as to why."

Cole's eyes narrow. "I used to believe all those stories you told me. About the Lady. About her friends. I don't anymore."

A wave of pain rips through my head. I squeeze my eyes closed, hoping it'll pass quickly. My thoughts are fragmented, scattered. Part of me struggles to stop the tears and wants to get down on my knees and beg Cole for forgiveness, for failing him.

The other part—

Ungrateful little shit. After everything I've done for him. He's just like the rest. Well, if he's not loyal to me, then I'll just have to—

Stop.

My fingertips dig into my temples, massaging. Cold sweat mixes with dried. The pounding finally subsides. I open my eyes, needing a minute for the blur to clear. When I'm finally able to focus again, Cole's holding out an object in his open palm.

A battered, round chronometer.

There's something familiar about it, but it's hard to concentrate through the brain fog.

"Take it," he says. "I don't need it anymore."

I reach out still trembling fingers and scoop it up, examining the battered casing and the burnt out digital display.

I know this piece.

"I gave this to you the day before the Ascension Ceremony, when I came to see you at the Priory."

Bitter memories eclipse the alien voices in my brain, and I embrace them, desperate and relieved to cling to something that is so irrevocably tied to me. But the price is pain. Another reminder of my failures.

"You never came," Cole says. "I waited for you. But you never came back."

He turns away.

His words sting. But the fact that he's carried this symbol of my broken promise to him for so long must mean something. There has to be a chance for us.

Forget him. He'll only slow you down, make you weak. Cut him loose.

That searing pain again. I bow my head against the throbbing. It seems to last longer this time.

"Your...nose..." Cole's voice sounds like its miles away.

The pain finally subsides. I swipe at the moisture coating my upper lip. Bright red blood.

I don't remember ever suffering a nosebleed before.

"Here." Cole hands me a rag from his pocket, and I wipe myself clean. What's happening to me?

The hatch bursts open, letting in searing light and heat, which hurts my eyes to look at. I can barely make out Digory's dark silhouette.

"Repairs are a bust," he announces. "We go on foot now. But there may be a clue as to why you led us here, Lucian. Let us go."

I join Digory in gathering supplies into our respective packs.

Cole grabs his own pack and pushes past me, as if he's afraid to be in the same room with me.

Not that I blame him.

Stuffing the chronometer back into my pocket, I follow suit, ignoring the ache in my head, following Cole and Digory into the scorching wilderness.

———

"This is where it lies," Digory calls over the moaning wind. "Not much farther."

Cole's perched on his shoulders. He hasn't said a word in almost an hour, when he protested letting me be the one to carry him. But it wasn't long before exhaustion overtook him, and Digory volunteered to hoist him the rest of the way.

Just as well. I'm not sure I trust myself to be alone with him any longer, not with those impulses to hurt him clouding my judgment. And the fact that I would ever even consider doing so tears at me more powerfully than those vultures circling silently overhead could ever hope to.

My leg muscles tense and tremble with fatigue as I follow them up the incline. We zig zag through the maze of boulders and dirt baking under the relentless sun, until we reach the shadow of a mammoth mountain.

Nexus Prime.

The name comes to me naturally, instinctively, and it takes a few seconds for the implications to sink in.

I've been here before. Not as Lucian Spark. In another life.

Queran Ember's life.

"I see it," I grumble, pushing past them, knowing there'll be a set of doors camouflaged by a rock formation, even before I spy the glint of sun on steel that Digory must have spotted from the transport.

Despite my weakness and dehydration, I rush forward, half-running, half-stumbling, until I reach a set of boulders nestled against the mountain's base.

Reaching out, I touch the hot stone. A flashflood of memories practically drowns me.

They're scared. The atmospheric conditions have grown dangerous. So much death and disease. War's wiping out the few that remain. Hunger and thirst are overwhelming. But there's a sense of relief.

Of hope.

We can wait here. Wait until the time's right and reclaim what belongs to us. To me. We can survive death, overcome it.

I can overcome death.

Become immortal.

My hands spring away from the rock, as if the memory itself has seared through my flesh.

Digory rushes up beside me. "Lucian, what is it? What have you found?"

For a moment it's as if I'm looking through two sets of eyes all at once. "This is where we—where they—sought refuge when things fell apart. Nexus Prime. The primary nerve center of the network of survivors, the repositories of civilization who went underground to wait out the Clathrate apocalypse and the Ash Wars."

"This is the place where the tech that controls the Hive was designed." Digory's gray eyes are wide open. He runs his fingers along the stone grooves.

"There are other people here, too, aren't there?" Cole's voice is barely above a whisper. "The ones that survived? And we'll be able to track the rest of the shelters from here, too." He looks up at me. "That's what Cassius wanted, right? To enslave them?"

"Yes," I finally say. "Or to wipe them out."

But there's something much darker here, too. I can almost see it.

If they try to take what belongs to us, they'll be destroyed, too.

Flashes of a huge chamber. Being blinded by gleaming silver. I can't make out the markings on the room or the cylinders, but a sense of overwhelming death presses into my chest, suffocating me.

Strangely, the visions fill me with exhilaration instead of fright.

"Are you remembering something else?" Digory's question brings me back to the here and now.

"No." The lie is out of my mouth like a reflex. And oddly, it feels right. Natural.

I stare at both my companions. The hulking, bald youth with the pale skin and storm gray eyes. The unkempt child, dark circles under its eyes, weak. Pathetic.

A wave of revulsion engulfs me. They're not my equals. Their company disgusts me.

I bury my face in my hands.

Get out of my head.

"What's wrong?" Cole's voice this time. Is that an actual hint of concern?

I open my eyes to meet their stares. "Leave me. I'm okay."

The intensity of the feelings dissipates, but the sensation remains, lurking in the corners of my brain, waiting for just the right moment when my guard's down to strike again.

The thought chills me, despite the desert heat.

"So where do we go from here?" Digory asks.

"Down below," I reply. "Way down."

I stare beyond the opening. Already the light's dimming and the wind's moaning, creating swirling particles of dust that obscure the horizon. "We've got a ways to go. I suggest we camp here for the night and recoup. There's a very long day ahead of us tomorrow."

"As you wish." Digory opens the packs and removes the sleeping bags.

Cole busies himself setting up the compact electrolantern. Then he pulls out the receiver from its battered case and turns to me. "Should we give it another try?"

I take it from him and switch the power on. "Battery's almost dead. Maybe we'll finally pick something up out here. Nothing to lose."

Ever since our escape from Haven, we've attempted to monitor both Thorn and Brigade channels and only succeeded in picking up static.

The three of us huddle in a semicircle while I try one channel after another.

I sigh. "Nothing but snow—"

"Wait." Digory adjusts some dials. "There is something—"

"I see it!" Cole fiddles with the antennae.

A pixelated image fills the small screen.

I recognize Brigade ships, zooming across the sky, followed by shots of Haven.

"—Torch Brigade has successfully liberated the internment camps at Haven from Sanctum control," the narrator of the newsreel explains, his voice cutting in and out. "Unfortunately, with the death of Sebastos Straton, and no one to lead them, the Sanctum forces have agreed to an armistice with the Thorn Republic."

"It worked! They were able to track the beacon." I can barely contain a grin. There's a rapid fire of images; Resistance ships and troops forming a perimeter around the massive Haven installation, interspersed with shots of medics tending to prisoners, some weeping, others cheering, at finally being liberated at last.

Cage's face appears. He looks battle worn, fresh cuts and bruises on his face, but his eyes are glowing with a fire that rivals the torch he thrusts high in the sky like a fiery weapon. "People of the Parish. The time to strike is now. Before the forces of The Thorn Republic and the remnants of Sanctum can regroup and ally against us. The Torch Brigade's recent victories are the beginning of their end!"

There's a montage of clips depicting the battle at the Cape, the rescue of prisoners and firefight at the Gorge, the most recent campaign against Haven, giving the Resistance countless more food and medical resources, plus stockpiles of weapons.

The camera's back to Cage's face. "We're coming for you, Thorn." He points straight ahead. "People of the Parish, join the Torch Keeper. Prepare to fight for our lives, for our liberty, against the Thorn Republic. Together, we can defeat tyranny once and for all."

A tide of guilt crashes into me. Would any of them really want to join me if they knew who I really was?

Cage continues his address. The camera slowly zooms out, revealing legions of resistance fighters and rescued citizens, all holding their glowing torches aloft, miniature suns in a sea of defiance.

My eyes scan the faces. "Is that Arrah? I think I see Dru and Corin."

But with so many faces and faulty reception, it's impossible to be sure.

There's a burst of static and the image disappears, replaced by the stark insignia of the Thorn Republic with a character-generated *Please Stand By* super-imposed on it.

"Maybe next time your Resistance will be able to broadcast longer before the republic intercepts," Digory says.

We switch channels, but there's nothing else being broadcast, just an endless, static blizzard.

I jam my thumb against the power button, switching it off. "We'd better get some sleep."

In minutes, we're all bedding down, Digory and I lying on either side of Cole, the three of us giving in to our weariness.

———

It's one of the most disturbing nights of my life. The dreams bombard my brain like an aerial raid, one explosive memory after another.

Mother is weak and useless. My father, arrogant and stern. Humiliating me constantly because I failed to live up to his standards. Always paling in comparison to my step brother.

Where once there was profound love for my brother, I've grown to hate the sight of him. Thinking he's so much better than I am. Stealing my father's approval.

But even then, we fought alongside each other in the Ash Wars.

I can taste the dirt and blood in my mouth. The explosions deafening in my ears. All around us the air itself is burning, scorching my lungs as I gasp for breath.

I've been hit. The pain in my side is intense. Warm blood oozes from the wound.

I'm so afraid. I don't want to die. Please don't let me die.

My brother swings my arm over his shoulder and pulls me with him through the sickening haze of fire and lethal explosions.

"I've got you, Queran!" he shouts.

He's not going to leave me. Relief fills me. The 'copter is just ahead. In a few seconds we'll be away from this horrible place.

Just as he shoves me inside, another explosion hits. He loses his grip, hanging from one of the 'copter's landing struts. The pilot, unaware, takes off and swerves into the infernal sky.

"Queran, help me," my step brother pleads, dangling from one of the 'copter's landing struts by one hand.

I hesitate an instant. He looks so helpless, so desperate. Not the arrogant war hero that's eclipsed me my whole life. Not the narcissist who's stolen my parents' love and admiration. It would be so easy to let him fall, to come back the victor for once in my life.

Before I can think it through it's too late.

A fireball engulfs him. His scream pierces the air. My eyes bulge as he roasts alive, his skin blackening and peeling away like the shavings of a sharpening pencil. He drops away—

My father's fist slams across my face, sending me reeling, toppling over my brother's casket at the memorial service.

There are screams.

"It should have been *him* that came back. Not *you*!" My father wails.

Through the blur of pain and tears, I spot my brother's hand, burnt to a crisp, reaching out for my own from the lid of his upturned coffin—

I spring up from my sleeping bag, coated in cold sweat, my heart thrumming.

Cole's clinging to me, restless, his eyelids fluttering, battling his own demons.

Holding him tight, I bury my face in his hair, sobbing. "You're okay, little brother. You're okay."

I rock him gently, until he relaxes, before tucking him back into his sleeping bag, like I used to before our lives were torn apart. I give him a kiss on the forehead, wiping away a shiny tear that plops above his brow.

Digory's sitting up. Even in the darkness, I can see his body trembling all over. He's in the throes of a massive seizure.

I crawl over to him, gripping his arm. "Digory. What's wrong?"

He stares at me, shaking his head. "It is all our…Digory's fault," he whispers. "They are dead because of him." He repeats this over and over again.

Grabbing his shoulders, I stare right into his eyes, which are glazed and bloodshot. "It was just a bad dream. Your Hive is okay."

Digory pulls away from me. "Not the Hive. That…family. The Tychos. Digory's parents. Our—his brother and sister. They are all dead because of us. Because he betrayed them."

He repeats the phrase, over and over.

He betrayed them.

This is the most helpless I've seen Digory since he returned to my life.

He tries to take my hand but he seems to have lost control of his motor skills. I grip him, holding him steady.

Not knowing what to say.

Instead, I just wrap my arms around him, holding him tightly against me.

We cling to each other like that until dawn, staring at the night sky.

But unlike long ago, this time the stars bring no comfort.

CHAPTER TWENTY

As the first rays of sunlight paint over the canvas of night, I stretch my body. It's stiff from Digory's weight and lying in the same position for so long. But every throb of my muscles and creak in my joints is worth the chance to spend one last night in close proximity to the people I care most about in this world. Once we enter that installation, there's no telling how much of me there'll be left.

It's getting harder and harder to keep Queran Embers at bay. He may just end up peeling away the rest of my skin—the rest of *me*—and discarding it, slinking free of my remains once and for all.

The image sends a bitter chill through me. I exhale a puff of frosty breath and disentangle myself from Digory, kneading the pins and needles from my still sleeping limbs. Even in the infant morning, he looks strikingly paler than before, the veins contrasted against his stark skin, most noticeable around his neck and temples. Dark circles cup his eyes, which stare at me, glazed and unblinking.

"You don't look so good." I reach out to touch his forehead and flinch. "You're burning up."

"It is nothing." He pulls away and springs to his feet in a lithe move. For just a moment, pain flashes across his face then vanishes. "Regeneration is taking just a little longer than usual, that is all."

"I don't think—"

"That is all. We had better get a move on. The day is wasting."

Without making eye contact, he busies himself with packing up the gear.

Hopefully, this place has some kind of med facility with something to bring down that fever. Not that I'd know what to give someone that's been altered like Digory has. But if he's right and Nexus Prime is where they developed the tech that transformed him—

He's right.

That thought. So confident. And so alien. My skin breaks out in bumps. It's like being infected with a parasite, burrowing its way through my veins, tunneling into my brain.

I steady myself against a boulder and wipe the sweat from my forehead, waiting for the wave of head pain and nausea to slowly subside.

You haven't won yet, Queran. There's still enough Lucian Spark in here to kick your ass.

Taking a deep breath, I hobble over to Cole, who's already rolled up his sleeping bag.

"How'd you sleep?" I ask.

His puffy eyes say it all. He shrugs.

"How bad were the dreams?"

Cole turns to the rising sun. "Bad." He looks my way. "Not as bad as yours, I think."

My muscles tense. I know Cole was there when Cassius told me who I really was, but considering his state, I've been hoping he was too brainwashed to process it. Denial can be very comforting at times. "What did you hear?"

He shakes his head. "*He's* getting stronger, isn't he?"

I can't hold his gaze. He knows. Of course he knows. I hunch down and grip his shoulders. "Yep."

I'm surprised when he pounds my chest with both his fists. Tears streak down his angry eyes. "And if he beats you, you're going to leave again. And then you'll never, ever come back."

Taking hold of his hands, I grasp them until the fury subsides. "We're going to leave here soon. And then things will get better."

Yet somehow, they always seem to get worse.

I stop myself from promising him anything. I've already broken too many, and he'd never believe me anyway.

I wouldn't either.

He shoves the electrolantern back in its case. "And then what? Go home? What is that now?"

"I honestly don't know, Cole."

He stares at me for a moment, eyes like glass.

"Thanks."

My brows arch. "For what?"

"For telling the truth."

"Come on," Digory calls.

We follow him through the craggy pathway winding up the peak, the three of us traveling in silence for hours until we reach a crevice in the mountain with a pathway cut into it. Cole pulls out the lantern and hands it to me, while Digory patches into one of the flashlight tools from the Flesher waist belt he retained from his Haven disguise.

Trudging the rest of the way, it's clear this isn't a natural tunnel, based on the nuts and bolts and steel reinforcements fused with the rock formations.

"It certainly looks like you know where you are going," Digory says to me. At least he doesn't sound upset anymore.

"I think I've been here before." I'm stepping faster now. Cole and Digory rush to keep up, just as fragments of memory plow through me like a raging river.

—breached our defenses, Sir." The Aide's voice is tremulous with panic.

My strides are fast and long. The body guards and members of the cabinet struggle to keep up with me. You can smell the fear seeping through their pores. Even in the ventilated tunnel pumping fresh oxygen through the ducts, it is still hard to breath. But even as my lungs burn from the effects of the fires outside, both from man-made war and nature's own climate rebellion, a surge of anger and excitement fills me with adrenaline and satisfaction.

I lean in close to one of the generals. "I would have liked a little more time but you know what we have to do."

"With all due respect, Sir," the Aide says from behind me, "we have to surrender. It's a perfectly viable option. Otherwise there'll be nothing left to govern."

He points to the body sealed inside the cryogenic tube hovering in the air between us. "I don't see why we're wasting valuable life support resources on someone that's beyond assistance and ignoring the millions of lives out there. You have to open the doors."

The words freeze me in my tracks as effectively as if I'd been stabbed. And in this case, particularly sickening, coming from someone from my supposedly trusted staff.

I grab the general's sidearm and turn to face the Aide, barely able to look him in the eye without disgust. "What you're proposing is treason. And you know how traitors are dealt with."

I turned back to the general. "You know what to do. Give the order."

My eyes study the interior of the stasis tube, and the charred mangled body within. The body of the man I loved, despite the fury of betrayal blazing inside of me.

Maybe there are benefits to be reaped from this tragedy after all.

My hand touches the cold glass, staring at the letters etched into its surface.

Case 1-Unit: Sowing

I look up. All my rage is directed at the Aide. My finger squeezes the trigger like a vise, spattering his brains on the cryotube's glass like gruesome rain—

A piercing blast shakes me back to my new life.

The memory of that all too familiar face sinks into the quicksand of my mind before I can retain it.

The tunnel dead-ends at a steel door.

Digory sidles up to me. "What is it?" In the metallic door's reflection, his distorted image looks more like a machine, while my likeness is a twisted, two-headed freak show.

"Through there," I say.

Touching the door's cold, smooth surface, I feel for some groove, a latch, some way to open it, but find nothing.

I slam my palm against it. "We're so close."

Digory approaches the door frame, digging his pale fingers into the rocky earth surrounding it. "Let us try."

He freezes in place. His eyes roll back into his head. Even though I've seen him in similar UltraImposer hibernation states before, it still tears me up inside, emphasizing all the suffering he's endured, much of which I'm responsible for.

His eyes flutter and he rips his hand free, dark blood oozing from his fingertips.

There's a flash of light and a low vibration. A stone panel slides out of place, revealing an oval, hand-sized screen.

"What's that?" Cole pushes forward and reaches for it.

Dread oozes from the pit of my stomach. "No, Cole! Wait—!"

Before I can stop him, his fingers graze the screen.

It erupts into bright red. An alarm pierces the tunnel. Strobe lights emerge from the ceiling, bathing the scene in a series of nightmarish fragments.

Warning! A voice blares from hidden speakers. *Unauthorized thermal scan detected. Intruders will be eradicated unless proper authorization code is entered in T-Minus three minutes.*

Another steel door slams down from the ceiling. Cole pulls me toward him and out of the way just as it seals behind us, cutting off any chance of retreat back outside the mountain.

Cole backs up into the corner. "I'm sorry. I didn't mean to."

"It's okay, Buddy. I know." My eyes shoot to Digory. "Any chance of you plugging back in and overriding the system?"

"Negative. As soon as it detected our system hack it triggered a virus alert and shut us out." His body's trembling and his breathing's completely out of whack. He pitches forward. I spring and catch him before he can hit the ground.

"Sorry we failed you," he groans.

I hold him upright and let him regain his balance. "It's okay. None of this is your fault."

When his eyes connect with mine, I can't help but feel that neither of us is really talking about his aborted attempt to infiltrate Nexus Prime's systems.

Two minutes, the computerized voice warns again. *Preparing to engage zero gravity contingency protocol.*

My eyes bounce between Cole and Digory. "Everyone grab on to something now."

The warning's barely out of my mouth when all of a sudden everything not bolted down, including us, rises into the air.

I miss grabbing the nearby railing, cursing under my breath while continuing to glide upward toward the darkness.

But my ascension's cut short. Cole's grabbed my right hand. Digory has Cole's other hand and has anchored himself to a support strut, the three of us forming a tenuous, floating chain.

My eyes dart around the chamber. "I'm surprised we can still breathe."

I begin to drift and Cole tugs me back. "As long as there's air we can breathe, even if gravity's gone."

"Which means this sealed chamber must be generating an artificial atmosphere to keep the oxygen from escaping," Digory chimes in.

I shake my head. "I don't get it. Why not just kill us?"

All around us, panels in the rocky wall open. Shiny steel nozzles erupt, their tips like ominous black eyes.

"I had to ask," I mutter.

Incinerators activated, the emotionless computer voice intones.

A blue glow appears on the tip of each nozzle, like pilot lights on a gas oven. Except these all detach from their hosts, floating silently through the chamber, celestial bubbles, getting closer with each breath.

Growing larger by the second.

Despite my fear, I stare at the globes, mesmerized by the beauty masking their deadliness. "So that's what fire looks like in zero gravity."

"Yes," Digory answers. "Normal fires force hot air to rise. Since there is no buoyancy or convection in zero gravity, the carbon dioxide waste surrounding the burning flames remains stagnant and cuts off the oxygen feeding the fire."

Cole nods. "That's why those globes keep getting bigger. The fire's searching for oxygen particles—"

"And the only thing between these fireballs and that oxygen is us," I finish. "Talk about your slow burn."

The lethal spheres close in all around us, like the jelly-like Medusozoa of the ocean's depths.

I catch sight of the blinking thermal panel by the door below me. So close, but impossible to reach. "I don't know what else to do."

"*You* don't. But *he* does," Cole says.

Digory and I exchange glances. My eyes meet Cole's. "If I go *there* again, I'm afraid I'll get lost and not be able to come back to you."

He squeezes my fingers. "You always show up, even if you're late. Besides, I'll be right here, waiting, like I always do."

My jaw clenches and I nod. "Digory. Try and pull us toward you. I have an idea."

Digory's arm muscles tense with the effort. Carefully, he draws Cole to him. A couple of times, we have to duck to avoid the hovering globes.

In seconds, the three of us are huddled together, holding on to the pillar. The spheres have all merged into a large mass on a direct collision course with our bodies.

Sixty seconds to input the authorization code, the computer announces.

Using our belts, we anchor ourselves to each other by the waist.

Digory braces against the wall.

I press my back against Digory's chest, holding on tightly to Cole, who's pressed against me in a similar fashion. "When I give the signal, kick us off as hard as you can toward the thermal panel on the door. It needs to be hard enough so the momentum will carry us across."

Digory nods against my neck, just as the giant sphere moves in.

"Now!" I shout.

My body's propelled forward. I spin and twist, narrowly avoiding the fireball. We sail past it, but I lose my grip on Cole.

"I got you." I reach flailing fingers toward him—

And he floats out of my grasp.

"Lucky!" The terror in his voice is like a livewire to my veins.

At the last second, his body snaps back where he's tethered to my waist.

But I can feel the belt giving way.

I slam against the exit door, my fingers dragging across the panel toward infinity—

Digory's body slams into mine, knocking me into the panel before I can float away.

Thirty seconds to input authorization code, the computer warns. *Twenty-nine. Twenty-eight. Twenty-seven.*

I slam my hand on the thermal screen. It flashes from red to green.

Thermal scan complete and confirmed, the computer voice announces. *Please enter security passcode.*

Cole's screaming. The tether joining us together begins to slide through my belt loop.

I squeeze my eyes tight to cut off the thought and concentrate as hard as I can on the past.

On *his* past.

It feels like my skull's being crushed. I reach into the bowels of my mind.

Pain wracks my body. My father—my other father— slammed a book down on my hand once, breaking my fingers—

Daddy's home from the factory. I run to him and he scoops me in his arms, twirling me around. I giggle and tell him to go faster—

I have two fathers. But only one of them loves me.

Ten seconds…, that cold voice drones from a million miles away…

—The young man looks deep into my eyes, caressing my face with warm fingers. "I love you so much, Queran," he whispers. "I don't care what our parents, or anyone else, says."

"Don't worry. No one will ever separate us. I promise."

Our lips press together, still sweet and succulent from—

The belt around my waist rips free. A child shrieks.

My mind tears away from the memory of that haunting kiss. My eyes spring open and my fingers fly over the keyboard, typing one word.

Manzana.

Identification verified, the computerized voice announces. The door slides open with a loud vacuum hiss.

I catch a glimpse of Digory grabbing Cole by the ankle. Then gravity kicks back in and the three of us tumble through the open door. There's a blast of searing heat as the massive fireball erupts just behind us—

The door slams shut again, sealing the fire out.

Both the alarms and strobe lights cut off.

I roll over and crawl to Cole. "Are you okay?"

He nods.

"Looks like I owe you yet again," I say to Digory.

"Lucian, what about you? Are you hurt?" Digory's voice sounds muffled to my addled brain, like it's coming from behind yet another steel door.

I turn to him but my balance is off. He stops me from toppling over, resting me on the ground.

"I'm…okay."

But it feels like my head's been cleaved in half. I rub my face until the sharp pain eases into a dull throb. When the nausea subsides, I open my eyes again, noticing the bright blood spattered on my hands.

Cole digs into his pack and pulls out a rumpled shirt. "Take this."

I dab at my nose, and he takes over, dabbing the blood from my face and wiping where it's trickled onto my suit.

I ruffle his hair. He doesn't try and stop me this time. Baby steps. "Looks like you're going to have to watch over both of us now."

"Guess so." He continues to dab at the blood without making eye contact. "It was worse this time."

At least Digory seems to be faring better. Barely. Together, he and Cole help me to my feet.

It looks like we're in some type of souped-up freight elevator, with another set of sealed doors on the opposite side. It reminds me of the lift back in New York City that led from the House of Worship into Sanctum. Makes sense since these facilities are connected. Smooth steel lines the floors, walls, and ceiling of the car. No buttons. No floor indicators.

I glance at Digory. "We need to figure out a way through that door."

He straightens to his full height, but he can't completely hide the flash of pain. "Let us do it."

Joining me, we both try the door, him using one of his accessories, me with one of the makeshift tools. No use. They won't budge.

Digory slams a fist against the door, only succeeding in bruising his knuckles.

Cole sighs. "Now what?"

There's high-pitched bleep, and a silver tube emerges from the ceiling with a blinking red nozzle at the end of it.

Instinctively, I grab Cole and push him behind me, just in case it's another defense mechanism.

"Please step forward for ocular scan." Our friendly computer is back.

"I've got this." Releasing my breath I move toward the scanner.

As soon as I'm within range, the red light stops blinking and aims a steady beam into my right eye.

Good morning, the pre-recorded voice greets us. *Welcome back, President Embers.*

CHAPTER TWENTY-ONE

President?

I can't help being amused, despite the circumstances. "Thank you," is all I can think to say.

Will the other two occupants require optical scans? the computer asks.

Cole and Digory exchange looks. Digory moves in front of Cole, his muscles tensing for a fight. They both stare at me.

If the system doesn't recognize them—

"Negative," I say.

Regulation number 62378 specifically states unidentified subjects will be classified as intruders, the computer drones on, *and must be immediately termin—*

"As the…President, I countermand that order. Proceed with override immediately. Understood?"

The scanning tube retracts. *Yes, of course, Mr. President.*

Is that a hint of humiliation in that artificial voice?

Digory nods at me. "That was very efficient."

I give him and Cole a half-hearted smile. "I guess there are some perks to being a dead guy."

Which level do you wish to proceed to? the computer inquires.

Damn. I don't even know exactly what the hell this place really is. "The survivors. I want to see the survivors."

Excuse me, Mr. President? the computer's voice modulator goes up an octave. *I'm having difficulty interpreting your request.*

"People!" I shout. "The staff. Personnel—"

Proceeding to personnel level immediately, the computer snaps.

In the system's apparent eagerness to carry out my orders, the car lurches and begins a nauseating, rapid descent.

As the seconds tick by, Digory catches my eye. "Judging from the speed we are going, this installation must extend even deeper into the earth than Sanctum."

"Someone wanted to make sure they were well protected from the Clathrate event and the Ash Wars." I shrug. "Probably me."

"*He's* not *you.*" Cole glares at me and looks away.

The car slows down and finally stops. The doors opposite the ones we entered grind open with a squeal.

Cole's eyes are wide. "Looks like nobody's been here in a long time."

Digory peers out into the shadows beyond the elevator. "We would surmise it has been centuries."

"At least." Joining him, I grip the door frame and glance both ways. "Digory, you bring up the rear and keep Cole between us."

"Yes, Sir. Mr. President."

I pause to stare at him. He's stone-faced, so I'm not sure if he's stating things in that unnerving, logical Hive way, or if he's simply teasing. As improbable as it is, I much prefer the implications of the latter, so I'm going with it.

"Let's go," I say, moving from the car and into the shadows.

Dim light flickers on off to the right, probably triggered by our presence, so I decide to head in that direction.

The walls on either side are covered with metal grids, as is the floor. Sparse lighting penetrates through every other grid, creating distorted shadows, trailing our movement like clinging nightmares. Probably emergency lighting powered by dying batteries.

I breathe in deep. "Is it just me, or does this air smell…stale?"

Digory pauses and cocks his head back, taking a whiff of his own. He bursts into a coughing fit, covering his mouth with his fist.

"What's wrong?" I ask. I move toward him.

He holds up his palm. "No need. Considering how deep under the surface we are, the air has probably been recycled many times over. There must be an intricate ventilation system filtering oxygen from the surface."

That still doesn't explain why it's affecting him, with his enhanced organ functions.

Cole leans against the wall. "If there are people here, why have they stayed hidden all these years?"

I shake my head. "After the atmosphere settled and the wars were over, you'd think they'd decide to go topside and have a look." I remember what Digory said about Sanctum severing communications with the Nexus deliberately. "Whatever the reason, we're about to find out."

The corridor opens up into a rotunda, surrounded by glass.

My next breath's a sharp intake. Through the clear windows, we can see level after level of the facility. Each of us presses against the glass to take a closer look.

From my vantage point, I can spot crates of canned food, hundreds—no thousands of them. An entire section looks like an elaborate forest, probably a greenhouse that's helping to keep this place oxygenated. The levels extend both above and below as far as the eye can see.

I can make out what appears to be a gymnasium, living quarters, and the sterile, white and steel of a medical wing. Digory's spotted it, too, and we exchange weary looks tinged with excitement. We're both in pretty messed up shape. Maybe there's something in these supplies that can take the edge off.

Despite the toll carrying around Queran Embers is taking on my overtaxed brain, the one medicine I crave most of all is answers.

"Over here!" Cole cries. He disappears behind an opaque glass door.

Digory and I rush over to the opposite end of the spherical chamber where Cole vanished. Inside, there's a treasure trove of rations strewn throughout the mess hall. Lush looking fruits and vegetables are being cut and placed on a platter by an automated machine, along with piping bowls of the most delicious smelling soup that's making my mouth water. Another dispenser spews water into frosty mugs.

As wonderful as it all looks and smells to my exhausted eyes, parched throat, and rumbling stomach, I can't help be a little creeped out by this ghostly banquet.

My eyes scan the commissary. "Something's not right," I squeeze out through clenched teeth. "A place this huge and no sign of living activity. Where is everybody?"

Cole eyes are riveted on the frosty mugs. "Maybe they're sleeping."

I cock my head. "This place has been buried here for hundreds of years, and it picks precisely this moment to activate and dispense rations? Kind of a coincidence, don't you think?"

"Maybe it was our presence in the installation that triggered this," Digory volunteers. "This commissary is probably programmed to dispense rations automatically."

"Possibly. Or it could mean something else entirely." That's what my gut's telling me, anyway.

Cole grabs one of the mugs and brings it to his lips.

I rush forward and grab his arm before he can drink. "Wait up. We don't know if this stuff is safe."

Digory picks up one of the mugs and takes a tentative taste. "My taste sensors are only picking up cold, filtered water. Nothing harmful."

No sooner has Digory finished his analysis, than Cole pulls away and gulps down the water. Digory and I join him. The icy water soothes my throat, and I practically guzzle down an entire bowl of the warm broth in seconds. Cole's chin drips with fruit juice. He grins at me as I wipe it with one of the cloth napkins from the dispenser.

At least we won't be dying on empty stomachs.

I haven't been this hungry since—

A memory—one of my own, not Queran's—hits me. My reunion with Cassius in the Prefect's quarters, when I was starving and gorged on his feast like a wild animal, just before he betrayed and condemned me to the Culling for the very first time. Suddenly, I'm not so hungry anymore.

When I look up, Digory's dangling a glistening slice of apple in front of my eyes. "We saved you the last piece."

I don't resist as he gently presses it against my lips. I take a bite, savoring the sweetness. Then quickly look away.

We eat the rest of our meal in silence.

When it's over, I move toward one of the side corridors.

"We'd better do some more exploring and see if we can find anyone."

I can hear their footfalls behind me as they follow me out of the mess hall.

One by one, we rifle through the adjacent chambers, checking out equipment and supplies, until we come to the very last one. The lights flicker on as we enter. I stop short as if I ran into a force field.

Embedded into the walls on either side are oblong, glass chambers placed vertically, one after another. Each one contains a body suspended in bluish fluid. A series of tubules that remind me of the tentacles of the Octopoda are attached to a facemask coiled around each figures' nose and mouth. Probably feeding them oxygen and nutrients.

Digory traces the glass of the pod nearest him. "Looks like we found our missing survivors."

"This facility must somehow be channeling the survivors' carbon dioxide to keep those plants alive." I lean in close to take a look at the young woman floating in the tube directly in front of me. She's probably right around my own age. "They've probably been in this suspended state since the Ash Wars. Waiting for some signal to emerge."

"A signal that never came," Cole adds.

As we walk further into the chamber and pass more and more of the encased survivors, I can't shake the feeling that there's something familiar about them.

"I've seen some of these people before," I finally say. "I'm sure of it."

Cole sidles up to me. "*You* have? Or *he* has?"

I dig my fingers into my temples, trying to make sense of the conflicting feelings. "I'm not sure. Both, I think."

Digory makes eye contact. "We think we know what you mean." He appears just as confused as I am.

My anxiety builds. I race down the aisles, faster and faster. Yes. I recognize these faces. They're Imps. Or at least some of them are. The others are recruits that never made it through the trials.

I pause and turn to Cole and Digory. "The recruits. They're all here. Everyone that's ever been drafted for the Culling."

"That is impossible," Digory whispers. But his expression lacks conviction.

Cole gazes up at the tube closest to him. "Why do they all look the same age as you?"

I shake my head. "They must have all entered cryo when they turned a certain age, just like all the recruits are drafted when they're sixteen, like Digory and I were."

Digory glances my way. "But you and Digory weren't supposed to be drafted. Were you?"

"I don't think *you* were." I leave the implication hanging in the decaying air.

We continue to examine the coffin-like cylinders. A deep cold slithers up my spine. More and more of these faces are becoming recognizable.

"That looks like Valerian." My words echo down the shadows. It *is* her, but it's not. She looks so young. And peaceful. A stark contrast to the woman with fire burning in her eyes during those last few moments of her life.

I spot random Imposers from the Parish, including Valerian's former partner, Arch. Studying the occupants on the opposite wall of this high-tech mausoleum, I start to detect a pattern of some sorts. "It looks like these specimens are grouped together in the same order they were recruited for the Culling."

Digory forges ahead of me. "We need to find out by whom and why. Maybe those answers will provide the key to discovering the nanotech that will allow the Hive to become autonomous."

When I study the next section of pods, I feel lightheaded, as if all the blood's been drained from me.

"What's wrong?" Cole's voice barely registers.

"I'd never forget these faces, no matter how young they are." I stare at three of the most vile people I've met during the course of my life.

Styles. Renquist. And Sergeant Slade.

What's most disturbing is that they seem so normal. Almost innocent. So different than the cruel sadists they became. Is the evil in their hearts even now manifesting while they slumber, a cancer eating away at their morality?

"I don't understand," Cole says. "If they've been here all this time, then who are the ones back home?"

"I don't know." I'm shaking—with rage, with bitterness. Whatever the hell this place is, this, this is my future. Slade and the others started out young like I am and became heartless monsters. That's my destiny, too. Tristin was wrong. There is no such thing as free will. It's all some bullshit illusion we delude ourselves with.

I let out the most pitiful laugh, laced with sorrow and hopelessness, a condemned man that's been told he only has a few days left to live.

Digory's cold hand grips my shoulder, trying to steady me. "What is wrong, Lucian?"

I can't bear to meet his eyes. "Lucian. That's what's wrong. Lucian Spark doesn't exist. He never did. I'm nothing but a freak. A lab rat. Someone thought it would be a good idea to revive a ruthless dictator and here I am. Ready to turn on everyone and everything I care about as soon as whatever wall's been blocking my memories comes tumbling down." I swipe at the blood dripping from my nose.

How much of others' blood have I spilled?

Digory squeezes my shoulders enough to cause pain. "Now is not the time to indulge in self-pity." He glances at Cole and lowers his voice. "The child needs you. And we—"

I rip free. "You *what*?"

"We do not have time to listen to this. You are supposed to be a leader of your people. The Torch Keeper, they call you. Act like it."

Another surge of anger broils me. Tears of rage cloud my vision. "You're one to be giving advice about being true to yourself. You don't even know what you are anymore."

He gives me his back as he moves toward Cole.

"You're not Digory Tycho. Are you even a man?" I call after him. "A machine? What the hell are you?"

He whips around. "At least we are not afraid to find out."

I regret my outburst immediately. "Digory, I'm sorry."

Let him go. You don't need him.

I press my palms against my temple. "Get out of my head."

"Stop it!" Cole shrieks. "Both of you stop it!"

I try to embrace him. But he pounds me with his fists. "I hate you! I… hate…you."

His struggles diminish and his resistance gives way, turning into choked sobs, his hot tears soothing against my cold neck. "I can't…lose you…again. Please stay. For me. Stay…Lucky…"

"It's okay," I murmur in his ear. "I didn't mean to frighten you. I'm sorry. For everything. I'm going to try real hard not to go away again."

We huddle together for a few minutes. I wipe his tears as he wipes my bloody nose. Patting his back, I stand. Gripping his hand, I pretend for a moment that things are the way they used to be, even though I know they never will be again.

I face Digory. "I didn't mean what I said. I'm just…with everything that's happening…I lost it there for a minute." I hold out my hand. "Are we good?"

He nods and squeezes my hand. "We understand." He nudges his head down the corridor. "We had better finish our sweep."

The three of us trudge down the rest of the chamber.

My eyes grow wider. One by one, I recognize the members of Flame Squad, floating in cylinders among the recruits they were drafted with. First Dahlia. Then Leander. Then Rodrigo.

And finally Arrah.

They may as well be resting comfortably in their bunks after a strenuous day of training.

Cassius should be here, too. Technically, he should have been Third Tier when I was undergoing Imp training. But for some reason, they skipped his Recruitment Culling and went right to Rodrigo's.

Why? And why isn't there a doppelganger of him here like all the others?

"They're exact duplicates." I say. "All of them. Part of whatever crazy experiment this is."

The same experiment that created me.

I rush ahead to the next section, where the recruits that were drafted with me should be.

In the shadows up ahead, the floor's wet. A breathing apparatus lies coiled on the floor like a snake. One of these tubes has recently been opened.

One of these ghosts is on the loose.

Something dashes out of the darkness and tackles me.

I tumble to the ground and hit the back of my head.

From miles away I can hear Digory's deep voice and Cole shouting. I struggle to pry my eyes open.

Above me a figure comes into focus. A figure holding a gun. "*Queran Embers*? It…can't be…"

I recognize that voice— and that face.

Ophelia Juniper, a former recruit who once tried to murder me.

CHAPTER TWENTY-TWO

The shock's like a hypo oozing with adrenaline, plunged directly into my heart. I push away. Hands hoist me to my feet. Digory and Cole.

"Are you hurt?"

I ignore Digory, don't even look his way. Instead my eyes are riveted on the pale young woman with the blood-red mane of curly hair and the weapon clutched in her hand, aimed directly at me.

There's no way Ophelia could have been revived like Cassius did to Digory back at Infiernos, when he pumped him up with drugs and converted him into an UltraImposer. No. The image of the Lady statue's stone spire gutting Ophelia through the heart is a frequent visitor in my nightmares. I recoil at the memory of that sickening sound of Ophelia's skull caving in on impact, splattering the statue's face in a bloody geyser.

I shake my head. "I saw you die, Ophelia."

She doesn't say anything, just continues to stare, her eyes at first questioning, then narrowing. She looks a little different. A few years older. Maybe more. Well she should, considering it's been two years since I watched her fall to her death.

I nudge my chin toward the gleaming silver weapon still clutched in her rigid hand. "I see you still want me dead. *That* hasn't changed. You'd actually be doing me a favor."

Cole shoves me. "Don't say that."

"The child is right." Digory moves slowly to my side, his hands raised. "No one needs to get hurt. We would just like some answers."

I cock my head at Ophelia. She continues to stare silently with that eerie calm. Her hair and skin are still damp from her recent thaw. My gaze wanders over to the countless pods. "It's okay. If she fires, I'm not so sure I'll die." I shrug. "Or at least, stay dead. Just like she obviously won't either."

She shoves the gun against my temple. "Maybe we can test your theory out. *You* first."

I take a deep breath. "If I were superstitious, I'd say Ophelia and I were trapped in some kind of metaphysical hell, destined to kill each other over and over again. What do you think, Ophelia?"

"Stop calling me Ophelia." Her voice is calm, no-nonsense. Dry even. No trace of the giddy, lepus-butchering, dainty, hand-hacking, ice-cold sociopath I remember so fondly. Instead, she looks...frightened?

"And you can't be Queran Embers," she continues. "No matter how much you look like him. You're too young."

I swallow my surprise. "Now there's an opinion that seems to differ from the general consensus. Refreshing. If you aren't Ophelia, then who are you exactly?"

"Breck Flannery. But that's the only one you get. I'm the one asking the questions here. And if I don't like your answers—," She sweeps us with her gun hand to make sure we get the point. "Who are you three?"

"Lucian Spark, here." I nod toward Cole. "That's my brother, Cole." Then I clap a hand on Digory's shoulder. "And this big guy over here used to be called Digory Tycho."

"Used to be?"

I sigh. "It's complicated. Just stick with Digory for now."

She scans Digory up and down. "You've been genetically modified. Haven't you? I see the distinct markers in your eyes. Nano technology."

Digory steps forward, ignoring Breck's weapon. "Yes. We require your assistance."

"You know something about the process Digory went through?" My heart starts to beat faster. "Maybe there's some way to reverse—"

She shoves the gone in my direction. "Keep your distance. This is a restricted installation. There aren't supposed to be any other survivors. How did a sorry lot like you breach security? And what do you want from us?"

Digory shoots me a look, then turns to this Breck. "By survivors, we assume you are referring to the Clathrate apocalypse that released the methane into the atmosphere and wiped out most of the planet's population, rendering the surface inhabitable. Is that correct?"

"Yes, of course." Her tone is borderline condescending, as if Digory's stating the most obvious fact ever recorded in the history of the universe. "What else would I be referring to?"

He leans in slightly. "That event occurred ages ago. Perhaps as long as a millennia. The surface has been capable of sustaining life for at least a few centuries now."

Her eyes grow wide. "That's impossible. We would have been alerted if that was the case. All of us would have been awakened from cryo." She's trembling.

"Why only you?" Cole asks.

Despite her *Only-I-ask-the-questions* rule, she addresses him. "To conserve resources, we all went into deep freeze when the catastrophe was at its worse. I was assigned to be resuscitated and check systems in the event of a breach."

Cole nods. "Us."

"If what you're saying is true," she continues, "and the surface has been habitable, it would mean some kind of massive system malfunction occurred, something we didn't plan for, maybe caused by the atmospheric conditions."

"Or good old-fashioned sabotage," I volunteer.

Her eyes whip around to me. She cocks her gun. "Maybe caused by you?"

I hold up my palms. "Whoa. Hang on. What I meant is we've visited another one of your facilities, a branch of the Nexus known as Sanctum. I can assure you they've been up and running and scavenging the surface for quite some time now."

She shakes her head. "You're lying. There's no way they can be functioning without our being aware of it. That's not the way it's supposed to work."

I sigh. "Then I suggest you tell that to Dr. Sebastos Straton. I'd venture he'd disagree with you."

At this, Breck's eyes open wide. "Don't you mean *Agusto* Straton?"

"Given how long you've been in stasis, the Sebastos Straton I met must be an ancestor of your guy." Pain knifes through my forehead and I manage to rub it away. "The good doctor tried to cut open my brain and get cozy with my hippocampus. But I guess the fact that you recognized me as the spitting-image of the not yet fully-grown Queran Embers would probably clue you in as to why he might do that."

"The Sowing," she mutters. "Clones replicated at the atomic level, capable of inheriting the memories of their progenitors genetically. The Straton I knew was trying to accelerate the memory retrieval process."

"Yes. And it looks like his descendants have continued his work. Since you know so much about the process, I'm guessing you were Sown, too."

She lowers her weapon ever so slightly. "No. I wasn't Sown. My entire team, which is still in stasis, as well as myself, all donated genetic samples to be harvested for the Sowing protocol. The situation is—was—dire. The fate of the entire planet was uncertain. The human race was on the verge of extinction."

Everything she's saying is starting to make sense. "And you wanted to—"

Live forever. Become immortal. Fulfill every person's secret desire.

"—*extend* your life cycles," I say, pushing the words through an onslaught of Queran's thoughts.

Breck's expression grows grave. "Not at all. We wanted the human race to survive by increasing a vastly depleted population that would take generations to regrow and retrain using traditional breeding methods. Cloning people at an atomic level so they would retain organic memories accomplished both those tasks. Imagine not having to expend resources teaching people technological, scientific, and agricultural skills because they can simply access prior memories stored in their own DNA. Passing on select memories through the Sowing was a carefully planned strategy to retain knowledge of our civilization, prevent it from being lost forever." She studies me now, eyes weary. "But during the wars there were rumors that some in high places had other ideas. Corrupt. Selfish. These individuals thought it was their right to continue to live, generation after generation, never relinquishing power, perverting the very ideals that we set out to protect, dooming us all to failure all over again."

I capture a deep breath and hold it prisoner for a few beats. "You mean people who resembled the hell out of me, like Queran Embers."

She looks away. "What can I say? I'll have to conduct preliminary tests, but if you were indeed Sown, then you're an exact duplicate of Queran Embers, replicated to the very core of his molecular level, right down to every last cell and memory. Not even a clone is that identical."

"But he doesn't remember," Cole speaks up.

At this, Breck's eyes bore into mine. "Not a thing?"

Digory and I exchange glances. I'm not sure how much to divulge of the procedure the Fleshers performed and the memory fragments I've kept silent about. After all, if Ophelia was cut from the same cloth as Breck, then according to the latter's own theories, she's not to be trusted. "I just remember strange fragments. Nothing really concrete."

Her smile's wistful. "Enough for you to find this hidden compound and get through the security protocols. It's only a matter of time before the rest of your memory returns. And then you'll really be him."

"Shut up." Cole hisses. "You're lying. Just like everyone else does. You're all liars."

"It's not that simple, Cole." I reach for him.

He moves away, retreating into the shadows.

Insolent, little—

A frightening jolt of anger tears through my brain and disappears like lightning.

Breck's right. I'm a ticking time bomb. When I finally go off, who knows how many people that I care about will be hurt in the blast?

Digory's rubbing his temples. His face looks even more drawn than before. He looks up at Breck. "You said that all of these cryogenically pre-served survivors like yourself were meant to serve as a template to per-petuate the human race."

"That's correct," she responds, relaxing her questioning policy. She's obviously disturbed by what we've told her.

Digory extends a hand to the rows of encased survivors. "So how do you explain how Lucian here, as well as copies of many of these others, including yourself, have existed for generations outside this complex? Who's responsible for sowing them and re-integrating them back into society if, as you claim, this facility has been in lockdown for centuries until our recent arrival?"

He may as well have tossed a live wire at her. Her eyes glow with excitement. "You've actually encountered one of my seedlings? What was she—what was *I*—like?"

I clear my throat. Despite everything Ophelia did, I can't bring myself to crush this untarnished version of her. "She was very driven. Very protective of her sister. Would do anything to keep her from harm."

Breck nods, her eyes clouding over. "As inspiring as that sounds, what you're implying is impossible. If there had been a prior breach of Nexus, we would have been aware of it, just like I was awakened by the system when you three arrived."

Digory purses his lips, and I can tell he's in a great deal of discomfort and is trying real hard to hold it together. "Yet logic dictates that someone did breach this facility and steal specimens. And whoever it was has been doing so for quite some time."

"Is there any way to check this installations records for any discrepancies?" I ask.

She pauses for a minute, confusion and suspicion melding in her eyes. "I suppose an inventory comparison of the specimens might yield some answers. Follow me."

Breck leads the way into an adjoining chamber filled with gauges and monitors. Accessing one of the keyboards, her fingers fly furiously over it. Every so often, she stops to shake her head. Finally, slams her hand down on the console. "This can't be right."

I move in to get a closer look. The information on the displays may as well be another language. Cryptic readouts and graphs.

I know exactly what they mean.

Breck tears her eyes from the monitors to face us. "An entire array of specimens is missing, corresponding to every survivor that's in stasis. The records indicate there was no breach. Someone was authorized to remove them."

"Who was it?" I ask.

"The information has been sealed. Some type of special order. I've tried to override the security settings, but it appears the original command has been purged from the system. Someone knew exactly what they were doing. At least I've reactivated the defense warnings so we'll know if anyone else comes calling."

Digory steadies himself against one of the consoles and turns to me. "Could Thorn be responsible?"

"It can't be Cassius. He's too young. This has obviously been going on since way before he was born." I stare at the bodies suspended in the opaque cylinders. "Unless—"

Digory's eyes squeeze shut. His face contorts, and he starts to teeter.

Breck's expression flashes concern. "What's happening to him?"

Digory grimaces and clutches at his head. I race over to catch him, before he can fall. When he coughs, petals of fresh blood bloom on his clenched fist. I hold him tight in my arms, his face ashen, straining to look up at mine.

"Lucian…we think this vessel is…seriously…malfunctioning." His eyes roll back. His head slumps forward. Spasms rock his body.

"Digory!" I struggle to hold him steady. "You said you were familiar with the nanotech they used to recreate him, Breck. Do something, please."

She holsters her weapon, grabs a tablet from the console, and enters some commands. In seconds, a hovering gurney zooms toward us and descends to ground level. Between the two of us, we push Digory's massive bulk aboard and it lifts off again. Then all three of us race to keep up with the transport. It jets toward the medical wing, depositing Digory into a pod. The machine seals. Diagnostic scans crisscross his body like a cocooning web.

I try to approach him, but Breck pushes me away.

"What's wrong with him?" I ask.

"You and your brother should wait outside," she barks. Then she rushes inside and seals the door, leaving Cole and I to wonder if we'll ever see Digory alive again.

CHAPTER TWENTY-THREE

The minutes camped out in the observation theater stretch into a lifetime. My forehead's numb from having it pressed against the cramped room's glass wall, staring out as Breck runs a batch of diagnostics on Digory's prone form.

The pain of losing him during the Trials, first during the sim where his heart stopped beating while mine broke, and then when he sacrificed his serum to save Cole, comes flooding back, as does the abject loneliness that followed, suffocating me, filling me with depression and rage. I can't go through that again. Even if Digory's changed, my feelings for him haven't, no matter how much I've tried to deny it since he's been back.

At one point, his lids flutter open, and we make eye contact. That imperfect coldness that I've been getting used to is still there, but there's a hint of something else on his face, too. An echo of the man that changed my life forever.

"Is he going to die?"

Cole's question rouses me like a splash of chilled water.

"No. I mean—why would you ask that?"

He shrugs. He's not looking at me, just staring through the plexiglass. "Because that's what happens to everybody. Mommy. Daddy. Mrs. Bledsoe. They all say they're going to love you forever. But the only thing they do is die." His gaze drops to his shoes. "When I grow up I don't ever want anyone to love me. Because if they do, I'll die, too."

I kneel in front of him. "Well I love you, buddy. I always will. And I'm still here."

"For now."

The doors hiss apart. Breck's standing in the threshold, looking flushed.

My muscles tense. "What's the verdict, doc?"

She shakes her head. "Inconclusive."

"What the hell is that supposed to mean?"

"It means that he's a new breed of nanotech. Different, and in some ways more advanced than the prototypes we were developing before the cataclysm. There are more tests to be run, and the personnel qualified to perform them are still in stasis."

"So unfreeze their asses and get them on it stat." I can feel the anger percolating in my blood, and I can't tell if it's all mine or his. Makes no difference. "All that matters is that Digory's in danger, and we're wasting precious time."

"It's not that simple," she continues. "We have certain protocols in place, and it's against regulations to awaken the others without proper authorization. I'm sorry, but your companion just doesn't fit the pre-determined criteria for violating established—"

"I knew there was a reason I never liked you." I grab her by the collar of her jumpsuit. "Screw your damn protocols. In case you haven't been keeping up with current events, this facility's already been breached. Specimens have been stolen. And let's not forget that somebody forgot to wake your collective asses up centuries ago. I'd say we're well beyond following rules." I lean in real close, tightening my grip, and spraying her with flecks of hot saliva. "I watched you die before. Now unless you want a repeat performance, I suggest you wake your team before I go all Queran Embers on your ass." I shove her away.

She glares at me, just like her clone, Ophelia, did on that stormy morning atop the statue of the Lady. "You've made your point. And admittedly there have been some unorthodox occurrences here." Now it's her turn to lean in close. "But don't be surprised if you regret your decision."

She turns toward the cryo chamber. I grab her arm.

"Can I see him now?" The tremble in my voice has shifted from anger to fear.

"Go ahead. I'll be a bit. But don't overexert him."

Cole tugs at her wrist. "Can I go with you? I want to see how it works." He nods at Digory then at me.

He wants us to be alone.

Breck nods and takes his hand. "Sure. C'mon."

They disappear into the corridor. I can't help feeling uneasy watching my brother walk away with someone's who's an exact duplicate of a girl that tried to murder him.

Taking a deep breath, I hit the door lock and enter the platform holding Digory's med pod.

He looks up at me, his gray eyes now murky.

I move in closer. "How's the pain?"

"Not as pronounced. But even more unsettling."

"I don't understand."

"It feels strange. Unfocused. This body's connection to the Hive is becoming...garbled. The sensation reminds me of how things used to be. Not being a part of the whole. Filled with weakness, vulnerability...," he looks at me pointedly. "Being human."

Sitting on the edge of the bed, I press my palm against his forehead, expecting it to be hot with fever. Instead it's like ice. "I suppose being human isn't all that it's cracked up to be, considering all the messed up things we do."

"Humanity is quite complicated."

His rare smile is cut short by a severe bout of coughing. I move close, helping to prop him up. He leans forward, hacking up his lung by the sound of it.

"Here, use this."

I grab a small, white towel from beside the bed and hand it to him. By the time his spasm has subsided, it's covered in rust-colored spots. My heart sinks. I dab at the dark blood spattered on his chin. "Breck and her team will find out what's wrong."

His icy hand covers mine. "Humanity's proclivity for lies and delusion is truly remarkable."

"I'm sorry," I whisper. My head slumps against the comforting mound of his shoulder.

Digory shifts his head against mine. "Do not feel bad. The pain we are experiencing is nothing compared to the pain caused by Digory Tycho."

My cheek presses against his. "What do you mean?"

"We have been unable to purge this vessel's data from our collective. It is resurfacing. Fragment by Fragment."

I take his hand. "We can't forget our past, Digory."

No matter how much we try.

His fingers slowly wrap around mine. "The Tychos held deep affection for their son, Digory. They coddled him. Spoiled him. Digory was brought up in luxury, welcomed in all the grand homes of the Establishment's elite. He never once knew hunger like you did. Like so many others. Yet it was never enough."

I lift my head. "I had no idea. How did your status change so drastically?"

"This vessel was always desperate for the Tychos' attention, always wanting to show how smart he was. He would always hear them…his parents…speaking in hushed voices. They didn't think their children could really understand what was going on, what they were secretly up to."

I sit up straight. "What do you mean?"

He's staring past me, and it's almost like I'm not even there. "It seems the Tychos, in addition to their wealth and prestige, possessed something else that began as an inconvenience and developed into something far more dangerous."

"Dangerous to whom, Digory?"

Still avoiding my gaze, he shifts his position. "Dangerous to the Establishment, as well as themselves. You see, they had these troublesome little attributes humans refer to as consciences."

He attempts another smile but it dies before it can flourish. "Apparently performing charitable works, donating to the homeless, making sure children received proper nutrition and an education despite their social status just wasn't enough for them."

Digory finally turns to me with a pleading look on his face that surprises me. "Why could they have not left well enough alone? Why did they want so much more? It makes no logical sense. That is when the clandestine visits started to happen. Strangers coming to the home late into the night. Digory's father disappearing for days. His brother and sister were too young to understand, but he did. He would creep out of bed and listen in the shadows. He pieced together what they were up to, the risks they were taking, which could destroy the entire Tycho family."

My mind and heart are in a race. "The resistance. Your parents were involved, weren't they?"

"Yes. Digory was a child. He was not sure at the time what it all meant. All he knew from everything he had heard was that it was something terrible. That the entire family could all be punished, shelved, for what they were doing."

I nod. "That's true. That's exactly what would have happened."

He squeezes my hand. "That is when Digory became angry. So very angry. He thought if they cared so little about their children's welfare, it was up to him to save the Tycho family." His gaze drops to his lap. He begins to cough again, violently.

I hold him, patting his back. "You have to take it easy and not exert yourself. Just lie down and get some sleep and we'll finish this conversation later." I grab the glass of ice cold water sitting on a nearby table and bring it to his lips.

He takes a few gulps and pushes it away. "No. We need to purge this information from our system. We need to tell you."

He settles back onto the bed. "Lucian, Digory did something humans would consider terrible."

I bring the sheet up to his neck. "Don't do this to yourself. You were only a child. What could you have possibly done that was so bad?"

His eyes glisten. He flinches—from physical pain, emotional, or both, I'm not sure. "He told."

From the haunted expression on his face those two words seem like the most damning words ever uttered in human history. I've witnessed Digory in pain before. But this—this is something so much more devastating than physical suffering or fear of death. This is torment of the very core, the very soul if one believes in such things. Seeing him in such profound inner turmoil, shreds me.

I hold him tight, trying in vain to absorb his anguish into my own being, my forehead pressed against his. "Please don't do this to yourself."

"He told," he repeats. His voice is hollow, as if every single emotion has been scooped out and trashed. "Digory told one of his instructors at the Instructional Facility, who then called him into his office and had him repeat it to an emissary from the Citadel. After that everything happened so fast."

We're embracing each other fiercely now, as if we're both afraid to let go, clinging to each other to hold onto one last scrap of sanity.

My fingers trace concentric circles on the coldness of his bare skull. "Don't think about any of it now. That all happened so long ago. It doesn't matter now."

"But it does. These impulses, these feelings…it all seems as if it just happened. We are experiencing it as an observer and intricately involved with it simultaneously. We can feel all that dread rushing through our system like a highly toxic virus, compromising our harmony. Our unity."

"I'm so sorry."

Digory nods. "Once Digory realized that maybe he should have kept quiet, everything began to spiral out of control." He clutches both my hands now. "He was very afraid. All he wanted was someone to talk some sense into his parents, set them back on the right path, stop them from being so selfish. It was only later, after it was all over, after there was no way to take any of it back, that Digory realized he was the one being utterly selfish."

"You were just a kid—"

"A kid that prided himself on how intelligent he was. A kid that thought he was better than others and deserved all his material possessions. A kid too stupid to realize, or maybe just too blind with jealousy, to realize the consequences of his actions. After Digory betrayed his parents, he panicked. He pleaded with them not to hurt his family, and they assured him that his family's reputation and legacy would not be harmed in any way. Behind closed doors, he was hailed a hero for coming forward and doing his patriotic duty."

"Digory. I'm so sorry."

"He never saw the Tychos again. Shortly thereafter, they were involved in one of the Establishment's many 'accidents,' including the two younger children. Digory was spared. That was his reward. To have his family's reputation remain intact publicly by keeping their involvement in the rebellion quiet, and not have the Tycho name besmirched by treason. Digory became the sole remaining heir to what little of their wealth was left after the bulk was appropriated by the Establishment, of course."

He turns and looks deep into my eyes, tears streaming freely down his face. He touches them and stares at his moist fingertips, as if beholding something alien, something long forgotten. "How do humans do it?"

"How do we do what?"

"Open your eyes each day, live your lives, despite the onslaught of memories, despite all the pain gnawing at you, tearing up your insides every second of your existence. Being part of the Hive is so much more peaceful, so much more logical. This emptiness—this loneliness is unbearable."

I pause to collect my swirling thoughts. "You make a very good point. It seems I've been thinking about that for most of my life. But recently it's becoming more like an obsession. Sometimes, I'm not sure if the only reason I get up in the morning is just out of habit, a routine that's deeply ingrained, or if it's because of my brother, you know? If I were gone what would happen to him? Maybe it's kind of selfish, but I think if you can make a difference in just one other person's life, touch them in even the most minute, positive way, then it kind of makes up for all the dark stuff. So in some ways, humanity is like a hive, too, people feeding off each other to justify their existence." I shrug. "Or maybe I'm just rationalizing the irrational. Going crazy."

He shakes his head. "The fact that you are consciously worried about losing your mind makes it more than likely that you are not."

"Digory, I need you to promise me something."

"What is it?"

Bowing my head, I press my palms against my forehead, slick with sweat. "If you notice anything—and I mean anything—that I do that may pose a danger to my brother, you have to take whatever action necessary to keep him safe."

I can tell he's straining to keep his upper body upright. "What are you talking about? You would never inflict any harm on that child. We have seen how much you care about him, how far you are willing to go to protect him. It does not make any sense—"

"Just promise me. Again. Please."

He nods. "Done."

A surge of relief washes over me. I slump back against him. "Thanks. And I'm sorry for the things I said earlier, the way I snapped at you."

"Do not worry. We have all been under intense pressure for quite some time now. It is a very human quality to vent frustrations on others. And we understand that reconciling this vessel's current state with the person you used to know is probably very unsettling."

"That's the thing. My anger was never about you or anything you did. Watching you struggling with your memories and coming to terms with who you used to be is like holding up a mirror to myself and not being able to deal with what I can see."

"And just what is it that you see, Lucian?"

"Someone I don't know anymore. Someone that absolutely terrifies me."

We lie next to each other in the darkness, not saying a word, just listening to each other breathe.

CHAPTER TWENTY-FOUR

The voice snaps me fully awake.

"—your brother's perusing the medical library, Spark. He's got quite the aptitude. And the team's been de-iced and briefed."

And instantly it feels like I must be dreaming.

Breck, our mirror-image of Ophelia is standing over the bed—

Along with two of my other dead friends and former recruits.

Gideon and Cypress.

I bolt up, my eyes straining against their sockets. "You can't be *them*."

"I'm sorry about the confusion," the one who could be Gideon's older twin addresses me. "Breck mentioned the possibility of us resembling people that you know. If it's any consolation, you look very much like someone we know, too." He extends a hand. "Cephas Decatur here." He drops it when I'm too stunned to shake it and turns to the Cypress doppelganger. "And this is my colleague, Saffron Clove."

She nods toward Breck. "Breck here's told us quite the story. If it weren't for reviewing the data logs and seeing your resemblance to Queran Embers for ourselves, we wouldn't have believed it was possible."

I scramble out of bed and stare at them, making sure my mouth isn't hanging wide open. "You're…*Saffron*…and *Cephas*…and *Breck*. I'm sorry but this is going to take a little getting used to."

Gideon—Cephas—looks concerned as he approaches Digory's bedside. "Are you feeling alright?" He turns to Breck. "This is the nano hybrid?"

She nods.

"That would be this vessel, formerly known as Tycho," Digory mutters, propping himself up on the bed.

I rest a hand on his shoulder. "Do you recognize them, too?"

"Yes. We recall them quite vividly." Despite the pain on his face, he manages to look amused.

Breck sighs. "As I explained, both Lucian Spark, here, and his companion, Digory Tycho, seem to have encountered our Repros on the surface."

At those words, Cypress and Gideon—Saffron and Cephas, or whoever the hell they are—turn to each other, their eyes ready to burst. Then they fall into each other's arms. Cephas grabs Saffron, lifts her, and spins her around.

"It worked." Tears stream from Cephas's eyes. "The Sowing's viable."

Saffron gives him a big kiss. "All our research wasn't in vain. There's still a chance."

He hugs her again. When they separate, they share a look, almost of embarrassment, as if they'd forgotten they weren't alone.

I squeeze Digory's shoulder.

Cephas clears his throat. "Our Repros—the people that you met who resemble us—how are they adjusting?"

"Were they the ones that told you about our facility here?" Saffron interrupts.

My throat locks up. I can't speak. All I want to do is hang on to this moment for just a few seconds longer, this one sliver of what might have been. My old team of recruits back together again: Cypress, Gideon, Ophelia, Digory, and myself. Only in this magical, alternate reality, Gideon isn't broken by abuse, he's strong. Cypress's eyes glow bright with hope, never having endured the scars of the Pleasure Emporiums, nor the experience of her children's deaths. Even Ophelia hasn't been wounded by a callous mother, groomed to survive, her mind fractured by a devotion to a poor, innocent sister that doesn't even exist.

But the illusion is shattered when I exchange looks with Digory. He's deathly pale and barely recognizable, lying in his bed. I can't even imagine how worn and jaded I must look, too. Ironically, it's Digory and I that are the more damaged, unstable ones this time around.

The players may change but the cycle never truly ends.

I swallow hard. "No. Your Repros didn't tell us how to find you."

"Lucian. We seem to be experiencing…another…glitch…" Digory's fingers dig into my arm. His body's wracked by a fresh wave of spasms.

"Digory, hang on." I grip his body, trying to hold him steady. But he's bucking like a wild Caballus. "Somebody help me!"

Cephas and Saffron move in, tightening the straps around Digory's body.

"I need ten ccs of Neuro-Sed," Cephas mutters.

Saffron throws open a shiny, steel box, grabs a hypo, and plunges it into an ampule of golden liquid. She thrusts the loaded needle at Cephas.

He grabs it and mutters, "Hold him steady," to me.

It's a struggle to keep Digory from moving. He coughs violently, spattering beads of blood on Cephas's white smock. Then Cephas jabs Digory's upper left arm with the hypo.

Everyone's quiet. Digory's movements gradually subside. The only sounds are his raspy breathing. I'm shell-shocked, gaping at the sight of Saffron wiping away the blood oozing from Digory's lips. His eyes are severely bloodshot. Looks like he's burst the blood vessels during his violent seizures. He looks so different, so frail compared to the UltraImposer groomed to withstand any physical onslaught.

"What's happening to him?" My own voice sounds like a stranger's to me. "Why isn't he regenerating anymore?"

Saffron and Cephas ignore my question, scurrying around Digory, attaching electrodes and I.V.'s to his body, hooking him up to monitors that fill the room with unnerving *bleeps* and *pings*.

Saffron shoves a tube into one of the gauges and turns to her companion. "We need a complete blood culture and Nano work-up stat."

"Already on it." Cephas spears another of Digory's veins with a fresh hypo, drawing dark blood into the plunger.

My anger and fear bubble over. "What the hell you doing to him?"

Cephas glances at me then shoots Breck a stern look. "Get him out of here now."

I shake my head. "I'm not going anywhere until—"

Breck clutches my arm. "If you want Tycho to have a fighting shot, the team needs room to work. Let's go."

I'm in a haze as Breck pulls me from the chamber and into an adjoining room, maneuvering me onto the examination bed. "He's not going to make it, is he?" I mumble.

"Hard to say." She wraps a blood pressure cuff around my arm and activates it. "We'll know better once the results of the battery of tests they're performing are in. Those two are the best in their field. If Tycho has a chance, they're definitely it."

The monitor bleeps and Breck removes the cuff and examines the readout. "A little on the high side but that's to be expected considering your stress levels. What about your headaches? Getting worse?"

I nod. "It seems the more I remember, the more intense they are."

She shakes her head. "Not surprising. The Sowing was never intended to be used to download a complete consciousness into a new body, only certain skill sets and knowledge to help rebuild the population. There's supposed to be safeguards involved to filter the information into the brain. Looks like someone's stripped those away those in your case, causing your physical symptoms. Your mind's overwhelmed with processing too much too soon."

"The Fleshers…the nanotech race…removed some of the filters in my brain so I could remember enough to find this place. They thought you would have the answers that might allow them to function autonomously. They want freedom. They're tired of their glorified slave status beholden to their masters. Can't say I blame them."

Breck's expression brightens. "So the nanotech's becoming self-aware? That was always something we speculated about. It's one of the complexities of developing new life."

"The created become the creators," I mutter.

"What was that?"

I sigh. "Humans playing deities is a dangerous game. We may have the intelligence to create a new species. But we sure as hell lack the wisdom to guide them."

She opens a cabinet, studies its contents, and pulls out a bottle of pills. "These can help with the pain until we can find a more permanent solution to manage your condition."

I take the bottle from her and examine the label. "Will these also suppress the memories?"

"Yes. Consider them a sort of dream suppressant, acting to bury those memories deeper into your subconscious—"

I shove the bottle back into her hand. "Sorry. That's not an option any longer."

Breck looks confused. "I don't understand. If the memories are causing you pain, why would you want to continue to endure them, especially if their ill effects can create irreversible damage that may prove to be life threatening?"

"Because buried in those memories is something very important. Something to do with this place. Something that could involve major repercussions for the war effort. I'm not just talking about the effects on the original survivors in the Nexus." I glance upward. "The people living up there are at risk, too. I can feel it, lurking just beyond the veil of my subconscious. There's something about this place that can tip the balance of humanity's survival, and not necessarily in a good way." My head throbs again. I clutch the ends of the examining table, squeezing my eyes shut until the pain subsides to a dull ache.

Breck taps my arm. "Here. Take this." She hands me a cloth and touches her nose.

Hot blood pools at my upper lip even before I dab my nose with the cloth. I stare at the fresh blood for a moment while the dizziness passes. Then I hop off the bed. "I need some air."

Before she can protest, I hit the release on the door and march out of the room, desperate to escape the claustrophobic confines and reach the openness of Nexus Prime's central core.

No sooner do I arrive there, blaring alarms pierce the quiet, echoing throughout the installation.

Cole emerges from the hallway, running to me. "What's going on?" he shouts over the shrill din.

All I can do is shake my head.

Attention, a synthetic voice declares from the complex's speakers. *Intruders have breached the installation's security perimeter and are closing in.*

The huge screens on every level spring to life with static and then an unsettling image.

A squadron of Thorn Republic attack ships.

My heart thunders. "They found us."

Breck bursts into the core, Saffron close on her heels. Cephas must have stayed in the medical wing to look after Digory. The two young women stare at the Squawkers and Vultures flitting across the surface like angry insects.

"Who are they?" Saffron asks, her eyes glued to the screens.

"Looks like an advance scouting mission from the Thorn Republic."

They both gape at me.

I purse my lips. "Meet the enemy."

"Maybe they're *your* enemy," Saffron says. "But they don't even know we exist. They might not mean us any harm."

The screens fill with the sight of the weapon hatches on the fighters sliding open. "I'd rethink that position if I were you."

An intense flash momentarily blinds us. The images on the screens distort in a burst of static. Through the haze I can make out a stream of charges spewing from the aircrafts' underbellies.

Instinctively, I grab Cole. "Brace yourselves."

Loud explosions rock the complex. The monitors and control consoles spark. The force of the blast nearly knocks us all off our feet."

I hold Cole tight. "You okay?" I mutter in his ear.

He nods into my cheek.

Breck shoots me an accusing look. "How did they know we were here? You must have brought them."

"I swear I don't know. But we have more important things to worry about, like jamming their transmissions before they can request reinforcements."

"I'm on it." Saffron's already punching commands into the keyboard.

Breck's busy checking gauges and readouts. "Looks like the agro sector's sustained heavy damage. Level Six generator is at fifty percent capacity and dropping fast. Ventilation on levels Ten through fifteen's been severely compromised."

I point Cole toward the exit. "Get back to the research center and lay low in one of the reinforced observation towers."

He shakes his head. "I'm staying here."

I pull him away, but he grabs on to one of the consoles. "I said go, damn it! It's too dangerous!"

But Cole won't let go. "No. You're not going to get rid of me, too. I'm staying."

My hands let go. I sigh. "Okay. But stay where I can see you."

"Kay."

Breck points at the nearest screen. "They're prepping to make another pass."

The Vultures swerve in the distance in a smooth arc, swarming back toward Nexus Prime's airspace.

I join Saffron at the main com. "What kind of defenses you got?"

"We've got artillery turrets stationed all across the perimeter. They should be able to lock onto incoming aircraft."

The fighters zoom across the horizon. Nexus Prime's gun turrets trail them with a barrage of firepower. A few of the aircraft erupt, glowing like fireflies before bursting into balls of flame and disintegrating. But most of the small, sleek ships dart past and around the turrets, under and over, avoiding the blasts altogether.

My fist slams against the console. "It's no good. Those automated guns of yours look like they were designed for a large scale attack. The Thorn ships are too agile. We need something more maneuverable."

Breck highlights an area of the holographic map. "We've got drones. But none of us have military training. And the team that does is still in deep freeze. By the time we thaw them out of cryo—"

"Looks like I'm your best shot, literally," I say. "Give me drone access stat."

A series of explosions rocks the complex. Overhead lights burst. Concrete gives way. Steel beams topple. For a few tense seconds, the facility's pitch black. Then the emergency lights come on, bathing us in shadows and a sickly, swirling amber glow.

Breck shoots Saffron an anxious look. The latter nods.

With a few quick movements of her fingers, Breck brings the drone system online and hands me a portable screen. "It's all yours, flyboy."

This tech's arguably hundreds of years older than what I'm used to, if not more. In some ways, it's surprisingly more advanced. Between my Imp and Resistance military training, though, I should be able to make up for the lack of hands-on experience using this system. Theoretically.

On the surface, the attack fleet is systematically knocking out the gun turrets. One by one, they're engulfed in blinding explosions, toppling over, the impact sending violent aftershocks reverberating down into the bowels of the complex. Wisps of obsidian smoke ooze through the vents.

Saffron's face grows pale. "They've taken out all of the turrets except for the main one. Now we're practically defenseless. One more blast like that and the cryostations will be severely compromised."

Compromised? Why is it people feel the need to soften harsh reality. "They'll die. And so will we."

Studying the readouts, I try and slow my breathing to quell the rising panic. The system shouldn't make that much sense to me. Yet—

I know this system like the back of my hand.

For once, Queran's intrusion in my brain is a welcome one. Rather than fight it, I open myself up to it, fusing his knowledge of Nexus Prime's systems with my own combat experience.

"Here we go." My fingers fly over the controls, releasing my own squadron of attack drones into the sky. It actually feels like I'm in the pilot seat again. I maneuver each of my drones into attack formation, guided missiles locking onto the heat signatures of the Thorn ships.

"Let's see how much *they* can take." I fire one of my drone's weapons into an oncoming Squawker, clipping it in the wing. The craft spins out of control colliding into another. A Vulture is caught in the fiery wake, and the three craft disappear in a cloud of flame and blackness.

"Gotcha." Punching in more commands, I position the drones into a deadly perimeter, closing in on the enemy aircraft like a noose, trying to herd them away from the complex.

But these pilots aren't going down without a fight. They're good.

And they're so many.

One by one my drones go down.

"Time to change tactics." I aim each remaining drone on a collision course with the fleet.

It's a huge gamble. If I'm wrong, we'll be completely defenseless.

Except I'm not really defenseless, am I? I have the power to stop them. All of them

Just give the command.

Intense pain stabs my skull, bringing on choppy waves of dizziness and nausea. The control screen disappears in a blur, replaced by flashes of oblong silver, their bright gleam knifing into my brain. There are hundreds, maybe thousands of them, all lined up and waiting. Waiting for me to set them all free.

We're ready, Mr. President.

My hand looks older and steadier. I press my palm against the cold, black box.

Then come the screams. Growing more intense. Filling my head with satisfaction and agony—

The memory flickers out, leaving me reeling. Warm blood trickles from my nostrils onto the tablet.

"Spark, you okay?" Breck rushes to my side, helping to prop me up.

I slump against the console.

"I'm good." Despite how sick my mind and spirit feel, I hit the command deploying the drones on a suicidal course with their targets.

A series of bright, orange explosions fills the screens. One by one, the drones impact against the Squawkers in their one-way missions.

The blips representing the drones and the enemy ships disappear from the readouts.

Saffron squeezes my arm. "It worked. Looks like you've taken them all out."

Her words echo down the tunnels of my memories. I've heard them before, only then, they didn't fill me with relief, just a sense of impending dread.

Like the sight of the black smoke dissipating on the screens.

And the soft bleeping coming from the instruments, growing stronger each second.

"There's still one ship left." I stare at the lone craft, a huge Scavenger cruiser, emerging from the blackness. From the trail of dark exhaust it spews in its wake, it's obviously been damaged. But it's still limping along, slowly but steadily.

Heading right for us.

Breck's face is like solid granite. "It's coming in hot. Fully weaponized. Headed straight for the life support generators. Deep impact estimated within five minutes."

I shake my head. "What about the gun turret. Can't we use it to take them out before—"

"That's a negative," Breck responds. "Looks like the relays between the command station and the artillery centers have been damaged. There's no way to align the turret's targeting sensors."

I study the readings. She's right. "Looks like somebody's going to have to get to the surface, bypass the turret's auto targeting systems, and blow that ship old school."

Saffron and Breck exchange anxious looks. I open a metal case laying near the console and throw in a bunch of tools from nearby shelves.

"You'll never make it in time, Spark." Breck's voice is quiet and emotionless. "You don't even know how to navigate the complex well enough to reach the surface."

I force a smile and a wink. "You forget just who I am."

She gives a curt nod. "That's what worries me."

Grabbing the case, I turn toward the exit and find Cole blocking the way, staring at me with glassy eyes.

"You don't have to promise me anything this time," he says. "Just try to come back soon."

It's hard to swallow the lump in my throat. "I'll try my best."

I dash out of the control center.

The maze to reach the main gun turret is a blur. I try and block out everything and let my inherited memories guide me. The irony of Queran Embers doing something good for a change fuels me. I sprint down one corridor and then another, dash into one of the lifts, enter a code, and punch the button to the artillery level.

Impact in two minutes. Breck's voice booms throughout the complex's audio system.

After a dizzying high-speed ascension, I burst free of the elevator into the simmering heat of the hazy desert, and onto a very narrow path leading into a crevice in the mountain. My momentum almost sends me careening off the ledge, which overlooks a drop of hundreds of feet.

One minute until impact, Breck announces from the elevator's speakers. The rest is cut off when the doors *woosh* shut.

No matter. I don't need any more warnings to emphasize what's at stake. All around me, the sky's filled with a terrible rumbling, like endless thunder. An enormous, dark shadow eclipses the searing sun above me. Overhead, the crippled Scavenger continues its deadly run toward Nexus Prime.

Squeezing into the narrow crevice inside the mountain that camouflages the main gun turret, I get stuck for a moment. Cursing, I squeeze my way through, ignoring the jagged rocks tearing at my suit and cutting into my skin.

The tunnel finally opens up. I pull myself through, ripping open the tool box, using the sharp instruments to pry open the panel. There's a series of wires of all different colors. Somehow, I know exactly which ones to pull and replace, plugging in the portable terminal.

What do I have? Maybe fifteen seconds left?

Ignoring the panic, I power on the portable terminal, my fingers jabbing furiously at the keys. There's a loud creaking. The gun turret slowly rotates, locking onto the falling Scavenger.

It's almost like the day's turned into night. The huge craft blocks out everything, falling rapidly now, almost on top of the life support generators.

Time's up.

CHAPTER TWENTY-FIVE

I jam my finger on the firing trigger.

The turret spits out explosive charges at the invading Scavenger.

Covering my ears, I fall to the floor, wedging myself against two massive boulders.

The explosions are defeaning. A mixture of steel, rock, and earth pelts down around me. Shielding my eyes, I peek out. The Scavenger erupts, disintegrating in clouds of fire and smoke.

I slump against the mountainside, allowing myself some relief.

I did it.

No. Queran did it.

The life support systems aren't in danger any longer. Nexus Prime will survive yet another day.

My respite dies a very quick and painful death.

Zipping away from the remnants of the downed Scavenger carrier is a group of tiny emergency escape pods. Though they have no weaponry and have a limited flight range, they're still equipped with com systems capable of sending out a distress beacon that'll alert the rest of the Thorn battalions to our position. And we have no guns left to stop them from clearing our jamming range.

In a little while, the airspace will be crawling with reinforcements. All I've done is prolong the inevitable blood bath.

I activate my Com Stream. "Couldn't down the Scavenger before it released its emergency evac crew. How long before they're out of jamming range?"

The com unit hisses and crackles. "Just under thirty seconds." Even through the unsteady signal, Breck's voice radiates hopelessness.

Can't say that I blame her. "We need to salvage what we can from the data records and get the hell out of here before—"

"We can't just leave everyone behind here to die."

"Wait a minute," Saffron's voice interrupts Breck's. "Scanner just revealed a fleet of ships heading our way."

Her warning is moot. I can already hear the steady thrum of engines rapidly approaching. My eyes search the sky, fixating on the squadron of ships zooming through the clouds to meet the escape pods. "Not sure how they got here so fast when the escape ships have barely made it past the jamming range, but it looks like it's already too late."

"Someone doesn't have too much faith, Mate," a familiar voice crackles through my resistance com band.

"Cage! How the hell did you find us?" A rush of jubilation and excitement re-energizes me.

"You can thank Dru. She injected Tycho with a tracker when he was in our custody, just like the Thornies did. Now hang on and let the big blokes show you how it's done." I can picture the infectious sly grin on Cage's face as he says those glorious words.

"Spark, who are these people?" Breck asks, her voice tinged with surprise and relief.

I smile at my com. "Just some old friends."

"*Old*? Who the hell's he calling *old*, Dru?" Arrah.

"Well you are my old lady," Drusilla teases on another channel.

"Cut the chatter you two," Dahlia breaks in. "We've got work to do. We can catch up with the Fifth Tier later. Nice to hear your voice, Sparkles."

I chuckle. "Yours, too, D."

"Time to sweep up this mess, people," Corin shouts from another cockpit transmitter.

The old gang's back together again. More resistance fighters swoop down toward Nexus, creating a perimeter. The new arrivals intercept the pods and escort them to the surface.

I wave my arms at the incoming ships, exhilarated at the sight of my friends—my people—joining me at last.

They aren't really my friends anymore, are they?

Trying to shake the thought away, I mutter into my Nexus Com, "Roll out the welcome mats. We've got company."

But I can't shake that last, relentless thought from my brain.

———

The remainder of the day's spent integrating the resistance crew into Nexus Prime's facilities. At first, Breck and Saffron are very skeptical about hosting all these strangers, a sentiment seemingly shared by Rios and the rest of the resistance crew. But with me acting as intermediary in the main conference center, both sides exchange information, reluctantly at first, but then more openly as the proceedings continue.

Croakley and the council fill the Nexus crew in on the atrocities committed by the Establishment and Thorn Republic, complete with holos, docs, and eyewitness testimonials. But the real turning point comes when the evidence against Straton and Sanctum is presented, corroborating all the horrors I've already informed the Nexus team of. That's when Breck and Saffron begin to earnestly share the history of Nexus and the Clathrate Apocalypse, as well as the devastation of the Ash Wars that spurred its creation.

By the end of the hours long session, Rios begrudgingly gives me a nod and stands to address the group. "It seems like we owe Commander Spark here a debt of gratitude for bringing both sides together in this most crucial hour."

There's thunderous applause, which makes me very uncomfortable. After it's all over, I make some small talk, and politely excuse myself to find Cole and check on Digory and my friends.

I enter the small sleeping quarters Cole's currently sharing with Corin. "What took you so long?" He's lying down on the bottom bunk while Corin's on top, oblivious to my presence, busy working on some gadget that bleeps and buzzes.

I smile, plopping down next to Cole. "I told you I'd try."

His arms wrap around my neck tightly. "I'm sorry."

"You have nothing to be sorry about. Ever."

"It's working!" Corin leaps down from his bunk holding out his project.

It's a tray with a few dark gloves, and some small cases with clear lenses and tiny ear pieces.

"What's it do?" Cole asks.

He's beaming. "It's a com system I've been working on. The lenses actually transmit audio and video and are undetectable in body scans. Each fingertip accesses different channels by pressing against the thumb. So you can send and receive transmissions without anyone else being aware of what you're doing." He holds out the devices. "Why don't you guys give it a test drive?"

Cole and I don the devices and take turns using them. I'm surprised to find myself tuning into Cage, Arrah, Dru and Dahlia, assisting the others get situated in bunks and doling out food rations.

I pat Corin's shoulder. "Great job. It'll come in handy on our next mission." I turn to Cole. "You going to be okay here, buddy? I just have something I need to take care of."

Cole nods. "Sure. I hope he's all right, too."

Nodding, I exit the room, the door sliding shut on their excited chatter. Doing my best not to attract any attention, I make my way to Cephas Decatur's lab. I spy him and Digory speaking through the glass. Digory nods solemnly.

I knock on the door before entering. "Sorry to bother you."

"Not a problem," Cephas says. "I was just leaving."

As he passes me, I take hold of his arm. "Thanks for keeping the Queran thing and Digory's presence under wraps until I can figure out how to smooth it over," I say low enough so Digory can't hear.

"I understand," he says. "But we're running out of time."

Then he's gone.

I turn to Digory, pleased to see him on his feet and dressed in a jumpsuit instead of his hospital gown. "Looks like someone's feeling a lot better."

"The doctor gave us something to help control the symptoms."

"Symptoms of what?" I move in closer.

"It does not matter."

"It does to me."

Digory rests his hands on my shoulders. "Lucian. We have to leave here now."

"I know you're concerned about Rios and the others, but I'll find a way to make them understand." I rest tentative hands on his waist.

"It has got nothing to do with that. It is the Hive. They need me."

"So you got what you want, the key to your autonomy, and you're just leaving."

He lets go of me. "We know this is hard to understand after everything we have shared. We can see why you and this vessel grew so close before. But that can never be now. We all have different destinies."

Pain and fury swirl in my gut, especially since there's a part of me that knows he's right.

"You have to do what you feel." My voice is hoarse. "When are you leaving?"

"Right away."

A fresh wave of pain seeps into my still opened wounds. "I guess this is goodbye then." I turn my back on him, unable to stare into his eyes. "Take care of yourself, Digory."

Then I'm out the door, fists clenched, teeth digging into my upper lip until I taste warm blood.

He's not worthy of me. Of course he betrayed me like all the rest. Forget him.

My com bleeps to life. "Spark," Cage says. "You'd best come down to the control center, Mate."

"On my way."

Forcing myself not to think about anything else, I make my way to command central, where Cage is waiting with Arrah, Dahlia, Dru, Rios, and a team of techs.

I approach the monitors they're all staring at. "What's up?"

"Looks like some kind of virus has infected the systems," Arrah says.

"Everything's shutting down," Dru continues. "Your Nexus pals aren't sure what's triggered it. They're investigating the servers now."

There's something very familiar about the unintelligible code displayed on the screens.

I know this code. It's a failsafe.

A failsafe *I* built into the system, so very long ago.

Focusing on the monitors, I punch in commands on the keyboard. "Don't worry, I think I know what's wrong." In seconds, the systems start coming back online.

"How did you do that?" Rios asks, his question laced with suspicion.

I shake my head. "I've been here longer than you. I've had more time to study their systems."

There's a series of loud bleeps. "What's happening now?" Dahlia asks.

Data is rapidly streaming on every single monitor creating a strobe effect. I recognize glimpses of silver, as well as a map displaying a myriad of locations, all connected to Nexus Prime.

Breck and Saffron burst into the control center. "Someone's accessing the servers, downloading and deleting files," Breck cries.

The screens go black, followed by static, and then a face appears on every single one of the monitors.

Cassius Thorn.

"Greetings from the Thorn Republic," he says with a smile. "I must say I was rather dismayed at the less than hospitable welcome my ships received upon entering your airspace. Unfortunately, that's an action that will have consequences."

His face fills me with rage. "What do you want, Cassius?"

"Funny it should be you that asks, Lucian. I actually would like to inform your friends of the traitors in their midst."

"What traitors?" Rios barks.

Cassius licks his lips. "At this very moment, your former ally turned Flesher conspirator, Digory Tycho is hidden in Nexus, harbored here by the one you call Lucian Spark."

"Tycho's here?" Cage asks, his eyes fill with shock and accusation.

"Yes," I say. "But I can explain everything."

"Go ahead then," Cassius cuts in. "Tell them how you knowingly used Tycho to access your memories so he would bring you here to obtain this place's secrets all for yourself. Fortunately, the nanotech inside Tycho allowed me to track him here and stop you before you could betray your friends."

Arrah grips my arm. "*Betray your friends*? What the hell is he talking about, Spark?"

Cassius shakes his head. "And therein lies the heart of the betrayal. You all know him as Lucian Spark. That's just not the case."

I push past Arrah to stare at the main screen head on. "Cassius, don't do this. You said you wouldn't." I realize as the words escape from my throat how incriminating they must sound to the others.

But Cassius won't be deterred. "All this time the resistance hasn't realized that they've been harboring their greatest enemy right under their noses. An enemy that makes a mockery of your entire movement and will destroy you all."

Rios pushes me out of the way and approaches the main monitor. "We're listening."

Cassius leans into the screen. "Lucian Spark is Queran Embers, founder of the very Establishment you've been fighting. The information he just transmitted was the classified locations of the other installations in the Nexus, as well as the coordinates for an arsenal of nuclear warheads."

"Liar! I haven't transmitted anything. You're trying to set me up." My heart's pounding like it's about to explode.

Sighs and chuckles erupt. Even Rios shakes his head. "It appears that you've lost your mind, Thorn."

Cassius smiles. "I'm sure once you've seen the evidence you won't doubt my sanity, General."

For the next few agonizing minutes, the screens fill with details of the Sowing experiments, including the history of Queran Embers, complete with photos of his youth. The resemblance is undeniable.

When it's over, not a sound can be heard. Rios turns to Saffron and Breck. "Is this possible?"

Breck looks at me gravely. She thinks I betrayed them, transferred the Nexus files to Cassius. She turns back to Rios. "Yes. It is."

The look of shock and horror on my friends' faces is unbearable.

Cage takes a step closer. "Is it true? Are you really bloody Queran Embers?"

After an eternity I can only say one word. "Yes."

Rios draws his weapon. "Take him into custody."

An explosion rocks the control center, knocking everyone off their feet. Beams come crashing down, smashing into smoking computer banks. Cassius's face disappears. The lights flicker off, replaced by the swirling red of emergency strobes. Through the grit and smoke, I make out Digory standing at the level above, another grenade held in his fist. He disappears into the shadows.

Was he the one that set me up and transmitted those files? Is he still working with Cassius? Or did he just give me a chance to escape? As everyone stirs in the chaos, I crawl through a broken duct, into a side hallway. Rising on shaky legs, I sprint through a maze of corridors, ignoring the shouts. My former comrades are already hot on my tail. But they don't know this place like I do.

After all, I helped design it.

Attention! Rios's voice blares through the coms. *Lucian Spark is wanted for treason and should be taken into custody by any means necessary for interrogation. Repeat. Apprehend Lucian Spark at all cost for interrogation!*

They've all turned against me. Just like before. But I don't need them anymore.

I'm just about to access a hidden elevator to the surface when someone dashes out from the shadows.

It's Cole.

"Here," he says, throwing me a small, silver box. "You'll need this."

Our eyes connect for one moment. Then he runs away, and I dash inside the elevator which whisks me to a hidden hangar containing my transportation out of this mess.

As the resistance pilots scramble to their ships, I'm already up and away from Nexus Prime, speeding into the darkening skies.

An enemy of the Thorn Republic, the Flesher regime, and the Resistance, with nowhere to hide.

PART III

DESTINIES

CHAPTER TWENTY-SIX

Just like I was able to pilot the drones by siphoning Queran's memories, I again tap into that same dark well, combining that arcane knowledge with my own piloting skills to navigate the systems of this antique heap. According to the gauges, I have just enough fuel left. The same can't be said of my spirits. That's okay. I just need to focus on one, final task.

I bite my lower lip. This whole odyssey began back in the Parish, with me purposely breaking curfew in order to get caught by Imps and taken into the presence of my once trusted soul mate, Cassius Thorn.

And now, after all that's happened, here I am completing the cycle that changed my life forever, piloting this piece of junk into Thorn airspace, in hopes of getting captured and taken before Cassius one last time.

Ironically, Cassius is the only one left I can turn to. The resistance will never trust me again, no matter what I say. And my friends—those terrible expressions on their faces—I've lost them forever, too.

All I have left now are memories. The memories of another lifetime. Where once I fought them, deluding myself that they weren't part of me, I embrace them now, peeling away the last layers that separate Lucian Spark from the ghosts of the past.

Every bit of pain, jealousy, and betrayal I experienced as Queran churns through me, filling the numbness and empty void that was once Lucian Spark. I know why Queran—why I—did what I did. That obsessive quest for power all makes sense. It's all so freeing. I don't have to rely on anyone else ever again or beg for their approval. Nor am I emotionally vulnerable to people that don't have my best interests at heart. Everyone who's ever hurt me will pay the price.

Beginning with Cassius Thorn.

He's made a big mistake by awakening me at last.

Whatever time I have left will be spent on utterly destroying him and his republic, including his underlings, Delvecchio and the others. And when I'm finished with them I'll turn my vengeance on—

A barrage of images and feelings makes my head spin. Cole's face. Digory's. Then Cage, Arrah, Dru, Dahlia, Corin—

The headache's intense. Once again, warm blood oozes from my nostrils and seeps between my lips. I savor the coppery taste. It conjures flashes of gleaming silver.

Missiles.

The ones I ordered to be deployed against my enemies.

The ones I will deploy again and again, until there's no one left to oppose me.

No one left to hurt me.

A sensor *bleeps.*

Unidentified ships approaching, the computer nav's crackly voice announces.

On the scanners, a squad of Thorn Republic cruisers zooms my way. Instead of firing, they pull back, disappearing into the horizon.

"Looks like you're waiting for me," I mutter.

The Parish looms ahead. The place I once called home.

The place where it all ends.

With no one to stop me, I maneuver the ship past the familiar smoke stacks of the Industrial Borough, which cough up puffs of blackness like dying lungs rasping their final breaths.

Swerving past the Dome of the Citadel, I soar over the rubble of my former neighborhood, flying over the sewage treatment centers, steering the craft over the cemetery and woods. I finally set down by the banks of Fortune's River.

The ship's engines sputter and die.

Fuel's almost gone. But that doesn't matter.

I'll never be leaving here again.

Leaning back in my seat, I take a deep breath and catch sight of something forgotten in the co-pilot's seat.

It's the small, silver box that Cole tossed me before I escaped. Grabbing it, I pop the lid open and stare down at its contents.

A black glove, along with a tiny case of clear lenses. Corin's device. What did he call it? An Opticom? The one the resistance planned on using during their next mission.

I'm about to close the lid, but I can't quite bring myself to do it. Instead, I slip the glove onto my right hand and insert the lenses over my eyes.

Could it possibly be functional?

I press the tip of my index finger against the thumb.

A small rectangular window opens in the lower right corner of my field of vision. It's completely disorienting and uncomfortable at first. My eyes flit from side to side, up and down. The image retains its relativity and aspect ratio.

"—once we get through the access tunnels underground and emerge from this duct right into the main server room."

It's Cage's voice, even though I'm seeing images of Arrah, Dru, Dahlia, and a few other members of my former squad standing at attention, including Rios. This must be Cage's Opticom unit, feeding me footage from his own cam.

Rios pops in a fresh ammo cartridge. "Is everything set with your contacts, Private Ryland?"

Drusilla zips her pack closed. "My Worm contacts will meet up with us at the rendezvous point and supply us with the proper I.D.s and codes to gain access, Sir."

"Are you sure we can trust them, Dru?" Dahlia asks.

"They have no love for the Thorn Republic, I can tell you that. Besides, with the Culling on ice, they've learned to adapt their skills from assuming Incentive identities to infiltrating government facilities quite nicely."

Arrah's face is rigid. "How much of a window do we have to introduce the virus into their computer network before they pick up our scent?"

"Not much," Cage continues. "But we only need a few minutes to compromise their entire defense grid."

When I press my third finger into my thumb, the view point changes. Cage's face fills the box in my field of vision now. "The moment the Thorn fleet's systems are infected, our own ships will begin bombardment of the Citadel, while our ground troops strike from these strategic locations."

As Cage points out these areas on a holo map, I find that if I roll my third finger up and down my thumb, the image zooms in and out, autofocusing. It's almost better than actually being there.

The image pans right, then left. The user must be shifting his or her head. I'm able to see the others and deduce that the third finger must control the feed for Arrah's unit.

My ring finger presses against my thumb, changing the channel again.

"So it looks like this entire plan hinges on our little team here." Dahlia's voice. Her camera pans the team's faces. So Cage's com is the index finger, Arrah's is the third finger, and Dahlia's unit is controlled by the ring finger. It takes me a few moments, but in no time I develop a rhythm of tapping and rolling my fingers against my thumb which allows me to follow all their interactions, as if I were still a part of their group, instead of the outsider I've become.

Dru squeezes Arrah's hand. "Time to get this show going."

Cage grabs his gear. "Anyone have any last words before we take off?"

Dahlia's eyes pivot from one to another. "Here's to making it back in one piece." She pauses for a moment while the others cheer the sentiment. Then the Company's mood grows somber. "All of us. Wherever we may be."

Do they know I can hear and see them? It doesn't really matter one way or another. I'm not a part of anything anymore and can never be again.

"Saddle up, people," Rios barks. "It's time."

They slap each other's backs and scramble inside their ship.

When I press my thumb against the palm, I instantly get a fourth set of feeds from inside a cockpit.

"Pilot Lignier initiating engines," Corin announces. He flips a few switches on his console and his fighter's engines roar to life.

He's part of the airstrike.

It dawns on me that I haven't tried the last channel yet. My little finger settles against my thumb. I hesitate. What's the point? That life is over now. I can't afford to let anything pull my focus from what I have to do.

I'm just about to rip off the glove when the sound of another engine catches my attention. I clench my fist, cutting off the Opticom's feeds.

Outside the cockpit window, a sleek ship hovers overhead, then descends alongside my own vessel. There's no point in grabbing my weapon. If they wanted me dead they'd have blasted me out of the sky the moment I entered Thorn airspace.

The ship's gangway extends. I brace myself for the inevitable onslaught. Instead of a squad of Imps, a long shadow stretches through the hatch, followed by its owner, a solitary figure that stands there, unmoving.

Waiting for me.

My fist jams against the hatch release switch. I stride out of the cockpit, down the gangway, and come face to face with Cassius Thorn.

Straining my eyes, I pick out the Imps positioned at a distance among the trees, sharpshooters ready to spring to action if I should make any threatening moves toward their leader, no doubt.

"I knew you couldn't stay away," he says.

My gaze drifts back to Cassius. "You didn't really leave me with any other choice, did you?"

His expression's vacant. "There's always a choice, Lucian." He motions toward the river. "Walk with me?"

Instead of answering, I trudge past him, my boots crunching the dead leaves as I make my way down to the river bank, relishing the chilly wind against my cheeks.

He catches up to me, scoops up some pebbles from the ground and tosses one of them into the river's current. "I was so young the last time the two of us stood here."

"Sixteen years old and ready to take on the Trials and the whole world. I remember too well."

His smile's wistful. "You were only fourteen. Just a baby."

Our eyes meet. I can't help notice the dark circles under his. "I think we both know I'm much older than that now."

Cassius shakes his head. "I wasn't really speaking of my chronological age anyway. It was more like my spirit. I still had blinders on back then." He's staring at the choppy river flow now. "Sometimes I wonder what things would be like if I'd never taken them off. If I could unsee what I've seen."

"And just what is it you've seen, Cassius?"

He tosses another pebble into the river. It manages to skip a few times over the chaotic stream before sinking into the depths. "What would you say if you found out during the Trials that you were nothing but an experiment, and that the parents you loved so much were merely monitoring your brain, seeing how much pressure they could apply before memories of a previous life surfaced?"

"You were Sown, too? A Repro?"

His eyes narrow. "Abomination is a much more accurate term. But after dear old dad died in the trials and I emerged victorious, I started doing some digging and discovered some very startling and valuable information."

"I take it this information is what got you appointed Prefect, the youngest prefect ever, only two years after you completed the Trials?"

"Yes." Cassius flings another pebble into the river, this time managing to make it skip four times before it disappears in a white cap. "Following the leads I got from my adopted mother, I started investigating things and gathering evidence while stationed at the Citadel. It wasn't long before my diligence paid off, and I discovered who it was that actually gave birth to me."

Little by little the pieces of the puzzle are all starting to form a clear mosaic. There's only one person that had the authority to pull strings and expedite Cassius's rise in rank so quickly.

"Prime Minister Talon. She was your mother. And you murdered her."

Cassius pauses in mid toss. "No. She wasn't my mother. A mother is someone that's supposed to care for you, nurture you. Love you." He finishes his toss, only this time the pebble immediately plunks down into the river like a heavy anchor. "Talon was just a vessel, an unfeeling incubator that carried an implanted embryo. An experiment. Me."

"Not surprised. I never pegged Talon as the motherly type." I toss my own pebble in after his.

He nods. "You see, in her younger years, just before she became obsessed with her political aspirations, Talon was part of a secretive study conducted by a conclave embedded deep within the Establishment since its founding." He turns to me. "Since you founded it."

Flashes of memory ignite through my brain. I remember something about appointing a special council that would be responsible for reintegrating the Sown into society.

A secret order embedded in the Establishment's religious Foundation, hidden in the bowels of the Priory.

A powerful sect dedicated to bringing about my own resurrection.

"I can see by your expression that it's starting to come back to you, Lucian. Or have you embraced Queran yet?"

I ignore the taunt. "So Queran founds the Establishment, then he sets up this secret society hidden in the Priory to use genetic samples stolen from Nexus to revive the survivors and achieve a level of immortality. But something went wrong, didn't it?"

My temples start to throb and my heart's racing. Why can't I remember?

"Something did go wrong, Lucian. Very wrong. It seems the first test subject they attempted to resurrect wasn't entirely stable." He purses his lips, staring at the rippling river. "This specimen was an amalgamation of the genetics of several different candidates. The test subject couldn't handle the onslaught of a myriad of memories. He suffered from terrible hallucinations, the onset of a bipolar condition and acute schizophrenia." Cassius turns to me. "But instead of treating this pitiful creature and finding a way to alleviate its misery, do you know what they did?"

Another wave of pain and nausea hit me. My eyes squeeze closed. When the wave passes, I force myself to meet his gaze again. "They killed the subject. Then attempted the revival again."

Of course I know. I'm the one that issued that edict to make sure all the kinks in the process were ironed out before it was attempted on Queran Embers.

Before it was attempted on me.

Cass's eyes are glassy shards. "Yes. They murdered that poor specimen, which would have been a mercy had they left it at that. But then they revived it. And killed it anew. The cycle of death and rebirth, over and over and over again." His shoulders hunch. "Each rebirth and death, this specimen remembered every... single... agonizing second of suffering it had endured in its prior incarnation. They didn't care. This was just genetic material to be dissected, studied, and discarded."

I nod slowly. "Until something began to change."

"It did. After each subsequent Sowing, the specimen, designated Case 1-Unit: Sowing, began to stabilize. Began to learn." He smiles. "Eventually, after the original team of scientists succumbed to the ravages of time and died out, subsequent personnel grew lax. They allowed their little experimental freak some freedoms." He leans in close. "They had no idea that Case 1 had learned the virtues of extreme patience. Eventually Case 1 sabotaged their experiments by destroying data, corrupting and stealing the other genetic samples, setting back the Sowing research decades."

My mind's racing. "The personnel running the Sowing program must have realized what was going on and shelved this subject permanently."

"Oh, yes. They did. But not before Case 1 had altered a few labels on certain samples, preserving his own genetic material so it would be unwittingly revived. The irony is, Case 1 knew that, as the Sowing became more viable, his participation in the experiment must come to its inevitable conclusion. But he wanted to live now. Live and come back, one last time—to destroy all of it so no poor creature would have to endure that kind of unnatural suffering ever again."

We stare at each other for a very long time without saying a word. The only sound is the roar of the rushing water crashing round the river bend.

"It's *you*," I finally say. "You're Case 1-Unit: Sowing. Case 1-U.S... Cassius."

Cassius' eyes are moist. He lets out a laugh, not one of malice, more like relief. "In the flesh. As Case 1, I made sure my specimen was named appropriately and introduced into the Talon family, one of the most powerful political dynasties in the Establishment. I wanted to position myself in the place where I could do the most damage upon my return. Despite all my planning, I didn't count on what it would feel like when I was unwittingly revived as a different specimen. All those horrific memories came rushing back during the mental and physical stress I was subjected to during the Trials."

My mind flashes to all the specimens we discovered at Nexus Prime, including Breck, Saffron, and Cephas. "Every Imposer recruit that endured the Culling during the Trials. They were all Sown as part of this same experiment, Repros purposely subjected to physical and mental torture to unlock their genetically inherited memories—"

"And create an elite strike force of loyal followers for President Queran Embers to command upon his return," Cassius finishes. "After I endured the Culling, those emerging memories led me to Straton and Sanctum, and we began to share classified information to destroy your Establishment."

"Until you betrayed Straton, too."

"Sanctum was only a tool to achieve what I couldn't singlehandedly." Cassius swipes his hand over his eyes. "I can still hear them, you know? Every single genetically grafted memory crying out in my mind. All of them. Even when I'm asleep." He laughs again.

"Cassius, I'm—"

"Don't even think of saying you're sorry." His eyes narrow to slits. "You're responsible for all of it. It was Queran's decision to begin experimentation on me after he nearly killed me during the Ash Wars. Can you imagine what it must feel like to discover that the boy you loved more than anything in the entire world is the same monster who condemned you to generations of pain and suffering?" He smiles. "It has quite an effect on you."

"Why don't you just kill me now and get your revenge over with?"

Cassius shakes his head. "Haven't you been listening? This has never been about revenge. I want to stop it from ever happening again. And you're the key, Queran."

"What the hell do you mean?"

"The codes to launch nuclear strikes against every single hub of the Nexus are buried in your subconscious. With the entire Nexus destroyed, every single piece of data necessary to implement the Sowing ever again will be obliterated."

"Nuclear strikes? If you do that you'll destroy all those dormant survivors that have been waiting for ages to be rescued. It's mass murder, Cassius."

He shakes his head. "Surely, you of all people aren't going to give me a lecture on morality? Didn't you order strikes against those you perceived as a threat to your stockades of provisions during the Ash Wars?"

I remain silent.

"Tell me, just how many deaths are you responsible for? Hundreds of thousands? Millions? Your hypocrisy would be amusing if the stakes were not so high."

I swallow hard. "You're the one that's being hypocritical. You claim everything that you've done is to prevent others from suffering the horrible fate that you have, yet you're willing to destroy countless innocent lives to attain that goal. Besides, *I* never ordered any strikes."

Cassius sighs. "I thought we'd worked through the denial stage. Every single cell and memory in that body you're wearing belongs to Queran Embers. That's who you are."

Pain sears my brain. Images flash.

A boy a little older than me, about fourteen or fifteen, with auburn hair and green eyes, entering the foyer of a palatial manor. My home. He's with a woman. His mother. And she's just married my widowed father.

My father turns to me, his smile cold. "Meet your new stepbrother, Queran."

My new stepbrother.

Lisandro.

I rub my temples until the throbbing subsides to a dull ache and the memory fades. "We knew each other before all of this. Before the Ash Wars."

Cassius moves in closer, his eyes pleading. "Trust me, I understand your conflict. There was a time after I discovered the truth about you that I didn't want to accept it either. I still thought I could save the boy I'd grown to love with all my heart." He takes my hands, and I'm too numb to stop him. "But I was devastated by the fact that you can never escape who you truly are."

I stare deeply into his eyes. "Neither of us can."

He clears his throat and turns to face the turbulent waters of Fortune's River again. "I think it's quite fitting that we should have this enlightening exchange at this specific spot. Do you remember that day? When I left you to embark on the Trials?"

I nod, even though he's not looking at me. "We thought we might never see each other again."

"Neither of us had absolutely any idea how prophetic our fears would prove to be." His words sound brittle, as if all the emotions have leaked away. When he turns to me his skin looks ashen, his eyes wet and weary. "That was the very last time that Cassius Thorn and Lucian Spark ever faced each other. Those two ceased to exist that day, if they ever truly existed at all."

The wind picks up, moaning through the dying trees and echoing the deep melancholy that chills my bones.

Dead leaves swirl about Cassius. "This was the exact spot where we once promised we would never forget each other, no matter what happened. Now, I make you a new promise. I promise to utterly destroy the evil that you represent, no matter what it takes or how I may feel."

I smile. "And I promise that you'll die trying, no matter what I have to do."

He presses a button on his wrist band.

The rust-colored leaves crackle around us. A platoon of Imps emerges from the trees and surrounds us, their weapons trained on me.

"It's time for us to go," Cassius says.

Taking a deep breath, I allow the soldiers to lead me to the ship and up the gangway, cuffing me into my seat. In moments, the engines rev and we lift off from the clearing.

I glance out the porthole, taking in what will probably be my last glance of Fortune's River, gazing at the foaming current, violently churning its way around the bend and colliding against a fork. Some of the waters rush to the left, heading back toward the remnants of my old tenement, the former life of Lucian Spark, while the rest of the river plunges toward the right, toward the Citadel of Truth and my life as Queran Embers.

If I was a pebble cast into this maelstrom, which way would the current carry me?

CHAPTER TWENTY-SEVEN

The Vulture swoops toward the towers of the Citadel. My mind races with anger and anxiety. Twiddling my thumbs, I catch sight of the Opticom glove I'm still wearing. Corin was right. When the Imps searched and scanned me for weapons, they didn't detect it.

Clenching my fist, I activate the unit, tapping my fingers against my thumb.

The box in the corner of my field of vision appears. Once again, I maneuver my index, third, and ring fingers into a steady rhythm to follow the feeds.

Cage and the rest of the crew are just landing their transport on the outskirts of the Parish.

Arrah hops out of the hatch. "Do you think they picked us up on their scanners?"

Joining her, Dahlia checks her holocam. "That would be a negative. My scans show we're clear."

Another group of a half-dozen black clad figures rushes to greet them. This must be the Worm team.

The leader, a slender young woman with cropped dark hair, checks her chron and steps forward to meet Rios. "We're running out of time."

"We're ready."

Another Worm, a young man who reminds me of the ill-fated Tim Fremont from that long ago alley, rushes up to the others. "We've got company. Recon patrol's heading this way."

The Worm leader scrambles into the abandoned power relay station, with Cage and the rest of the ground assault team slinking into the darkness after her.

"Time to blend in with the shadows, people." Dru tosses each of them a pair of the Shadow tech night vision goggles, which they quickly don.

Cage is busy with a blow torch, cutting an opening into the metal hatch leading into the access tunnels.

"You think we could hurry this up a little?" Dahlia's weapon is drawn, ready to take on the new arrivals. "Now would definitely be good."

Looking up, Cage gives her a wink. "Just a few more minutes, mates."

He finally kicks a metal panel out of the hatch. "Let's go."

They all drop into the darkness.

Remembering the fourth channel I never activated, I press the tip of my little finger against my thumb.

Someone's piloting a ship, but I can't tell who it is. All I can see are the legions of Flesher ships flitting past the cockpit windows.

They must be heading to the Parish for the armistice ceremony. But something about their formations doesn't feel right.

Before I can figure it out, the Vulture I'm aboard dives into the hangar bay atop the Citadel and descends to the landing platform. The engines cut out. A group of Imps surrounds me. I clench my fist to disable the opticom. The guards uncuff me from my seat, pull me to my feet, and drag me toward the gangplank.

"There's no need for brutality." Cassius sidles up to me and the Imps retreat. "I'll take it from here."

One of the Imps steps forward, looking uncomfortable. "Sir, are you sure—?"

"I said I can handle him." His words cut like glass. "Let's go." His tone's soft but firm.

Cassius leads me away and into his private lift. It whisks us toward the top of the Citadel's Dome. The doors slide open and we exit onto the observation level, a huge rotunda that overlooks every corner of the Parish.

There are only two Imps standing guard inside.

A figure emerges from the shadows.

Prior Delvecchio.

I smile at him. "It looks like the two of you have gotten pretty cozy. Why am I not surprised?"

The Prior's skull-like face stares at me intently. "Praise the Deity for returning you to us, my son."

"I may be a lot of things, but your son isn't one of them."

I turn to stare out the panoramic windows and activate the opticom.

Cage is sprinting down the underground shaft. The rest of the team's close on his heels. "We're almost there, mates!"

"Get those server room doors open," Arrah calls.

The Worms move into position, entering a series of codes by the panels near the door and swiping an access card in the slot.

For a few seconds, nothing happens.

Then the doors slide partially open, the gap just wide enough for the team to squeeze through.

"We're in." The Worm leader disappears inside and everyone follows.

Drusilla's already removing the computer virus chip from a small case in her satchel. She hands it to one of Worms, who inserts it into a slot on the main frame. Dahlia glances at her holocam. "Let's go people. The attack squadrons are expecting our signal stat."

They hustle to hack into the defense system and plant the virus.

And I can't help but smile.

"Now why don't you spare us all any unpleasantness and provide me with the access codes to the entire Nexus, Queran," Cassius says.

Clenching my fist to cut off the signal, I turn once again to face the two people I want to destroy most in the world. "I'm never going to give up my secrets to any of you. I'll die first. You should both already know that."

Cassius exchanges a smug look with Delvecchio before facing me. "I would have thought that now that Queran was back in play you wouldn't be so naïve."

My confidence buckles. "What do you mean?"

He studies my face. "Just like you had your own spy, my *trusted* Valerian, infiltrate our ranks, what makes you think we didn't have one of our own amongst your allies—oh, excuse me, I meant your *former* allies, in the Resistance?"

As much as I've tried to sever all my physical and emotional ties, my heart still races when I think of him. "Digory?" I whisper. "He's *still* working with you?"

Cassius takes a deep breath, then exhales. "That would be the logical choice. But you know me better than that. When have I ever had only one iron in the fire? I needed someone more closely connected to the rebels and with a little more clout than Tycho to serve my purposes." He grips my shoulder. "Besides, in case you haven't noticed, Tycho is dying. His body's rejecting the nanotech, exactly as it was meant to do, once he was of no further use to me."

Another remaining fragment of Lucian Spark dies at this latest revelation. It's such a tremendous relief being free of the emotional shackles that have bound me all my life. I glance at Delvecchio. "That's exactly how he'll deal with *you* once he doesn't need you any further."

I squeeze my hand closed. The resistance team's feeds reappear. They're still deep in the tunnels.

Cage glances at the Worm busy at work on the keyboard. "How's it coming, Mate?"

The young man turns and smiles. "We're almost in—"

"Too bad." Rios fires his weapon.

The impact sends what's left of the Worm tecchie's head smashing into the monitor. Rios snatches the virus chip from its slot.

"What the hell are you doing, General?" Arrah shoves her weapon directly at him.

Then the entire team's surrounded by a pack of snarling, drooling Canids.

"They'll tear you apart before you can get your first shot out," Rios says.

As if in response, the Canids' growls grow louder, reverberating in my ear piece. The sharp sound of boot heels precedes the appearance of a squad of Imps. They outgun the resistance strike team three to one.

"Throw down your weapons," the lead Imp commands.

Cage, Arra, Dru, Dahlia, and the others exchange glares with the Imps. They toss their weapons to the ground.

Drusilla turns to Rios. "Why are you doing this?"

Rios shakes his head. "My son, Rafé. They said I could be with him again."

"And you bloody believed them?" Cage spits out.

Rios gets right in his face. "If they have the power to bring back a monster like Queran Embers and slip him right under our noses, make us trust him, why couldn't they do the same for my son?" He shakes his head. "The resistance is finished. We never really stood a chance."

"You're the one that's finished, arsehole!" Cage lunges at him.

Rios fires another shot. Cage crashes to the ground.

Dahlia drops to her knees by his side, shielding him with her body. "Leave him alone. He's wounded."

Arrah spits at Rios. "You dishonor Rafe's memory."

Drusilla holds her back. "It's a mercy he isn't around to see how far his father's fallen."

Straightening his uniform's collar, Rios addresses the Imp leader. "I need to speak with Thorn."

The soldier activates his wrist com.

There's a loud bleep a few feet from me.

Cassius grins. "I think I'll put this on screen so you can see the magnitude of the insurrectionists' failure for yourself."

He activates his own wrist com and an image appears on the screens before us, the exact scene I've been monitoring on the opticom's feeds. Cassius smiles at Rios's weary face. "Good work, General."

Rios moves in closer to the transmitter, until his face blocks everything else out. "I've fulfilled my end of the bargain, Thorn. I transmitted the data from Nexus Prime and made it look like it was Spark's doing, as you ordered. The strike team's been neutralized."

"So resourceful. It's a pity I didn't enlist your services before that debacle at Fort Diablos. It would have been a very different outcome."

"When do I get to see my son? You promised I would join him."

Cassius sighs. "And so you shall, General."

The blast echoes through the Citadel's speakers and in my earpiece. The screen's spattered with Rios's skull and brains. Then it goes dark.

Cassius shakes his head. "Poor man. Way too gullible. I guess the love of a parent will do that." He stares at me for a long moment before continuing. "Now that the noble General Rios has betrayed the resistance strike team, the mission to take out our defense main frame is a complete failure. This war is over."

"What happens to the rest of the team?" I ask before I can stop myself.

"Lucian Spark's terrorist friends, Cage Argus, Arrah Creed, Drusilla Ryland, and Dahlia Bledsoe are among our new captives." He emphasizes every syllable of their full names, as if to magnify their import. "Along with the Worm vermin, of course."

My hand balls into a fist, cutting off the feeds. "What are you going to do with the team?"

He exhales. "You need to let go of the past, especially since it's not *your* reality. Forget Lucian Spark and embrace who you truly are. Queran Embers."

"What are you going to do with them?"

Cassius shifts his gaze to the panoramic vista. "They'll be interrogated to see if we can glean any useful information from them before they're publicly executed as traitors to the regime."

Delvecchio steps forward, his hands clasped as if in prayer. "But that's inconsequential compared to the gift their failure has given to us."

I would love to give the good Pryor a little gift of my own, involving my hands and his throat. "What are you talking about?"

Cassius points to the horizon, where the Industrial Borough continues to poison the air with its billowing death clouds. "The resistance fleet is about to realize its horrific blunder."

Delvecchio nods. "An entire battalion of the Flesher abominations is moving in on them as we speak, cutting off any chance of escape."

"While the entirety of the Thorn Republic fleet prepares to attack from *this* side of the Parish's city limits," Cassius adds. "We've known they were coming all along, thanks to Rios."

My eyes grow wide. "The resistance fighters will be overwhelmed by such a massive strike force coming at them from both sides. They'll be wiped out."

Delvecchio opens his arms. "Finally ushering in an era of absolute peace and order."

"With no one to oppose either of you." My voice sounds hoarse.

Cassius moves in close. "Of course, if you allow yourself to shed your Lucian Spark persona, once and for all, and become Queran Embers, you can tell me what I need to know and I may yet be able to arrange amnesty for your misguided friends. They'll have to remain under supervision, of course, but at least they'll live. Think of it as your last act of mercy to them as Lucian Spark. As always, the choice is yours."

My mind's a tumult. If I allow myself to completely embody the essence of Queran Embers, my captured friends might survive. But I'll condemn possibly hundreds of thousands of dormant survivors in the Nexus to their deaths by providing Cassius and Delvecchio with the launch codes.

If I refuse Cass's proposal, my friends will certainly die, as will the entire resistance, destroying any chance of anyone challenging his reign of blood.

I'm damned either way. All the choices I made in the Trials seem like a drop of water in a vast ocean of impossible decisions.

"Perhaps a taste of what's at stake will help your thought process reach the appropriate conclusion." Cassius activates his com unit. "Transmit the resistance all clear signal and begin the attack."

My fist activates the opticom unit once again. This time I select Corin's channel.

He's staring at the cockpit monitor display, which blinks green. "The strike team's successfully compromised the entire Thorn fleet's nav systems. Their ships are defenseless. Repeat. Their ships are defenseless."

"All craft move in." Croakley's voice commands through the cockpit's speakers.

Corin lets out a loud *whoop*. He soars through the skies with the rest of the fleet and into Parish airspace. "Closing in on main targets." Flipping a few switches on his console, Corin stares at the readouts. "Something's not right. Scans show we have enemy ships on a direct intercept course."

Dozens of Vulture and Squawker squadrons are now visible through Corin's cockpit, zigzagging across the sky, spewing bursts of gunfire at the approaching resistance forces. A ship erupts in a ball of fire just outside Corin's. He veers sharply to escape its path. His console sparks and the craft rocks violently. "I've been clipped, but still in one piece."

Corin soars over an oncoming Squawker, narrowly avoiding a barrage of gunfire. Then he dives under the enemy ship, inverting his own craft in a dizzying maneuver. He blasts the Squawker out of the sky with his rear gun turrets, before spinning away toward the Parish's city limits.

But he realizes something an instant later that I already know.

Flesher ships break through the clouds, launching their own attack.

"Sanctum fleet's blocking our retreat," Corin yells into his mic. "This whole thing's one mother of an ambush!"

All around him, ships explode, from ammo bursts and collisions, creating a hellish sky that rains fireballs and debris onto the city.

"—no....chance....escape..." Croakley's com transmission is overpowered by static and explosions.

Cassius grips my shoulder. "It appears the rebellion is officially over."

CHAPTER TWENTY-EIGHT

"If we're going to go out," Corin barks into his mic, "we may as well take as many of them with us as we can."

Cheers and shouts of agreement overwhelm the cockpit speakers. Corin joins the other ships, trading firepower with the Thorn and Flesher fleets.

Tuning out the opticom, I glance out the observation decks' viewscreens. From this vantage point, the swarms of ships outside look like they're engaged in an elegant, fiery dance of deadly beauty, their contrails and blasts painting the sky in a brilliant fireworks display.

Cassius notices me staring. "It's only a matter of time before the resistance ships are wiped out. You still have the chance to save some lives. Just tell me what I wish to know, and it will all be over."

A huge burst fills the expanse of glass separating us from the carnage outside. The sight is all too familiar. As Queran, I remember watching my forces decimate all those others, desperately trying to steal our provisions. How dare they raid my stockpiles? That's what the lazy and the weak do. Live off the hard work of others, parasites leeching off the system, draining the resources of those more important, more worthy—

I force myself to look away from the destruction. If I give in and become Queran, what's happening outside will be nothing but a minor skirmish compared with what I'll be capable of. The thought fills me with such satisfaction that it terrifies me at the same time.

A fresh feeling of serenity and resolve fills me. "No," I say at last. "I won't give you the codes."

Cass's face is weary. "In your obsession to remain Lucian Spark, you don't realize how much your stubbornness is an intricate part of Queran Embers."

I allow myself the luxury of a grin. "Then you know that trying to change my mind is an exercise in futility. Just the idea of watching you squirm is motivation enough to remain silent."

He shakes his head. "Fight it as much as you'd like, but you *are* Queran—with one critical flaw."

"And what might that be?"

"Queran was wise enough to realize that personal attachments can have an extremely detrimental effect on one's judgment. He purged himself of that liability. Of all people, I should know." He sighs. "Unfortunately for you, that's a lesson you haven't mastered yet." Cassius waves an arm toward the aerial attack. "The ambush of your resistance fleet, while satisfying on a strategic level, is a tad too abstract to obtain the results I was hoping for."

My eyes flit to my glove. If he only knew just how close I was to what was going on he'd realize just how much he's underestimated my determination.

"I think it's time we made the *incentives* a little more personal, just like the good old days." He activates his com unit. "Escort the prisoners that were apprehended in the main frame attack to Town Square for immediate public execution."

Every muscle in my body tenses. I try not to give Cassius the satisfaction of betraying the torrential storm of emotions flooding my gut. I hold his gaze, even as I activate the opticom, staring past him at the feeds belonging to the strike team. At first, I glimpse nothing but darkness.

Did the Imps discover the opticom units and confiscate them?

The image flickers. Cage, Arrah, Dru, and Dahlia are bunched together in a transport vehicle, along with the surviving Worms. I try hard not to cringe at the sight of their bloodied and swollen faces. Looks like the Thorn Agents haven't wasted any time interrogating them.

Dahlia readjusts the makeshift bandage around Cage's arm. It looks like its sopping with dark wetness. "How're you holding up, soldier?"

Cage's smile seems like a real effort. "Not too bad, considering I think I've lost a few pints of blood." He grimaces as she tightens the bandage. "Speaking of pints, what's say you and me grab a pint of Wanderer's Brew after this party's over?"

Dahlia focuses her attention on his bandage. "You asking me on a date?"

His eyes squeeze shut. "Timing's not ideal, I know, but I figured I'd play the 'go out with the poor bloke before he carks it' card while I still had the chance."

"I'm not sure about a cark, but I'm going to shove a cork in your mouth if you don't stop talking like that," Drusilla chimes in. "We're all going to get through this."

Arrah squeezes her hand. "I love you, Dru."

Drusilla shakes her. "Don't. Not now. I can't…" She buries her face against Arrah's shoulder.

The transport grinds to a stop.

"It's main event time," a burly Imp snorts.

They're all dragged off the craft, through the huddled masses gathered in Town Square, and shoved toward the dais where so many recruits were condemned to the Trials.

Explosions and whirring ships rock the skies, eliciting gasps and a hubbub of whispering voices from the throng of spectators. It's obvious many of them have either been dragged from their homes or have rushed here in a panic over the aerial engagement thundering above.

In the observation deck, one section of the glass window glows, projecting a holographic feed from the Town Square cameras. It provides a wide angle view of the chaotic scene in glorious detail.

Cage, Dahlia, Arrah, Dru, and the Worm team look like they can barely stand. They're held at gunpoint in front of the anxious crowd.

In the observation deck, Cassius steps away and into the spotlight of a hovering holocam. His live image is projected onto the dais next to the captives and on every single jumbotron surrounding the packed square.

"Greetings, citizens of the Thorn Republic," he begins his address. "It is regrettable that on this day where we have gathered to commemorate the Armistice between our nation and the inhabitants of Sanctum, the insurrectionists have chosen this opportunity to wage war, in their final, futile attempt to disrupt order."

A wave of hushed murmuring passes through the crowd.

Cassius silences the disruption with a wave of his finger. "I stand before you all now to assure you that there is no need to panic. Even as we gather here, the terrorist attack has been thwarted, and the new alliance forged between our republic and Sanctum is working together to vanquish the plague of rebellion amongst us once and for all."

If Cassius expected cheers he couldn't have been more wrong. Instead, the multitude remains silent. The only sounds are the blasts from the air strikes, booming like a breaking storm.

After the uncomfortable silence, Cassius resumes his diatribe. "Standing before you are the latest prisoners of war, caught trying to infiltrate our great city's defenses, which, if successful, would have rendered our forces vulnerable to destruction."

Despite their condition, Cage and the others hold their heads high.

Even with one eye swollen shut, Cage manages a quip through blood-crusted lips. "It's all right. You can hold the applause. Save it for when you stop being cowards and stand up to these monsters and show them you bloody matter—each and every one of you."

I feel a stabbing pain in my gut, a dark premonition. Cage is trying to expedite his execution, go out on his terms in the hopes of sparking a reaction from the frightened throng.

Reflexively, I activate the more intimate feeds of the opticom.

The Imp nearest Cage shoves him to the ground and aims his gun right at Cage's head. Cage closes his eyes and smiles.

"No!" Dahlia pushes Cage out of the way.

The blast rings out, echoing through Town Square.

Reeling from that terrible sound, I brace myself against the nearest column.

Someone—Arrah or Drusilla, I can't be sure—cries out.

Cage grips Dahlia close, his eyes wide and wet. "Why'd you go and do that for?" he whispers. "I had everything under control."

Blood's streaming from a gaping wound in Dahlia's chest. "It's…not… so bad," her voice is little more than a gurgle, "besides…couldn't let you… show…me…up…," she grips his shoulder and looks up at the sky. More ships fly by, firing at each other. "…shooting…stars," her eyes glaze over. Her head slumps into Cage's shoulder, still at last.

I have no tears. Only rage. After all Mrs. Bledsoe did for Cole and me, I failed her and her daughter.

No. Lucian Spark failed them both. He's too weak.

Cage lifts Dahlia's head and strokes her cheek. He presses his quivering lips against hers. "See you real soon."

"Sooner than you think," the lead Imp snarls, hauling Cage to his feet.

Arrah and Dru rip free of their captors and position themselves in front of Cage, forming a human shield.

"You'll have to go through us first," Arrah hisses.

"My pleasure," the Imp aims the muzzle of his gun straight at her forehead.

I lunge forward. "Cassius."

"Hold your fire and await my command," Cassius says into his com, cutting off his transmission.

The glow from the holo bathes Cassius's silhouette in a sickly, amber light. "I know this is a difficult decision for Lucian Spark to make, but you're only delaying the inevitable. The more you resist, the more pain you're forcing yourself to endure, and the lives of your friends become expendable. You can end it all right now by letting go and telling me what I need to know. I'll give you a few minutes to think it over, before resuming the executions."

Turning away from him, I scramble to distance myself from that scene, I need to escape it, whether from guilt or indifference, I'm not sure anymore.

Instead, I find myself accessing Corin's opticom feed. I'm immediately thrust into the adrenaline rush of the aerial raid. The view beyond the cockpit's window is a dizzying array of rolls, spins, and explosions.

"—losing too many ships!" a fellow pilot's voice crackles through Corin's console speakers.

"Stay in formation!" Corin shouts. "We just need to keep them busy a little longer until Cage's strike team can take their systems offline—"

I bite into my lower lip. He has no idea what's happened. None of them do.

Another series of explosions strike all around Corin's ship.

"—not going to hold out much longer—" Croakley's voice.

One of the Flesher vessels is on a collision course with Corin's ship, while the monitors show a Thorn ship approaching Corin from behind, weapons blazing.

Corin adjusts his controls. His ship does a three hundred and sixty degree spin, avoiding blasts from both ships, and then suddenly dives, leaving the Flesher vessel to fire and obliterate the Squawker.

Corin lets out a victorious yelp, but it's short lived. A blast from another ship sends his craft into a tail spin. "I've been hit." Warning sirens blare through the cockpit. Emergency lights flash. "I'm going down."

The view outside the cockpit is nothing but black smoke.

Swallowing the bile burning my throat, I quickly switch the feed.

I'm looking through the cockpit of another ship. From the pulsating, organic matter surrounding the interior, it's definitely a Flesher vessel. But why would a Flesher be utilizing opticom tech?

Swerving from the raging battle, the ship's pilot guides it into the hangar bay of a much larger vessel that I've never seen before. The entire docking area is alive with thick, undulating membranes. These spread out web-like from support struts hewn from bone, and wrap around control consoles, feeding them energy in the form of vein-like cables and dark fluids.

Fleshers glide about, some on legs, while others dart on wheeled extremities and tentacular appendages. I recognize a few of them. The four Hive members who are all that remain of the Fallen Five recruits. They stand majestically, taking in the carnage of the aerial battle displayed on the bridge.

Every single Flesher stops what they're doing and turns in unison to stare at the new arrival wearing the opticom unit.

There's only one being that can be commanding their attention like this, and even before I see his face reflected on the metallic chest plate of the Flesher he faces, I know that it's Digory Tycho, come home at last.

Digory's face looks completely emotionless once again. It's as if all the experiences we shared since I broke him out of the brig and we arrived at Nexus Prime have been wiped clean. Maybe he's already undergone some type of upgrade and embraced the machine side of him completely.

He communicates with the other Hive members in silence, then turns to the nearest, glowing console and presses his fingers into the film of gook covering it. The substance pulsates and shimmers. I can really see his face now, His eyes are rolled back into his head, exposing nothing but white. Any semblance of humanity he had left has been completely stripped away as he communes with this living vessel.

The screen to the right of the console comes to life. It's my eyes that open wide now. I can't understand the readouts, but from the display, it's clear that this ship is spooling up every single one of its power reserves, heading on a collision course with the main resistance carrier, the Lady Liberty. The impact will be disastrous and will cripple the Torch Brigade, leaving survivors to be picked off by the Thorn ships like pesky flies.

Fury and despair tear at my insides. I clench my fists, not caring that the feeds are cut off. None of it matters anymore.

"Well, my son?" Delvecchio asks. "Have you made your decision?"

The pain in my head's excruciating. I wipe away more hot blood from my nose, smearing my bloodied hand against my chest. Cage, Arrah, and Dru will be slaughtered, just like Dahlia was, with no chance of completing their mission and taking the Republic systems off line. Corin's probably already dead, another casualty of this senseless war, waiting in vain for a reprieve that will never come.

And Digory's about to wipe out what's left of humanity's only hope against the machinations of Cassius and Delvecchio, effectively ending my brother's life. I feel more weary than I ever have in my entire life. Maybe Digory has the right idea. He's embraced who he truly is at last. Maybe there's a peace there.

I look up at Delvecchio, then turn to Cassius, staring deeply into those venomous green eyes, seeing more clearly now than I ever have before.

"I've made my decision," I say. "If you want Queran Embers, you shall have him."

CHAPTER TWENTY-NINE

A look of relief washes over Cassius's face. "You're finally being reasonable."

I shake my head. "You misunderstand. I'll embrace being Queran. And speaking for him, the answer is *no*. You will never take what belongs to me."

Cassius doesn't seem surprised. He activates his com. "This is how it's done, Queran."

The fury inside me ignites to a blaze.

"Execute the prisoners," Cassius orders. "Beginning with the Worms."

There's a barrage of gunfire, and the Worms collapse in a bloody heap.

I lunge for Cassius, but the two guards intercept me, pulling me away.

On the holo, the Imps grab Cage, Arrah and Drusilla, shoving their weapons against the prisoners' temples.

Before they can fire, a roaring sound fills the square. It sounds like a ship's about to crash into the crowd.

Except it's not. The sound's coming from the spectators themselves.

En masse, the onlookers fling themselves onto the dais. Male and female, old and young, they pull each other up by their arms, legs, even hair, tumbling onto the platform like an oncoming human tide, with the surprised Imps caught in the surge. The mob rushes the Imps, who push the prisoners aside and begin firing.

"Stay the hell back," the lead Imp shouts. He blasts several people in his path, including a boy no older than fourteen or fifteen, who collapses from the dais with a large, smoking hole in his chest.

The crowd holds back for a moment, then pounces on the soldiers, clawing, biting, ripping through anything in their path. Hundreds of them, factory workers, teachers, farmers, medtechs, children, grab the guards, tearing them apart, united at last in vengeance and blood lust against their oppressors. More shots ring out as reinforcements arrive, but they're vastly outnumbered. The screens fill with images of tangled limbs, blood spatters, cries of anguish and rage, even as the pandemonium continues in the skies above them.

While Cassius and the guards stare in awe at the chaotic scene, I activate the opticom. "This way. C'mon!" Arrah shoves an Imp out of her way.

She and Drusilla each have one of Cage's arms wrapped around their shoulders. They haul him away from the scene and into an alley.

"It's no use," Cage mutters. "Without the virus we can't take out the defense main frame."

Dru shakes her head. "Give me some credit. You don't think I made a copy of the virus?"

An Imp grabs for her. She kicks him in the gut and seizes his weapon, using it to shoot a few more of his comrades, who collapse at her feet.

"That's my girl." Arrah grabs two of the weapons, tossing one to Cage.

"We've got to get back to the server," he grumbles. "I know a short cut." He pauses for a moment, glancing back at the rioting behind them. "Dahlia…"

Drusilla slaps him on the back. "We can't go back. But we can go forward and carry out the mission for *her.*"

He wipes his eyes and leads the way through the backstreets.

Explosions strike all around them, sending concrete and stone raining through the air.

I can barely make out their images through the clouds of black smoke and dust obscuring everything.

What I can see fills me with conflicting emotions. Bloodlust, hope— and dread.

As Cage, Arrah, and Drusilla battle their way back to the main frame, I catch vivid glimpses of the carnage surrounding them. It's as if I'm right there with them, dodging falling debris, ducking out of range of ear-piercing weapons blasts, trading shots with Republic agents.

For the first time ever, the citizens of the Parish have come alive as a cohesive unit. Gone are the looks of fear, the numb expressions created by years of repression, intimidation, and torture. Instead, their eyes are wide with primal energy, their teeth bared like animals defending their territory and fighting for survival. Young and old, women and children— they charge the enemies with stolen weapons, makeshift spears, home-made grenades. After a lifetime of being ground under the heavy boots of the Establishment, only to find themselves under the choke hold of Cassius Thorn and the sadistic religious doctrine of Delvecchio, they've finally reached their breaking point and decided to strike back against their oppressors, regardless if it costs each and every one of them their miserable lives.

"We're almost there." Cage leads the trio down another alley. He swears at the burning wreckage of a neighborhood tenement blocking their path.

A weapon's blast strikes the concrete wall, inches from Arrah's head. "There must be another way around."

"Looks like we've got company." Drusilla opens fire on an approach-ing squad of Imps.

She's joined by Cage and Arrah. The three of them take cover behind one of the ruined concrete slabs obstructing their retreat.

"We can't afford to be wasting so much time," Arrah takes out two of the Imps with her pulsator, but five more take their place.

Cage fires round after round, taking out maybe a dozen of the agents, but they keep coming. There's an unmistakable sound of a sharp *click*. "That's it. I'm out, mates," he mutters.

"That makes two of us." Drusilla tosses her spent cartridge behind her.

"I don't know about you two, but I'd rather not be taken alive." Cage punctuates his words by spitting out a wad of blood.

Arrah holds up a small, black, oval device. "My last grenade."

The three of them share a solemn look.

Cage nods. "Make it count."

The Imps must have figured out they're out of ammo. In unison, they rush in for the kill. Arrah turns to Dru, tears in her eyes.

They pull each other close, sharing a deep kiss. "I love you, Dru. I always will."

Drusilla smiles at her, wiping her cheeks. "Love you, too. My girl til the end."

When she pulls away, Drusilla's clutching the glistening grenade instead. She tosses Cage the virus chip.

Arrah's eyes are stark. "What are you—?"

Dru pushes away from her. "Carry out the mission. I've got this."

Before Arrah and Cage can stop her, Dru sprints toward the oncoming squad and leaps.

The agents fire. Arrah's agonized shriek carves right through me. Drusilla's body is riddled with bullets, spraying arcs of blood into the hazy air. A defeaning blast engulfs Drusilla and the squad. Clumps of flesh, bone, and blood spatter the alleyway.

For a few moments, the feed cuts out, replaced by static.

First Dahlia. Now Drusilla. How many more of the people I called friends will be gone when this is all over? And what makes it worse is that I'm too numb to feel anything anymore. Or maybe it's just that I don't care? That I never really did?

The world of Queran Embers is a much less complicated place to live in than Lucian Spark's, filled with a lifetime of pain and loss. At least in Queran's there are no delusions of morality, masked by meaningless attachments. Simple. Efficient.

When the feeds return, Cage is practically dragging Arrah away from the scene.

"Get your damn hands off me!" She punches him repeatedly, but he won't go.

"I know what you're feeling," he says. "But if we don't go now she'll have bloody died in vain."

She tries to bite him, but he backhands her. "Get a grip. She's gone. We've got a job to do, Soldier."

Arrah takes another look at the grisly scene and nods.

Cage gives her a fierce hug. They push away and take advantage of the reprieve they've been given, staggering away from what's left of the bodies, into the alleyway and down another side street, picking up speed as they go. Along the way, they stoop to scoop up weapons and supplies from the bodies strewn about.

"Such a waste." Cassius's voice brings me back to the Citadel's observation tower. He's studying the screens. Each one is broadcasting scenes of republic agents trying to contain the relentless mob. "Useless bloodshed. The end result will be the same." His gaze wanders over to me. "I underestimated you. You could have avoided all this bloodshed. But you're already too much like Queran Embers to care."

I shut the opticom's feeds off. "No matter what I would have told you or not, Cassius, the end result would be the same."

Cassius doesn't seem to appreciate my sense of irony. "Maybe when Fortune's River flows red with the blood of all your friends you'll be persuaded to see reason at last."

He taps his com unit. "Forget trying to round up any prisoners. No need to ask any questions. Shoot any citizen violating curfew on sight."

As if the Imps needed any more encouragement.

The view of Town Square on the holos is one of total devastation. Bloodied bodies are scattered everywhere, military and civilian alike. The dais is a crimson stream dripping rivulets of darkness into the now wet cobblestone. Outstretched limbs reach out from under toppled pillars. Others lie contorted into unnatural shapes, trampled under the weight of the furious stampede.

Judging from the views on most of the still working monitors, the rest of the Parish is faring much worse.

Cassius's usual calm has developed a noticeable chink. As he checks in with his people for status reports, he grows visibly shaken.

"Say again?" He barks into his com.

"—plant workers have commandeered… we're under attack—" the voice on the other end is drowned out by an explosion, replaced by the steady crackle of static.

It makes no difference that the connection's been lost. From our vantage point high above the Parish, we feel the vibration of the blast. The smoke stacks of the Industrial Borough erupt into a fiery vortex. The western most stack lurches into the next one, which careens into the next, and so on, creating a domino effect of roaring flames and dark, billowing destruction.

"We need reinforcements!" Another Imp cries.

From the holos, it appears she's stationed at the water treatment facility. Gunfire and screams fill the speakers. The troops stationed at the plant continually fire their weapons, taking down countless civilians. But they're vastly outnumbered.

"—lost control of the center—" her head dissolves in a violent explosion.

That's when the tanks explode, releasing rampaging water through the entire complex. The flood engulfs the Imps and workers alike, sweeping them away in a sea of screams.

The holo cuts off.

Cassius bows his head.

"What's the matter?" I ask. "Seems like you underestimated the effects of your new order. People would rather die than live in your brave, new world, Cassius."

He ignores me, instead concentrating on filtering through updates from his underlings.

Seizing the opportunity of his distraction, I once again activate the opticom, hesitant to see what's happened to the others, but unable to resist at the same time.

I'm surprised and relieved to find that Corin's feed is still active.

Somehow, he's managed to set his damaged ship down on the hull of a Vulture.

He's toggling the switches of his communicator, obviously searching for a working channel. "Lady Liberty, do you copy?"

His only response is a stream of static. The craft's close proximity to the Vulture must be jamming his com unit.

"If anyone can read me," Corin continues, "my ship's guidance systems have been damaged. I'm not going to be able to fly this thing."

He continues to try and hail the Resistance, even as the Vulture he's hitched a ride on changes course.

Through Corin's cockpit, I catch a bird's eye view of the once opulent homes of the elite on the port side, now engulfed in flames. Throngs of civilians storm through the gates, engaging the stationed troops at point blank range.

On the starboard side, the harbor's ablaze with burning ships and smoking, collapsed docks.

There's another pop of static. Croakley's voice comes through Corin's cockpit speakers. "This is the Lady Liberty. We read you, Corin. Our ship's weapon systems have been damaged. We're waiting for reinforcements until we can get the systems back on line. But there's a Vulture craft approaching. Scans show its forward batteries are spooling up. We're running out of time."

I can see the Liberty now, outside the Citadel's windows.

And the Vulture rushing to destroy it.

"Corin, is that you?" Cole's voice crackles through the coms.

"Affirmative, Little Man," Corin replies. "You onboard the Liberty?"

"Yes. Do you know what's happened to my brother?"

Corin's voice drops. He realizes exactly what I do. "That's a negative. Just hold on. We're on our way." He flicks off the com.

My blood freezes. I can't breathe.

Cole, along with Croakley and the entirety of Lady Liberty's crew, are seconds away from death.

CHAPTER THIRTY

I try to pull away from the guards, but their grip's too tight. "Cassius. Please. Don't fire on that ship."

He turns to me, eyes narrowed. "Where's your cockiness now, Queran? Why should I spare that vessel?"

"I'll tell you what you want to know."

Cassius shakes his head. "I'm not sure what's so special about that ship. But if it's something that you want so desperately, then destroying it might just be the final impetus you need to shed your pitiful former existence once and for all."

He jams a finger onto his com system. "Fire at will."

The Vulture's shadow falls over the Lady Liberty.

"I swear I'm going to destroy you." My voice is eerily calm, even though I'm dying inside.

On the opticom's feeds, Croakley sends out another transmission through Corin's cockpit speakers. "This is the Lady Liberty. We can't hold them off. It's been an honor and a privilege serving with you all."

Corin flicks the switch on his transmitter. "Lady Liberty hang on. I have an idea."

"Targeting the Lady Liberty now," the Vulture commander relays through Cassius's com.

My heart's about to burst through my rib cage.

Corin's activating his ship's remaining missiles—

"Our target is locked," the Commander announces. "Firing in three… two…"

Corin jams his finger against the firing button and hits the eject mechanism.

The Vulture detonates, splitting into two pieces, spewing its crew into the sky in a brilliant display of blazing sparks. The forward section of the craft nosedives right into a squadron of Squawkers, disintegrating them all.

Cassius slumps against the console, shock, confusion, and anger warring on his face.

I'm finally able to breathe again. "Looks like this just isn't your day, Cassius."

He whirls on me. "You really think your friends have a chance? You should know that I always have a back-up plan."

Before I can ask, Cassius punches in a new channel on the holocam. The three dimensional image of a familiar ship's bridge appears in the air between us.

It's the Flesher's Hive ship.

Digory's standing still, face unreadable, eyes unblinking. Flanking him, two on either side, are the four original Fleshers.

"Initiate the next phase of the attack sequence." Cassius announces quite casually.

Next phase? What the hell? Cassius has been conspiring with the Hive behind Straton's back all this time. Not surprising. But Digory never told me a thing. Here I was feeling sorry for him, deluding myself I could reach him. He's been playing me this whole time.

What tears at my gut the most is the way Digory just stands there and nods. If he sees me, he doesn't acknowledge my presence in the slightest. "Commencing deployment stat." His fingers glide over the console, dipping into the ship's biofluid. The panel in front of him pulsates rapidly.

I step closer to the projection so I'm face to face with Digory's image. "So it was all a lie, wasn't it?"

Finally, his empty eyes make contact with my own. "I am only doing what needs to be done."

His words strike a chord deep within me. I remember saying the exact same thing another lifetime ago to justify—

My head throbs. I can't completely block out the sounds and images: piercing screams, crowds of panicked people, a blinding mushroom cloud obliterating everything—

As angry and hurt as I am by Digory, I empathize with his position completely. A soothing calm overtakes me.

I would do the same thing. I *have*. But every action has a counteraction. *I am only doing what needs to be done.*

"One day I'll be saying those words to you, Digory." I turn away, unable to bear the sight of him at that moment.

Or is it just the part of me I see reflected in him that I can't stand to look at?

Cassius points toward the three-dimensional images displaying the different sectors of the Parish. "Time to quell this futile uprising once and for all."

All around the city, the sewer grates explode, adding to the storm of debris and shrapnel from the aerial and ground assaults. Dark plumes ooze from the newly created openings.

And something else.

Large silhouettes appear through the billowing smoke, dark, twisting shadows, buzzing and whirring with bright glowing lights.

Fleshers. Legions of them pouring into the Parish streets like nightmares unleashed.

A smug look creeps across Cassius's face. "The civilians won't stand a chance against their firepower."

My eyes are glued to the holos. Imps and civvies alike cower and crawl from these monstrosities of flesh and steel. "What about your own troops? Don't you care?"

He sighs. "That's what I've been trying to tell you all along. None of that matters anymore. Only the endgame."

New skirmishes break out all across the city and around its perimeter. Imps turn from the civvies and open fire on the invading horde instead. But most of their blasts make little impact on the Fleshers' exoskeletons.

Cassius's eyes are riveted on the holos, glowing eerily in their light. "It will all be over soon."

Once again, I squeeze my fist closed and press my fingers against my thumb to activate the opticom feeds.

Cage and Arrah huddle behind the mangled hull of a downed Squawker, engaged in a firefight with a couple of Imps guarding the relay station. The aerial bombardment continues around them, blowing chunks from the pavement and surrounding buildings, leaving nothing but smoking husks.

Arrah's eyes scan the skies. "Our people can't hold out much longer."

Cage's response is a blast of his pulsator, which takes out one of the Imps. "Looks like the odds just got a little better."

"Let's rush him." Arrah's about to spring, when Cage grabs her.

A squad of Imps appears from behind them, brandishing their weapons and preparing to fire.

"At least we tried." Cage grabs Arrah's hand.

Before the Imps can shoot, a group of civvies leaps from the roof of a dilapidated building, ambushing them.

Arrah covers Cage with blasts from her pulsator, while he dashes toward the relay station.

"Entering the initiation codes now." Cage's fingers work the keypad.

A cloak of darkness eclipses the light behind them. They both whirl to find a battalion of Fleshers surrounding them.

They don't even have time to surrender. The Fleshers fire their weapons.

The image flickers and dies.

Blinking the stinging wetness from my eyes, I jam another finger into my thumb and switch to Corin's feeds.

He's tangled in the remnants of his glider, working to pull himself from a pile of rubble. His hands are scratched and bloodied from clawing at the wreckage. That's the least of his worries, though.

A swarm of Fleshers trundles toward his location, firing at everything moving in its path.

One of the Fleshers' treads runs right over a civilian holding up his hands in surrender, cleaving him neatly in half. The unfortunate victim's guts spill from his severed midsection. The Flesher rolls on, its tracks leaving a bloody, grisly trail to mark its passing.

The Fleshers are almost on top of him. Corin manages to yank himself free. He plays dead, panicked breaths hissing loud and fast in my earpiece.

As soon as the Flesher pack moves past, Corin springs to his feet and scrambles over and around mounds of bodies and debris. He's dashing toward a spherical pod, half-buried in the rubble, surrounded by tangled, lifeless limbs.

It's an escape pod. I recognize the markings of the Lady Liberty. My pulse pistons.

No sooner does Corin reach the pod than Cole's face appears in the porthole.

Corin tugs at the latch but the pod's hatch remains sealed. "Don't worry. I'm gonna get you out of there." He glances behind him. More Fleshers rumble through the streets, firing at anything moving.

A group of Imps runs by, ignoring Corin and the escape pod as they trade blasts with the encroaching Fleshers.

After several more attempts to pry open the pod's jammed hatch, Corin pulls out a small, silver, spherical device from his pack and turns back to the porthole.

"Listen up, Cole. I want you to move as far back as you can and lie on your stomach with your hands over your head."

My chest and gut feel like they're in an ever-tightening vise.

Cole nods and mouths "okay" through the glass before he disappears from the window.

Corin wastes no time attaching the explosive charge to the pod's door. When he turns around again, he lets out a small gasp. The entire area's crawling with Fleshers. The somber expression on his face tells me he's probably thinking the same thing I am. Even if he manages to set Cole free, the odds of the two of them making it out of there alive are infinitesimal.

Grotesque shadows engulf Corin and the pod. I manage to catch glimpses of Fleshers raising their appendages, ships roaring by above, and Corin's panicked face reflected in the porthole.

Another blast erupts on the feeds, completely obscuring the image. There's a burst of static. The entire image cuts to black. My sweaty fingers try to adjust the device, bring the feed back. Nothing. It's useless.

I slump in my captors' grasp. They're all gone. Dahlia, Drusilla, Cage, Arrah, Corin.

And now my brother, Cole.

Something snaps inside of me. Cassius was right. Cole was my anchor, the last and most important link tethering me to the mundane and pathetic existence of Lucian Spark. The intense pain of this loss splinters what's left of the dam in my brain holding Queran Embers at bay. All that hurt, all that rage bursts through, filling every vein, every cell with an overwhelming desire for vengeance.

And the two foremost targets of my wrath are clearly visible to me now, despite the haze in my head and the burning tears streaming down my face.

That thing that was Digory Tycho stares right at me through the holo. Blood's trickling from its nostrils and its lips, but it doesn't appear too concerned, continuing to integrate its systems with that of the Flesher Hive.

I was so wrong to ever think I could reach this soulless machine. Digory died long ago back in Sanctum. Hell even before that. During the Trials. What came back was an obscene creation, wearing the remnants of his body in an effort to cause me pain and keep me off balance. My feelings for Digory don't matter anymore. They've been nothing but a liability to me, and it's freeing to finally let go.

Many more lives will be lost today because of this abomination.

Lives that could otherwise serve the greater good.

Lives that could otherwise serve me.

Which brings me to the one person who I'll take the most pleasure in destroying.

Cassius Thorn.

Everything about him since the first day we met has been a complete lie. There was a time that I trusted him more than anyone in the entire world. But he turned on me, just like they all do, eventually. Because of him and everything he's done, all my plans are in jeopardy. My vision for a new society has been compromised. And that's something that I simply can't tolerate. There's a price to pay for defying me, and Cassius has earned retribution ten fold.

"You've done an excellent job," he says to the Tycho thing now. "The republic agents and citizens alike never saw it coming. It's time to move on to the next stage of our enterprise. Have your forces finish their sweep and mop up the last of the insurrection."

"Initiating final sequence now," the Tycho thing's voice is more emotionless than ever.

Cassius turns to me, his eyes oozing with satisfaction. "And so it is done. By the time the Hive completes its sweep, there will be nothing left to oppose me. Except of course, you."

"It always does seem to come down to you and me, doesn't it?"

He moves in closer to me. "We may not be the same people we once were, but there's no reason why we cannot work together to resolve this pointless conflict and forge a new and better future."

"I prefer my independence."

The guards aren't ready for my attack. Yanking one of my arms free, I grab the other's side arm, shoot one, and then the other. They both collapse at my feet.

Cassius goes for his own weapon, but I jam the barrel of my gun into his forehead.

"Don't even try. Drop your weapon and kick it across the room."

He follows my orders, letting go of his gun and sending it spinning across the room with the toe of his boot. "This is all such a waste. If you kill me, you'll never leave this place alive. Think about what you're doing."

A chuckle escapes me. "Oh, I've had plenty of time to consider my options, Cassius, and unfortunately, none of them include forging an alliance with the likes of you. Unfortunately, for you, that is."

Something cold presses against my neck.

"I suggest you drop your weapon at once and release him, my son."

I'd never forget the terrible timbre of that voice.

Prior Delvecchio.

"What's to stop me from shooting Thorn before you shoot me?" I ask.

"Nothing," Delvecchio responds, "except for your admirable sense of self-preservation. Once Thorn is disposed of, your bargaining abilities will be greatly diminished. Observe."

The cold steel lifts from my neck.

There's a blast which nearly blows out my eardrums.

Cassius's eyes open wide. Then he collapses onto the floor.

If there's anyone more surprised at Delvecchio's actions than I am, it's Cassius.

Despite the trickle of blood spurting from the wound in his arm, his eyes are narrowed into slits. He slides his body backwards until it's pressed against one of the marble columns. "You'll pay for this, old man," he hisses through clenched teeth.

My eyes pivot from Cassius to Delvecchio. "I can't say I'm completely surprised. I always knew you two would turn on each other. I just didn't think it would happen so soon." I nod at Delvecchio's still raised weapon. "What are you waiting for? I'm sure you've been anticipating this moment for quite some time. Go ahead. Take another life for your bloodthirsty deity."

Delvecchio releases a drawn out breath. "My poor, ignorant child. You still do not realize your significance in all of this." He waves his arms, encompassing the entire Parish in this gesture. "Today marks the culmination of years of hard work in service to our almighty Deity."

Cassius and I exchange glances. It's obvious that for once, he isn't quite sure what's going on. His usual cool, confident arrogance has been replaced by confusion and anxiety. Slowly, he braces against the pillar and pulls himself to his feet.

I turn back to the Prior. "Perhaps you should enlighten us as to your deity's divine intentions. After all, neither Cassius nor I are what you'd call the spiritual types."

Delvecchio's smile would chill the frost off a snowflake. "It was no coincidence I chose Calliope Spark as the vessel to deliver the Holy progeny."

Calliope Spark. That name rattles my core. She was my mother. Lucian Spark's mother. No. She only carried him. Me. Why is everything so foggy? "Don't ever mention my mother's name again."

"Of course," Delvecchio continues, seemingly oblivious to my request, "it wasn't completely my decision. The hand of the deity guided mine in making the selection and fulfilling His will." His reptilian eyes focus on me now. "She was such a beautiful creature, you know. Even as a child, before she blossomed into womanhood." His eyes grow dark as another memory slithers through that sickened mind. "Of course, had she not saddled herself with the undeserving filth that was Lazaro Spark, she could have avoided all that suffering and lived a much different life."

Lazaro. My father. Memories of both my former parents chisel their way through the ice enveloping me, one painful blow after another. I squeeze my eyes shut, straining to will them out of my brain, my heart.

Let go. There's nothing you can do now. They're both gone.

As is my little—

My eyes spring open and glare. I take a step closer to Delvecchio, heedless of the gun still clutched in his long, bony fingers. "The next time your filthy lips utter anyone in my family's name you die."

Delvecchio shakes his head. "Don't you understand? They were never really your family."

"I'm warning you, shaman," I spit, relishing the welcome feel of the fury boiling in my veins.

"I'd listen to him, Delvecchio," Cassius chimes in. "We both know what he's capable of."

Delvecchio ignores him. "I thought you wanted to know the truth, my son."

I scoff. "That forked tongue of yours has never tasted truth. Just get on with it and end this farce."

The Prior clears his throat and continues. "As a young acolyte, I was entrusted by the former Prior with the secret that had been passed down for generations. Through science, our deity had managed to create eternal life, a gift that would be bestowed on only those of the true faith, until the time when our great deliverer would join us in flesh and blood once again."

Cassius laughs. "Of course. One of the scientists who oversaw the Sowing project was a member of your glorified cult and stole the genetic material from Nexus. I suppose you can add thievery to your growing list of virtues."

Delvecchio scowls. "We are not thieves. We are the protectors of the Holy seed, our mission to protect the Deity's progeny until the time he would walk amongst us once more." He points to the destruction taking place outside the Citadel's windows. "That time is at hand now."

My mind's racing. "So you're the one responsible for my mother being impregnated with the Sown genetic material of Queran Embers."

He nods. "Yes. She was having tests performed at one of the MedCens. While she was sedated, the procedure was performed. She never knew."

My eyes are glued to Delvecchio's skinny throat, calculating how loud the *pop* will be when I snap it. "There's a word for people who violate and impregnate others without their consent."

"I came to her beforehand," he continues, "to try and make her see the error of remaining with the man you knew as your father."

"But she rejected you, didn't she?" Cassius asks. "Overcome with revulsion, no doubt."

"And you retaliated against her," I finish. "Ruined her life by forcing me into it."

Delvecchio's eyes burn like brushfires. "I made her a saint. In time, she will be revered as the mother of our deliverer. There will be song and prayer commemorating her throughout the ages. I saved her from the condemned life of obscurity she would have had at the side of your false father."

"That's perverted logic, even for you." I'm seething. "So that's it? I'm Queran Embers, your resurrected deity, standing once again before you in corporeal form. That's what this has all been about?"

"I'm afraid you think too highly of yourself, boy," a new voice proclaims from the darkness. "That honor belongs entirely to me."

A figure moves out from the shadows.

Queran Embers.

CHAPTER THIRTY-ONE

For a few seconds, I think I must be losing my mind, that it's just another one of the vivid flashbacks assaulting my addled brain. Except there's none of that feeling of intense pain. No excruciating headaches that feel like my brain's hemorrhaging the essence of Lucian Spark with each piercing throb. No memories bursting free of the mental grave buried deep inside me. I can barely feel anything at all through the shock that's numbing my body and hitting the gas on my lungs and heart.

"Judging from that look on your face, you weren't expecting me." Queran's tone is unnatural, like his voice has been processed through a myriad of electronic filters.

At first glance, it appears that the man before me could be a Flesher. His entire body's shrouded in some sort of black bio-suit, his head encased behind a clear, sealed helmet. Tubes that look like giant veins protrude from the areas on the suit where his vital organs would be, over his heart, lungs, kidneys, and intestinal tract. These artificial arteries coil their way into various silver control boxes located around the waist, equipped with bleeping monitors and gauges.

I glance at Cassius. He's more ruffled than I ever remember seeing him. For once, he's not in total control of a situation and I can't help but revel in his misery, even though it hurts to try and wrap my head around what's going on.

"You didn't know?" I ask him.

All he can do is shake his head, his eyes riveted on this monstrosity before us.

A burst of nervous laughter escapes me. "I've lost it completely."

There's an uncomfortable underlying slurping sound created by the machinery churning the thing's bodily fluids. This is accompanied by the faint wheeze of oxygen pistoning through lungs, and the unnerving rhythm of a heartbeat.

"Your eyes aren't deceiving you," he rasps.

That face is the most disturbing part of all and nearly causes me to bolt from this place.

It's *my* face—or at least the face I will have if I live another thirty or so years. Instead of my jet black hair, this man's hair is streaked with salt and pepper. Where my olive-skinned complexion's still smooth, illness has speckled his flesh with splotches of pale discoloration. Harsh lines dig into the outline of his jaw.

His grin frosts my blood. "I am definitely who you think I am."

Protruding from his throat is a pulsing, gray device, which explains why the voice is eerily distorted. Disease has apparently claimed his vocal chords as well.

"It can't be." I can barely hear the sound of my own voice.

His eyes crawl all over my skin. "You know I speak the truth. Don't fight it, boy."

As unsettling as his appearance is, it's the eyes that are almost too much to bear. Whatever malady has ravaged this body, it's leeched the dark brown color he must have once shared with mine and coated them in a sickly, translucent film. All the pain, all the anger and cruelty that's plagued my resurfacing memories, is deeply etched in those terrible eyes, an entire lifetime of vengeance and deceit reflecting that sick, twisted mind.

A reflection of the darkness that festers within me.

"You're...." What I'm seeing is so inconceivable that my mind struggles to convey the rest of the words to my lips.

"Queran Embers in the flesh." When he spreads his arms, it's accompanied by the soft whir of the servomotors powering the limbs of his suit. "I can understand your surprise."

"You died. Centuries ago."

"Yet here I am." He sighs, a sickening gurgle that makes the hair on my body stand on end. "Do not believe everything you hear." He moves forward, trundling along on encased, motorized legs that slam into the marble floor with each step. "And now that I have returned, things are going to change."

Delvecchio drops to his knees and bows his head. "Praise to the almighty Deity, resurrected at last."

Queran bows his head. "Your holy purpose has now been served. Your order has paved the way for my return for centuries, continuing the experiments while preserving my body in the secret chambers of your Priory, awakening me from cryo when the time was right, and granting me access to this very tower via the hidden catacombs. Behold, paradise at last." His machine powered arms grab the shocked Delvecchio around the neck and twist.

Crack!

The Prior's lifeless body slumps to the floor.

I swallow to try and hydrate my parched throat. "How did you come back?"

Our eyes meet. I flinch but force myself to hold the connection. He's staring at me with an eerie fascination. One of his encased fingers reaches out, stopping just short of my cheek. "I can't believe how young you are. I can barely remember my life at that age." Those milky eyes cloud over even more.

At first I mistake his look for anger. But then his reaction becomes crystal clear. It's envy and bitterness. The same emotions I struggled with when Cole and I were starving, and I had to scavenge through dumpsters for scraps to stay alive. Had I never been recruited and escaped the daily grind of Parish life, who knows what lengths I would have gone to in ensuring our continued survival?

Queran catches me staring, and I look away. "Do not become too attached to youth, boy. I assure you, it's quite fleeting. And by the time you learn to appreciate it, it's already become a shadow."

"So the Sowing wasn't enough, Queran?" Cassius finally asks, his voice regaining some of his lost confidence with each word. "You had to find some other way to cheat death."

Queran's treads revolve and spin him around to face Cassius. He pauses at the sight of him, and his oxygen and heart gauges go into overdrive. "I have always been a man that prefers to keep his options open. You strike me as that same sort of person, Thorn is it now? I remember when your name was—"

"Yes, my name's Cassius Thorn." Despite the pain he must be in, Cassius pulls himself to his full height and meets Queran's stare. "It's a name you should get very used to, at least for the very limited time you have left on this humble plane of existence."

Queran's mechanized laugh is a horrible mix of wheezing and deep gurgling. "In my lifetime I've encountered countless young men like you, arrogant, overconfident fools that are too clever for their own good." His eyes crawl back and forth between me and Cassius. "Needless to say, none of them outlived me. And I do not see that trend changing any time soon."

"So you had your genes Sown," I interrupt. "But you took other measures to preserve your legacy."

"Yes." His treads pirouette slowly around Cassius until he's directly in front of me. "After the Ash Wars, when I emerged from stasis and founded the Establishment, there was an outbreak of a highly contagious biological agent that caused mental instability, eventually leading to homicidal behavior and death. Fortunately, the outbreak was contained with an acceptable number of casualties." He touches his chest. "Unfortunately, not before I was exposed. On the brink of death, I was placed in cryogenic suspension and confined to a top secret location until such time that an anti-virus could be developed." He focuses on Cassius. "The true nature of the disease's origin was never discovered. But I had my theories."

Cassius' eyes could burn a hole through Ember's suit. "Consider it a parting gift."

Despite the throbbing in my head, my mind's fitting in the missing pieces. "Asclepius Valley," I say to Cassius. "That virus my team and I were exposed to while trying to retrieve the GX07 to counter the Biological Magnetic Pulse, last year. The disease infected all those scientists and their families stationed there. Turned them into savage killers. That's what Embers is talking about, isn't it. That was all you?"

"Yes, it was," he says, matter-of-factly. "I thought it would be poetic justice to finish what I'd started so long ago against Queran's legacy when I was nothing but Case 1, the lab rat. Asclepius Valley was what you'd call a trial run." He smiles and focuses his attention on Queran. "Little did I know I'd have a much sweeter target. I may yet get to finish what I started."

"You always were prone to delusions, even when we were children," Queran says. "I can assure you I have a permanent cure for that."

"What about all those people that died because of your little experiment?" I spit the question at Cassius. "You weren't there. You didn't see their faces, all that suffering. You turned them into little more than rabid Canids who had to be put down. All for some petty revenge over something that happened ages ago. You're the monsters that need to be put down," I turn to Queran. "Both of you."

The veins in Cass's temples throb, his face red. "You can quit the self-righteous act. You're an extension of him. As such, you're responsible for all the lives he's destroyed. You're no better than either of us. You're a monster, too."

"Shut up. None of this has anything to do with me. You've done nothing but inflict harm on my own friends and family."

Cassius moves toward me. "I was only doing what must be done to destroy his legacy." His eyes flit to Queran and back to me. "Your legacy. I had no choice."

"There's always a choice." My blood's on fire.

A blinding explosion outside the panoramic windows interrupts us. We all turn to stare at the battle still raging across the skies.

Above the Citadel, the Lady Liberty's sustained a massive hit. The vessel begins to cant and drop.

Reflexively, I activate the opticom.

It takes me a moment to figure out the display on Cage and Arrah's channel. It's the badly damaged server room. The image is on its side, as if the opticom's wearer were lying on the ground. Aside from the Fleshers milling in the background, dark fluid flows into the cam's range. The image remains static. Lifeless.

Blinking away the wet rage from my eyes, I flick to the next channel, Corin's. All I can see is the dark interior of the escape pod, the hatch still smoking from where it's been blown open. Hordes of Fleshers darken the horizon. The light filters through the mangled hatch, reflecting on a small object.

The chron I gave Cole. It's dented and flecked with blood.

My finger's numb as it jams on the last channel.

Digory studies the holo of the Parish map, monitoring the attack. Battalions of Fleshers tear through the streets, consuming everything in their wake like a swarm of locusts. The last semblance of humanity has left his face. He's gone now.

Forever.

"Your resistance is dying," Cassius says to me. "It won't be much longer." His eyes lock onto mine. "I suppose I no longer need *you* to give me those codes. Why settle for a copy when I can get them right from the original source."

Queran touches my shoulder. "I admire your fortitude. You are just like I used to be. Idealistic. Head strong. But I am afraid there can only be one of us."

His words penetrate the numbness. "What are you saying?"

"He means," Cassius interjects, "That he no longer has any use for you."

Queran's eyes look me up and down, admiringly. "On the contrary. He still has the most vital use of all, and his sacrifice will not be in vain." He cups my face in those cold, metallic hands. "You will always be a part of me and will continue to live inside me, I promise you."

I pull away from his grasp. "I don't know what the hell you're talking about, but I'm done with you. Both of you. And all of this."

Cassius's entire expression changes. A satisfied look spreads across his face. He closes in. "Don't you see? Now that he's been resurrected he doesn't plan on sharing his power. There is only one use you have for him now."

The truth hits me before Cassius can continue. I whirl to face Queran. "My vital organs. They're an identical match for you."

Queran nods. "Yes, that is true. The virus has compromised most of my vital tissues, confining me to this infernal device." He glides closer. "But through you I can function again, as I once did, retaining my dignity and commanding the respect I deserve."

I take a step backwards. "So what happens to me? I just become a living organ donor to be disposed of once there's nothing left. What about my life?"

A look of frustration and pity spreads across Queran's face. "Don't you understand what I've been saying? *You* are *me*. Everything I am, all of my memories, my experience, my deepest secrets, they live inside of you. Our relationship is perfectly symbiotic. You will continue to live inside of me."

My back presses against one of the marble columns. "What about Lucian Spark's life? His experiences? The memories of his family and friends? What happens to all of that? It just ceases to exist like it never really mattered? Like I never really mattered?"

"Did you ever really?" Queran's eyes ooze contempt now. "You can imagine my disgust when I discovered that I'd been reborn as a common street urchin, living in squalor, barely surviving, watching the people you claim to love die all around you. You call that a life worth remembering, Lucian?"

His words shake me to the core. I remember lying awake some nights, wishing my parents had never had me and burdened me with the responsibility of having to take care of my little brother. Even with Mrs. Bledsoe's help, the weight of the responsibility was crushing. It would have been much easier to hop on a freighter, run away, leave everything behind me.

But at the end of the day, sitting at the side of my brother's bed, tucking him in and reading him those stories, all those feelings would wash away. He was the only thing making that miserable life worth living, the spark of hope in the overwhelming darkness trying to suffocate me on a daily basis.

Now that light's gone, snuffed out in this senseless war, another casualty, along with the lives of everyone I care about, Cage, Arrah, Drusilla, Dahlia and Corin, all gone because of their association with Lucian Spark.

Maybe Queran's right. Maybe the legacy of Lucian Spark isn't really worth preserving after all. It would be so easy to just give in to the inevitable and let myself be absorbed into who I really am instead of clinging to the façade of a pitiful, false existence.

And it would be far less painful to forget all the excruciating pain, the terrible losses I've suffered.

"I can understand your conflict," Queran speaks up as if reading my mind. "Once the process is complete, none of what's plaguing you now will matter anymore. You will finally find peace. Isn't that what you really want after all you've endured?"

Who better to understand what I'm feeling than an older, wiser version of myself?

Queran extends a mechanized hand. "Come with me now and begin a new life, unshackled from the burdens of a past best forgotten."

I glance at the holos and outside the tower's windows, taking in all the destruction surrounding us. When I turn back to Queran, I begin to move closer, extending my own hand to take his—

Cassius grabs me from behind. Cold silver presses against my neck.

A sharp blade's poised against my jugular. Its serrated edge digs into my skin with every breath I take.

"I think this game has gone on long enough," Cassius rasps into my ear.

I twist my neck ever so slightly. "Cassius, what are you—?"

"Shut up."

Panic and anger fill Queran's face. "Careful now. There's no need for any hasty decisions. I am sure we can reach a mutually satisfying compromise."

Cassius leers at him. "Now that I know there isn't anything you wouldn't do to preserve this body," the blade nicks my throat, drawing blood, "I want you to input the launch codes on that console right now. If you don't, I slit his throat and toss the body from the tower. There will be no vital organs left for you to harvest, and you'll be forced to live whatever remaining days you have left in the confines of that stinking suit."

Queran's eyes smolder like bonfires. "You wouldn't do that. Once you kill him, you're a dead man. And I'll make sure your suffering is prolonged before your eventual demise."

Cassius laughs. "As long as I've prevented you from fulfilling your agenda, I'll die a happy man, although I wouldn't count my survival out if I were you. You have no idea who you are dealing with." He nudges his chin toward the console. "You have five seconds to input those codes before I start cutting."

The look on Queran's face is one of pure hatred. His gaze shifts between Cassius and myself.

"Time's up," Cassius announces. The blade pierces my flesh—

"Wait." Queran trundles over to the console and enters the codes.

Missile launch countdown has been activated, the computer announces. *The Nexus facilities will be impacted in T-Minus Ten minutes.*

CHAPTER THIRTY-TWO

The blade relaxes against my throat. "Excellent," Cassius crows. "I knew your instinct for self-preservation would ultimately trump whatever scant ideologies you might possess, Queran. Despite the centuries, you still remain a selfish coward. That hasn't changed."

Adrenaline surges through my body. Involuntarily, I activate the opticom.

On Corin's channel, he and Cole emerge from the pod's supply compartment they've been hiding in.

I release a deep breath. They're both still alive. There's still a chance they can make it through this.

Other citizens huddle close by, fear and desperation plastered on their faces.

Corin shields Cole with his body. "Whatever happens to me, Little Man, you just run as fast as you can and hide."

"No more running." Cole grabs his hand. Then he stares down their attackers and begins to chant.

"A spark does smolder deep within,
While Winter's blow doth burn the skin...,"

Corin's voice joins his.

Look toward the Sky, a flame held high,
The Season chars, its ashes nigh..."

The survivors beside them all lock hands, standing their ground and forming a growing human chain as they, too, take up the song.

"Keep it lit, Keep it burnin'
All the dreams, all the yearnin',
Ole leaves will fall, New moons arise,

The Keeper sings, the Season cries..."

Heart racing, I quickly flick to the other channels. The same scene is repeating throughout the Parish, the chorus growing louder and louder, rising above the chaos of the aerial battle as the united crowd surges forward to meet their attackers head on.

I flick to the last channel.

Digory's convulsing face is reflected on the monitor before him. Blood oozes from his nostrils as the seizure gets worse.

"We did it, Lucian." He smiles. "*I* did it." He collapses against the console.

I'm stunned by the mention of my name. And that expression on Digory's face. So full of pain. So full of relief.

And then I realize, Digory's been monitoring me all this time, the same way I've been observing him.

The Fleshers aim their weapons—

And freeze in their tracks.

"What the hell are you waiting for?" Corin shouts at the biomachines. "Go on now and get it over with you metallic piles of shit."

The taunt seems to have its desired effects. But instead of firing on the citizens, the Fleshers whirl and discharge their weapons at the squads of Imps scurrying about like rodents, instead. The civilians seize the opportunity to grab weapons from the dead and dying Imps and join their strange new allies to wage war on Thorn agents.

The tide of this bloody battle has turned.

All because of Digory. He must have infected the Flesher Hive with his illness, freeing them of their programming, and finally giving them the autonomy that they've always craved.

Corin lets loose a triumphant whoop. "Looks like there's been another regime change, Little Man."

Cole's one step ahead of him. He tosses Corin a weapon from one of the fallen Imps, after securing one for himself. Then he scoops up the battered chron and stuffs it into his pocket. "C'mon!"

With the Fleshers providing cover, Cole and Corin blast their weapons and join the alliance of civvies and Fleshers waging war.

A surge of hope fills my heart. I switch the opticom's feed to Cage and Arrah's channel.

"Cage, let's go." Arrah drags his prone body toward the main server.

It seems like they've only been playing dead at the hands of the Fleshers to buy themselves time. A grin spreads across my face.

The biomachines ignore them as they stagger toward the computer terminal, both bloodied and bruised.

"I'm not sure why those things aren't attacking," Arrah says. "Let's just unleash the virus while we've got the chance."

"Already on it." Cage shoves the chip into slot and begins inputting keyboard commands.

Outside the Citadel's tower, the fleet of Thorn carriers surrounds the devastated Lady Liberty.

Cass's lips brush my ear. His dagger cuts deeper into my throat. "How fitting that the last thing you should see is the complete annihilation of your insurrectionist fleet, along with the destruction of all your friends."

On the holos monitoring the Thorn fleet, a power surge registers on the readout displays. All ships batteries target the resistance fleet, initiating a countdown to fire. The already crippled Torch Brigade won't survive the blast. My renewed sense of hope teeters on the brink of despair as I my attentions flits back and forth between the attack on the fleet and the opticom channels.

"What are you two blokes doing here?" Cage looks up from installing the virus to see Corin and Cole racing toward him and Arrah.

Corin smirks. "Why should you two get to be the only ones to play?"

Arrah shakes her head as she studies her com. "There's a battalion heading straight for us. They'll be here before the virus upload's complete."

Corin grins. "Then we'll just have to slow'em down."

Cole tosses charges to him and he wastes no time planting them in the hallway just outside the server room's doors.

They're running out of time. The Thorn fleet has reached maximum firepower.

"That's it. Virus is almost uploaded. I'm blowing the hallway now. Take cover!" Cage flicks the switch on the remote detonator.

Nothing happens.

Arrah studies the small black box. "The detonator's been damaged. We're out of time. Someone's going to have to stay behind and trigger it manually."

Cage's eyes lock with hers. "Looks like that someone's going to be me." His eyes sweep Cole and Corin. "Just make sure you get these two clear of the blast."

"Forget it, Cage," Arrah snaps. "I'm staying."

He grabs her by the collar. "We don't have time to argue—"

Gunfire blasts down the hallway. Corin whirls, grabs Cole, and pushes him out of the way of the next blast. Blood gushes from the new wound blooming across his chest like a lethal flower.

Cage drops to his knees and scoops Corin in his arms. His eyes fill with wetness that cuts through the grime coating his cheeks. "Hang on, Mate. We're gonna get you back to base—"

Corin grabs his hand and coughs up a gout of blood. "You're such…a bad…liar…" his smile reveals bloody teeth. "We both know….I'm done playin'…" He looks up at Arrah. "Now get me to that detonator….and make sure you get…the kid…out…"

"No. We can't leave him," Cole punches Cage and tries to wriggle out of his grasp. But Cage carries him away.

Arrah buries her face in her hands. Then she nods and carries Corin over to the detonation switch. She gives him a fierce hug and kiss before sprinting away to join the others.

"Prepare to fire," The Thorn fleet commander orders through the bridge speakers at the Citadel.

On the opticom feeds, Corin smiles at Arrah, Cage, and Cole from a distance. Another stray shot hits him in the neck. He slumps forward, jamming his hand on the control switch in his death throes.

My whole body's tense. I switch off the opticom feeds, unable to bear them anymore, and gaze at the holos.

"Something's wrong!" the Thorn fleet commander shouts.

One by one, the guidance systems on the Thorn craft shut down, powering down the ships' defenses and weapons' systems. All the vessels begin to drift aimlessly, some crashing into each other. More massive explosions fill the skies.

Seizing advantage of this unexpected reprieve, the remaining resistance ships swoop in and bombard the drifting Thorn battalions with all their firepower. Guided missiles zig zag across the horizon like fiery comets, erupting in brilliant arrays of color and smoke, even as they disintegrate their targets.

"What is this?" His hold on my neck tightens, making it difficult to breathe.

"Looks like you underestimated your opponents." The satisfaction drips through Queran's tone, despite the voice-modulation. "Your entire world is crumbling around you, Thorn."

Five minutes left until Nexus missile launch.

Cassius sighs at this announcement. "Actually, it's everything *you* built that's about to crumble, Queran. First Nexus, and then the Establishment. But first," he pushes the tip of the blade against my throat, drawing blood, "I'm going to make sure you will never be able to return. This time, your death will be final—"

An explosion rocks the tower. The power flickers. Through the windows, a Thorn carrier hurtles toward the surface, trailed by chunks of debris from the Tower's antennae. Shards of glass and superheated metal spray through the chamber. I seize advantage of Cassius's temporary distraction and ram an elbow into his ribcage where Delvecchio shot him.

He yelps and loosens his grip, just enough for me to grab hold of his arm and yank it away, spinning and kicking him in the gut. But his grip's too powerful. We both topple onto the ground. I'm trapped underneath his weight, grabbing his wrists as he attempts to jam the dagger in my chest. Being on top gives him the edge. The blade dips closer to my chest.

His eyes are molten pools. "Why...did you make...me do this...?"

Hot drool flows from his lips onto my cheeks. His face grows crimson. He forces the tip of the blade into my skin—

Focusing all of my energy, I knee him in the groin, thrusting my hands upward, ramming him in the forehead with the dagger's hilt. I hurl him off me and roll out of his reach.

We both spring to our feet, facing each other.

He peels the remnants of his tattered shirt away. Blood's oozing from the wound in his chest down to his abdomen. Yet he's grinning at me. "Not bad. But the end result's going to be the same."

I curl my hands into fists. "This has been a long time coming, Cassius. It ends now."

Our eyes deadlock for a moment. We charge toward each other like wild animals.

Just before we make contact, I leap and spin, clipping his chin with a kick of my foot.

Arching his body backwards at the last second, he escapes the full impact of the blow and drops to his knees.

His fists pummel my gut.

Something cracks, and I double over in pain.

Cassius is relentless. He grabs a broken support strut and wields it like a club toward me. I duck, just as it smashes into the marble column where my head was a split-second ago.

He wipes the blood from his chin. "You're quick, I'll give you that. But I was always quicker." The smile disappears from his face, smothered in rage. "I can't believe I struggled over sparing your life when I discovered the truth. That I had pity on you." Pulling the club free, he raises it again. "I assure you, I won't be making that mistake again."

Cassius swings the club down. I roll out of the way and it smashes into the marble floor. Before he can launch another attack, I smash my foot down on a fallen plank, which catapults a hunk of still smoldering metal debris directly at him.

It hits him in the face. He cries out in pain, swatting at the burning fragments. I leap and tackle him full-force. The impact sends us both crashing through one of the tower's already cracked windows.

We crash onto a rickety circular platform around ten feet in diameter, connected to the control room by a narrow beam. Jutting from the center of the platform is a towering communications spire.

Our bodies intertwine. We come to a rough stop in a tangle of limbs, broken glass, and debris, facing each other, buffeted by the winds

"I never wanted things to end this way," he groans. "I really did love you."

I feel like I've been run over by a Trundler. All my limbs ache. My insides feel like they've been squeezed in a vise. "Why?" Is all I can muster the energy to whisper.

"The more we love someone, the deeper the pain they can inflict."

Staring into his eyes, it's all coming back to me. "When I was… Queran….my father married your mother when we were both fourteen. You were…Lisandro. *My* Lisandro."

His smile is caked with blood. "Step brothers who eventually grew to love each other much more deeply than two people ever could."

Unfathomable pain fills me, not from my wounds, but from somewhere deep inside of me, a vault in my brain I've never accessed as Lucian Spark. "It was me, wasn't it? I was the one that decided to use you as Case 1. I'm the one responsible for all the pain you endured even though I loved you more than anything in the world."

He struggles to move closer to me. "That's right. You condemned me to an existence of eternal suffering."

"But why would I do that?" I feel I already know the answer to this question, but I can't bring myself to face it.

Cassius crawls closer. His breath's hot in my ear. "Maybe you'll remember when you watch Tycho die. I made sure I programmed the nanotech in his body to make him suffer even more than I ever did. And when the excruciating pain is finally too much for him to bear and he succumbs, you'll know it's because of you and everything you've done."

A gush of anger fills me. "I hate you." Rolling on top of him, I wrap my hands around his throat, squeezing them tighter and tighter.

He tries to claw my fingers away, but my grip's relentless. Not only has Cassius caused me so much pain and grief, he's also destroyed the lives of those I love the most. Cole and Digory.

With an earsplitting crack, the already damaged platform beneath us gives way. I struggle to hold on to the communications spire with one hand, hanging on to Cassius with the other, both of us dangling hundreds of feet in the air.

"Queran…Lucian…whoever you are…help me," he gasps.

"That's it," Queran says behind me. "Finish him off. Take your revenge."

My mind exists in two places at once. Holding on to a young man. Cassius. His face burned. Pleading with me…

"Lucian, please…"

Queran, help me.

Last time, jealousy and envy ruled my emotions. I loved him so much. But he was going to go away and leave me. After everything we shared—

It's all coming back to me now. So vivid. Like it just happened.

The heat searing my skin from the inferno below. I'm barely clinging to the inside of the ship's open hatch as the attack craft zooms through the ash and haze. My hand's slick with sweat. I grip on to his, struggling not to let go.

"Queran," he shouts over the roar of the flames and the aircraft's engines. "I can't hold on much longer."

My arm feels like it's being ripped from its socket, but still I hold on. He's the man I love, after all, even though he's gone behind my back, earned my father's favor. I'll pull him into the ship, and we'll both be safe. And then he'll go on to join my father and take everything away that should rightfully be mine. It's so unfair. I earned it. I'm the one that endured all of my father's drunken beatings, the broken bones, the public humiliations. All I ever wanted was his approval. And now this young man that's my brother, my lover, my best friend—he's going to take all that away from me.

Unless—

"I can't hold on much longer," Cassius groans. Falling debris from a destroyed Vulture barely misses him. The wreckage spirals downwards, hundreds of feet, marking the path that Cassius will soon follow with contrails of black smoke. He looks up at me, his eyes glazed with fear. "Lucky…please…"

My eyes meet his, burning with wet fire.

"I'm sorry," I whisper to that other, long ago Cassius.

Panic dawns on his face as he realizes what I'm about to do. "Please, Queran. You don't have to choose this. I love you."

The bottom of his suit catches fire. He begins to wail. The flames consume him—

His burning body morphs into Cass's, who's struggling to hold on to my grip, our sweaty fingers starting to slip.

Once again, instead of Cassius, I see his other self, suffering in pain as he pleads with me to save his life. "Queran, it hurts...it hurts so much...if you ever loved me help me now...please...I'm begging you..."

"Lucky!" Cassius cries. "I'm begging you. Don't let me fall. I know I've hurt you. Have pity on me. Please."

His image blurs into that of the other young man, screaming in agony, half his body consumed by flames.

I hesitated too long. Letting go now will be an act of mercy, I lie to myself.

The second I release my grip, I realize it's a mistake, but it's too late. He falls away from me, engulfed in flames, letting loose an agonized wail.

My fingers loosen on Cassius's hand. After everything he's done to me and those I love, all the hurt, the betrayals, I'll finally have my revenge. I'll finally be—

Exactly what he's become.

"Let him go," the older Queran, my future self, calls from behind me. "You can't change who you are. You didn't have a choice then. You don't have a choice now."

"No." My grip tightens on Cassius's hands. "You're wrong, Queran. There's always a choice."

With everything I have left, I haul Cassius back onto what's left of the platform, drag him across the narrow beam and back into the safety of the control room.

We both collapse next to each other.

Cassius looks at me, confused, angry, his eyes welling with tears. "You saved me. After everything I've done to you. That's not possible. That's not how things are supposed to go. Why?"

I feel strangely at peace. "You gave me an apple once."

He stares at me and opens his mouth. But no words come.

"I agree with Thorn," Queran grumbles. "This is not how things are supposed to go." His face is trembling with rage. "You are definitely an inferior copy, Boy, unworthy to carry on my legacy. I'll make sure not to damage your vital organs when I terminate you."

Queran pulls out a hypodermic from a hidden compartment in his suit and lunges at me.

"Lucky!" Cassius pushes me out of the way and takes the brunt of the injection in his throat.

I pounce on Queran, tearing at his life support mechanisms, dislodging tubes. Fluids spray everywhere. Queran spins on his hydraulic mechanisms and shrieks, an awful, guttural sound. I dig my fingers into his suit and continue to claw, determined to destroy the darkness, the darkness that lives deep inside me, all the while knowing it will always be a part of who I am.

Queran's movements slow as his life functions dwindle. Exhausted, we both tumble to the ground.

The only sounds are his rasping breaths and the pounding of my heart in my ears.

I remove his protective helmet, gazing at that pale face, the diseased and pock-marked skin. A face that might have been me once and could still be.

The Nexus missile launch will initiate in two minutes, the computerized voice announces.

Queran smiles, foul fluid dripping from his lips. "You've lost. I wanted all of them to die, anyway."

Nodding, I grab the last of the cables feeding him oxygen and twist them, cutting off his supply.

His eyes open wide, full of fear. "Why? You could have been so powerful. All that I am…is what you could have been…"

Hot tears flow down my cheeks. "And *I* am all that *you* will *never* be."

The once great and feared Queran Embers's eyes glaze over. His breathing stops. Forever.

Rushing over to the computer console, I enter the codes that have now come back to me, consciously accessing Queran's memories for what I swear will be the very last time.

Nexus attack has been overridden, the computer announces. *Missile launch aborted.*

With the remnants of humanity out of harm's way, I locate all the files on the Sowing protocol and purge them completely from the system.

My fingers tap the keyboard, issuing one final order.

On the holos, all the facilities in the Nexus network appear, finally online once again. The Nexus facilities, long buried underground, begin to rise out of the earth at last.

According to the readouts, hundreds of thousands of survivors are awakening from their endless slumber to face a brand new world.

I can't say it's a better world than what they've left behind, but it'll have to do.

"Lucky..." Cass's voice sounds weak.

As I stagger back toward him, I glance at the holos.

Practically all of the Thorn fleet has been either destroyed or boarded by the remnants of the resistance, working in tandem with the newly liberated Fleshers. The Parish is little more than smoking ruins and unrecognizable streets, littered with blood and bodies. It strikes me as odd that in war, where factions battle for supremacy, they all find equality in destruction and death.

Above, resistance ships soar through the skies in formation, sounding victory beacons. There's a growing rumbling, and at first, to my dulled senses, it sounds like an approaching storm. But then it becomes clearer. Cheering. Cheering from the survivors. I can hear them from below, the sound growing louder and louder. On the holos, they march en masse, hand in hand through the streets, a massive wall of human and machine, heading this way, toward the Citadel of Truth, the symbol of their oppression at the hands of the Establishment and Thorn Republic for so long.

Somewhere in that crowd is my brother. And my remaining friends, Cage and Arrah. As I stagger toward Cassius, I try to activate the opticom, but can't get a signal. I rip off the glove and the earpiece, stuffing them in my pocket. I can only hope they are among the throng of survivors, liberated at last, free to start new lives and close the door on the darkness that's shrouded them for their entire existence.

Soon they'll arrive here and find Cassius and me, the faces of tyranny.

Exhaustion and pain take their toll. I drop to my knees and crawl the rest of the way to Cassius.

When I touch his forehead, it's already burning hot, his eyes bloodshot, lips cracked.

He grips my hand. "I was wrong about you. I thought you were *him*. But your life, the people you love, have made you someone else. Someone better than Queran could ever be."

I shake my head. "But everything that made Queran the tyrant that he was...all that darkness lives inside of me. Who's to say that one day—"

"It won't," he whispers. "There's the potential for darkness in every single one of us. We all decide if we're going to turn away from it or embrace it. Today, *you*, Lucian Spark, made *your* choice."

"You were a good man, once, Cassius. I *remember*."

When he chuckles, blood bubbles at the corner of his lips. "Isn't it ironic? When I discovered who we both used to be, I became obsessed with foiling you, with destroying everything that Queran Embers represented. And in the process, I became *him*, and *you* became the man I *used* to be." He smiles, and reaches up a trembling hand to touch my cheek. "So maybe a part of me will live on in you after I'm gone." His voice is raspy and quavers as he begins to sing.

"Keep it hot', Keep it searin,'
The fire bright, the dark a'fearin,'
Ole Stars will fall, new Suns arise,
The Torch holds strong, the season dies."

A mixture of foam and drool spews from his lips. I prop his head up and hold him tight. "Hang on Cassius. You're going...to be fine."

"Who's the liar now, Lucky?" His face contorts for a moment. "Even if I could survive this, I think the sound of that approaching mob has sealed my fate." When he looks back up at me, I see desperation in his eyes. "You've been given a rare opportunity, Lucky. The chance to see your future self and change your fate. Not many people can say that." He squeezes my hand tighter with both of his. "Don't waste the opportunity."

Where once I felt rage and the desire for vengeance, all I feel for Cassius now is sorrow and pity.

His breathing eases a tad. "You and Digory... were good together."

My heart feels like it's breaking at the sound of Digory's name, and I tense. Then Cass is convulsing, and I'm doing everything I can to hold him steady. "It's all right. Don't fight it."

"I know I can never ask you for...forgiveness...," he whispers.

There's a loud crashing sound coming from the levels below. Then the sounds of distant gun shots, followed by a cacophony of footsteps and murmuring. I glance at the holos to see the crowds pouring into the Citadel, ripping down flags, knocking over monuments, and barreling through the Imps that have remained loyal to the end.

They're here. And they're thirsty for the blood of the two people that enslaved them with deceit and treachery. There's no escape.

For either of us.

I lean down and brush my lips against his. "Forgive me, Lisandro."

When he opens his mouth again, no sounds comes forth, but his eyes haunt me with gratitude.

He pulls me close, clutching at me. "You have to…leave…now."

Pulling out a small, silver remote from his pocket, he activates it before I can stop him.

The tile beneath me slides open, and I fall into a small duct hidden underneath the floor. I try to pull myself out but don't have the strength. From where I'm crouched, I can still peer over the rim to see him staring at me.

Cassius smiles, like he did in the old days, before the Trials. "I always… plan for… contingencies. My escape route…is now…yours."

"Why?" I barely have the strength to speak.

"I can't… afford to be… Lisandro…anymore. I've made…my choice…"

Amazingly, he pulls himself to his feet, his limbs trembling as he fights to stay erect.

The crowd bursts into the chamber, tearing through the furnishings, smashing the consoles.

They're heading in my direction, and I don't care.

"It's me you want," he calls to them. "Cassius Thorn."

They stop in their tracks and turn toward him. Then they attack, engulfing his entire body like a swarm of locusts.

All I can see is blood oozing out from beneath the mob's feet where Cass's body should be, spreading across the marble.

There was a time when the thought of seeing him lying there dead would have filled me with triumph and satisfaction. But that's not who

I am anymore. Now it just makes me sick and sad. I make out one of his arms sticking out from beneath the horde, bent unnaturally and out-stretched toward me. The growing pool of dark blood reaches his fingers, still clutching the remote, and covers them as it continues to flow in my direction.

It's as if he's offering me a bright, crimson gift, like that little boy so long ago, crouched outside my windowsill. Making sure I wasn't frightened. Making sure I was safe.

His fingers spasm and click the unit. Then the floor gives, and I drop into the darkness, squeezing my eyes shut, as the crowd's roar fades into the distance.

But all that matters is the boy and that apple.

CHAPTER THIRTY-THREE

"We have to smuggle him out of the city."

The familiar voice rouses me from sleep. It's Cage. Someone shushes him, and he lowers his voice so I can't make out the rest.

I'm lying on a lumpy cot in a small, dingy room. I know this place. I was here not too long ago. With Digory. My old abandoned tenement in the Parish. It's somehow survived the latest onslaught of war and remained relatively intact, despite the peeling plaster and haze of dust covering everything.

Everything comes back to me in a rush. Queran. Aborting the missile strike against Nexus. Cassius and our final exchange before he faced the vengeance of the bloodthirsty mob.

Cage and the others must have found me where Cass's escape tunnel deposited me and spirited me away to this place. Rather than being grateful, all I can think about is Digory. I wish Cassius would have just left me in the tower to face my fate. But if Cage managed to survive, then Cole—

When I try to raise myself to a sitting position, sharp pains fill my head like a rampaging electrical storm. The room blurs. I feel nauseous and double-over, dry heaving. Eventually the wave subsides but the dull throbbing persists. Even though my encounter with Queran is over, the scars of that confrontation remain just as strong as ever. Somehow, I know I'll carry them with me the remainder of my life.

Bracing myself against the cot, I lift up and make my way toward the door, ignoring the stiffness of my aching muscles. Taking a deep breath, I pull it open and hobble into the outer room.

You'd think I was waving a gun. The conversation comes to a dead stop. Cage, Arrah, and Croakley are seated at a small, wooden table, staring at me. The only sound now is the crackling of flame in the small fireplace, which casts flickering shadows on their somber faces.

I attempt a smile. "Do I talk in my sleep?"

Cage rushes from the table and wraps me in a bear hug. "It's so bloody good to see you moving around, Mate."

I kiss the warmth of his cheek. "I missed you, too."

Peering over Cage's shoulder, I see Arrah smiling at me, her eyes moist. She rushes over. "You gave us quite the scare, Fifth Tier. Of course, we had to bail you out of trouble as always."

I wrap my arms around her, squeezing tightly. "I wouldn't want to disappoint."

She gives me a peck on the forehead. "How are you feeling?"

"I've definitely been better. But seeing you guys sort of makes up for it." I wink, more to alleviate their concern than a reflection of how I'm actually doing.

Croakley nods at me. "We're glad to have you back, Commander Spark."

"Thank you, Sir." I turn back to Arrah and Cage. "Where's Cole? Is he—?"

Cage cracks a smile. "No worries, Mate. He's out with an escort to gather some of the supplies the resistance is distributing to survivors. He'll be around soon, and I'm sure quite happy to see you."

Looking around the dilapidated hovel, I take in the cracked windows, the missing floor tiles, the lack of lighting. "What are we doing here? Why haven't we gone back to base?"

An uncomfortable look passes between Croakley, Arrah, and Cage.

Arrah forces a smile. "You first. Fill us in on what happened in that tower before we found you."

She and Cage hustle me into one of the unbroken chairs, and I proceed to tell them my story—at least most of it. There are some details that cut too deep to go into. Those I'll take with me to my grave. But I share the gist, the appearance of Queran Embers, the missile strike on Nexus, inputting the codes and aborting the launch.

"What about the bodies?" I ask when I'm finished. "Cassius and Queran. What did they do with..." I don't have the stomach to finish the question.

Croakley sighs. "Last I heard they were on exhibition where the Town Square once stood." His eyes drop, and it's clear he finds the implications as distasteful as I do.

"The survivors needed a way to vent their anger," Cage says.

I shake my head, despite the pounding. "It's wrong. Not even Cassius deserves to be desecrated after death."

Arrah takes hold of Croakley's hand across the table. "Surely the evidence corroborates his story. There would be no victory without Lucian. They have to be made to see that."

My eyes bounce between them. "What are you talking about? Tell me. I deserve to know what's going on. I think I've earned it."

Cage wraps an arm around my shoulder. "Yes, you sure have, Mate." He turns to Croakley. "Tell him."

Croakley closes his eyes for a moment. When he opens them, they're filled with great sadness. "After Thorn revealed your...history...publically, you've become somewhat of a—"

"I'm a pariah now," I finish. "I figured as much. They don't trust me because of my connection to Queran Embers. They're suspicious of me, and I don't blame them one bit. It's going to take time and a lot of tact to make them understand the truth."

Cage pats my back. "It's more than that, Mate. The officers loyal to Rios. They've spearheaded a movement against you."

My eyes narrow. "Movement? What kind of a movement?"

Arrah's shifts her gaze to me. "They've formed a tribunal."

Croakley scoffs. "Tribunal! Lynch mob is more like it."

Cage nods. "They've already started holding court, trying people for war crimes. Just a bloody formality because they've already been judged guilty before the procedure's even begun."

"In all fairness," Arrah says, "most of those that have already been convicted were indeed monsters."

"But Lucian isn't," Cage snaps. "He's a hero, and none of us would even be here if it bloody weren't for him."

I pull back from the table, taking it all in. "So am I supposed to assume the Resistance has deemed the Torch Keeper public enemy number one?" I grin. "That's a twist."

"This is serious, Lucian." Arrah rubs her eyes. "They're searching for you. With Queran and Cassius dead, they need someone living to rest all the blame on. Who better than the spitting image of the tyrant who started this whole mess? They're going to kill you, and we're not going to just sit on our asses and let that happen."

Now it's Croakley's turn to grin. "As Arrah has so colorfully stated, we have made plans to smuggle you out of the city where you and your brother will be free to head west. With any luck, they'll give you up for dead in a few months, and this will all be over."

I rest my elbows on the table's warped wood. "Except for the part where I won't have a place in helping to structure this new government and my brother and I will have to live the rest of our lives looking over our shoulders, in case someone should pick up our trail, correct?"

"I won't lie to you," Croakley says. "The likelihood of you ever being able to show yourself in these parts again without any serious reprisals is highly unlikely."

"Thanks for being honest with me."

Cage rests his palms on his forehead. His eyes glisten. "They never did find Tristin's body. But I heard she didn't make it."

I come over to him, slinging my arm around him. "There's something you should know."

He listens quietly as I tell him about Tristin's death and placing her body in the Tycho tomb. "I'm so sorry."

He gives me a hug. "I'm so glad she wasn't alone and was at peace when it happened, Mate."

I hold him as he weeps on my shoulder.

Footsteps approach the front door. I tense as it opens.

We all let out a collective sigh of relief. Breck and Saffron enter, followed by Cephas, who's walking hand in hand with Cole.

When Cole's eyes meet mine, it's like tapping into a reservoir of energy I didn't know I had. Suddenly, the throbbing head and physical pains don't register. We rush into each other's arms, and I scoop him up and spin him around. The movement makes me dizzy, but I don't care.

"Are you okay?" I ask, setting him down.

"I'm good," he says. "I've been waiting for you to wake up. What took so long?"

"You know me. Just being lazy, Buddy."

He nods. "They told me we're going away on a long trip."

"Yes, we sure are. Just me and you. You up for it?"

Cole hugs me tight. "We have to go, right? If we stay here, something bad's going to happen to us, isn't it?"

I stare into his eyes. "Don't worry about that. Go get your things ready. I'll be there in a bit to tuck you in, unless you think you're too big for that now?"

"Only if it makes *you* feel better." He scampers off.

"Thanks for looking out for him, guys." I grip Cephas's, Breck's, and Saffron's hands in turns. "I owe you."

"You saved the Nexus," Saffron says. "I'd say we're even."

"Nice to see you back on your feet." Breck smiles, but her eyes are tinged with uncertainty.

Cephas adjusts his glasses. "How are you feeling?"

"Not so hot," I admit.

"If you don't mind, we'd like to run some more blood work. Purely as a precautionary measure before you embark on your long journey."

"Sure, just give me a little bit, will you?"

"Of course."

The trio drifts over to Jeptha, and they begin murmuring in voices too low to make anything out.

I wrap my arms around Cage and Arrah. "There's something I need to ask you. It's about Digory. Did they ever find…?"

Cage and Arrah exchange a grave look.

"We found this." Cage pulls out a familiar black box. "The opticom unit you had on when we discovered you at the Citadel. It was actually this signal that helped us track you in that secret tunnel."

"There's something else," Arrah adds. "An incoming message on the opticom that's addressed to you."

———

The dawn dabs the sky and trees with soft highlights of orange and pink. Fortunately, the cemetery was far enough on the Parish outskirts to be mostly unaffected by the battle. From my vantage point atop a tree twisting over the wrought-iron fence, I watch as the small Flesher craft descends, hovers for a moment, and then perches on the roof of the Tycho mausoleum.

Cage has already removed Tristin's body from the vault and buried her in a small plot beside Jeptha and her mother. It's gut wrenching enough I had to watch Dahlia, Dru, and Corin's services from a distance, hidden among the trees and shadows as the small resistance team laid them to rest. There's no way I could stay away from this meeting now, even if I wanted to. Despite Cage and Arrah's repeated warnings not to come because I could be found and arrested, they finally and reluctantly agreed, vowing to keep a look out nearby and warn me if anyone approaches.

I spring from the tree and follow the stone steps leading to the Tycho tomb. The Fleshers have provided a dangling, organic ladder which lifts me to the rooftop. The Fallen Five await, four standing tall, the fifth, Orestes, encased in his pod. The five are connected by undulating tentacles to a second pod. The moment I see Digory's body lying peacefully inside the transparent tube, I lose it completely. My body heaves. Tears stream uncontrollably down my face.

I recall vividly the last time we were both in this place. All I want to do is crawl into that glass coffin beside him and shut out the rest of the world forever.

But I can't. Cole needs me. Now that he's finally coming around I can't abandon him.

My fingers graze the cold glass of Digory's resting place. I wish I could touch him.

The pod begins to glow, and a holographic image appears just above it.

It's Digory. He looks so pale and weak, as if every breath is a monumental effort. He must have recorded this right after he transmitted the auto nanos to the Hive. Yet still he manages a smile.

"Lucian. We wanted this vessel to deliver our message in person, but unfortunately, that was not possible, and the one you know as Digory Tycho had to be placed in hibernation to heal, and fully integrate with the Hive, a process that could take many of your years."

I lean against the pod to steady myself.

"We want to thank you so much for everything you have done and for helping us understand the virtues of humanity. You have shown us that despite the dark and destructive parts of human nature, your race is also capable of great understanding, compassion, and forgiveness." He smiles again. "Because of you, the screams are finally gone."

My body's shaking, and it feels like my legs are going to give way.

The image of Digory's face moves in closer. "Do not be sad. If you should ever find yourself alone and grieving, look to the millions of stars in the sky. We are *all* one big Hive, Human and Bio-Mech organism alike. Your light will always shine inside us, as ours will glow inside you. We do not know what our race's destiny may hold, but we know it will be a more enlightened one having been a part of your journey." His fingers reach out as if to touch me. "Having you be a part of *my* journey."

The image flickers and dies.

Silently, the Fleshers nod and re-enter their ship. I grip Digory's pod one last time before it glides inside and the hatch seals.

I back away as the ship lifts off and soars into the sky, disappearing into a sea of clouds.

"Goodbye, my love."

My vision blurs again, and I swipe a hand over my eyes. But it's not just the tears. Everything's going fuzzy. The pressure in my head grows unbearable. This time it's not a passing wave.

I smile, despite the pain. "I'm ready."

———

Cephas enters the room, holding some scans in his hand. Even before he can show them to me, I already know what he's going to say.

"How much time do I have left, doc?"

He sets the scans aside on the bed. "It's hard to say. This malignancy is growing at an alarming rate. I've never seen anything like it."

The drugs I've been given are barely keeping the pain at bay. "A biproduct of the Sowing process, I take it. And activating Queran's memories. I've been dying for quite some time now, haven't I?"

"Unfortunately, yes." He purses his lips. "The Sowing was never intended to be used the way Queran and his people did. I'm convinced that if I had more time to study these results, I could formulate some treatment plan, come up with a way to arrest the condition—"

I smile despite the pain. "We both know I'm not going to last long enough for that, Doc."

Saffron shakes her head. "Maybe we can try some experimental procedures. It's a longshot but—"

"No. Queran's already cheated death one too many times. Enough is enough. I'm ready now. I think I've been for quite a while."

Breck squeezes my hand. "I'm truly sorry, Lucian. We'll do our best to make you comfortable."

"Thanks. I really appreciate that."

———

I've started losing count of the days now. How many has it been? Three? Four? Maybe it's the meds that are making things so hard to keep track of. I can't be sure.

My vision's starting to go, too. Something about the pressure building in my brain. Most of the time now I only see shapes. But it's the voices that are comforting. Arrah and Cage barely leave my side now. Their voices are so soothing. Even Croakley's good-natured sparring with Cephas, Saffron, and Breck makes me feel good, especially on the really tough days, when I can't keep anything down and all I want to do is end things.

Of all the voices, the one I miss the most is Cole's. He never comes. I can understand why. I promised him I wasn't going to leave him again and…well…I'm breaking my word to him once more.

Only this time, I'm never coming back.

I get his anger, but it breaks my heart and I agonize for him and how frightened he must be. Some days I'm so saddened that I can't stop crying, and all I can do is pray to some invisible deity to make it all end so I won't have to feel anything anymore. But it doesn't end, and I curse myself for daring to hope that maybe there *is* something else after this, even though logic tells me it can't be so. I don't care if there's nothing else. Utter and complete blackness will do just fine.

Anything but this.

Cephas, Saffron, and Breck have respected my wishes and not poked or prodded me with any needles. But sometimes I sense them observing me, as if they're taking mental notes of my condition and assessing treatments.

It can't have been a week, can it? I can just make out the blurred silhouette of Arrah and Cage sitting at my bedside. "How's Cole?"

"He's not saying much these days," Arrah says.

"I'm going to make him come in here, Mate," Cage says.

I touch his hand, unable to squeeze it. "Leave…him…be. Promise me that you guys will…take care…of him. Please…"

"Of course we will," Cage's words choke.

Touching his face, I can feel wet warmth that's so soothing against my ice-cold fingers.

They're both holding my hands now. "I know you both lost people you loved…Dru…Dahlia…Corin…but you have to keep going…even on the days you don't feel up to it…every breath you take, everyone you meet…. everything you experience…it's a tribute to them. Remember that."

"We'll remember, Fifth tier." Arrah's lips press against my forehead.

I smile. "Looks like…I'm not going to…come in first…this time."

It's getting harder and harder to catch my breath. I can barely see their shadows now.

"We love you, Mate," Cage whispers. "Always." His lips brush against mine.

"Be happy," I say. "For me."

"We will," Arrah says.

"Lucky?" A new voice.

That voice. Why does it sound so familiar? I know that voice.

It's Cole.

"I'm right here, Buddy."

I can feel the shifting on the bed. Arrah and Cage must have moved away and let my brother takes their place.

"I'm sorry I couldn't come before." Cole's voice is soft, the best sound I've ever heard.

"That's okay, Buddy. You're here now. Thank you so much for coming."

He takes my hand. My tears flow freely now.

Cole buries his face against my chest. "Does it hurt?" he whispers in my ear.

"Just a little," I whisper back.

"I'm sorry I was mad. I don't want you to go away and leave me."

"I don't want to leave you, Cole. I swear it. You have to believe me."

Cole kisses my cheek. "I do. And I want you to know if going away will make you feel better, it's okay. You don't have to stay for me. I won't be mad. I promise."

"I love you, little brother."

"I love you, too, Lucky. Forever."

I can't see him at all, but I imagine his little face as I wipe the tears from his eyes. "Don't cry, big guy."

"I'll tell you a story, so you can go to sleep," Cole says.

"That would be very nice," I answer.

He takes both my hands in his. "There once was a brave boy, named Lucky. One day, the Great Lady lost her torch, and she could no longer watch over the great city she protected."

"What did she do?" I whisper.

"Because Lucky had so much courage, she made him the Torch Keeper of the Kingdom, and he set out with his friends to find the fire…"

I close my eyes, drifting into the most peaceful sleep ever.

CHAPTER THIRTY-FOUR

Home.

So cold. Stinging my skin. Stark white clouds smothering me. Can't breathe. Feels like I'm weighted down in a cold, dark sea filled with a bitter taste.

Hiding behind my mother's skirt as a squad of Imps marches down our street.

My head throbs with each click of their boots on the pavement, like large mallets tearing chunks from the cobblestones.

Then there's a rush of air and blinding flashes of light. With each blast an image—

a memory—mine or the Other one's?

Teaching Cole how to tie his shoes…the wonderful musty smell of the old books in the dusty archives where I apprenticed under…Mister… Croakley?…yes…catching fireflies behind the old dump with…the boy with the auburn hair and green eyes…his name's on the edge of my tongue, then there's that medicinal taste…the other boy….golden hair, brilliant blue eyes…sharp pain knifing through my head and chest… being recruited…friends…some gray with death…Cypress? Gideon? Ophelia—

But there are others not dead. The girl with the caramel skin and piercing dark eyes—

Arrah.

The images flutter…faster and faster like the shuffling of a deck of cards…overwhelming me…suffocating me…yet warming me despite the intense cold.

It's as if my whole life has been compressed into a matter of seconds—all the knowledge, all the feelings—the joy, the sorrow…fear…hope—crammed into a tiny spring-loaded box that finally bursts open—

I spring up, gasping for breath, body shaking uncontrollably, nausea ripping through me. I vomit what seems like every last drop of fluid from deep inside me.

It takes a moment for my surroundings to soak in. I'm essentially strapped to a bed, tethered to tubes and wires in what appears to be a sparse hospital room. The bright overhead light is too harsh for my eyes, and I look away.

Cold air nips at my skin. The stench of my own sick now covering the front of my hospital gown, the steady hum and vibration of the equipment—

What's happened to Cole? And where the hell am I? The instruments look very different than what I'm used to. I don't recognize this facility from any of the resistance bases. Nor does it look like anything I've seen in the Parish, or even the Nexus.

How am I still alive?

The door *wooshes* open. A tall young woman enters. She's wearing stark white medical scrubs.

"Where am I?" My voice is hoarse and filled with fear.

She shoots me a look—nervous, fearful? About what?

Adrenaline rockets through my system. I can hear the bleeps of my pulse start to floor it on the machines.

"You need to relax." The young woman hurries over to my bed, checking the instruments registering my vitals. She produces a wash cloth and wipes away my mess with gloved hands. I try to focus on her name tag until it finally becomes clear.

A. Messenger.

She makes notes on a three-dimensional holographic clipboard. She notices me staring, stops what she's doing and smiles. "Feeling better?"

I nod. "So you must be my doctor."

"Yes. One of them, actually. You need to be very careful exerting yourself. Even though the nerve stims have been used regularly to prevent atrophy, your muscles need some time to regain their former strength."

"Look, Doc. I appreciate your help. But I've got to get back to my friends. In case you haven't heard, there's a war going on and—"

"The war's over. Has been for quite some time." She suddenly finds her clipboard interesting again.

I sit up. "Over? Then…we *did* win? I mean, did the Torch Brigade…?"

Her eyes meet mine again. "Yes. The Establishment, Sanctum, the Thorn Republic—all of it's gone." She grips my hand. "The people of the Parish and Nexus—we're all free."

I study the pained expression in her eyes. "What is it you're not telling me? And where am I? How come I don't recognize this place?"

"It's…complicated. I'm not sure how much you'll be able to grasp all at once."

"First off, how am I even still breathing? Last time I checked, I was terminal. There isn't any cure for what I've got."

She stands and faces away from me. "There wasn't—twenty years ago."

Silence. Neither of us says anything as the import of her words seeps into every single one of my pores.

The doctor turns back to me. "When you died, you were placed into cryogenic sleep until a cure for your condition could be found."

Anger heats my blood. "I told Cephas and the others I didn't want to be a guinea pig."

Dr. Messenger's eyes meet mine. "Actually, though the Nexus teams spearheaded the efforts to arrest your condition, it was the dedicated work of a young researcher that provided the breakthrough for your cure."

I shake my head. "Great. I'll have to thank him or her personally."

"I'm afraid that won't be possible. You see, ever since your arrival, you've been under quarantine." Messenger looks extremely uncomfortable. "Not only for your own protection, but to prevent…unrest in the general populace as well. The researcher has never had any actual contact with you."

I shake my head. "This can't be real. This is some sort of trick."

She ignores me and checks my file. "You'll be pleased to know that your friend, Arrah Creed, has spent years serving in the rebuilding of the nation and is now the President of the Reunified Statehood. She and her wife will be flying in to see you tomorrow night before the inaugural ceremony at York City."

"Twenty years," I finally say. "I've been asleep for twenty years..."
An entire lifetime gone.

———

As relieved as I am to know that the horrors of the Establishment and the Thorn Republic are no more, there's a part of me that's in deep mourning, a sadness clinging to me like a winter's chill you can't shake no matter how close to the hearth you huddle. I've been asleep over half of my existence. Hearing the story of what happened after those dark days of the rebellion is not the same as living it. Everyone I care about—the entire world—has left me behind. I'm an oddity now, a relic of a dark past. I can see it in the curious faces of the doctors, nurses, and orderlies who cater to me, especially the younger ones.

That's him? That's the Torch Keeper?
He's just a kid.

Watching the television news reports, the updates on all the upcoming preparations for the inaugural ceremony, I'm overwhelmed by how different everything is. At one point, there's a news clip of an interview with Arrah from the Presidential suite. She's at once instantly recognizable and a total stranger. The three-dimensional definition on her face is so clear, I can make out the gray hairs, the fine lines etched into her once creamy smooth skin. Even her eyes aren't the same. Where once they shared the same story as mine, it's obvious they've witnessed so much more, and she's had to make much tougher decisions as the leader of this new country than she ever had before, even during the Trials.

It's me who's the stranger.
I don't belong here.
I never will.

Dusk approaches. Everyone around me is so consumed by excitement with tonight's event, they don't even notice when I open the locker containing my personal effects. Not much really, except the old battered chron I gave Cole, and the opticom.

I slip on the clothes I was wearing when I first went into deep sleep. It's like slipping on my old life, snug and familiar, despite the wrinkles and rips.

I'm just about to leave when Messenger enters the room. It only takes her a split-second to assess the situation. "I'm afraid I can't let you go, Lucian."

"I appreciate everything you've done for me. But it's not really your choice."

She taps her ear. "We have a Code Seventeen situation in med lab eight. Proceeding to administer stabilizing dosage," she says to whoever's listening on the other end of her communication device.

Lab? The image of another place floods my burdened brain cells. The laboratories in that place—Asclepius Valley—where the Establishment experimented with biological warfare.

Whoever's in charge here is experimenting on me as if I were a lab rat. Who knows? Maybe they're planning on using the agent I've been infected with to hurt more innocent people.

Without looking me directly in the eyes, Messenger pulls out a small, clear, cube, filled with a glowing green liquid, and approaches me. "Nothing to worry about. This injection will help you to sleep."

I nod. As soon as she's close enough, I grab the cube from her hand, and jam it against her own throat instead.

Her eyes blossom with shock and horror as the liquid is absorbed into her system. "Patient has broken...quarantine...," she manages to sputter into her com before collapsing.

Catching her and setting her on the bed, I grab her small, silver valise, and stuff the mini-projector containing my medical files, as well as my personal belongings, inside.

Sirens blare. The room's bathed in the dizzying amber glow of emergency lights. All my muscles are sore and feel like they've rusted shut. Standing on my feet is an ordeal. But I can't stay here. I stumble toward the exit.

Adrenaline pushes me forward. I barrel down the corridor to the right. One sign reads *Croakley Memorial Hospital*. A blur of grey glad figures heads in my direction. I swerve to my left, running faster, crashing through carts of medical instruments, shoving personnel emerging from other rooms out of my way.

All I can think about is escaping this strange place—getting back to my friends.

Getting back to my brother.

This is all some crazy lie.

I reach another intersection. Personnel lunge at me from either side, cornering me. There's only one way left to go. Bounding into a stairwell, I head up as far as I can go and burst through the rooftop doors, a dozen of the medical personnel pursuing me.

I turn to face them.

"I know you must need me alive for something or I'd be dead already. Stay away from me or I'll jump."

Am I bluffing? I'm not so sure. If I'm carrying a biological weapon of some kind inside my blood, maybe it's best if I do jump. I back against the wall, feeling the wind beating at me. There's nowhere to go except down.

A tall man emerges from the crowd. Early forties? Dark hair streaked with gray, wearing glasses. His eyes are filled with fear, but also... compassion?

"It's all right," he says. "We understand your confusion. We're here to help you. I promise."

He takes a step forward and I scramble up the ledge, clutching the valise. "I mean it," I croak.

I turn away and glance at the vista below me.

My breath catches in my throat.

The building I'm perched on overlooks an immense body of water. But it's not the rippling waves shimmering in the brilliant morning skies that take my breath away. It's the sight of the Lady herself, rising once again over the crystal blue waters.

The last time I saw her erect, she was canting noticeably, her body pocked with holes and cracks, covered with moss and algae like varicose veins, her crown of stars broken and jagged. Even in that condition, she managed to maintain her dignity, holding her torch high.

Then she was obliterated by Cassius's forces, nothing left but a smoldering pile of rubble.

But now, her body's been reborn, all smooth, gleaming copper, sparkling in the sunshine, standing straight as an arrow. Around her, construction crews hover about her in tiny, sleek craft like fireflies, removing the scaffolding surrounding her newly built facade. With most of the skeletal framework gone, it appears like the Lady's broken free of her prison at last, defying all those who fought to contain and destroy her.

"You can trust me. Please, Lucian."

The man with the glasses and compassionate eyes holds out his hand.

It's Cephas Decatur. Twenty years older.

It's all true.

I wipe my face and stare into his eyes. "You should have let me go."

Then I let myself drop into the sea.

———

That must be it up ahead. I stay hidden among the trees as I approach the small, brick house.

I'm on running on pure adrenaline now. Somehow, despite my weak muscles, I managed to swim to one of the small, nearby islands surrounding the Lady. Apparently, it houses researchers and their families, according to Messenger's files. Those keeping me hostage might think that I drowned, but it's only a matter of time before they discover that's not the case.

It must be an hour or two before I see him come out to the backyard. Using the opticom to zoom in, I recognize him instantly, the wavy dark hair, brown eyes the color of sweet chocolate. Only he's a man now.

My little Cole, all grown up.

The researcher who, according to the files, was responsible for finding the cure to my condition.

Laughter. A child's.

A little girl comes skipping out of the house, her dark hair in pig-tails. She must be the same age Cole was the last time I saw him.

She tugs his hand. "C'mon. I wanna play the swings. Push me, Daddy."

Cole chuckles. He lifts and spins her, then boosts her into the seat. "Okay, Sweetheart. Just for a little while. Then we have to help Mommy with dinner. It's a special night tonight. Grandpa Cage is coming for a visit."

I can't hold it in any longer. I weep silently, slumping into a sitting position on the grass, thinking of all the years I've missed, watching him become a husband and father, a man that's selflessly dedicated his life's work to go into medicine and help save countless lives, judging from his bio in those files.

I'm not sure how long I hide there watching him push her on that swing, hot tears streaming at the sound of their joy and laughter.

What can I possibly have to offer him now, except a connection to the tainted legacy of Queran Embers?

Besides. He probably forgot me long ago.

Cole scoops his daughter into his arms. "Time to get ready, Lucy."

A hint of a smile touches my lips. I wait until they go inside, then dart into the backyard and leave the small object on the swing.

There's movement, and I scramble away before I can be seen, hiding once again in the trees.

Cole comes back out. "I don't think you left your doll out here, but I'll check, honey. You go take your bath."

He walks over to the swing set. The seat is still swaying slightly from when I brushed it getting away. Cole stares at the sky. There's no breeze.

I tense as he picks up the small object I've left behind.

The battered chron I once gave him so many years ago.

He studies it, eyes moist, searching the tree line. "Lucky?"

Then I leave my brother for the final time.

————

I pull the hood of my cloak over my head to obscure my face. I can't take any chances of being recognized before I can get away.

The crowded streets feel like a maze. Everyone's boarding the shuttles to make it across the harbor to the new city's dedication ceremony tonight.

I push my way through. The further I go, the more overwhelmed and disoriented I become: the strange architecture, the unfamiliar styles of clothes, music that I've never heard before, the throngs of people talking and laughing, so connected to everyone else. Unlike me. I can't breathe. Panic sets in. I feel like a little child who's lost his parents in the crowd. Only it's not just my parents that I've lost.

Rounding a corner, I brace myself against the side of a building, looking up at the twilight sky. All those stars up there, thousands—and one in particular that catches my eye, burning brighter than the others, a twinkling beacon in a vast ocean.

Memories of a night long ago on an observation tower staring out to sea surface in my mind.

I need to get out of here and there's only one place left I can think to go.

Running on raw energy, I make my way to the harbor and one of the sea glider rental vendors along the docks. The proprietor, a pudgy, middle-aged man wears a name tag that says Charlton. He's surrounded by three black, miniature Canids that stare at me with gleaming eyes.

Charlon chuckles. "Don't worry. My dogs don't bite."

"*Dogs*?" I guess these must be a new, tamer breed than what I'm used to.

"Hop in. We'll have you at the city in no time."

"That's not where I'm headed." I point to the monument overlooking the river. "Can you please take me to *her*?"

When Charlton attempts to collect payment, I slip the Torch Keeper ring my friends gave me on that long ago birthday from my finger and hand it to him.

His eyes flame. "Hey! This is a real collector's item!"

"Keep it. I won't need it anymore."

Then I'm gliding over the waves until I reach the small island and my one familiar friend.

The Lady.

I look up at her towering face. "Hello, old friend."

Sure, most of her is new. But according to the enormous plaque at her base, some of her original parts were salvaged from the rubble and mixed in with the new. Like myself, the battered and worn queen has been resurrected and raised in this strange, new place.

There must be thousands of names engraved on the plaque. The heroes of the resistance. I don't stop searching until I find four particular ones.

Corin Lignier.

Drusilla Ryland.

Dahlia Bledsoe.

Tristin Argus.

My fingers trace each of their names. It's so unfair that I'm standing here, and they're not.

Once inside, I forgo the lift, opting instead to climb the spiral staircase, rising from the darkness.

I can't shake the feeling that someone's following me. Have Cephas and the others realized I didn't drown? Are they tracking me now, hoping to take me back and lock me away, or even silence me, before the entire population discovers that their most hated enemy, Queran Embers, has returned?

I emerge into the bright light of the Lady's torch.

"I knew you'd come here," a voice says behind me.

I turn and watch as the dark, hooded silhouette comes into focus.

My muscles tense. Ready to fight til the end.

"Who are you?" I ask.

"Just one of a million stars."

No matter how many years it's been, I recognize that voice.

I approach him tentatively, reach out, and pull his hood back.

Digory Tycho smiles at me, looking every bit as young and handsome as he did when he tackled me in that alley back in the Parish, a literal lifetime ago. Gone are the ravages of the nanotech that transformed his body. The pale skin is back to its familiar, smooth bronze. The shaved head is now resplendent with shimmering golden locks. But it's the eyes that take my breath away. The dark gray turbulent storm that plagued them for so long is over, replaced with the brilliant blue of the first day of springtime.

Now I'm the one who can't blink.

"Did you miss me, Lucky?"

I can't breathe. "Is this really happening?"

His smile is brilliant. "What do you think?"

We fall into each other's arms, our hot tears intermingling. For the first time since my resurrection, I feel truly connected.

Truly alive, like I finally belong somewhere.

I force myself to pull away and look into those beautiful eyes. "How did you...?"

He blinks the tears away. "I seem to have this problem not fitting in. First as a member of the Elite. Then as a member of the Resistance. Then as a Flesher. There was one thought, one emotion, I could never quite purge from my consciousness in the Hive. A thought so powerful, it was disrupting the entire collective. *You.* Lucian Spark. The Hive gave me the choice to stay with them or return to my other life." He grips my hands. "I chose to come back. For almost twenty years I've been in stasis while my body was regrown, dreaming of my past. Dreaming of you. Once I was free, I began searching for you, using all the tech I'd learned from the Hive. I knew they were hiding you. When you activated that opticom, I traced it right to you."

I wipe fresh tears from Digory's eyes. "What's wrong?"

He presses his forehead next to mine. "This body...this flesh...they're not the same. Yes, it's my genetic material, but these hands aren't the same ones that held you before. These lips aren't the same that kissed you. In some ways, I'm a stranger."

"We're both strangers in this place."

"Then we'll just have to be strangers together."

I grip him harder. "I don't give a damn about your hands or your lips." I press my hand against his heart. "Only what's in *here.*"

He kisses me, long and sweet, as if it were the first time. In some ways, it is. "The one thing that hasn't changed is how much I love you. That will never change."

"I love you, too. I have no choice."

Digory reaches into his cloak and pulls out two familiar silver objects in his cupped hand.

My eyes grow wide. "Our old I.D. tags. I haven't seen these since we were captive in Sanctum."

"The Hive returned them when I chose to leave. They're a little worse for wear, but I guess we all are."

He carefully places the chain with his name tag on it around me. It feels cool and comfortable. I return the gesture by taking the one with my name and fitting it over his broad neck.

We hold each other for a long time, not saying a word.

"Do you still remember?" he finally asks.

"I guess I always will, for as long as I live. It's a wound that will never completely heal. And maybe that's a good thing. A reminder to keep me focused. But *his* memories have faded, just fragments in the occasional nightmare." We both stare across the glittering waters at the brand new city before us. "Even still, I can never be a part of all *that*, Digory. You understand, don't you?"

He pulls me closer. "We'll head West. There's a whole new world out there for both of us to discover."

I turn back to take in the skyline. "So where does our tale go from here?"

Digory kisses me again, softly. "Someone once told me not every story has a happy ending. But some of them do. And those are the stories that *need* to be told."

As we hold each other tight, the cityscape before us erupts in a gleaming display of colorful lights. The inauguration is underway. The dawn of a new hope for the future. Fireworks crisscross the sky like flaming comets, intermingling with the dazzling canvas of stars above, until the horizon is a blazing glow that engulfs us in its warm brilliance, growing brighter and more intense by the second, until it's blinding.

It feels like the first bright day of a brand new life.

"Do you think humanity will ever learn from its mistakes?" Digory asks.

My hand melts into his. "I want to believe."

I choose to believe.

THE END

CPSIA information can be obtained
at www.ICGtesting.com
Printed in the USA
LVHW05s0117050718
582631LV00003B/554/P